SAN FRANCISCO
STORIES

For you, Richard,

With fondest memories
of San Francisco and
us in it.

Love,

'96

Panama Pacific International Exposition, 1915

SAN FRANCISCO STORIES

Great Writers on the City

Edited by John Miller

CHRONICLE BOOKS

SAN FRANCISCO

Printed in the United States of America.

Library of Congress Cataloging in Publication Data

San Francisco stories : great writers on the city / edited by John Miller.
  p. cm.
  ISBN 0-87701-669-0
  1. San Francisco (Calif.)–Literary collections. 2. American literature–California–San Francisco. 3. San Francisco (Calif.)--Description. I. Miller, John.
  PS572.S33S27   1990
  810.8′03279461–dc20   89-25337
                                                            CIP

Distributed in Canada by Raincoast Books,
8680 Cambie Street, Vancouver, B.C. V6P 6M9

10 9 8 7 6

Chronicle Books
275 Fifth Street
San Francisco, California 94103

Table of Contents

Special thanks to Frank Miller

Introduction

John Miller

L I V I N G   O N   a fault line is no easy business.

It helps if you live in a postcard town like San Francisco, everybody's favorite city, where folks are happy and healthy, where cable car rides afford one sunny, breathtaking view after another, and where every night the sun sets gently over the Golden Gate.

But, as we have from time to time been reminded, San Francisco *is* smack dead on a fault line. It is also on the edge of a continent, dangling precariously over the Pacific. And it is the golden city of the far west, the destiny that America made manifest. Some people think that it is precisely these characteristics, this hanging-onto-the-precipice, get-it-all-before-it's-gone quality that accounts for the vibrant, quirky writing that comes from San Francisco.

Eccentric San Francisco has fascinated travelers since the 49ers rode roughshod over gold-laden hills. They were soon followed by the writers, who arrived, notebooks in pockets, to find out exactly how far west you could go. What happens when you get all the way out here? And where do you go next? The number of works here by authors who are just passing through, who arrive, observe, and slip away speaks for itself. Even those who stay retain a certain stridency of voice, a vitality that cannot be refined out.

This collection turns the postcard of San Francisco over and allows us to read the messages on the back. That is, we've decided to pass by travel-brochure descriptions in favor of writing that shows the secret city—the side alleys of Amy Tan's 1950s Chinatown; the hills of North Beach from inside Ken Kesey's reeling magic bus; the back pew of William Saroyan's Blood of the Lamb Gospel Church on Turk Street in 1929; the Castro district's evolution from a sleepy little neighborhood to a vanguard gay community. It's not all blue skies and cable cars, but this is the city with its multiple personas—dark as well as alluring.

Everybody has a different story to tell, but if you stir them all into one big gumbo, it starts to become clear why San Francisco is so appealing.

And if somebody made you sum it all up, you might choose a letter Dylan Thomas penned to wife Caitlin in 1950. For this troubled poet, the city was—as it is to many—a mecca, a glimpse into a sunny future, into what life could be like:

> You wouldn't think such a place as San Francisco could exist. The wonderful sunlight there, the hills, the great bridges, the Pacific at your shoes. Beautiful Chinatown. Every race in the world. The sardine fleets sailing out. The little cable-cars whizzing down the city hills. The lobsters, clams, & crabs. Oh, Cat, what food for you. Every kind of seafood there is. And all the people are open and friendly. . . . You will love it here. I am madly unhappy but love it here, I am desperate for you but *know* that we, together, can come here. I love you. I love you. I love you.

SAN FRANCISCO STORIES

Ken Kesey's Magic Bus, 1967. Photograph © Gene Anthony, 1980.

T O M   W O L F E

Black Shiny FBI Shoes

T H AT ' S   G O O D   thinking there, Cool Breeze. Cool
Breeze is a kid with three or four days' beard sitting next to me on the
stamped metal bottom of the open back part of a pickup truck.
Bouncing along. Dipping and rising and rolling on these rotten
springs like a boat. Out the back of the truck the city of San Francisco
is bouncing down the hill, all those endless staggers of bay windows,
slums with a view, bouncing and streaming down the hill. One after
another, electric signs with neon martini glasses lit up on them, the
San Francisco symbol of "bar"–thousands of neon-magenta martini
glasses bouncing and streaming down the hill, and beneath them
hundreds, thousands of people wheeling around to look at this
freaking crazed truck we're in, their white faces erupting from their
lapels like marshmallows–streaming and bouncing down the hill–
and God knows they've got plenty to look at.

That's why it strikes me as funny when Cool Breeze says very
seriously over the whole roar of the thing, "I don't know–when Kesey
gets out I don't know if I can come around the Warehouse."

"Why not?"

"Well, like the cops are going to be coming around like all feisty,
and I'm on probation, so I don't know."

Well, that's good thinking there, Cool Breeze. Don't rouse the
bastids. Lie low–like right now. Right now Cool Breeze is so terrified
of the law he is sitting up in plain view of thousands of already startled
citizens wearing some kind of Seven Dwarfs Black Forest gnome's hat
covered in feathers and fluorescent colors. Kneeling in the truck,
facing us, also in plain view, is a half-Ottawa Indian girl named Lois
Jennings, with her head thrown back and a radiant look on her face.
Also a blazing silver disk in the middle of her forehead alternately
exploding with light when the sun hits it or sending off rainbows from

the defraction lines in it. And, oh yeah, there's a long-barreled Colt .45 revolver in her hand, only nobody on the street can tell it's a cap pistol as she pegs away, kheeew, kheeew, at the erupting marshmallow faces like Debra Paget in . . . in . . .

—Kesey's coming out of jail!

Two more things they are looking at out there are a sign on the rear bumper reading "Custer Died for Your Sins" and, at the wheel, Lois's enamorado Stewart Brand, a thin blond guy with a blazing disk on his forehead too, and a whole necktie made of Indian beads. No shirt, however, just an Indian bead necktie on bare skin and a white butcher's coat with medals from the King of Sweden on it.

Here comes a beautiful one, attaché case and all, the day-is-done resentful look and the . . . shoes—how they shine!—and what the hell are these beatnik ninnies—and Lois plugs him in the old marshmallow and he goes streaming and bouncing down the hill . . .

And the truck heaves and billows, blazing silver red and Day-Glo, and I doubt seriously, Cool Breeze, that there is a single cop in all of San Francisco today who does not know that this crazed vehicle is a guerrilla patrol from the dread LSD.

The cops now know the whole scene, even the costumes, the jesuschrist strung-out hair, Indian beads, Indian headbands, donkey beads, temple bells, amulets, mandalas, god's-eyes, fluorescent vests, unicorn horns, Errol Flynn dueling shirts—but they still don't know about the shoes. The heads have a thing about shoes. The worst are shiny black shoes with shoelaces in them. The hierarchy ascends from there, although practically all lowcut shoes are unhip, from there on up to the boots the heads like, light, fanciful boots, English boots of the mod variety, if that is all they can get, but better something like hand-tooled Mexican boots with Caliente Dude Triple A toes on them. So see the FBI—black—shiny—laced up—FBI shoes—when the FBI finally grabbed Kesey—

There is another girl in the back of the truck, a dark little girl with thick black hair, called Black Maria. She looks Mexican, but she says to me in straight soft Californian:

"When is your birthday?"

"March 2."

"Pisces," she says. And then: "I would never take you for a Pisces."

"Why?"

"You seem too . . . *solid* for a Pisces."

But I know she means stolid. I am beginning to feel stolid. Back in New York City, Black Maria, I tell you, I am even known as something of a dude. But somehow a blue silk blazer and a big tie with clowns on it and . . . a . . . pair of shiny lowcut black shoes don't set them all to doing the Varsity Rag in the head world in San Francisco. Lois picks off the marshmallows one by one; Cool Breeze ascends into the innards of his gnome's hat; Black Maria, a Scorpio herself, rummages through the Zodiac; Stewart Brand winds it through the streets; paillettes explode – and this is nothing special, just the usual, the usual in the head world of San Francisco, just a little routine messing up the minds of the citizenry en route, nothing more than psyche food for beautiful people, while giving some guy from New York a lift to the Warehouse to wait for the Chief, Ken Kesey, who is getting out of jail.

About all I knew about Kesey at that point was that he was a highly regarded 31-year-old novelist and in a lot of trouble over drugs. He wrote *One Flew Over the Cuckoo's Nest* (1962), which was made into a play in 1963, and *Sometimes a Great Notion* (1964). He was always included with Philip Roth and Joseph Heller and Bruce Jay Friedman and a couple of others as one of the young novelists who might go all the way. Then he was arrested twice for possession of marijuana, in April of 1965 and January of 1966, and fled to Mexico rather than risk a stiff sentence. It looked like as much as five years, as a second offender. One day I happened to get hold of some letters Kesey wrote from Mexico to his friend Larry McMurtry, who wrote *Horseman, Pass By,* from which the movie *Hud* was made. They were wild and ironic, written like a cross between William Burroughs and George Ade, telling of hideouts, disguises, paranoia, fleeing from cops, smoking joints and seeking satori in the Rat lands of Mexico. There was one passage written George Ade-fashion in the third person as a parody of what the straight world back there in the U.S.A. must think of him now:

"In short, this young, handsome, successful, happily-married-three-lovely-children father, was a fear-crazed dope fiend in flight to avoid prosecution on three felonies and god knows how many misdemeanors and seeking at the same time to sculpt a new satori from an old surf—in even shorter, mad as a hatter.

"Once an athlete so valued he had been given the job of calling signals from the line and risen into contention for the nationwide amateur wrestling crown, now he didn't know if he could do a dozen pushups. Once possessor of a phenomenal bank account and money waving from every hand, now it was all his poor wife could do to scrape together eight dollars to send as getaway money to Mexico. But a few years previous he had been listed in *Who's Who* and asked to speak at such auspicious gatherings as the Wellesley Club in Dah-la and now they wouldn't even allow him to speak at a VDC [Vietnam Day Committee] gathering. What was it that had brought a man so high of promise to so low a state in so short a time? Well, the answer can be found in just one short word, my friends, in just one all-well-used syllable:

"Dope!

"And while it may be claimed by some of the addled advocates of these chemicals that our hero is known to have indulged in drugs before his literary success, we must point out that there was evidence of his literary prowess well before the advent of the so-called psychedelic into his life but no evidence at all of any of the lunatic thinking that we find thereafter!"

To which he added:

"(oh yeah, the wind hums
time ago—time ago—
the rafter drums and the walls see
. . . and there's a door to that bird
in the sa-a-a-apling sky
time ago by—
Oh yeah the surf giggles
time ago time ago
of under things killed when
bad was banished and all the
doors to the birds vanished
time ago then.)"

I got the idea of going to Mexico and trying to find him and do a story on Young Novelist Real-Life Fugitive. I started asking around about where he might be in Mexico. Everybody on the hip circuit in New York knew for certain. It seemed to be the thing to know this summer. He is in Puerto Vallarta. He is in Ajijic. He is in Oaxaca. He is in San Miguel de Allende. He is in Paraguay. He just took a steamboat from Mexico to Canada. And everyone knew for certain.

I was still asking around when Kesey sneaked back into the U.S. in October and the FBI caught up with him on the Bayshore freeway south of San Francisco. An agent chased him down an embankment and caught him and Kesey was in jail. So I flew to San Francisco. I went straight to the San Mateo County jail in Redwood City and the scene in the waiting room there was more like the stage door at the Music Box Theatre. It was full of cheerful anticipation. There was a young psychologist there, Jim Fadiman—Clifton Fadiman's nephew, it turned out—and Jim and his wife Dorothy were happily stuffing three I Ching coins into the spine of some interminable dense volume of Oriental mysticism and they asked me to get word to Kesey that the coins were in there. There was also a little roundfaced brunette named Marilyn who told me she used to be a teenie grouper hanging out with a rock 'n' roll group called The Wild Flowers but now she was mainly with Bobby Petersen. Bobby Petersen was not a musician. He was a saint, as nearly as I could make out. He was in jail down in Santa Cruz trying to fight a marijuana charge on the grounds that marijuana was a religious sacrament for him. I didn't figure out exactly why she was up here in the San Mateo jail waiting room instead except that it was like a stage door, as I said, with Kesey as the star who was still inside.

There was a slight hassle with the jailers over whether I was to get into see him or not. The cops had nothing particularly to gain by letting me in. A reporter from New York—that just meant more publicity for this glorified beatnik. That was the line on Kesey. He was a glorified beatnik up on two dope charges, and why make a hero out of him. I must say that California has smooth cops. They all seem to be young, tall, crewcut, blond, with bleached blue eyes, like they just stepped out of a cigarette ad. Their jailhouses don't look like jailhouses, at least not the parts the public sees. They are all blond wood, fluorescent lights and filing-cabinet-tan metal, like the Civil Service exam room in a new Post Office building. The cops all speak soft Californian and are neat and correct as an ice cube. By the book; so they finally let me in to see Kesey during visiting hours. I had ten minutes. I waved goodbye to Marilyn and the Fadimans and the jolly scene downstairs and they took me up to the third floor in an elevator.

The elevator opened right onto a small visiting room. It was weird. Here was a lineup of four or five cubicles, like the isolation booths on the old TV quiz shows, each one with a thick plate-glass window and behind each window a prisoner in a prison blue workshirt. They were lined up like haddocks on ice. Outside each window ran a counter with a telephone on it. That's what you speak over in here. A couple of visitors are already hunched over the things. Then I pick out Kesey.

He is standing up with his arms folded over his chest and his eyes focused in the distance, i.e., the wall. He has thick wrists and big forearms, and the way he has them folded makes them look gigantic. He looks taller than he really is, maybe because of his neck. He has a big neck with a pair of sternocleido-mastoid muscles that rise up out of the prison workshirt like a couple of dock ropes. His jaw and chin are massive. He looks a little like Paul Newman, except that he is more muscular, has thicker skin, and he has tight blond curls boiling up around his head. His hair is almost gone on top, but somehow that goes all right with his big neck and general wrestler's build. Then he smiles slightly. It's curious, he doesn't have a line in his face. After all the chasing and hassling—he looks like the third week at the Sauna Spa; serene, as I say.

Then I pick up my telephone and he picks up his—and this is truly Modern Times. We are all of twenty-four inches apart, but there is a piece of plate glass as thick as a telephone directory between us. We might as well be in different continents, talking over Videophone. The telephones are very crackly and lo-fi, especially considering that they have a world of two feet to span. Naturally it was assumed that the police monitored every conversation. I wanted to ask him all about his fugitive days in Mexico. That was still the name of my story, Young Novelist Fugitive Eight Months in Mexico. But he could hardly go into that on this weird hookup, and besides, I had only ten minutes. I take out a notebook and start asking him—anything. There had been a piece in the paper about his saying it was time for the psychedelic movement to go "beyond acid," so I asked him about that. Then I started scribbling like mad, in shorthand, in the notebook. I could see his lips moving two feet away. His voice crackled over the telephone like it was coming from Brisbane. The whole thing was crazy. It seemed like calisthenics we were going through.

"It's my idea," he said, "that it's time to graduate from what has been going on, to something else. The psychedelic wave was happening six or eight months ago when I went to Mexico. It's been growing since then, but it hasn't been moving. I saw the same stuff when I got back as when I left. It was just bigger, that was all—" He talks in a soft voice with a country accent, almost a pure country accent, only crackling and rasping and cheese-grated over the two-foot hookup, talking about—

"—there's been no creativity," he is saying, "and I think my value has been to help create the next step. I don't think there will be any movement off the drug scene until there is something else to move to—"

—all in a plain country accent about something—well, to be frank, I didn't know what in the hell it was all about. Sometimes he spoke cryptically, in aphorisms. I told him I had heard he didn't intend to do any more writing. Why? I said.

"I'd rather be a lightning rod than a seismograph," he said.

He talked about something called the Acid Test and forms of expression in which there would be no separation between himself and the audience. It would be all one experience, with all the senses opened wide, words, music, lights, sounds, touch—*lightning*.

"You mean on the order of what Andy Warhol is doing?" I said.

. . . pause. "No offense," says Kesey, "but New York is about two years behind."

He said it very patiently, with a kind of country politeness, as if . . . I don't want to be rude to you fellows from the City, but there's been things going on out here that you would never guess in your wildest million years, old buddy . . .

The ten minutes were up and I was out of there. I had gotten nothing, except my first brush with a strange phenomenon, that strange up-country charisma, the Kesey presence. I had nothing to do but kill time and hope Kesey would get out on bail somehow and I could talk to him and get the details on Novelist Fugitive in Mexico. This seemed like a very long shot at this time, because Kesey had two marijuana charges against him and had already jumped the country once.

So I rented a car and started making the rounds in San Francisco. Somehow my strongest memories of San Francisco are of me in a terrific rented sedan roaring up hills or down hills, sliding on and off the cable-car tracks. Slipping and sliding down to North Beach, the fabled North Beach, the old fatherland bohemia of the West Coast, always full of Big Daddy So-and-so and Costee Plusee and long-haired little Wasp and Jewish buds balling spade cats—and now North Beach was dying. North Beach was nothing but tit shows. In the famous Beat Generation HQ, the City Lights bookstore, Shig Murao, the Nipponese panjandrum of the place, sat glowering with his beard hanging down like those strands of furze and fern in an architect's drawing, drooping over the volumes of Kahlil Gibran by the cash register while Professional Budget Finance Dentists here for the convention browsed in search of the beatniks between tit shows. Everything was The Topless on North Beach, strippers with their breasts enlarged with injections of silicone emulsion.

The action—meaning the hip cliques that set the original tone—the action was all over in Haight-Ashbury. Pretty soon all the bellwethers of a successful bohemia would be there, too, the cars going through, bumper to bumper, with everybody rubbernecking, the tour buses going through "and here . . . Home of the Hippies . . . there's one there," and the queers and spade hookers and bookstores and boutiques. Everything was Haight-Ashbury and the acid heads.

But it was not just North Beach that was dying. The whole old-style hip life—jazz, coffee houses, civil rights, invite a spade for dinner, Vietnam—it was all suddenly dying, I found out, even among the students at Berkeley, across the bay from San Francisco, which had been the heart of the "student-rebellion" and so forth. It had even gotten to the point that Negroes were no longer in the hip scene, not even as totem figures. It was unbelievable. *Spades*, the very soul figures of Hip, of jazz, of the hip vocabulary itself, man and like and dig and baby and scarf and split and later and so fine, of civil rights and graduating from Reed College and living on North Beach, down Mason, and balling spade cats—all that good elaborate petting and patting and pouring soul all over the spades—all over, finished, incredibly.

So I was starting to get the trend of all this heaving and convulsing in the bohemian world of San Francisco. Meantime, miraculously, Kesey's three young lawyers, Pat Hallinan, Brian Rohan, and Paul Robertson, were about to get Kesey out on bail. They assured the judges, in San Mateo and San Francisco, that Mr. Kesey had a very public-spirited project in mind. He had returned from exile for the express purpose of calling a huge meeting of heads and hippies at Winterland Arena in San Francisco in order to tell The Youth to stop taking LSD because it was dangerous and might french fry their brains, etc. It was going to be an "acid graduation" ceremony. They should go "beyond acid." That was what Kesey had been talking to me about, I guess. At the same time, six of Kesey's close friends in the Palo Alto area had put their homes up as security for a total of $35,000 bail with the San Mateo County court. I suppose the courts figured they had Kesey either way. If he jumped bail now, it would be such a dirty trick on his friends, costing them their homes, that Kesey would be discredited as a drug apostle or anything else. If he didn't, he would be obliged to give his talk to The Youth—and so much the better. In any case, Kesey was coming out.

This script was not very popular in Haight-Ashbury, however. I soon found out that the head life in San Francisco was already such a big thing that Kesey's return and his acid graduation plan were causing the heads' first big political crisis. All eyes were on Kesey and his group, known as the Merry Pranksters. Thousands of kids were moving into San Francisco for a life based on LSD and the psychedelic thing. *Thing* was the major abstract word in Haight-Ashbury. It could mean *any*thing, isms, life styles, habits, leanings, causes, sexual organs; *thing* and *freak; freak* referred to styles and obsessions, as in "Stewart Brand is an Indian freak" or "the zodiac—that's her freak," or just to heads in costume. It wasn't a negative word. Anyway, just a couple of weeks before, the heads had held their first big "be-in" in Golden Gate Park, at the foot of the hill leading up into Haight-Ashbury, in mock observance of the day LSD became illegal in California. This was a gathering of all the tribes, all the communal groups. All the freaks came and did their thing. A head named Michael Bowen started it, and thousands of them piled in, in high costume, ringing bells, chanting, dancing ecstatically, blowing their minds one way and another and making their favorite satiric gestures to the cops, handing them flowers, burying the bastids in tender fruity petals of love. Oh christ, Tom, the thing was fantastic, a freaking mindblower, thousands of high-loving heads out there messing up the minds of the cops and everybody else in a fiesta of love and euphoria. Even Kesey, who was still on the run then, had brazened on in and mingled with the crowd for a while, and they were all *one,* even Kesey—and now all of a sudden here he is, in the hands of the FBI and other supercops, the biggest name in The Life, Kesey, announcing that it is time to "graduate from acid." And what the hell is this, a copout or what? The *Stop Kesey* movement was beginning even within the hip world.

We pull up to the Warehouse in the crazed truck and—well, for a start, I begin to see that people like Lois and Stewart and Black Maria are the restrained, reflective wing of the Merry Pranksters. The Warehouse is on Harriet Street, between Howard and Folsom. Like most of San Francisco, Harriet Street is a lot of wooden buildings with bay windows all painted white. But Harriet Street is in San Francisco's Skid Row area, and despite all the paint, it looks like about forty winos crawled off in the shadows and died and turned black and bloated and exploded, sending forth a stream of spirochetes that got into every board, every strip, every crack, every splinter, every flecking flake of paint. The Warehouse actually turns out to be the ground-floor garage of an abandoned hotel. Its last commercial use was as a pie factory. We pull up to the garage and there is a panel truck parked just outside, painted in blue, yellow, orange, red Day-Glo, with the word BAM in huge letters on the hood. From out the black hole of the garage comes the sound of a record by Bob Dylan with his raunchy harmonica and Ernest Tubb voice raunching and rheuming in the old jack-legged chants—

Inside is a huge chaotic space with what looks at first in the gloom like ten or fifteen American flags walking around. This turns out to be a bunch of men and women, most of them in their twenties, in white coveralls of the sort airport workers wear, only with sections of American flags sewn all over, mostly the stars against fields of blue but some with red stripes running down the legs. Around the side is a lot of theater scaffolding with blankets strewn across like curtains and whole rows of uprooted theater seats piled up against the walls and big cubes of metal debris and ropes and girders.

One of the blanket curtains edges back and a little figure vaults down from a platform about nine feet up. It glows. It is a guy about five feet tall with some sort of World War I aviator's helmet on . . . glowing with curves and swirls of green and orange. His boots, too; he seems to be bouncing over on a pair of fluorescent globes. He stops. He has a small, fine, ascetic face with a big mustache and huge eyes. The eyes narrow and he breaks into a grin.

"I just had an eight-year-old boy up there," he says.

Then he goes into a sniffling giggle and bounds, glowing, over into a corner, in among the debris.

Everybody laughs. It is some kind of family joke, I guess. At least I am the only one who scans the scaffolding for the remains.

"That's the Hermit." Three days later I see he has built a cave in the corner.

A bigger glow in the center of the garage. I make out a school bus . . . glowing orange, green, magenta, lavender, chlorine blue, every fluorescent pastel imaginable in thousands of designs, both large and small, like a cross between Fernand Léger and Dr. Strange, roaring together and vibrating off each other as if somebody had given Hieronymous Bosch fifty buckets of Day-Glo paint and a 1939 International Harvester school bus and told him to go to it. On the floor by the bus is a 15-foot banner reading ACID TEST GRADUATION, and two or three of the Flag People are working on it. Bob Dylan's voice is raunching and rheuming and people are moving around, and babies are crying. I don't see them but they are somewhere in here, crying. Off to one side is a guy about 40 with a lot of muscles, as you can see because he has no shirt on—just a pair of khakis and some red leather boots on and his hell of a build—and he seems to be in a kinetic trance, flipping a small sledge hammer up in the air over and over, always managing to catch the handle on the way down with his arms and legs kicking out the whole time and his shoulders rolling and his head bobbing, all in a jerky beat as if somewhere Joe Cuba is playing "Bang Bang" although in fact even Bob Dylan is no longer on and out of the speaker, wherever it is, comes some sort of tape with a spectral voice saying:

"... The Nowhere Mine... we've got bubble-gum wrappers..." some sort of weird electronic music behind it, with Oriental intervals, like Juan Carrillo's music: "... We're going to jerk it out from under the world ... working in the Nowhere Mine ... this day, every day ..."

One of the Flag People comes up.

"Hey, Mountain Girl! That's wild!"

Mountain Girl is a tall girl, big and beautiful with dark brown hair falling down to her shoulders except that the lower two-thirds of her falling hair looks like a paint brush dipped in cadmium yellow from where she dyed it blond in Mexico. She pivots and shows the circle of stars on the back of her coveralls.

"We got 'em at a uniform store," she says. "Aren't they great! There's this old guy in there, says, 'Now, you ain't gonna cut them flags up for costumes, are you?' And so I told him, 'Naw, we're gonna git some horns and have a parade.' But you see this? This is really why we got 'em."

She points to a button on the coveralls. Everybody leans in to look. A motto is engraved on the bottom in art nouveau curves: "Can't Bust 'Em."

Can't Bust 'Em! . . . and about time. After all the times the Pranksters have gotten busted, by the San Mateo County cops, the San Francisco cops, the Mexicale Federale cops, FBI cops, cops cops cops cops . . .

And still the babies cry. Mountain Girl turns to Lois Jennings.

"What do Indians do to stop a baby from crying?"

"They hold its nose."

"Yeah?"

"They learn."

"I'll try it . . . it sounds logical . . ." And Mountain Girl goes over and picks up her baby, a four-months-old girl named Sunshine, out of one of those tube-and-net portable cribs from behind the bus and sits down in one of the theater seats. But instead of the Indian treatment she unbuttons the Can't Bust 'Em coveralls and starts feeding her.

"... The Nowhere Mine ... Nothing felt and screamed and cried ..." brang tweeeeeeng "... and I went back to the Nowhere Mine ..."

The sledge-hammer juggler rockets away—
"Who is that?"
"That's Cassady."

This strikes me as a marvelous fact. I remember Cassady. Cassady, Neal Cassady, was the hero, "Dean Moriarty," of Jack Kerouac's *On the Road*, the Denver Kid, a kid who was always racing back and forth across the U.S. by car, chasing, or outrunning, "life," and here is the same guy, now 40, in the garage, flipping a sledge hammer, rocketing about to his own Joe Cuba and—talking. Cassady never stops talking. But that is a bad way to put it. Cassady is a monologuist, only he doesn't seem to care whether anyone is listening or not. He just goes off on the monologue, by himself if necessary, although anyone is welcome aboard. He will answer all questions, although not exactly in that order, because we can't stop here, next rest area 40 miles, you understand, spinning off memories, metaphors, literary, Oriental, hip allusions, all punctuated by the unlikely expression, "you understand—"

1968

San Francisco, 1858.

ROBERT LOUIS STEVENSON

Arriving in San Francisco

W H E N I awoke next morning, I was puzzled for a while to know if it were day or night, for the illumination was unusual. I sat up at last, and found we were grading slowly downward through a long snowshed; and suddenly we shot into an open; and before we were swallowed into the next length of wooden tunnel, I had one glimpse of a huge pine-forested ravine upon my left, a foaming river, and a sky already coloured with fires of dawn. I am usually very calm over the displays of nature; but you will scarce believe how my heart leaped at this. It was like meeting one's wife. I had come home again – home from unsightly deserts to the green and habitable corners of the earth. Every spire of pine along the hill-top, every trouty pool along the mountain river, was more dear to me than a blood relation. Few people have praised God more happily than I did. And thenceforward, down by Blue Cañon, Alta, Dutch Flat, and all the old mining camps, through a sea of mountain forests, dropping thousands of feet toward the far sea-level as we went, not I only, but all the passengers on board, threw off their sense of dirt and heat and weariness, and bawled like schoolboys, and thronged with shining eyes upon the platform and became new creatures within and without. The sun no longer oppressed us with heat, it only shone laughingly along the mountain-side, until we were fain to laugh ourselves for glee. At every turn we could see farther into the land and our own happy futures. At every town the cocks were tossing their clear notes into the golden air, and crowing for the new day and the new country. For this was indeed our destination; this was "the good country" we had been going to so long.

By afternoon we were at Sacramento, the city of gardens in a plain of corn; and the next day before the dawn we were lying to upon the Oakland side of San Francisco Bay. The day was breaking as we crossed the ferry; the fog was rising over the citied hills of San Francisco; the bay was perfect—not a ripple, scarce a stain, upon its blue expanse; everything was waiting, breathless, for the sun. A spot of cloudy gold lit first upon the head of Tamalpais, and then widened downward on its shapely shoulder; the air seemed to awaken, and began to sparkle; and suddenly

"The tall hills Titan discovered,"

and the city of San Francisco, and the bay of gold and corn were lit from end to end with summer daylight.

1879

DYLAN THOMAS

Letters to Caitlin

about April 5 1950

M Y L O V E my Caitlin my love my love
thank you (I love you) for your beautiful beautiful beautiful letter and (my love) for the love you sent. Please forgive, Cat dear, the nasty little note I sent about your not-writing: it was only because I was so worried and so deeply in love with you. This is going to be the shortest letter because I am writing it on a rocking train that is taking me from San Francisco–the best city on earth–to Vancouver in Canada. And with this tiny, but profoundly loving, letter, I also send you a cheque to Magdalen College for £50 & a cheque for £15 to you: that £15 seems an odd amount, but God knows how much is in the Chelsea bank. I unfortunately can't find the Dathan Davies bill you sent, so can you pay it out of this. Please, my own sweetheart, send all the bills & troubles to me after this. And I hope the cheques are met. The train is going so fast through wonderful country along the Pacific coast that I can write no more. As soon as I get on stationary land I will write longly. I said San Francisco was the best city on earth. It is incredibly beautiful, all hills and bridges and blinding blue sky and boats and the Pacific ocean. I am trying–& there's every reason to believe it will succeed–to arrange that you & me & Colum (my Colum, your Colum,) come to San Francisco next spring when I will become, for six months, a professor in the English department of the University. You will love it here. I am madly unhappy but I love it here. I am desperate for you but I *know* that we can, together, come here. I love you. I love you. I love you. I am glad you are stiff & staid. I am rather overwrought but am so much in love with you that it does not matter. I spent last evening with Varda, the Greek painter, who remembers you when you were fifteen. I wish I did. A long letter

tomorrow. O my heart, my golden heart, how I miss you. There's an intolerable emptiness in me, that can be made whole only by your soul & body. I will come back alive & as deep in love with you as a cormorant dives, as an anemone grows, as Neptune breathes, as the sea is deep. God bless & protect you & Llewelyn & Aeron & Colum, my, our, Colum. I love you.

Dylan

P.S. Write, air mail, to the above address. I return to S. Francisco in a week.
P.S.S. Darling, I realise fifteen pounds is inadequate, but let that big £50 get thro' the bank alright & then I can send more. I can send you a cheque in dollars next week, which you can cash through the account of my poor old man or through Ivy.

I love you.

Caitlin Thomas
7th April 1950

Caitlin. Just to write down your name like that. Caitlin. I don't have to say My dear, My darling, my sweetheart, though I do say those words, to you in myself, all day and night. Caitlin. And all the words are in that one word. Caitlin, Caitlin, and I can see your blue eyes and your golden hair and your slow smile and your faraway voice. Your faraway voice is saying, now, at my ear, the words you said in your last letter, and thank you, dear, for the love you said and sent. I love you. Never forget that, for one single moment of the long, slow, sad Laugharne day, never forget it in your mazed trances, in your womb & your bones, in our bed at night. I love you. Over this continent I take your love inside me, your love goes with me up in the aeroplaned air, into all the hotel bedrooms where momentarily I open my bag—half full, as ever, of dirty shirts—and lay down my head & do not sleep until dawn because I can hear your heart beat beside me, your voice saying my name and our love above the noise of the night-traffic, above the neon flashing, deep in my loneliness, my love.

Today is Good Friday. I am writing this in an hotel bedroom in Vancouver, British Columbia, Canada, where yesterday I gave two readings, one in the university, one in the ballroom of the Vancouver Hotel, and made one broadcast. Vancouver is on the sea, and gigantic mountains loom above it. Behind the mountains lie other mountains, lies an unknown place, 30,000 miles of mountainous wilderness, the lost land of Columbia where cougars live and black bears. But the city of Vancouver is a quite handsome hellhole. It is, of course, being Canadian, more British than Cheltenham. I spoke last night – or read, I never lecture, how could I? – in front of two huge union jacks. The pubs – they are called beer-parlours – serve only beer, are not allowed to have whiskey or wine or any spirits at all – and are open only for a few hours a day. There are, in this monstrous hotel, two bars, one for Men, one for Women. They do not mix. Today, Good Friday, nothing is open nor will be open all day long. Everybody is pious and patriotic, apart from a few people in the university & my old friend Malcolm Lowry – do you remember Under the Volcano – who lives in a hut in the mountains & who came down to see me last night. Do you remember his wife Margery? We met her with Bill & Helen in Richmond, and, later, I think, in Oxford. She, anyway, remembers you well and sends you her love.

This afternoon I pick up my bag of soiled clothes and take a plane to Seattle. And thank God to be out of British Canada & back in the terrible United States of America. I read poems to the University there tonight. And then I have one day's rest in Seattle, & then on Sunday I fly to Montana, where the cowboys are, thousands of them, tell Ebie, and then on Monday I fly – it takes about 8 hours – to Los Angeles & Hollywood: the nightmare zenith of my mad, lonely tour.

But oh, San Francisco! It is and has everything. Here in Canada, five hours away by plane, you wouldn't think that such a place as San Francisco could exist. The wonderful sunlight there, the hills, the great bridges, the Pacific at your shoes. Beautiful Chinatown. Every race in the world. The sardine fleets sailing out. The little cable-cars whizzing down the city hills. The lobsters, clams, & crabs. Oh, Cat, what food for you. Every kind of seafood there is. And all the people are open and friendly. And next year we both come to live there, you

Cable car on Telegraph Hill.

& me & Colum & maybe Aeron. This is sure. I am offered a job in two universities. When I return to San Francisco next week, after Los Angeles, for another two readings, I shall know definitely which of the jobs to take. The pay will be enough to keep us comfortably, though no more. Everyone connected with the Universities is hard-up. But that doesn't matter. Seafood is cheap. Chinese food is cheaper, & lovely. Californian wine is good. The iced bock beer is good. What more? And the city is built on hills; it dances in the sun for nine months of the year; & the Pacific Ocean never runs dry.

Last week I went to Big Sur, a mountainous region by the sea, and stayed the night with Henry Miller. Tell Ivy that; she who hid his books in the oven. He lives about 6,000 feet up in the hills, over the blinding blue Pacific, in a hut of his own making. He has married a pretty young Polish girl, & they have two small children. He is gentle and mellow and gay.

I love you, Caitlin.

You asked me about the shops. I only know that the shops in the big cities, in New York, Chicago, San Francisco, are full of everything you have ever heard of and also full of everything one has never heard of or seen. The foodshops knock you down. All the women are smart, as in magazines – I mean, the women in the main streets; behind, lie the eternal poor, beaten, robbed, humiliated, spat upon, done to death – and slick & groomed. But they are not as beautiful as you. And when you & me are in San Francisco, you will be smarter & slicker than them, and the sea & sun will make you jump over the roofs & the trees, & you will never be tired again. Oh, my lovely dear, how I love you. I love you for ever & ever. I see you every moment of the day & night. I see you in our little house, tending the pomegranate of your eye. I love you. Kiss Colum, kiss Aeron & Llewelyn. Is Elizabeth with you? Remember me to her. I love you. Write, write, write, write, my sweetheart Caitlin. Write to me still c/o Brinnin; though the letters come late that way, I am sure of them. Do not despair. Do not be too tired. Be always good to me. I shall one day be in your arms, my own, however shy we shall be. Be good to me, as I am always to you. I love you. Think of us together in the San Francisco sun, which we shall be.

I love you. I want you. Oh, darling, when I was with you all the time,
how did I ever shout at you? I love you. Think of me.

Your

Dylan

I enclose a cheque for £15.
I will write from Hollywood in three days.
I will send some more money.
I love you.

1950

ANTHONY TROLLOPE

Nothing to See in San Francisco

M Y W A Y home from the Sandwich Islands to London took me to San Francisco, across the American continent, and New York,–whence I am now writing to you my last letter of this series. I had made this journey before, but had on that occasion reached California too late to visit the now world-famous valley of the Yo Semite, and the big pine trees which we call Wellingtonias. On this occasion I made the excursion, and will presently tell the story of the trip,–but I must first say a few words as to the town of San Francisco.

I do not know that in all my travels I ever visited a city less interesting to the normal tourist, who, as a rule, does not care to investigate the ways of trade or to employ himself in ascertaining how the people around him earn their bread. There is almost nothing to see in San Francisco that is worth seeing. There is a new park in which you may drive for six or seven miles on a well made road, and which, as a park for the use of a city, will, when completed, have many excellencies. There is also the biggest hotel in the world,–so the people of San Francisco say, which has cost a million sterling,–5 millions of dollars,–and is intended to swallow up all the other hotels. It was just finished but not opened when I was there. There is an inferior menagerie of wild beasts, and a place called the Cliff House to which strangers are taken to hear seals bark. Everything,–except hotel prices,–is dearer here than at any other large town I know; and the ordinary traveller has no peace left him either in public or private by touters who wish to persuade him to take this or the other railway route into the Eastern States.

There is always a perfectly cloudless sky over head unless when rain is falling in torrents, and perhaps no where in the world is there a more sudden change from heat to cold in the same day. I think I may say that strangers will generally desire to get out of San Francisco as quickly as they can,—unless indeed circumstances may have enabled them to enjoy the hospitality of the place. There is little or nothing to see, and life at the hotels is not comfortable. But the trade of the place and the way in which money is won and lost are alike marvellous. I found 10/a day to be about the lowest rate of wages paid to a man for any kind of work in the city, and the average wages of a housemaid who is, of course, found in everything but her clothes, to be over £70 per annum. All payments in California are made in coin, whereas in the other states of the Union except California, Oregon, and Nevada, monies are paid in depreciated notes,—so that the two dollars and a half per day which the labourer earns in San Francisco are as good as three and a quarter in New York. No doubt this high rate of pay is met by an equivalent in the high cost of many articles, such as clothing and rent; but it does not affect the price of food which to the labouring man is the one important item of expenditure. Consequently the labouring man in California has a position which I have not known him to achieve elsewhere.

In trade there is a speculative rashness which ought to ensure ruin according to our old world ideas, but which seems to be rewarded by very general success. The stranger may of course remember if he pleases that the millionaire who builds a mighty palace is seen and heard of and encountered at all corners, while the bankrupt will probably sink unseen into obscurity. But in San Francisco there is not much of bankruptcy; and when it does occur no one seems to be so little impressed as the bankrupt. There is a goodnature, a forbearance, and an easy giving of trust which to an old fashioned Englishman like myself seem to be most dangerous, but which I was assured there form the readiest mode of building up a great commercial community. The great commercial community is there, and I am not prepared to deny that it has been built after that fashion. If a young man there can make friends, and can establish a character for honesty to his friends and for smartness to the outside world, he can borrow almost any amount of money without security, for the purpose of establishing himself in business. The lender, if he feel sure that he will not be robbed by his protege, is willing to run the risk of unsuccessful speculation.

As we steamed into the Golden Horn (*sic*) the news reached us that about a month previously the leading bank in San Francisco, the bank of California, had "burst up" for some enormous amount of dollars, and that the manager, who was well known as one of the richest men and as perhaps the boldest speculator in the State, had been drowned on the day following. But we also heard that payments would be resumed in a few days; and payments were resumed before I left the city: that no one but the shareholders would lose a dollar, and that the shareholders were ready to go on with any amount of new capital; and that not a single bankruptcy in the whole community had been caused by this stoppage of the bank which had been extended for a period over a month! How came it to pass, I asked of course, that the collapse of so great a monetary enterprise as the bank of California should pass on without a general panic, at any rate in the city? Then I was assured that all those concerned were goodnatured, that everybody gave time,—that bills were renewed all round, and that in an hour or two it was understood that no one in San Francisco was to be asked for money just at that crisis. To me all this seemed to be wrong. I have always imagined that severity to bankrupt debtors,—that amount of severity which requires that a bankrupt shall really be a bankrupt,—is the best and indeed the only way of ensuring regularity in commerce and of preventing men from tossing up with other people's money in the confidence that they may win and cannot lose. But such doctrines are altogether out of date in California. The money of depositors was scattered broadcast through the mining speculations of the district, and no one was a bit the worse for it,—except the unfortunate gentleman who had been, perhaps happily, removed from a community which had trusted him long with implicit confidence, which still believed him to be an honest man, but which would hardly have known how to treat him had he survived. To add to the romance of the story it should be said that though this gentleman was drowned while bathing it seems to be certain that his death was accidental. It is stated that he was struck by apoplexy while in the water.

I was taken to visit the stock-brokers' Board in San Francisco,— that is the room in which mining shares are bought and sold. The trader should understand that in California, and, still more, in the neighboring State of Nevada, gold and silver mining are now very lively. The stock-jobbing created by these mines is carried on in San Francisco and is a business as universally popular as was the buying and selling of railroad shares during our railway mania. Everybody is at it. The housemaid of whom I have spoken as earning £70 per annum, buys Consolidated Virginia or Ophir stock with that money;—or perhaps she prefers Chollar Potosi, or Best and Belcher, or Yellow Jacket, or Buckeye. She probably consults some gentleman of her acquaintance and no doubt in 19 cases out of 20 loses her money. But it is the thing to do, and she enjoys that charm which is the delectation of all gamblers. Of course in such a condition of things there are men who know how the wind is going to blow, who make the wind blow this way and that, who can raise the price of shares by fictitious purchases, and then sell, or depreciate them by fictitious sales and then buy. The housemaids and others go to the wall, while the knowing men build palaces and seem to be troubled by no seared consciences. In the mean time the brokers drive a roaring trade,— whether they purchase legitimately for others or speculate on their own account.

The Stock Exchange in London is I believe closed to strangers. The Bourse in Paris is open to the world and at a certain hour affords a scene to those who choose to go and look at it of wild noise, unintelligible action, and sometimes apparently of demoniac fury. The uninitiated are unable to comprehend that the roaring herd in the pen beneath them are doing business. The Stock Exchange Board in San Francisco is not open to strangers, as it is in Paris, but may be visited with an order, and by the kindness of a friend I was admitted. Paris is more than six times as large as San Francisco; but the fury at San Francisco is even more demoniac than at Paris. I thought that the gentlemen employed were going to hit each other between the eyes, and that the apparent quarrels which I saw already demanded the interference of the police. But the uproarious throng were always

Snowstorm in downtown San Francisco, 1882.

obedient, after slight delays, to the ringing hammer of the Chairman and as each five minutes' period of internecine combat was brought to an end, I found that a vast number of mining shares had been bought and sold. Perhaps a visit to this Chamber, when the stock-brokers are at work between the hours of eleven and twelve, is of all sights in San Francisco, the one best worth seeing.

1875

ISHMAEL REED

The Moochers Have a Crisis

THE COMMITTEE meeting was to be held at the Gross Christian Church, San Francisco's truly avant-garde center of worship. The first thing you came upon was the entrance, over which could be seen a sign spelling out "PEACE" in the manner of the garish neon signs one saw at the bottomless topless clubs on Broadway. Rev. Rookie's church was a reconverted niteclub. Inside he stands behind one of the long elegant bars which has been restored to its original furnishings. On the walls are black light psychedelic posters of Harry Belafonte, Sammy Davis, Jr. (the name of Jefferson Davis' body servant, incidentally), and Quincy Jones. Whenever "Q" came to the Circle Star Theatre, Rev. Rookie would be right there, in the front row, whooping it up, yelling such colorful expletives as "right on," and "get down," which he would say twice, "get down, get down." Another one of his expressions was "can you dig it?" Quite effective when used sparingly, which Rev. Rookie didn't. Cats were circling the room. Moochers love cats, perhaps because you have to be crafty and dexterous and phony-finicky to be a Moocher, winning your territory inch by inch. Rev. Rookie had a motley congregation and really didn't care about their life styles. He had twisted old John Wesley's philosophy so that he had forgotten the theology he started out with. Rev. Rookie was real ecumenical. Gushing with it. I mean, he ecumenicaled all over himself, but he wasn't one of these obvious old-fashioned preachers. No, when he spoke of God, he didn't come right out and mention his Hebrew name. God, for him, was always a "force," or a "principle."

The Christians looked the other way from their maverick minister in San Francisco; after all, he was packing them in, wasn't he? Why, Rev. Rookie would get up in his mojo jumpsuit and just carry on so. He employed $100,000 worth of audio-visual equipment with which to "project" himself, plus a rhumba band (he couldn't preach); it was the tackiest Jesus you'd ever want to see. Rev. Rookie wasn't no fool, though. He had won a place for himself in the Moocher high command along with Maxwell Kasavubu, the Lit. teacher from New York; Cinnamon Easterhood, hi-yellow editor of the *Moocher Monthly,* their official magazine; and Big Sally, the poverty worker. The crisis meeting was being held to see what was to be done with Papa LaBas, the interloper from the east.

Big Sally arrived first. Big old thing. Though her 300 ESL Mercedes was parked outside, Big Sally insisted upon her "oppression" to all that would listen. She had a top job in the 1960s version of the Freedmen's Bureau, which was somewhat surprising since the poor had never seen Big Sally. Never heard of her either. Although she was always "addressing myself to the community," she spent an awful lot of time in Sausalito, a millionaires' resort. A Ph.D. in Black English, her image of herself was as "just one of the people"; "just me" or "plain prole." Big Sally took off her maxi coat which made her look like a Russian general and then slid onto one of the barstools and continued her knitting; she was always knitting.

"WELL, HOW YOU, SALLY? WHAT'S THE NEW THANG? WHAT'S WITH THE HAPPENINGS?" Big Sally looked at Rev. Rookie as if to say "poot."

"I guess I'll get by."

Rev. Rookie knew better than to scream on Big Sally. She had a habit of screaming on you back. She'd rank you no matter where you were; in the middle of the street, usually, telling all the traffic your business.

The next Moocher to show up was curly-haired grey Maxwell Kasavubu. Trench coat, brown cordovans, icy look of New York angst. He slowly removed his trench coat and put it on the rack; he smiled at Big Sally.

"Hi, Rev., Sally." Rev. Rookie lit all up; Sally blushed and fluttered her eyebrows.

Rev. Rookie rushed over to one of his church's biggest contributors, slobbering all over the man.

"HEY, BABY, WHAT'S GOING ON?" he said, placing a hand on

Max's shoulder. Max stared coldly at his hand, and, meekly, Rev. Rookie removed it.

Sally continued knitting. Rev. Rookie paced up and down behind the bar. Max sat for a moment, contemplatively inhaling from his pipe, occasionally winking at Big Sally. Soon Max rose and went over to read some of Rev. Rookie's literature which was lying on the bar top: *Ramparts* and *The Rolling Stone*. Max stared at them contemptuously for a moment, then slammed them down.

"WOULD YOU BROTHERS AND SISTERS LIKE TO HEAR SOME LEON BIBBS?" Rev. Rookie asked.

Big Sally made a sound like *spitsch,* lifted her head and stared evilly, stopping her knitting, staring disgustedly at Rev. Rookie for a long time.

"I don't feel like hearing no music now," she said.

The door opened and in walked Cinnamon Easterhood, hi-yellow editor of the *Moocher Monthly.* He walked in all tense and hi-strung in a nehru suit, clutching a wooden handbag which the men were wearing or carrying these days. He looked so nervous and slight that if you said boo, he'd blow away. Accompanying him was Rusty, his dust-bowl woman of euro descent, wearing old raggedy dirty blue jeans, no bra and no shoes. She immediately got all up in Sally's face.

Big Sally showed the whites of her eyes for a real long time. "Uhmp," she said. "Uhmp. Uhmp."

"Sally, lord, you sure is a mess," Cinnamon Easterhood's wife said, looking like the history of stale apple pie diners, confidante to every Big-Rig on the New York State freeway.

"HEY, PEOPLE. I FEEL GREAT NOW. ALL MY PEOPLE ARE HERE. WHY DON'T WE LIGHT THE FIREPLACE AND ROAST SOME MARSHMALLOWS? MY UKULELE AND PETE SEEGER RECORDS ARE OUT IN THE VW. " Ignored. And here he was the chairman of the Moochers, second only to Minnie herself.

Cinnamon was over in the corner, congratulating Maxwell Kasavubu on his startling thesis, now being circulated in literary and political circles, that Richard Wright's Bigger Thomas wasn't executed at all but had been smuggled out of prison at the 11th hour and would soon return. Cinnamon was doing most of the talking, saying that he thought the idea was "absolutely brilliant," or "incredibly fantastic."

Max examined his watch.

"Well, I guess it's about time we began the meeting," he said in his obnoxious know-it-all New York accent. As usual Max talked first.

"I've been thinking about our problem and think I can put some input into the discussion. After Ed was murdered, we thought it would take people's minds off gumbo and renew the interest in Moochism, but this hasn't been the case. The community's infatuation with cults and superstition should have run its course by now. But now we have this LaBas. A name that isn't even French and so you can see how pretentious he is."

"It's patois." Big Sally, expert on Black English, put in her input.

"What say, Sally?" Max said, smiling indulgently.

"I said it's patois."

"Well, whatever, the man has presented us with some problems."

"*Spitsch!*"

"Did you want to say something, Big Sally?" Max said, mistaking this sound for comment.

"Nothin, Max. 'Cept to say that I concur with your conclusions. Things was moving nicely till this LaBas man come in here, but it seems to me that we ought not be sitting here talking bout our problems but bout our conclusions, I mean about our solutions."

"TELL IT, SISTER. TELL IT," Rev. Rookie hollered all loud.

"Our solutions is an inescapable part of our problems, and they are one in the part the woof and warf of what we're going to be about. Now, are we going to be about our problems or are we going to be about solutions?"

Hi-yellow, pimply-faced and epicene, rose to speak.

"But—"

"I ain't through. Now, I ain't through. Let me finish what I'm saying and then you can have your turn to talk, cause ain't no use of all us talking at one time, and so you just sit there and let me finish."

Maxwell signaled him to sit down.

"When it comes your time, then you can have the floor, but long as I'm having the floor I think everybody ought to treat me with the courtesy to hear out my views, cause if you going to dispute my views you have to hear me out first—"

"But I was only being practical," Easterhood protested.

"Practical? You was only being practical? If you was only being practical, then look like the first practical thing you would want to do would be to hush your practical mouth so I can talk."

Easterhood's wife was just beaming at all that good old down-home rusticness coming her way. She just leaned back and said, "Sally, lawd. Sister, you sho can come on."

"Takes Sally to just cut through all the bullshit and get right down to the nitty gritty," Maxwell said.

"TELL IT LIKE IT T/I/S/MAMA," Rev. Rookie said.

"That's mo like it. Now, as I was saying, we don't have to worry about this LaBas man, and was going on to say that what we need is somebody to replace that hi-yellow heffer," Big Sally said, her eyes rolling about her head.

Easterhood smiled a good-natured Moocher smile but secretly wanted to crawl on his belly out of the room. He didn't mind all this downhomeness, but, shit, he had an M.A.

"Hi-Yellow Heffer?" Max asked. "What's with this hi-yellow?"

"THE SISTER IS CALLING SOMEBODY A COW," Rev. Rookie explained to Maxwell Kasavubu.

"O, you mean heifer," Maxwell Kasavubu said.

"Whatever you call that old ugly thang. Think she cute. Drive up here in that sport car and when she come start talking that old simpleass mutherfuking bullshit make me sick in my asshole."

"RUN IT DOWN, SISTER, RUN IT DOWN TO THE GROUND," Rev. Rookie said, jumping up and down.

"But which sister are you referring to, Big Sally?" Max asked for clarification. He always asked for clarification, not one to be swept away by emotions as the "minorities" were. They got "enthused" real quick, but when you needed someone to pass out leaflets or man a booth, they were busy or tired or it was so and so's turn to do that.

"Minnie," Big Sally blurted out.

"Minnie?" Cinnamon said, jumping from the couch where his wife Rusty sat guzzling beer, eating Ritz crackers as if they were the whole meal and grinning squint-eyed over what Sally was saying.

"Minnie? Did I hear you right?" Cinnamon Easterhood said, grinning.

"You hearrrrrrrrd, me!" she said, cutting a rough glance his way.

"Well, you have to admit Minnie is a bore. Only a handful turned out for the last rally," said Maxwell.

"That's crazy, we need her. The sister has a fine mind," Cinnamon protested. "She's writing an article in the *Moocher Monthly* magazine on the morphological, ontological and phenomenological ramifications in which she will refute certain long-held contradictory conclusions commonly held by peripatetics entering menopause. Why the dialectics of the –"

"Big Sally, did you want to say something?" Max said, noticing Sally's impatience – impatience being a mild word. Frowns were proliferating her forehead.

"As I was saying before I was so rudely interrupted, we don't need no ontology, we needs some grits, and Minnie ain't bringing no grits. Ain't no ontology gone pay our light bill. P.G. and E. fixin to cut off our Oakland office. Disconnect. We need somebody who knows how to get down."

"Who would you suggest, Big Sally?"

"Street Yellings is the only one the people in the street wont. He the only man that can put this Moocher business back in business."

"Street!" Rusty said. "Street Yellings! Why, if you brought him back, everything would be so outtasite." She remembered his Wanted poster in the post office. The girls would go down there and get all excited. Somebody had painted horns on his head. Street made them want to say fuck. Say words like fuck. Made you feel obscene. Even the men. There was a way he looked at you. And when he made love she had heard from one of the women who had named a rape clinic after him – after he had your clothes off he would say, "Now Give Me Some That Booty, Bitch!!"

"I don't think he can articulate the Moocher point of view," Easterhood said.

"We don't need no articulate," Big Sally said. "Articulate we got too much of. We need someone to oppose that LaBas and them niggers over there in that gumbo business."

"I wish I had your gift, Big Sally – right down to brass tacks."

"Why, thank you, Max," Big Sally said, smiling.

"And as for you, Cinnamon, don't ever call Street inarticulate.

Why, if it wasn't for me convincing the Moocher Board of Directors to back that rag of yours, your verbosely footnoted monstrosity would have folded long ago. Street knows the poolrooms, the crap games, the alleys and the bars. He knows the redemptive suffering and oppression. We will offer Street Yellings the position. Is there any dissent?"

"You, Rev. Rookie?"

"WHATEVER YOU SAY IS FINE FOR ME, MAX," Rev. Rookie said.

"Mrs. Easterhood?"

"Do I look like a broomhandle to you, you four-eyed goofy motherfuka," Rusty says nasty as Max turns red as a beet. Big Sally starts to cackle.

"Please, dear, you'll upset Mr. Kasavubu," Easterhood said.

"I don't care, I'll spit on that fat worm."

"Let's not get carried away, Rusty. We'll remove the licorice sticks you enjoy so much," Max said.

"What did you mean by that, you poot butt?" Rusty said, leaping from the sofa.

Easterhood looked real simple, like a Bunny Berrigan adaptation of a Jelly Roll Morton hit.

"I get sick of your pompous insane cock-sucking remarks," Rusty bellowed.

"BROTHERS AND SISTERS. WE MOOCHERS DON'T GET INVOLVED IN PETTY INDIVIDUALISTIC CLASHES. WE ARE TOGETHER FOR ONE CAUSE. WE MUST LEARN TO SUBMERGE OUR DIFFERENCES." (Guess who.)

Rusty was sobbing, curled up in Big Sally's lap. Big Sally was comforting her.

"Just don't ask me up here any more. I am not a Mrs. Rusty Easterhood, I'm a person. You men think it always has to be your way. Do your housework, raise your children. Well, I'm sick of it; I want to play tennis, express myself, visit motels. Big Sally," she says, looking up to her, "you busy this evening?"

"Look, it's hot," said Maxwell Kasavubu, so sensible, so cool at these times. "We've gone through a difficult transition from an obscure Telegraph Avenue notion to a movement to be reckoned with.

I'll fly to Africa, pick up Street tomorrow."

"But what do you make of Street's criminal record? You remember how he murdered that brother and escaped from jail," Easterhood asked. "The editorial board of the *Moocher Monthly* has had a change of viewpoint concerning the effectiveness of the charismatic lumpen."

"That doesn't count. Just another nigger killing. What's a nigger to the law?" Max said.

Rev. Rookie, Sally, Rusty and even Cinnamon gave Max a momentary hostile look. But when he asked, "Did I say something wrong?" they outdid each other trying to put him at ease. All except Rusty. She didn't owe him anything.

1974

FRANCES FITZGERALD

The Castro

IN THE second week of July in 1984 fourteen thousand reporters made their way to the Democratic Convention in San Francisco. Some of them were actually going to sit in the new Moscone Convention Center and listen to speeches; the rest were going into the streets, for mayhem was predicted. In previous weeks there had been a spate of press stories about "the unconventional city" with its bohemian subcultures and weirdo life-styles. As the flower children had long since gone, what they referred to, for the most part, was the gay community. San Francisco journalists did the best they could to defend the city from its "negative stereotype" with articles about the "driving pertinence" of its tolerance and its diversity for the country as a whole. But they, too, were battening down the hatches. The week before the convention, Jerry Falwell was to bring a road show of New Right personalities to discuss "family issues" and to denounce what he called San Francisco's "Wild Kingdom." His Family Forum seemed to be a probe designed to draw a group of transvestite nuns on roller skates, the Sisters of Perpetual Indulgence, within the range of the nightly network news cameras. In fact the Sisters had announced plans for a puke-in and an exorcism of Falwell. More important, a gay rights march was planned for the convention itself, and it was generally supposed that a horde of witches, warlocks, drag queens, leather men, and so on would descend on the convention center and embarrass the Democrats.

In the event, however, the speeches inside the convention center and the nomination of Geraldine Ferraro as the vice-presidential candidate were rather more spectacular than the goings-on outside in the streets. Guerrilla theater groups did turn up at the Family Forum to perform their tribal rites, but there were probably more police than demonstrators in attendance. And Falwell, who sent his youngest son out into the Castro to report on the "Wild Kingdom" came back with disappointingly few details for the *Moral Majority Report*. The gay march from the Castro to the convention center was orderly and not at all colorful. There were contingents of gay union members and nuclear freeze supporters; there were groups of gay parents and gay businessmen in three-piece suits; there were Democratic clubs, human rights coalitions, and medical groups, including a contingent of men with AIDS. In the lead were the sixty-five gay elected officials, gay delegates, and gay alternates to the convention. The march, one of the delegates told the press, was not a protest but a show of support for the Democratic party. Gay men and women have become "a part of the problem-solving family of the Democratic party," said City Supervisor Harry Britt.

Of course the parade organizers and gay Democrats had put a good deal of effort into seeing that the march turned out as it did. But an era was nonetheless over, and the march was a sign of the times. The gay rights movement continued, but gay liberation, the last wave emanating from the seismic disturbances of the sixties, had worn itself out by 1984. What it left in San Francisco was a small gay city—a city of perhaps 100,000 men and women with political organizations, newspapers, professional associations, businesses, churches, cultural institutions, and recreational facilities. A survey done by a market research corporation of gay men in San Francisco that year revealed a good deal about that city, or rather about the male part of it. From a survey sample of 529 gay or bisexual men researchers found that 78 percent had arrived since 1969, and most of them were living as openly gay men. About half of them lived in the Castro proper and its adjacent neighborhoods; about 80 percent lived in three major gay enclaves. The city was still young—half of the men were in their thirties—and it was prospering. Over half of the men were working in managerial or professional positions—or they had businesses of their own. Forty-three percent of them were making $25,000 a year or more (as opposed to 28 percent of San Franciscans generally), and 39 percent of those living in the Castro proper were making $30,000 or more. The vast majority of them lived in one- or two-person households, and just over half of them had a "primary relationship" with another man. But the city was not growing: immigration had dropped off considerably in the past few years, and thus possibly the population was the same or not much greater than it had been in 1978. It was also aging. A generation of gay men had come to San Francisco, and the next generation was not replacing it (only 18 percent were in their twenties). The gay community was thus becoming a minority in the sense that it had not been one while on the increase. And it was accepting its status as such. It was still powerful politically, but the old militance had gone. Even for those who lived there, the Castro was no longer the shining ideal. If anywhere, West Hollywood, where homosexuals won the majority of seats on the city council in 1984, now held claim to the title of the gay Camelot.

The looks of the Castro proper had changed quite noticeably since 1978. The main street, which six years ago had been in lively transition between hip and chic, now had an uneven and unlived-in look to it. Boutiques selling trendy clothes and expensive home furnishings had crowded out a number of the neighborhood stores; a building and an alleyway had been turned into a boutique mall. The gay bars were still there, but one had become a video discotheque and several of the others had acquired the tired, seedy air of those North Beach bars too long at the center of the tourist routes. Restaurants on the street now advertised pretentious "Continental" food on huge, engraved menus. A chain bookstore had replaced the gay political bookshop, and a new brick-and-plate-glass office building now occupied a whole block on the corner of Market Street. There were noticeably more women in the street—several of the boutiques sold women's clothes—and while the men still wore tight blue jeans and T-shirts, the Castro styles had grown vague and confused. The one shop selling gay leather gear looked musty by contrast to the shops selling three-hundred-dollar suede jackets. In the Folsom District, straight restaurants and discos were crowding the gay bars out.

On the bulletin board at the corner of Castro and Market were fliers from the Alice B. Toklas and the Harvey Milk Gay Democratic clubs. Half of the officers of both clubs were now women—and the same seemed to be true of most of the gay, now "gay and lesbian," social-service groups. Asking around for the veterans of the Harvey Milk campaigns and the Castro marches, I found that some of them had moved away, left the scene, while others had moved into the political mainstream. Cleve Jones was now working for Art Agnos, the state assemblyman who had won his seat for the first time by defeating Harvey Milk. Jim Rivaldo and Dick Pabich each had successful political consulting businesses and were at work for liberal candidates around the state. Bill Kraus worked for Congresswoman Sala Burton. Anne Kronenberg spent several years working in city government, no longer riding a motorcycle to work. Randy Shilts, who had written a biography of Harvey Milk, *The Mayor of Castro Street*, was now a reporter on the *San Francisco Chronicle*. Calling my friends, I found Peter Adair working on a film about antinuclear-war protesters, Ken Maley working on earthquake preparedness measures, and Armistead Maupin finishing another book in the *Tales of the City* series and horribly depressed. Another friend of his had come down with AIDS.

AIDS – the Acquired Immune Deficiency Syndrome – had hit the Castro hard. As of July 30th, 1984, 5394 cases had been recorded nationally, 634 of them in San Francisco. New York alone had a higher number of cases than San Francisco (about a third of the total), but its population was ten times as large. San Francisco had by far the highest number per capita, and a great proportion of them came from the Castro and the surrounding neighborhoods; as was not the case in other cities, virtually all of the victims were gay men.

The disease had been identified only three years earlier. In the spring of 1981 health officials at the Centers for Disease Control (CDC) in Atlanta had received reports of an outbreak of an unusual form of pneumonia and a rare form of skin cancer – both of them in these cases deadly. What the victims of the two diseases had in common was that all of them were homosexual men – and their immune systems had broken down. Setting up a task force, CDC officials contacted physicians across the country and in ten weeks found that 108 gay men had been stricken; some had died as long as two years before, their deaths written off to the proximate causes (as, pneumonia) or unexplained. By December 1981, nearly a hundred cases of immune system breakdown had been reported – twenty-four of the total in San Francisco. As the months passed and the number of cases grew, it appeared that the disease struck not only gay men but also drug addicts who used intravenous needles, hemophiliacs, and other blood transfusion recipients; also the sexual partners, and occasionally the children, of AIDS victims. There was also an outbreak among Haitian refugees in the United States. Studying the incidence of these cases, epidemiologists came eventually to believe that the disease was caused by an infectious agent, probably a virus, and was transmitted through blood, semen, and perhaps other bodily fluids. In August 1982, what had been called "the gay cancer" or "the gay plague" CDC researchers now officially dubbed the Acquired Immune Deficiency Syndrome. But the disease itself remained a mystery.

In April 1983 researchers at the Pasteur Institute in Paris announced they had isolated what they supposed to be the AIDS virus. While French researchers identified it as such, the American medical establishment preferred to wait until the National Health Laboratories offered a conclusion; that came a year later when Dr. Robert Gallo of the National Cancer Institute identified the retrovirus HTLV–III as the AIDS virus. It proved to be virtually identical to the one found at the Pasteur Institute. In the meantime, however, epidemiologists learned a good deal more about the disease. They were able to state with some assurance that the disease was infectious rather than contagious: that is, it could be transmitted only through the exchange of bodily fluids and not through the air or by casual contact. The recipients of anal sex were, they thought, particularly at risk probably owing to the delicacy of the rectal tissues; but all forms of sex involving the exchange of bodily fluids (even possibly saliva) carried the risk of transmission. Later, when the virus was isolated, researchers discovered that HTLV–III was associated with another group of infections that were not always deadly; they also found the virus, or rather its antibodies, present in the blood of a large number of people who did not have any disease. It was thought that AIDS itself might strike particularly at those in poor health, or those whose immune systems had already been assaulted by other infections, such as the related hepatitis B virus. But this was not clear. It seemed probable that the virus alone was enough to cause the disease, but if there were any other factors involved, they remained unknown.

Of all the epidemic diseases AIDS was in many respects the most terrible. In the first place, the mean incubation period for it (as was later discovered) was about five years. What this meant was that an individual could have the virus for a few months or possibly up to fourteen years before the first symptoms (such as fatigue, glandular swellings, and weight loss) manifested themselves, and during that time it was altogether possible that he or she could infect others without knowing it. Once AIDS was diagnosed, the victim might have six months, a year, even three or four years to live, but no one had yet survived for more than five years. As there was no cure, the victim had simply to await the onset of one or more diseases that his or her system could not fight off: meningitis, perhaps, or pneumonia, or the rare skin cancer, Kaposi's sarcoma. The appearance of a small purple skin lesion usually heralded the latter—and was in many cases the first sign of AIDS; and as the cancer developed, the lesions spread on and through the body. Kaposi's sarcoma was, in the case of AIDS patients, not only excruciatingly painful but mutilating.

As AIDS moved relatively slowly through the body, so it moved relatively slowly through the population. And in this respect it was also excruciating. Gay men across the country could watch the number of cases grow inexorably month by month, starting with a few, then multiplying into large numbers. In San Francisco, one of the cities where the disease was first noticed, there were 24 cases in December 1981, 61 cases six months later, and 118 cases the following December—and so on. Proportional to the population, the numbers advanced the most rapidly in the close-knit community of Castro. In March 1983 it was estimated that 1 out of every 333 gay men had AIDS; a year or so later, it was 1 out of 100. An epidemiological survey published in 1985 indicated that 37 percent of gay men in San Francisco had been exposed to the AIDS virus; the figure later climbed to over 50 percent. How many men would end up contracting the disease, no one could predict with any certainty, but AIDS researchers thought it possible that the Castro would be literally decimated in the course of the next decade: 1 out of 10 men would die. The gay carnival with its leather masks and ball gowns had thus been the twentieth-century equivalent of the Masque of the Red Death.

In fact the Castro had become something like the Algerian city of Oran that Albert Camus described in *The Plague*—a city separated from the outside world, where death and the threat of death hung over everyone. By 1984 there were few gay men who did not know someone, or know of someone, who had been struck by AIDS. Most of the victims were in their twenties, thirties, and forties—men in the prime of their lives. Very often they were athletic, ambitious, good-looking men who one day found a purple spot somewhere on their body. The purple spot was the nightmare that haunted the sleep of the Castro. Waking up in the morning, men would search their bodies for it; not finding it, they would search again the next day. Those who found it went on to a new series of nightmares. In the city there was a counseling service, the Shanti Project, where AIDS patients could go to imagine their deaths and take control of their fears in order to live and die as best as possible. Not everyone had the strength for that; not everyone could reconcile themselves to dying while all those around them went on with their lives.

The Castro became a city of moral dramas—dramas that involved not only the victims but their lovers, their parents, and their friends. There were hundreds of stories told. One young man had a lover who deserted him as soon as the news came, saying that he didn't love him anymore—he had found someone else. More often the story was of faithful lovers: one was of a man who nursed his sick friend at home even while he began to suffer from AIDS himself. One young man—so it was said—had parents who had never acknowledged his homosexuality and who, when they heard of his sickness, cut him off and cast him out of the family. Another young man had a mother who moved into his apartment with him to nurse him, and because neither had much money, they lived mostly on gifts of food and money from his friends. A lot of mothers came to San Francisco.

There were stories of landlords who evicted AIDS patients, health workers who would not touch them, and employers who asked them to leave. But most of these stories dated from the early years when the fear of infection was the greatest. In general San Franciscans behaved well. There was no panic, and though some people blamed gay men collectively, people tended to show generosity and compassion to the afflicted men they knew. The city government—led by the mayor—reacted swiftly and generously to the crisis, appropriating $4 million, $5 million, and then $9 million annually for AIDS education, health care, and research. As AIDS patients did not have to be hospitalized for most of the period of their illness, it created an outpatient health care program—a model of its kind and one that could be used in treating victims of other lingering diseases. A network of social-service organizations–the Shanti Project, the San Francisco AIDS Foundation, and Hospice–had city funding to provide emergency housing, counseling, help with medical bills, and home care for AIDS patients. And hundreds of volunteers, both gay and straight, turned out to staff them. San Francisco took care of its AIDS patients better than any other city in the nation and its newspapers, particularly the *Chronicle*, covered the AIDS crisis thoroughly and well. The one ugly note was that incidents of violence against gay people increased measurably. There were stories of juvenile gangs attacking Kaposi's sarcoma patients on the streets, calling them names and beating them.

Most gay men in the Castro, of course, went on with their lives. In the spring of 1984 most of the people I knew there did not talk about AIDS very much. Some of them had already thought themselves through it in some detail. They had decided what they would do with six months or a year to live, and they had imagined how their friends, lovers, and families would react. They had made their wills and settled their accounts. As a result, AIDS no longer preoccupied them. All the same, it was a part of their lives and something they considered before making any long-term commitment. When I told Peter Adair that Armistead was thinking of going to London, Adair replied quickly, "I'm not sure I would do that. I don't think I'd leave San Francisco. If we leave here, we just take the disease with us." Armistead, I explained, was not thinking of going to live in London–he was just planning a few weeks' holiday with a friend. He, too, had considered the responsibility.

The moral drama for gay men in the Castro was something like that for Camus's characters, but it had other dimensions. The plague, after all, threatened everyone in the city–men, women, and children; it struck randomly and killed its victims in a matter of days. Whether people behaved well or badly did not matter in the sense that little or nothing could be done about it. That was Camus's premise: the plague–which was morally meaningless–simply ran its course and subsided. It merely showed how men behaved when faced with a mortal danger they could not affect. Camus's priest, Father Paneloux, who had preached the plague as the wrath of God, abandoned his faith after watching a small child die horribly of it. But AIDS was different. In the first place, it singled out gay men and drug abusers. In San Francisco it struck gay men almost exclusively for the first three or four years. Then one female prostitute came down with it, and it began to appear that heterosexuals could pass it on through sexual contact. Still, its epidemic proportions owed directly to the level of promiscuity within the homosexual population. Fundamentalist ministers who preached God's wrath could thus continue to see the epidemic as God's punishment for the transgression of His law. In addition, all others who harbored negative feelings about homosexuality or sexual promiscuity could now see those feelings as justified. Gay men thus had to face a new form of social condemnation – as well as the disease itself. In the Castro those who had spent a good part of their lives in the struggle against the sexual taboo now had to acknowledge that the sexual liberation they had fought for so strenuously – and on which they had laid their claims of being the avant-garde of a national revolution – had deadly consequences. What was more, they had to face the fact that they were giving the disease to one another.

Quite early on in the epidemic it became clear that gay men could affect the course of the disease: they were responsible for their own lives and for those of others in a way that the citizens of Camus's city were not. But the responsibility was of a strange sort. At least before a test for the AIDS virus was developed and put to use, the responsibility was collective and statistical. That is, an individual gay man could choose to exercise it by forgoing high-risk sex, and it might make no difference to him or to anyone he knew. Even celibacy might not save his life if he had the virus already – though of course it might save the lives of others. On the other hand, it might make no difference if he engaged in high-risk forms of sex with one, two, three, or many other people, since not everyone had the virus and not everyone who had the virus would contract the disease. The only certainty was statistical: if a sufficient number of gay men refrained from high-risk sex with new partners, then the spread of disease would abate. The number of AIDS cases would eventually rise or fall in direct proportion to the choices made. Thus, beyond the individual dramas going on in the Castro, there was also a collective moral drama which involved all of its inhabitants. And because the Castro was an important part of San Francisco, it involved not only gay men but also city officials and to some extent the press and the public at large.

When I returned to San Francisco in June 1984, a battle was raging in the city over public health measures. The struggle had begun about a year before. Until then the gay organizations in San Francisco – as elsewhere – had put all their efforts into obtaining federal government funding for medical research. The federal government had responded sluggishly to the AIDS crisis. The Reagan administration had no sensitivity to gay or inner-city problems, and was in any case attempting to cut back on all forms of social spending. And there were bureaucratic tangles. By the spring of 1983, however, the U.S. Department of Health and Human Services had identified AIDS as the number-one priority, and the Congress, thanks in large part to the California delegation, had appropriated $26 million for AIDS research. In May, Mayor Feinstein had declared an AIDS awareness week, and six thousand people had marched from the Castro to the Civic Center to show their concern and to keep up the pressure for government funding. At that point, however, members of the Harvey Milk club and others raised a new and, as it turned out, bitterly divisive issue.

By the spring of 1983 epidemiologists had produced abundant evidence to show that AIDS could be transmitted through sexual contact involving the exchange of bodily fluids. Their findings had appeared in the regular press, both local and national. Yet a survey made by three gay psychotherapists including Leon McKusick of the University of California, San Francisco, suggested that only a minority of gay men in San Francisco had heeded the implicit warnings. Of the six hundred men who answered the survey questionnaire, only 30 percent said that they had changed their sexual behavior because of AIDS; one in fourteen said that they had actually increased their involvement with high-risk sex. The survey was not a statistical sample of the whole gay population, but it offered some numerical evidence for what AIDS researchers believed from their experience to be the case: most gay men had not yet taken the danger seriously enough, and some did not even know it existed. The responsibility, as far as AIDS researchers and the Harvey Milk club people were concerned, lay first and foremost with the city health department and the gay organizations—neither of which had made any effort to educate the community on the sexual transmission of the disease.

In the July issue of *California* magazine, reporters Peter Collier and David Horowitz documented the case for a public health scandal. Until May, the reporters found, there was not a single piece of health department literature in the city clinics warning gay men about the sexual transmission of AIDS. The literature the department put out all went to reassure the general public that AIDS was not infectious and could not be transmitted by casual contact. Most gay newspapers in the city did not print the epidemiological information available in the regular press, and the gay medical and political organizations, which had called vociferously for government funding, did little to advertise the dangers of the epidemic or the ways in which gay men might protect themselves. Not only that, but they seemed to be engaged in an attempt to suppress information about the spread of the disease.

In January two researchers from the University of California Medical Center had been ready to release their findings showing that AIDS had been diagnosed in 1 out of every 333 single men in the Castro area. They had held a meeting and discussed their findings with members of the gay doctors' association, the Bay Area Physicians for Human Rights (BAPHR), and health activists from the Kaposi Sarcoma/AIDS Foundation and all three gay Democratic clubs. But the consensus at all the meetings had been against publishing them. Finally, two months later, the report was leaked to Randy Shilts and published in the *Chronicle*. Before Shilts ran the article, he received phone calls from a number of gay leaders, including the president of the Toklas club, who was also the cochair of the Coalition for Human Rights, asking him to suppress it on the grounds that it would hurt business in the Castro and reduce the chances for the passage of a gay rights bill in Sacramento. In *California* magazine Catherine Cusic, the head of the health services committee for the Harvey Milk club, charged, "There are leaders in this community who don't want people to know the truth. Their attitude is that it is bad for business, bad for the gay image. Hundreds, perhaps thousands, are going to die because of this attitude. The whole thing borders on the homicidal."

On May 24 the Harvey Milk club voted almost unanimously to put out a pamphlet warning of the sexual transmission of AIDS. Some of the Castro activists in the club—Ron Huberman, its chairman, Bill Kraus, Cleve Jones, Dick Pabich, and Frank Robinson—began to agitate within the 1983 gay community for further measures. In the weeks before the Gay Freedom Day Parade—the event that annually brought 100,000 to 200,000 gay people to San Francisco from elsewhere in the country—they tried to convince the owners of the gay bathhouses to post warnings about high-risk sex. According to Kraus, the bath owners were "totally incensed" by the suggestion. The Toklas club issued a statement disassociating itself from their initiative. Outraged, Kraus, Jones, and Huberman wrote a manifesto and sent it to the largest-circulation gay bar newspaper, *The Bay Area Reporter;* it was printed after a delay of six weeks. "What a peculiar perversion it is of gay liberation," they wrote, "to ignore the overwhelming scientific evidence, to keep quiet, to deny the obvious—when the lives of gay men are at stake." Harry Britt supported the manifesto signers and the drive to post warnings, but many other gay leaders denounced both as treasonous to the cause. "Labeling San Francisco as unsafe for our people is inaccurate and a direct attack on the social and economic viability of our community," the Toklas president wrote.

Just before the parade the mayor asked the city's public health director, Dr. Mervyn Silverman, to close the baths, and gay health activists asked him to pressure the owners into posting warnings. Silverman told the mayor, "It is not the bathhouses that are the problem—it's sex. People who want to have sex will find a way to have it." However, he agreed to ask the bathhouse owners to post warnings. There were further meetings between the owners and the health activists, and eventually a few notices appeared. Most of the gay leaders, however, continued to oppose the initiative. Konstantin Berlandt, the cochair of the Gay Freedom Day Parade, called the proposal to close the baths "genocidal"; his view of the educational effort was that "institutions that have fought against sexual repression for years are being attacked under the guise of medical strategy." For Berlandt, as for the leaders of the Stonewall Gay Democratic Club, the sexual transmission of AIDS was merely a "theory" designed to attack "gay life-styles."

Two or three months later, the health education policies of the city and of most of the gay organizations changed dramatically. By

June the city health department had put out risk guidelines on the sexual transmission of AIDS, and the gay health organizations were printing pamphlets discussing safe versus dangerous sex. The Toklas club and other groups that had fought to suppress AIDS information now earnestly did their part to disseminate it. As Catherine Cusic said, "They took the very positions they had trashed a few months before." There were no apologies and no explanations, but they proceeded, and the results were significant. In November 1983, a health department survey showed that 95 percent of the gay men in the city knew how AIDS was transmitted and knew of the risk guidelines. Attendance at the bathhouses and sex clubs declined—two bathhouses shut down for lack of business—and the VD rate had plummeted. The AIDS Behavior Research Project, a new organization headed by Leon McKusick, instituted a longitudinal study and found that gay men had significantly reduced their participation in high-risk sex.

All the same, a year later, in 1985, as the Gay Freedom Day Parade again approached, a number of health activists felt that the situation still did not warrant optimism. The toll of AIDS victims was still rising at a terrifying rate—the number of cases now doubling every seven or eight months. Roughly a third of the gay male population seemed unpersuaded by the educational campaign, and the indicators of change had come to a stop. Attendance at the baths was up slightly, and the rectal gonorrhea rate had leveled off. Among others, Frank Robinson, who had all but abandoned his science fiction writing in order to study AIDS and what it meant for the Castro, thought the efforts taken thus far were wholly inadequate. "The educational program is crap," he told me. "Look at the new AIDS Foundation posters. There's one with a photograph of two sexy naked men with their asses turned to the camera, and underneath there's a message about the joys of safe sex. Look, I've seen a lot of men with Kaposi's sarcoma. It's a hideous, disfiguring disease. A Hollywood makeup man couldn't duplicate it. There should be pictures of it. But the gay press has never carried a picture, and when *Time* and *Newsweek* did stories on AIDS, the worst they showed were the lesions on a leg."

To Robinson—as to a number of others—it seemed clear that something should be done about the bathhouses, glory holes, and sex

Gay rights demonstration, 1976. Photograph by Tom Levy.

clubs. The baths were a big business in San Francisco, far bigger than they were in most other cities; a lot of openly gay men went to them, as they did not elsewhere, and because of that, they attracted visitors from other cities. The owners asserted that there was no scientifically determined correlation between the bathhouse attendance and AIDS—or even bathhouse attendance and high-risk sex. This was true: a study had never been done. But the baths were facilities for multiple, anonymous sex contacts, and anyone who went to them knew that high-risk sex took place in them. And once the fuss over them had died away, most of the owners had ceased to post the risk guidelines in places where they could be seen. A year before the columnist Herb Caen had reported that a gay doctor had run into three of his AIDS patients in the bathhouse; he had ordered them out but they had refused to leave.

In fact for some months now gay health activists had been asking city officials to take action on the baths. They had given up on the gay organizations, for not even the gay AIDS specialists would make public statements about the dangers posed by the baths. The city, however, was no more responsive. The mayor and the president of the Board of Supervisors, Wendy Nelder, had both let it be known that they favored closing the baths, but both had declined to take action on the grounds that it was not a political matter but a decision for the public health authorities. Silverman, for his part, had said that it would be "inappropriate and, in fact, illegal" for him to close them. To Robinson this reasoning was implausible. "They closed the public swimming pools during the polio epidemic when they didn't know any more about polio than they now know about AIDS," Robinson said. "They license the baths—for fire hazards, cleanliness, and so on—so clearly they can close them." In March, Larry Littlejohn, a deputy sheriff and a gay activist of twenty years' standing, had decided to force the issue. Going down to City Hall, he filed a petition to put a proposition on the November ballot requiring the Board of Supervisors to adopt an ordinance prohibiting sex in the bathhouses. Littlejohn knew that if such a proposition were on the ballot, the great majority of San Franciscans would vote yes. (An *Examiner* pool taken in April showed that 80 percent of San Franciscans would vote yes.) He also presumed that the city and gay organizations would not allow the issue to come to a referendum. There followed a series of events that Robinson, for one, could not wholly account for.

In the two days that followed the Littlejohn initiative, there were gay organization meetings all over the city. The Harvey Milk club held a public debate on the issue. At it, Dr. Marcus Conant, the head of the AIDS Clinical Research Center at the University of California in San Francisco, made his first public statement on the baths. "We have to look at the possibility of closing the bathhouses and bookstores," he said. "I do not say *close* the baths. The word is *discussion*. We must begin the discussion of this problem." Bill Kraus and one of the University of California AIDS researchers spoke in support of Conant's position, but most of the other speakers attacked it. The next day Robinson was at a small gathering of doctors and Milk club people when word came from another small meeting via Dr. Conant that Dr. Mervyn Silverman was going to announce a decision to close the baths the next day. It was the consensus at both meetings that if the baths were to be closed, the initiative should come, or appear to come, from the gay community. At Robinson's meeting, several people asked for time to go back to their organizations and discuss the matter with their memberships. But there did not seem to be time. The group drew up a statement requesting Silverman to close the baths, and several people were dispatched to the phones to collect as many signatures as they could for it in twelve hours.

The next day Randy Shilts came out with a story in the *Chronicle* saying that Silverman, who had long resisted closing the baths, was now planning to close them at the request of fifty gay businessmen, physicians, and political leaders. That morning, however, Silverman announced at a press conference that he would defer his decision for a week or two; there were many factors involved, he said, "some of which have nothing to do with medicine." He assured the press that the decision was his alone, and not based on pressure from any group. Clearly, however, he was under a great deal of pressure. According to the Shilts story, he had consulted fifteen gay physicians and political leaders, and the majority had asked him to delay. According to the *Bay Area Reporter* he had spent the previous evening at a gay forum on the issue, where ninety out of a hundred people opposed any action on the baths. In addition, his press conference was attended by several bathhouse owners and a contingent of men dressed only in towels carrying a sign that read, TODAY THE TUBS, TOMORROW YOUR BEDROOMS.

A few days later, according to the press, Silverman called a meeting of AIDS experts on federal and state levels and including the coordinator of the AIDS task force at the Centers for Disease Control. The discussions were held behind closed doors, and the content of them was not disclosed. On April 10 Silverman held another press conference, where, flanked by gay doctors and health activists, he announced that he would draw up regulations banning sex in the bathhouses and sex clubs. The city attorney, he said, had advised him that an order regulating the baths had a better chance of standing up in court than an order to close them. Preparing the order, he added, would take some time partly because the Board of Supervisors would have to clarify the authority of the police and the health departments in the matter.

By June the issue was still not settled—the regulations were still not drawn up. The reason for the delay was not at all clear from press accounts; city officials seemed to be using the press to blame each other. Nelder, the board president, said that she was amazed that Silverman had not done anything about the baths. Mayor Feinstein let it be known that she was "livid" about the delay and wondered aloud why Silverman hadn't "the guts" to close the baths before the Gay Freedom Day Parade. Silverman, however, maintained that he was waiting for the Board of Supervisors to transfer the authority for regulating the baths from the police to the health department. The police chief, Cornelius Murphy, said that he did not want the police to go into the bathhouses—and that seemed entirely reasonable. Harry Britt, for his part, criticized Silverman for not acting "immediately and expeditiously" to close the baths, but on the other hand opposed any regulation of the baths on the grounds that regulation of sexual activity would be a serious violation of civil liberties. He introduced legislation to prevent the city from regulating them; meanwhile a board subcommittee voted to table hearings on the matter of licensing until after the Democratic Convention. (An uproar over the gay bathhouses was the last thing the mayor and the supervisors wanted with the national press in town.) From the press it looked very much as if no one was willing to take responsibility for closing the baths.

In June the nongay San Franciscans I talked to who had followed the controversy were outraged by the delays and by the apparent failure of political will. In April the mayor had candidly said that the issue was politically sensitive, and that she had to be cautious as some gays in the past had dismissed her comments on gay life-styles as patronizing. "I've got to be careful," she said, "and I recognize that." But the mayor—in the view of those I talked to—was not really to blame: the decision to close or regulate the baths was not a political matter, but a public health matter, and should be treated as such. One journalist—a woman now pregnant and soon to go to the hospital for the delivery of her first child—thought the public health authorities had a lot to answer for. "Look," she said, "the doctors and the health department people keep telling us not to worry about AIDS. They told us not to worry about going to restaurants since AIDS isn't contagious. They told us that with great certainty, but now they say saliva might transmit the virus. Then they tell us not to worry about the blood supply in the hospitals because not very much of it has the AIDS virus in it. Well, the one thing they do know is that AIDS can be sexually transmitted. And yet they won't close down the places where all the sex goes on. It's unbelievable."

On my way to an interview with Dr. Silverman, I, too, thought the public health director had a good deal to explain. Why had his department been so slow in putting out literature about the sexual transmission of AIDS? Why had he refused to consider closing the baths a year ago, then temporized in March of this year, then decided to go ahead after meeting with the national AIDS authorities? At the moment he seemed to be lost in a bureaucratic snarl and not at all eager to get out of it. He had said nothing in public about the health hazards of the baths—and nothing whatever to indicate that AIDS might be a health emergency. He seemed extremely sensitive to gay pressures, much more so than the mayor, though he did not hold a political office (the public health director was appointed by the city's chief administrative officer) and he did not seem to be running for anything. Many San Franciscans now blamed him for the fact that the baths were not closed. Even Frank Robinson blamed him, though he knew what the pressures were and knew there were legal problems as well. "In the end I have to fault Silverman," he told me. "In the end you have to act on principle. If you think the baths are a health risk, you have to close them and fight it in court. There is such a thing as a Hippocratic oath."

Silverman surprised me. I had imagined a bland, elderly bureaucrat, and he turned out to be a man in his mid-forties with longish hair and a beard: lively, humorous, direct. A child of the sixties, one would have said. He was, as it turned out, a former Peace Corps physician. His degrees were from Tulane University Medical School and Harvard University's School of Public Health, and he had been in San Francisco since 1977. He was, I discovered, a reflective man but also an activist—a man passionately committed to his work and to the cause of stopping the AIDS epidemic. In two hours he had convinced me not only that he was taking the right approach to the whole question but that it would have been very difficult to second-guess any one of the decisions he had made. "It's an extraordinary situation," he said. "In recent history I don't know that there's been a disease with so many implications. My medical training didn't begin to prepare me for the job I have to do. My job is to change people's behavior—to change their sex practices, for heaven's sakes. That's not a medical problem. It wouldn't be easy with any population, but among gay men the sensitivities are particularly acute. I may look as if I'm responding to political pressures, but what I'm responding to is opposition from the gay community. To succeed I must have their support—I must have their confidence that what I am doing is in their interests. If gays start opposing my decisions—if they start looking on me as a heavy father—then the whole issue of AIDS gets lost. The mayor seems not to understand this."

In fact Silverman—as I began to understand—had one of the most difficult jobs in the country, and one of the loneliest. The beginning of the AIDS crisis had felt like the first tremors of an earthquake; the doctors who watched the mysterious infection bring down new victims week by week had felt a heave of fear, for no one knew what it might do. When epidemiologists found that it was not contagious, Silverman—like his counterpart in New York—had put a great deal of effort into advertising the fact, for there had been a smell of rising panic in the city. There had been terrible incidents— landlords throwing AIDS patients out of their apartments, health workers refusing to touch them—and some talk of taking measures against the gay community. The panic had subsided, but Silverman still got letters asking him to quarantine all gay men—or send them away.

In the gay community the initial reaction had been one of incredulity. "A disease which killed only gay white men? It seemed unbelievable," one gay doctor told me, remembering the period. "I used to teach epidemiology, and I had never heard of a disease that selective. I thought, they are making this up. It can't be true. Or if there is such a disease, it must be the work of some government agency—the FBI or the CIA trying to kill us all." For those who were not doctors it was easier to believe that the medical profession was exaggerating the threat—or would soon have it under control if enough pressure were put. The alternative was accepting a terrible fear and a sense of contamination. While many individuals faced up to it, the gay organizations preferred to deny the scale of the epidemic and the evidence that it was sexually transmitted. (There were still, after all, many medical uncertainties.) At the same time there was a great deal of paranoia going around about the origins of the disease and the role of the government. Such was the outsider mentality in the Castro that a great many gay men took quite seriously the thought that AIDS might be a form of germ warfare targeted on the gay population by the FBI or the CIA. City officials, and indeed all nongay authorities, were suspect as well: if they had not invented the disease, they were probably using it to suppress "the gay life-style." Pat Norman, the city coordinator of lesbian-gay health services, wrote an article in the 1983 gay parade program suggesting that the medical profession was blaming AIDS victims for contracting the disease "because of their *assumed* sexual behavior and/or use of illicit drugs."

Faced with this reaction, Silverman soon realized that if he took a hard line, it would simply rebound against him: he could not force people to believe him or to do what was good for them, and he could not threaten them with the consequences of not doing so. Reining himself in, he formed an advisory committee of gay and nongay physicians and prepared for a gradual, long-term effort. He became grateful for the college course he had once taken in advertising. The first health department literature he was able to put out offered the advice: "Limit your use of recreational drugs" and "Enjoy more time with fewer partners." The appearance of these inadequate warnings represented a victory as they had been booed by gay audiences just months before. Over the months, and then the years, Silverman spent a great deal of time in the Castro going to meetings, discussion groups, benefit dinners, and so on. He got to know the doctors, the political leaders, and others of influence in the community, and gradually they came to trust him. The radicals often disagreed with him, but even they came to believe that he had no motive other than trying to halt the epidemic. Silverman for his part began to have a feel for the situation and for how the community worked. He watched attitudes change as the disease spread and the death toll mounted. The cry of protest from the Harvey Milk club people over city, as well as gay, policies on health education was what he was waiting for. The initiative had to come from the gay community, and in its wake, he could push forward. That the resistance of the other gay organizations had collapsed immediately thereafter was not perhaps so surprising as the leaders had been defending an illusion rather than a calculated policy. After that, Silverman, in cooperation with the gay organizations, had made a great deal of progress: the educational literature had proliferated, the warnings had become gradually blunter, and the community had responded. In the spring of 1984 Silverman decided to take a new step in the educational campaign. "The new literature is just going out," he told me in June. "We can now show pictures of people with AIDS. We couldn't before because people weren't ready for it, and if the receptors aren't there, it does no good. Besides, fear does not seem to have a very long-term effect on people's behavior."

The next stage, however, was going to be more difficult. Virtually all gay men now knew of the dangers, but still evidence suggested that roughly a third of them had not changed their behavior accordingly. Silverman thought that within the remaining third there were probably numbers of people who could never be persuaded to change. There were people for whom sex had become an addiction, like tobacco, alcohol, or drugs. There were people with death wishes and people who thought they would live forever. This was not, in Silverman's view, either remarkable or difficult to understand—certainly not given the number of people in the general population who continued to smoke or to drink and drive. People thought up all kinds of ways to justify their behavior. "Some people tell me they are so anxious about AIDS that they have to go to the bathhouses to relieve stress. Some people say the whole thing is a conspiracy. There are a lot of sexual radicals in this city; in fact there are probably more in San Francisco than anywhere else. San Francisco has always been the place for people who want a little bit more." Nonetheless Silverman thought there was some reason for optimism. Many more people could be persuaded to change their behavior: the proof was that every time there was a flurry of news about AIDS in the press, the indices changed for the better. And in the long run this would have an effect on the epidemic. "The rate of increase in AIDS cases has already tapered slightly, and that's something given the length of the incubation period. I think they could continue to taper down and eventually become flat." For that to happen, however, the public health director would have to have the support of gay organizations—and now the bathhouse issue threatened to destroy all the credibility he had built up.

Silverman had not chosen the issue. "When I began to think about it eighteen months ago," he said, "I realized that the baths were symbolic facilities. The freedom to have anonymous sex had become associated with gay liberation. The cry was, 'If you close them, we'll go to the barricades.'" No other city had closed its bathhouses, and, as Silverman knew, there was a strong rationale for not closing them. In New York and Los Angeles the working assumption in the public health departments was that if the educational campaigns succeeded, fewer and fewer people would go to the baths; on the other hand, if they did not succeed, and if the baths were closed by fiat, there would be an uproar and dangerous practices would continue anyway. The previous spring Silverman had suggested to the gay activists that they treat the baths as they treated other threats to the community and picket them. His suggestion was much discussed in the Castro, but the pickets did not materialize. With such small support Silverman decided he could not take action himself. But then in March, Larry Littlejohn had forced his hand with the ballot initiative.

From Silverman's perspective what had happened since was this: "After Littlejohn made his announcement, some people got together and said, 'Well, if the baths are going to be closed, better have

Silverman do it.' They assured me they would have community support, but when I called around the next day, I found the support wasn't there. So I decided to postpone my decision." (The same people called Randy Shilts to say that they had, or were in the process of getting, fifty signatures on a petition to Silverman. In fact the group got fifty people to sign, but some of these took their names off the next day, and the document was never made public.) Now unable to avoid the issue, but uncertain what to do, Silverman called a meeting of AIDS experts. "I thought at the time, maybe I shouldn't worry. We have a model program for AIDS in this city, and the bath issue has never even come up elsewhere. But we had a six-hour meeting, and to my surprise, there was unanimous support for an attempt to regulate sex in the baths. Not on medical grounds. The medical grounds were clear enough. But on public health grounds. On educational grounds. So I decided to go ahead. Then I met with gay community leaders and my advisory board of physicians and I told them what I was going to do. I promised them that the regulations would involve only high-risk sex in the baths but that I wasn't going to say that in making the announcements as I wasn't going to talk about masturbation at a press conference. Well, a number of the physicians came to the press conference and stood behind me while I made the announcement. But then seven out of nine of them defected because I didn't mention 'safe sex.'"

But the die was cast now, and Silverman had to proceed. What he needed was an order from the Board of Supervisors transferring the licensing from the police to the health department. The mayor had insisted on this in order to spare the police, and her chief, Cornelius Murphy, from any involvement with the baths. Silverman had gone along with this – though he thought it would be unnecessary to involve any police in the investigation. But the board seemed disinclined to issue the order. Part of the problem was Harry Britt. Britt, while criticizing Silverman for not closing the baths, was opposing any regulation of them. Apparently he was making a distinction in principle, but in introducing legislation to prevent Silverman from regulating them, he said that his measures would "kill the issue of whether the baths should be closed or not." The board subcommittee responsible for the matter seemed to be leaning in his direction. Apparently its members were under pressure from the gay community, and the mayor and the board president could not push them into it. The mayor added to Silverman's difficulties. Silverman had tried to convince her that the baths were not the heart of the AIDS problem, but he had not succeeded. As the daughter of one physician and the widow of another, she looked at the issue in purely medical terms: the baths were a health hazard and should be closed. "If someone were trying to commit suicide by jumping out the window, I would try to stop them. That's the analogy," she said. "The Public Health Director makes a political argument he should not be making. The baths are licensed by the city, a lot of young people from all over the country come here, and there's the possibility of spreading a fatal disease." Thus, while to many gay men Silverman was beginning to look like the patsy of the mayor for trying to regulate the baths after so many refusals to do so, he was also beginning to look to many other San Franciscans like a captive of the gay community.

This latter was a real problem. Before the AIDS crisis most San Franciscans had no notion of what went on in the baths and no idea of the extent of sexual promiscuity in the Castro. Now they were reading the Bell and Weinberg statistics—five hundred, a thousand sexual partners—in the newspapers and coming to the conclusion that gays were different from other people in more ways than one. Under the circumstances the idea that the city would condone the baths seemed quite fantastic. Because the mayor had always favored closing the baths, it was now Silverman who was getting the angry letters. And Silverman could not defend himself. He could not explain gay politics to straight San Franciscans—any more than he could tell the gay community why he had taken so many different positions on the bath issue. Further, he could not publicly attack the mayor or the Board of Supervisors.

Still, the most important issue as far as Silverman was concerned was the reaction of the gay community. Would it eventually accept his position on the bathhouses, or would it go to the barricades? At the moment the barricades seemed a distinct possibility. The Harvey Milk club people generally favored some form of action on the baths, but, once again, they were quite alone in raising their voices. The Stonewall Gay Democratic Club opposed the action. This was hardly surprising since it was in sexual, as in other kinds of politics, the most radical of the three. Two years before it had supported a drive to recall the mayor because its members objected to her veto of legislation introduced by Britt to give "domestic partners" of city employees the same rights to compensation as married partners. But the Toklas club also opposed the regulation of the baths; so did the gay Republican club, the Coalition for Human Rights, the gay doctors' association (BAPHR), the gay newspapers, the gay business association, and just about every other gay organization that could be named.

The opponents of the regulations I talked to explained their position in various ways. They brought up Silverman's own doubts about the effectiveness of such a measure in terms of the whole AIDS prevention program. But they made other arguments as well. Gerry F. Parker, for example, one of the founders of Stonewall and a member of the Castro generation, gave me a long speech on the subject. "I feel very strongly," he said, "that if we lose the battle for the baths, we lose the battle for free expression, free association, and privacy. Along with the church, the government has been the major force for repressing—for terrorizing—gays and lesbians. No scientific evidence definitely proves that there is a correlation between multiple sex partners and AIDS. If we close the baths, we're back to the fifties again with nothing but park sex for a certain percentage of the gay population—largely straight-identified gays. Dianne Feinstein is not just against the baths, she's against all kinds of things, like bookstores and peep shows. She wants to take the Wild West image away from San Francisco. She's just using AIDS to do this. She wants us to go back to the good little fairy days—and we're not going to go."

Jerry E. Berg, a prominent downtown lawyer in his late forties and a close associate of the mayor's, argued from the opposite end of the political spectrum. When I asked how the city had responded to the AIDS crisis, he said, "I'm pleased with what the mayor has done, both locally and nationally. She truly views it as a community problem." When I asked about the mayor's stand on the baths, he went on to say, "Well, the mayor knows the seriousness of AIDS and wants to do something about it and doesn't know what else to do. She sees the baths as designed for promiscuous sex. Well, I'd like to see them closed, too. But I take the civil liberties argument very seriously.

I don't think you can legislate morality. And there are economic interests involved. There is no proof that the baths are directly related to AIDS, and to close them would be a denial of due process. Also, much of the country looks to San Francisco for leadership on these issues. There's an enlightened leadership in this city, but not everywhere else. What if, let us say, Wichita were to close all the gay bars? It could happen. All kinds of things could happen. Look what happened to the Japanese in California during World War Two."

I went to see Michael England, the pastor of the Metropolitan Community Church in the Castro, to ask about the impact of AIDS on the gay community. I had no idea what his position on the baths might be. When the subject came up, England, a robust, energetic man in his late thirties or early forties, told me that he had been working closely with Dr. Silverman on the issue. "I trust Silverman," he said. "The man is not in any way a homophobe—his sole agenda is to save lives. If we had only spent the money and energy on it, we ourselves in the community could have gotten the bathhouses to serve an educational function—they would have been very useful in that way. But we didn't. Communication was screwed up and people got very paranoid. Now what people are hearing is prohibition and negativism. It makes them more scared and more ignorant. When Silverman made his announcement, a lot of people thought he had changed what he told us and was now trying to restrict all forms of sex. But I didn't think so. I thought he was simply being too conservative, medically speaking. The medical experts he called in constructed all kinds of scenarios about how any kind of sex could, under certain circumstances, spread AIDS. They took a much more restrictive approach than the one they would take to, say, drinking or smoking. I think BAPHR has made a lot of sense on this issue; they came out early saying that closing the baths was not the solution."

It occurred to me to say that many gay leaders seemed more concerned about the violation of civil rights than about dying of AIDS. England's reply was: "If I had to go back to living in the closet, I'd have to think very clearly about whether or not I'd rather be dead."

In fact the civil rights argument, as Jerry Berg made it, was not to be dismissed. Given feelings about homosexuality and the opposition to gay rights that still existed in large parts of the country, it was not out of the question that some city might use AIDS as a pretext to close gay bars or otherwise restrict gay men. (Indeed the threat of AIDS was put to service in defeating a gay rights bill in Houston the following January, and Houston City Council members listened to a social psychologist call for the quarantining of all gay men.) Concern for the legal and political precedent the city might create by closing the baths was thus legitimate. This being the case, however, the question was what strategy gay leaders should adopt vis-à-vis the baths themselves. Clearly, government regulation was not the best solution from anyone's point of view. San Francisco city officials would have preferred it if bath attendance had simply dropped off to zero of itself—or if the owners had turned their establishments into AIDS education centers. But the bathhouse owners had not done this on their own, and the gay leaders had not exerted enough pressure on them to make them do so. Now these same gay leaders were objecting to government action on the grounds that made little sense to most San Franciscans. The public perception was that gays were being irresponsible and not taking the most obvious measure to curb the epidemic, and, arguably, this public perception was more of a threat to gay civil liberties than any legal precedent the city might set by regulating the baths. Under the circumstances, it could be argued, gay leaders could best defend their civil liberties by supporting government action on the baths and taking their stand on principle somewhere else. This in any case was the position that many Harvey Milk club people took.

The civil rights argument was debatable politically, but rhetorically speaking, there was something quite suspect about it. In the past, gay liberationists, including Harvey Milk, had permitted themselves frequent recourse to the logic of the slippery slope: that is, if this or that measure was not defeated (the Briggs Initiative or the Anita Bryant campaign in Dade Country), the next step was the concentration camps for all gay men and women. It was one thing, of course, to say this for effect in front of a crowd of people, but it was another thing to deploy the logic in serious discussion, for the United States was not Nazi Germany, and there were many redoubts to be defended along the way. In addition, the civil rights argument was almost invariably accompanied by an assertion that there was no proof that the baths were related to the spread of AIDS. Gerry Parker went so far as to say that there was "no conclusive proof of the correlation between multiple sex partners and AIDS." Both statements were literally true in that statistical samples offer probabilities, not proofs— but they were at the same time wholly sophistical. And the very people who made these arguments otherwise acknowledged, implicitly, that there was some correlation between these things. Berg and England said that they thought the baths should be closed, and Parker, after telling me there was no proof of the correlation between multiple partners and AIDS, went on to talk about the sexual "irresponsibility" of the past "for which so many had paid a price."

In fact the arguments gay leaders made against the regulation of the baths seemed to confirm Silverman's view that the baths were "symbolic facilities." These days some small percentage of gay men in San Francisco went to the baths (between 10 and 15 percent according to surveys), and yet for most gay leaders they seemed to stand as synecdoches for gay sexual freedom. They were seen as sanctuaries in a hostile world. They were also perhaps the last defense against the fact that most forms of sex were now mortally dangerous. To read the gay press was to imagine that that was the case, for in speaking to the gay community, opponents of the regulations spoke at a far higher emotional pitch than they did to outsiders. In one issue of *BAR* there was a full account of the public meeting held by the Harvey Milk club at which Larry Littlejohn had announced his ballot initiative. Gerry Parker, according to the article, had gotten up at the meeting and "screamed" at Littlejohn, "What you are doing is going to be a political disaster. You have given the Moral Majority and the right wing the gasoline they have been waiting for to fuel the flames that will annihilate us!" In the next issue of *BAR* there were letters calling Littlejohn an "Uncle Tom," a "quisling," and an "Alice-in-Wonderland do-gooder" who "forced" other people "to behave in a manner deemed for their own good." The editorial in that issue dealt with the statement Robinson, Conant, and others had drawn up asking Silverman to close the baths. The statement was never published, but the editorial said:

The Gay Liberation Movement in San Francisco almost died last Friday morning at 11 a.m. [i.e., the time of Silverman's first press conference].
No, that's not quite it. The Gay Liberation Movement here and

then everywhere else was almost killed off by 16 Gay men and one Lesbian last Friday morning.

This group, whose number changed by the hour . . . signed a request or gave their names to give the green light to the annihilation of Gay life. This group would have empowered government forces to enter our private precincts and rule over and regulate our sex lives. . . .

These people would have given away our right to assemble, our right to do with our own bodies what we choose, the few gains we have made over the past 25 years. These 16 people would have killed the movement—glibly handing it all over to the forces that have beaten us down since time immemorial. . . .

The people of the community were quick to see what was being traded off, and have responded in anger and consternation. This office has received more mail on this issue than any other. Not one letter backed the collaborators.

Somewhere in the middle of the editorial was the charge: "The Gay Community should remember those names well, if not etch them into their anger and regret." There followed, in a box and in large type, the names of sixteen people. Among them were Ron Huberman and Carole Migden (the two leaders of the Harvey Milk club), Bill Kraus, Dick Pabich, Dr. Marcus Conant, Frank Robinson, Harry Britt, and "the traitor *extraordinaire,* Larry Littlejohn."

Rhetorical overkill had become something of a convention in the Castro, but I did not remember gay liberationists in the past attacking each other in this vitriolic a fashion. Randy Shilts, however, told me that such attacks had become fairly common ever since the beginning of the AIDS crisis. "There's a whole genre of political leaders who keep saying we're about to be put in concentration camps," he said. "Meanwhile they attack the messengers who bring the bad news about AIDS. Last year I ran a piece about that study on the incidence of AIDS in the Castro, and we at the *Chronicle* made a fuss when the bathhouse owners refused to put AIDS literature in the baths. All of a sudden it was like the McCarthy period. People all over the place were calling me a 'traitor to the gay community' and 'homophobic.' Among gays that's like being called anti-American. The Toklas club passed a resolution calling me the most homophobic person in northern California."

It was impossible to think about AIDS without strong feelings, and in the face of disaster, communities, like emperors, have often preferred to blame messengers rather than to take responsibility—and action. But the form gay anger took still had to be explained. Jerry Berg had suggested an answer to this when I asked him about the impact of AIDS of the community. "Generally speaking," he said, "there was a lack of personal definition of what it meant to be gay. Those who think that what binds us together is sex and not broader human qualities are very threatened by the disease. To them AIDS looks like a great threat to everything gay. Many of these people are quite hysterical, and there is a political craziness around. I have dear friends who are battling over the baths."

Reverend England suggested a further explanation in a roundabout way. England, as I discovered after going to see him, had denounced the attempts made to close the baths in a letter to *BAR* he had written with a fellow pastor of the Metropolitan Community Church. In that letter the pastors gave several reasons for their view that the attempts were "ill-advised." One of them was that " . . . airing of the issue through such a measure may further inflame public panic and give tacit permission to expression of homophobic feelings in repressive legal measures and even violence."

This was the usual slippery slope argument put in psychological terms. The pastors, however, concluded with an argument about gay psychology:

> Finally, we see such a measure as the product, in some minds, of our internalized homophobia, a tendency deep in some of us to see sexuality as evil and to scapegoat non-traditional forms of sexuality, instead of spending the effort to place them in loving and safety-conscious contexts.

The very complexity of the sentence suggested that it touched on a delicate issue. Given the context, England was accusing Little-john and the Milk club people of "internalized homophobia." But he had mentioned the same phenomenon to me in a much more general context. When I went to see him in his office, he had just been arranging a funeral service for an AIDS victim at which other AIDS victims would speak. Thinking of Father Paneloux in *The Plague,* I asked what a minister had to say to those living in the shadow of such a catastrophe. His reply followed my thought in that it concerned the Panelouxes of the Christian Right. "The Jerry Falwells of this country," he said, "are trying to tell us that AIDS is God's wrath – that God is punishing us for being homosexuals. As ministers we say that this is not the Christian point of view. God does not punish by disease. Divine love is unconditional, and it will bring good out of evil if we allow it to."

Surprised at the mention of Falwell, I asked him whether any of his parishioners took anything that the Christian Right said seriously.

"There's a lot of internalized homophobia in this community," he said, "and it's very hard to throw off. In the beginning many people believed that AIDS was a punishment. They thought it proved they were bad people or that sex was bad. The immediate reaction was 'I'm never going to have sex again.' But now there's been some turnaround on this. People are active in fund-raising and volunteer activities. But as pastors we still have to deal with the Christian Right. That's our most important task."

England was certainly in a position to understand the psychology of the Castro, and his description of it was wholly plausible. Indeed, some months later, Leon McKusick and three other psychotherapists working with gay men said much the same thing in an interview published in *BAR*. One of the important functions of coming out, after all, was to banish guilt by bringing "the guilty secret" into the plain light of day. The experience, though cathartic, was perhaps not always sufficient to remove every last trace of guilt, and in the face of AIDS, even those not normally in conflict about their sexuality might have this feeling all over again – and see AIDS as a punishment. According to the psychotherapists "AIDS-related stress" could create a crisis in which the individual fell into depression, resorted to defiant acting-out, suffered anxiety, or became paranoiac. In light of England's letter to *BAR*, it occurred to me that this "internalized homophobia" might be the key to the otherwise puzzling response of the community and many of its leaders to the AIDS crisis. England, who understood these feelings (neither he nor the psychotherapists as they were quoted ever used the word "guilt"), had himself tried to deal with them in a variety of ways. One way was to preach the gospel of a loving God who brought good out of evil. Another way was to charge that the message of guilt came from the Christian Right–and not from within. These were his conscious strategies. But he, like many other gay leaders, used other strategies without perhaps knowing it. One was to attribute violent homophobic feelings to the public at large (which would end in "repressive measures and even violence"). Homophobic feelings certainly existed in the public at large, but it was one thing to assess their consequences in a rational manner, as, for example, Berg had, and another to maintain that they would lead to general violence–and concentration camps for gay men. The slippery slope logic began with a projection. Another way was to attribute homophobic feelings to those who brought the bad news about AIDS or who publicly proposed that gay men curb their sexuality. This same form of projection turned the health authorities into punishing fathers. Seen in this light, the gay men who brought the bad news were doubly heroic, for they had first to overcome whatever residue of guilt they themselves felt about their sexuality and then to brave the verbal terrorism leveled at them. It was perhaps no coincidence that those who were able to do so were those who had been closest to the center of gay liberation.

England, when I went to see him, told me that he would be speaking at a panel discussion on the baths the next day in a downtown church. He had not, he said, reached a decision about the regulations, but he would probably defend Silverman's position at the meetings as there would be no one else there to do so. The next day, however, surrounded by opponents of the regulations, he attacked all those who favored government action. "In effect what they're saying is 'We know what's best for you,' " he said. "It's a heavy paternal message, and it caused me to be suspicious right away." This was precisely the reaction Silverman had feared, and coming from someone who had worked with him and trusted him, it boded ill for his move on the bathhouses.

On October 9, just about four months later, Dr. Silverman invoked emergency powers to close the baths and made a statement to the press in which he said that the baths and sex clubs were "fostering disease and death" and "literally playing Russian roulette with the lives of gay men." His move was unexpected. In August, at the request of

Harry Britt, a committee of the Board of Supervisors effectively killed legislation transferring the regulating authority over the baths to the health department. Silverman then reconvened his group of AIDS experts to ask them their advice. The group proved divided, but he decided nonetheless to proceed. In September he sent private investigators into thirty establishments (both gay and straight) to report on high-risk sexual activity, and with their report in hand issued an order to close fourteen baths and sex clubs as "public nuisances." The baths closed, but most reopened again after twenty-four hours to test Silverman's order. The mayor, predictably, was furious. Though it was the city attorney who recommended the legal strategy and took the case, she had said that if the choice was hers, she would simply have closed them on her own authority–presumably with a quarantine order. "If I were overturned by a court, so be it," she said. "The important thing is if you save lives, it's worth it, and I'm convinced you will save lives." She added that, "If this were a heterosexual problem, these establishments would have been closed a long time ago. But because this has been involved in politics, they haven't been closed."

On October 15 a Superior Court judge ordered nine baths and sex clubs closed temporarily pending a hearing on the city's request for an injunction. (He excepted bookstores and two movie theaters cited for health violations.) The bath owners prepared to dispute the order, backed by a number of gay legal groups. The Harvey Milk club, Dr. Marcus Conant, and Harry Britt came out in favor of Silverman's initiative, but the other two Democratic clubs, the Republican club, the Golden Gate Business Association, and the Bay Area Physicians for Human Rights denounced it. In the community the lines appeared firmly drawn in the same place they had been drawn in June. But when a coalition of these groups called a protest rally at Market Street and Castro on October 29, only three hundred people showed up. The gay leaders might protest, but the rank and file would not, it appeared, go to the barricades.

The hearings took place, and on November 29 Judge Roy Wonder of the Superior Court told the bathhouses they could reopen, but ordered them to comply with certain regulations, the most important of which was that they had to hire monitors and expel those of their patrons who engaged in high-risk sex. Judge Wonder had perhaps not spent very much time contemplating the working of bathhouses. In any case, the attorneys for both sides claimed victory, and the mayor, along with the *Chronicle* editorialist, objected that his order would create a "spying system" repugnant to all. The mayor was perfectly right, but at the same time it was unthinkable that the baths could remain open if the order was enforced. The city attorney requested a clarification of the enforcement procedures, and on December 20, Judge Wonder gave him the changes of wording he sought. The consequence was that while the bathhouse owners planned an appeal, all but one of the baths and sex clubs shut down.

What Judge Wonder's order seemed to demonstrate was that had Silverman simply closed the baths as the mayor had urged, his order would not have stood up in court. An editorial in the *San Francisco Examiner* pointed this out and argued that in view of the health emergency the only proper solution was for the Board of Supervisors to pass an ordinance closing the baths. The supervisors, however, were disinclined to such a move, and the mayor no more inclined to consider the justice of Silverman's position than she had ever been. The passage of a proposition she had sponsored on the November ballot now permitted her to take control of the city health department through the medium of a new health commission, whose members she had the right to appoint. In early December she gave Silverman a clear signal to resign by failing to include him in the planning for the new commission. Word was put out that the bath issue was not the only issue between them — earlier in the year, state investigators had found fault with conditions in one of the hospitals under his jurisdiction. But clearly the baths were the main issue, and most of the newspaper articles spoke of her displeasure with his "indecision and foot-dragging" in closing them. On December 11 Dr. Silverman resigned.

By the spring of 1985 there was ample evidence to show that Silverman's initiative on the baths had succeeded in all the ways he had hoped for it. While the bathhouse owners continued to press for an appeal, their case languished in the dockets, and eventually several of them sold off their buildings for very good prices. More important, the gay organizations did not go to the barricades; they did not turn on Silverman or the city government. In November the new *BAR* editorialist, Brian Jones, reproached a letter writer for calling people "the enemy" for wanting the baths closed; you might disagree with them, he said, but they are not the enemy. At no time did the protest reach the rhetorical level of the previous June, and as time went on, the issue simply faded away—even from the pages of the gay bar press. That both Superior Court judges involved in the case showed concern for the civil liberties issues involved took the force out of some of the protest. Then when it appeared that no other city would follow San Francisco's lead in closing the baths, most of those uniquely concerned with the consequences dropped their objections. "I opposed government regulations because I worried about the domino effect," one businessman told me. "But now the baths are closed, I'm delighted." Actually, the very day he said that, two bathhouses reopened: their owners were clearly testing the city's enforcement procedures. It made very little difference: the baths had lost their symbolic value. As before, the defenders of the barricades had simply melted away without apology or explanation.

Silverman's main purpose in taking action on the baths had been to move along the whole process of AIDS education. Six months later all the experts in the field I spoke with thought the purpose very well served. "I thought Silverman was wrong," Frank Robinson told me. "I, like the mayor, thought he could simply close the baths and have the order stand up in court. But the way he did it, the baths were closed with a minimum of community objection, and all the right results followed. The fallout was an *extreme* heightening of education. The education program is just about as good as you could get it, and the awareness just about as high as it could be." Leon McKusick of the AIDS Behavioral Research Project thought that the controversy itself had not been helpful but that the months of news coverage that accompanied it had had a significant effect. For two years now McKusick and his colleagues had been doing a study of some four hundred men, sending questionnaires out to them every six months, and the results of his last survey went to show that behavior had changed remarkably. His respondents reported that in November of 1982 they had had an average of six sexual partners in a month; in November 1984, they reported an average of two and a half. In the same period the mean number of unsafe sex acts they reported declined from almost five per month to less than one per month. The decline in both sets of figures had been very gradual in 1983 and very sharp in 1984. In another survey done for the San Francisco AIDS Foundation, 62 percent of the five hundred gay and bisexual men interviewed reported having had no unsafe sex outside a primary relationship in the previous month; nine out of ten reported having altered their high-risk practices in some way because of AIDS.

Though Silverman was now out of office (he remained temporarily as a consultant to the Health Department), his approach to AIDS education had now been taken up by the gay community itself. The San Francisco AIDS Foundation had employed a professional management consultant and engaged the services of a market research firm, the Research & Decisions Corporation. Sam Puckett, the management consultant, told me: "We take a factual, no-nonsense approach that the epidemic is not going away, and we want to solve it ourselves. Here we're not using health educators—there's not a Ph.D. in the place—we're doing market research and advertising. We've just spent a hundred thousand dollars on a market research survey to find out what people know and what they believe. Before, people were working in the dark, and there were so many sensitivities in the community that they were very cautious. But that time is over, and our new ad campaign has been very well received." The leaflets Puckett showed me were very different in tone from those of the year before. There was no coyness anymore. The headline on one of them was, THERE IS NO LONGER AN EXCUSE FOR SPREADING AIDS; its message was that the individual bore responsibility not just for his own life but for that of his partner—and for the life of the whole community. Under foundation sponsorship the Research & Decisions Corporation was now moving beyond advertising to start a series of rap groups in which gay men could discuss what AIDS prevention meant in their own lives.

In the space of a year the politics of the Castro had changed even more than the educational programs—though the two were very much related. In the first place, the Milk club people were no longer a besieged minority. In the six months since Silverman had made his move there had been a good deal of internal criticism of "the gay leaders" in the Castro. Randy Shilts had delivered the first broadside in an interview he gave to a gay skin magazine. In the interview, as excerpted in *BAR* in November, he started by attacking both the gay press and the gay leadership for lying to people and telling them only what they wanted to hear. He then called the gay leaders "a bunch of jerks who wrap themselves in silly, dogmatic rhetoric" and went on to say, "Let's not kid ourselves. The local Gay political scene is a loony bin. The community is top-heavy with Chiefs and not an awful lot of Indians. You are not dealing with normal people. These folks are crazy." The reaction to this in *BAR* over the next few weeks was very surprising. The editorial on the subject defended "the gay leaders" solely on the grounds that there had to be leaders in a democracy, and most of the letters praised Shilts for starting a "healthy and much-needed debate." The newspaper did not pursue the subject, but the debate must have gone on elsewhere, for by April a great many people I spoke with were critical, if not contemptuous of "the gay leaders." Jim Foster, the founder of the Toklas club, told me, "The message we've been putting out for years is ghettoization, isolation, and alienation from the larger community. The leaders only know how to lose. They never take responsibility, so it's always someone else's fault." Foster believed that gay politics as such were dead in the climate of the eighties; the solution was now to build philanthropies on the model of Jewish organizations.

Possibly "the gay leaders" represented the community better than Shilts or Foster was ready to admit, for the debate did not lead to personal recriminations, leadership struggles, or new divisions in the Castro. The Castro simply put some distance on politics and on the panicky crowd behavior of the year before. Shouts of "traitor" and "homophobe" were now rarely heard in the streets, and the political craziness surrounding AIDS had all but disappeared. It was not that there were no issues left. Far from it. The newly developed tests for AIDS antibodies in the blood raised civil liberties issues far more serious than the closing of the baths. (Could the test results be kept confidential? If not, should gay men take the tests, as positive results might subject them to discrimination by insurance companies, government agencies, the military, and so on?) But the gay leaders and the gay press generally discussed these issues in a rational manner without discovering "enemies" and building up factions. It was as if a boil had been lanced or a fever had broken. The Castro was at peace.

When I asked Leon McKusick what, as a psychotherapist, he thought had happened to the community, he said, "It's my hypothesis that the community has been going through the stages that individuals are said to go through when faced by a life-threatening disease: denial, rage, bargaining, and acceptance. The community has now accepted AIDS." The leaders had, it seemed, acted out this all-too-human drama and brought its members along with them.

But it was not only political attitudes that had changed, it was attitudes about life in general. There had been signs of this change the previous June – only at that point they had seemed incongruous. Then I had noticed that the gay leaders who most strenuously opposed government action on the baths sometimes talked about the impact of AIDS on the community in a strangely positive way. Gerry Parker, for example, said: "The AIDS crisis has gotten people to come together and look at themselves in the mirror and ask critical questions about their lives. In the seventies this was a very young society, and for the young the dream of the ghetto was a candy store, a romp. In the irresponsible seventies you used to see a lot of refrigerators with drugs in them but no food. Now people are concerned about health; there's a realization that we're all interdependent. It's the 'we' generation, not the 'me' generation anymore. People look for an inner purpose, and there's a lot of interest in Taoism and Buddhism. There was a time when we were cutting the edge of commercialism and fashion – that was a part of our being – but it's no longer true. Now we're into backpacking and wholesome relationships. The lesbian community is far ahead of us in many ways, particularly in its sense of cooperation and interdependence. There's a feminization process going on in the gay community now, and it's very healthy."

Parker had a declamatory style, and while listening to him make this speech, I felt increasingly irritated. In the first place, these sentiments seemed to fit rather badly with his contention that there was no proof of the correlation between multiple sex partners and AIDS. In the second place, much of it was clearly nonsense. Backpacking and Taoism! That was a counterculture fantasy, and one I assumed he was creating in a spirit of boosterism for my benefit. Only later did I begin to think this was not the case. Parker went on to say, "AIDS was a great and profound fear that affected all of us. We know more people who have died of it in the past two years than have died in our lifetimes. I witnessed a number of people going through it, and the encouraging thing is that we found a connection. They were strong people and they had bright outlooks. The political people gave me sage advice on the direction the movement ought to take right up to their last hours."

Parker's description of the AIDS victims rang a bell. The regular San Francisco press had done a number of profiles of AIDS victims, the journalists in every instance choosing admirable young men with wonderful families and fine careers, and generally glossing over the terrible fear and suffering they went through. The gay press usually printed obituaries of the AIDS dead written by their lovers, but in the case of gay activists, the editors themselves would write the obits using much the same language Parker had used: the men had fought and died heroically in the service of their cause. This ennobling of the dead was clearly some form of compensation for the horror or contempt with which the world at large regarded them. Now a similar form of explanation – or mythology – seemed to be growing up around the impact of AIDS on the community as a whole. Right after telling me about the "political craziness" AIDS had engendered, Jerry Berg, for example, said: "My own view is that AIDS is a terrible tragedy, and yet one which offers real opportunities for personal and collective growth. My friends are taking a new look at their relationships, at the meaning of love and intimacy, and they are making choices. It's very positive and exciting. Of course, large numbers will continue to die, but the threat of the disease has given us all a new perspective on life. It's growth-producing, and most people who have had it have grown into grace."

Growth, a new maturity, a new intimacy, a sense of interdependence were phases I heard again and again in the Castro that year, and often from the very same people engaged in the fratricidal struggle over the baths. Many of my friends satirized this kind of talk. When I asked Larry Glover – now working as a bartender – about the "new intimacy," he said, "It's just like the fifties again: people getting married for all the wrong reasons." Larry did not mean his remark to be taken seriously so much as he meant it to be subversive of the new mythology he saw the community weaving around itself. Larry did not understand people who talked about all the wonderful things that were happening as a result of AIDS.

In the late fall of 1984, however, a McKusick study and the Research & Decisions Corporation survey for the AIDS Foundation came out with some data suggesting that at least some of what Parker and Berg had been saying about community attitudes was, or was becoming, true. The surveys showed that "the new intimacy" had little basis in fact: gay men were not any more involved in "primary relationships" than they had been in the past. About half of them had such relationships and half did not: the figures remained virtually unchanged in two years. According to the Research & Decisions survey, however, respondents in a large majority said they would like to be in a committed relationship—preferably monogamous, and one that would last. Respondents in an equally large majority said they had more concern than formerly about the community as a whole. The studies also indicated that there was a good deal more concern about general health, diet, and exercise in the gay community, and a good deal less drug and alcohol consumption and less interest in impersonal sex. Asked to rate the sentence "Because of AIDS many gay men are changing their lives for the better" on a scale of one to ten, respondents gave it a 7.2 rating, whereas they gave the sentence "AIDS is damaging the gay movement by limiting people's sexual freedom" a rating of only 3.8. Conceivably a number of the respondents told the researchers what they thought they ought to say. All the same, they had created a positive vision for themselves. They had made a decision to focus on the good that might come out of the evil of AIDS. This vision was a consolation, but it was also an antidote to the notion that AIDS was a punishment—a notion that, as Reverend England suggested, lay so deep as to be unavailable to reason. And it helped people act against the threat of AIDS.

By April 1985, the looks of the Castro had changed once again. They had changed so quickly that even its residents pointed it out to me. On a weekday morning or afternoon the people on the main street included numbers of older people and women with children. These people had not just moved into the area; rather, they had taken up doing their shopping and socializing on the main street again. The tourists had vanished, and with them a number of the most expensive gift stores and clothing boutiques. The Castro was a neighborhood once more. The gay bars were still there, and on Saturday mornings the street would fill up with young men. But now the only remarkable thing about these young men was their numbers. Very few—perhaps one or two in a crowd—wore leather or one of the other sexual costumes. Most looked like all other men of their age, and most were clearly doing Saturday errands, having been at work all week. The Castro was still a gay neighborhood, but it had lost its "gender eccentricities." It was a neighborhood much like the other white, middle-class neighborhoods surrounding the downtown.

Sam Puckett, a resident of the Castro, but one slightly older than most of its inhabitants, said something to me which might have been an epitaph for the old Castro: "During the seventies the gay movement here created an almost totalitarian society in the name of promoting sexual freedom. It evolved without any conscious decision, but there was so much peer pressure to conform that it allowed no self-criticism or self-examination. At some point there would have to be less sexual, political, and visual conformity. People grow up and change. But AIDS forced a reexamination in the way that few issues do. What we're seeing now is a revolution. We're seeing a reevaluation of life and relationships and what being gay is all about. We haven't got the answers yet, but at least the questions have been posed."

Puckett's observation about the breakdown of conformity seemed to me to be true on many levels. A sign of the times was a theater piece put on by the major gay theater group in the city, Theatre Rhinoceros. The piece was a series of sketches about the ways that AIDS had entered people's lives, and many of them broke the mold: they are dramatic rather than melodramatic and they explored the nuances of real feeling rather than the sentimental cliché. My friend Peter Adair, who was filming the production for a documentary, told me that the producers had held open casting calls in "the community" and that most of the people involved—actors, writers, and so on—had some experience with the disease. On Peter's film the cast members and others talked about the way AIDS had affected their lives: one man had an AIDS-related condition, and several had lovers or friends die of it; one of the directors was a Shanti volunteer and one actor—a young comedian—was a nurse in the AIDS ward of a hospital. By some extraordinary coincidence the director and the actor-nurse had taken care of the same patient. They remembered him well, for the man had been full of bitterness, rage, and aggressive self-pity. Indeed, he seemed, they said, to have only ugliness inside of him. Profoundly shocked by the patient, the young nurse had gone to the hospital therapist to find out how to cope with the man but also how to deal with his own emotions. The company was now building a sketch around the incident in which the young actor would play himself. "I learned something from it," the actor said gaily on camera. "I learned that just because someone's dying doesn't mean he can't also be an asshole."

Going around to see my friends, I found that many of them were working in one way or another on AIDS. Randy Shilts, of course, had been writing about it for years in the *Chronicle* and now he was writing a book. But Peter Adair had been making a film on nuclear weapons protesters, and Ken Maley's work had for a long time centered on earthquake prevention measures. Now both of them had come back to the disaster closest to them: the real thing as opposed to its substitutes. Adair had made a public-service film for those thinking of taking the AIDS test, and was now involved with the Theatre Rhinoceros production. Maley was, among other things, working on AIDS awareness programs with Jim Rivaldo. Armistead Maupin had returned from England and was traveling around the country talking to gay groups; he would entertain them, but he would also urge people not to deny their homosexuality or to deny the threat of AIDS. Adair told me that gay men in San Francisco probably spent 60 percent of their time thinking about AIDS: after all, about that percentage of them probably had the virus by now. But my friends did not seem obsessed by the subject—and perhaps it helped that they were dealing with it professionally. In any case, life went on.

As Peter, Ken, and Armistead had come back to look the monster in the face, so they, along with many other gay men, had come back in other ways as well. For the past two or three years many people had in one way or another withdrawn from the community: some had actually picked up and left the Castro, or left the city. For some time it had seemed to me possible that "the community" would break up, and that gay institutions—other than those concerned with AIDS—would simply dissolve. But now it seemed that many people had come back—as they told the researchers they would—and the hive was humming again. Armistead, for one, had resumed his duties as Gay Personality and had recently officiated at the ceremony welcoming back to San Francisco the two gay hostages from the June, 1985 TWA hijacking to Beirut. The two hostages, openly gay, had lived in fear that their captors would recognize them as such, for under radical Shi'ite law homosexuality was a crime punishable by death. Their captors, however, had never suspected anything of the sort, for the two men had been dressed in Castro Street gear—olive drab fatigue trousers and tank-top shirts—and the militiamen had taken them for macho toughs. "It was an only-in-San Francisco story," Armistead said. "You couldn't have made it up."

Armistead was, as usual, full of stories, many of them unprintable, about the new gay social institutions and the ingenious ways people had found to have safe but nonetheless impersonal sex. "It's the tribal rites," he said. "People get nostalgic for them." I asked him about the story of the man who bit a policeman. The newspapers had it that a San Francisco policeman had been bitten three times by a man who was resisting arrest; the man had later told the police that he had AIDS. The district attorney then considered changing the charge from assault to felonious assault with a deadly weapon. "Ah, yes," Armistead said, "I heard that, and I was already to get on my high horse and go out and protest police behavior when it came out that the policeman was openly gay. He had gotten his job on the force only after an antidiscrimination suit. No one knows whether the man who bit him was gay or not, and he's refusing to take the AIDS test."

Armistead seemed to me very much back in form. His *Tales of the City* books were selling very well in the bookstores, and now a major production company wanted them for a television series. "They seem serious this time," Armistead said. "But it's a little late. San Francisco isn't at all the place that it was in the mid-seventies—full of odd and unconventional people. Now everyone's so madly dressed for success. But at least they can handle the gay character. After all, every soap opera on television has a gay character in it now. So perhaps we did make some kind of a dent. That's why I go around to places like Texas and Indiana telling people they shouldn't cut themselves off from their heterosexual friends. I tell them it's fun to be an exotic bird."

An era was over, and yet the Castro seemed much as it had been in the very old days when Ken and Armistead and Steven and Daniel had thought of it as their stamping grounds and a small fraternity. The crowds had gone, political enthusiasms had abated, and personal relations—friendships—had come again to the fore. It was now the pattern in the Castro for men, whether they were living with someone or not, to have a number of very close friends with whom they spent the holidays, in whom they could confide, and who would take care of them if necessary. This was the family the Castro had developed, and it was—Armistead's stories notwithstanding—stable and domesticated. But then the people of the Castro had grown up together, and they had a great deal more in common now than the fact of being gay. Indeed, the people they had very little in common with were gay men in their twenties—for whom Harvey Milk was a myth and the clone style as antiquated as high-button shoes. There was only ten years' difference between them, but when men of the Castro generation talked about the younger men, grumbling that they took "gay" for granted and were not pulling their weight, they sounded like codgers talking about the decline of the work ethic. Steve Beery, Armistead's friend, who himself did not look much more than thirty, told me his revelation about the generation gap. Steve still lived on the Filbert Steps opposite Ken and Daniel. One day, when he was at home sick, he looked out on the steps and espied a beautiful young man taking a lunch break with his shirt off in the sun. The young man looked with great interest at Steve, so the next day when he came back at lunch hour and looked in Steve's direction again, Steve invited him up to the apartment. "I was thinking . . . well, you can imagine what I was thinking," Steve said. "But the guy just kept sitting there in the chair talking about one thing and another. As he was leaving, he asked me for a date. A date! I was shocked. He was, I gathered, looking for commitment. He was looking for a lifelong partnership."

1986

ALICE B. TOKLAS

What Is Remembered

I WAS born and raised in California, where my maternal grandfather had been a pioneer before the state was admitted to the Union. He had bought a gold mine and settled in Jackson, Amador County. A few years later he crossed the Isthmus of Panama again and went to Brooklyn, where he married my grandmother. There my mother was born. When she was three years old, they went to Jackson.

When they arrived in San Francisco all the bells were ringing. My grandmother said it was not a holiday, what were they celebrating? Two horse thieves are being hanged on Lone Mountain, was the response. It was an unpleasant welcome and my grandmother never forgot it.

As my grandfather's mine was not worth working, he sold it and bought a large tract of land in the San Joaquin Valley and turned to ranching. Later his stepsister's husband acquired a piece of land near his. It was they who organized the opposition to the Southern Pacific railroad and the defense against its laying tracks to carry the San Joaquin Valley harvest east. They were violently opposed to its having a monopoly, and they placed a barrage of farm implements across the road. The engine was forced to stop before it. The next day, however, it drove into the barricade and the railroad men laid tracks beyond. This constituted a right of way. Frank Norris took this as the theme for *The Octopus,* the first novel of his trilogy on the history of wheat.

There were no suitable schools in Amador County for my mother and her sister, nor music for my grandmother. So my grandfather moved his family to San Francisco, and while he built a home for them they lived at the Nucleus Hotel. The home he built on O'Farrell Street was where they lived for many years. The two girls grew up there and were married from there, I was born there, and later the two grandparents died there.

My mother with a group of ladies brought Emma Marwedel, a pupil of Froebel, to San Francisco, where in a large garden a schoolhouse had been built and the first kindergarten in the United States established. There I went mornings and learned to read and to write German and English, a great deal of geography, and some arithmetic.

It was when I was seven or eight that my grandmother talked to me about music and took me to hear it. The first singer I remember was Judic, a gay though very old Parisian light opera singer. She wore an immense turquoise brooch surrounded by diamonds presented to her by the Emperor Louis Napoleon. That was my first introduction to the War of 1870.

There was then and for many years after a stock company, the Tivoli Opera House, that gave opera the year round, performing everything from *Aïda* to *Les Cloches de Corneville*. I enjoyed them all equally. It was there that I heard *Lohengrin* for the first time. Luisa Tetrazzini sang Violetta at the Tivoli, her cadenzas being so sensational that she was engaged for the Metropolitan Opera of New York.

My grandmother started to give me piano lessons and told me that she and her three sisters had been pupils of Friedrich Wieck, the father of Clara Schumann. When one of the sisters became a concert pianist in Vienna her parents disinherited her. Then she married an army officer, which was the last we heard of Tante Berthe.

When I was nine years old my father took me to spend the night with my grandparents. This was always a pleasure for me. The next morning my father called for me saying, I have a surprise for you, there is a baby brother for you to see. Is it Tommie? I asked.

Tommie was a small marble Renaissance head my mother had, for which I had a passionate attachment. No, I don't think so, my father answered. You will see.

When I did see the small red-faced thing, I was ready to burst into tears. I wanted to kiss my mother and confide my horror to her. He is red like a lobster, I said, are you going to love him? Taking me in her arms she said, Not like you, darling, you will always come first. And I was satisfied.

It was at this time that my parents decided to go to Europe to celebrate the golden wedding anniversary of my father's parents.

My mother and I found New York very cold. On a chair with runners a cousin pushed me on the frozen lake in Central Park, whilst my father and cousins skated, making figures on the ice.

To get to the steamer we were obliged to be ferried to Hoboken. The boat got stuck and it was necessary to cut away the ice. But on the steamer on the Atlantic the sun shone, and for the twelve days of the voyage I played on deck.

At Hamburg where the steamer landed we went to see the Rentz circus, where not only trained horses but elephants danced to the music of a big blaring brass band.

From Hamburg we went to Kempen in Silesia, where my father's numerous family welcomed us and we were joined by the cousins and an uncle and an aunt from New York and two uncles from New Mexico.

My father's father was a gentle kindly person. He read aloud to me Grimm's fairy tales, frightening by comparison with those of Hans Christian Andersen and those of Perrault which I had already known. As a young man he had gone from home on a voyage to Portugal and in '48 he had clandestinely left his wife to go to Paris to fight on the barricades. My grandmother, not sympathizing with this escapade, had notified the bank in Paris not to honor her husband's cheques, thus obliging him to return to Kempen.

My grandfather enjoyed painting and gave one of the pictures he had painted to my father. It was a lively scene of two Polish cavalrymen with several wounded and dead Russian soldiers on the ground. The Poles were slashing at the two remaining Russians with broad swords.

My grandmother was a large, handsome, imperious woman who wore very long diamond earrings. In her white hair, piled very high, were artificial lilacs. She and my grandfather lived to be over eighty years old and died within a day of each other.

From Kempen my father drove us in a four-in-hand to Stettin to see a companion of his lycée days. It was at Stettin, at a restaurant, that some Polish officers asked my mother's permission to give me a glass of champagne so that everyone might toast the United States.

From Kempen we went to Vienna, and from there to Pest where my parents had some friends. In the music room the young people were dancing with Hungarian officers. For them I danced the cachucha and waltzed with the daughters of our host, Stephanie and Melanie, becoming quite dizzy as they did not reverse.

From Pest we went by way of Vienna and Dresden to England. My mother had found in Kempen a young Polish governess for me who was a pleasant companion, but as she spoke English perfectly I didn't learn any moré Polish than my father had already taught me, "The Lord's Prayer" and "God Save Poland," which I forgot over a half-century ago.

In England we went to stay with my mother's uncle, who had married a Scotchwoman. They had two little daughters, Violet and Adela, about my age, and lived in the country. After a few days my parents decided to leave me there and go to London. The two cousins were sweet companions. But one night Violet woke me and said, Come quickly, Adela is walking in her sleep on a balcony without a railing. Adela had her eyes open but evidently was not seeing where she was nor where she was going. It was frightening but romantic.

Not as frightening, but quite as romantic, was the elephants' tusk jelly served to us children by an Indian colonel for tea when we were driven over to visit him.

From England we went back to Hamburg to stay with my mother's other uncle, a doctor who lived with his wife and widowed daughter and two very large black poodles that sat on their haunches immovable while we were being served my first frozen puddings. I remember a Nesselrode and a Himalaya. The poodles were each then given a large tray of coffee with milk. When they had finished this, the valet removed these trays and replaced them with two other trays. It was many years later, when Gertrude Stein and I had a poodle, that I understood this effort to control their greed.

In Hamburg the Polish governess and I said a tearful farewell, for my parents were taking me back to America on the same boat that had brought us. General Lew Wallace, the first of my authors, was on board. He had been our ambassador to Turkey and had written *Ben Hur*. He gave me an inscribed copy.

Soon after we returned to San Francisco, I was sent to Miss Mary West's school. A little girl in my class asked me if my father was a millionaire. I said I did not know. Had we a yacht? she continued. When she learned we hadn't, she lost interest. My mother said it was time to send me to another school where the little girls would be less snobbish.

The new school, Miss Lake's, was a gay happy one. At once I formed a close friendship with a radiant, resilient, brilliant little girl, Clare Moore, which was to last until her death only a few years ago. After school hours we read the same books, the stores of Juliana Ewing and Louisa Alcott, a sordid dull English novel, *The Lamplighter,* by Miss Cummins, and a story "Honor Bright" that I tried unsuccessfully many years later to find for Gertrude Stein. Then we read Dickens, commencing with *David Copperfield.* I preferred *A Tale of Two Cities* and *Great Expectations.*

My mother gave me a membership card to the Mercantile and Mechanics Library where novels were soon replaced by biographies and memoirs, and at home I had Shakespeare and some poetry.

I remained at Miss Lake's School for four years. Then my father decided we would go to Seattle to live. Two fires and the collapse of a boom had reduced his income seriously, and he hoped to extricate himself from these difficulties there. After we had moved, a committee of San Francisco bankers came to investigate the financial situation in the Northwest. One of them asked my uncle in Spokane how his mining stock was getting on. Very nice and quiet, I thank you, my uncle, not a great talker, replied.

That autumn, I went to Miss Mary Cochrane's School. She and her two sisters were the staff, and all these three knew was what they taught us. They were from the Shenandoah Valley and remembered the Civil War, which was the occasion of considerable bitterness between the Misses Cochrane and their Northern pupils.

While I was at Miss Cochrane's School, Coxey's Army was marching on Washington. My father was one of a committee who tried to keep the men on their farms by giving them implements and maintaining prices for their harvests.

My mother was an ardent gardener, and she planted around the house on a hilltop where we lived small beds of many different flowers. She liked making bouquets with original combinations, particularly Homer roses and hops. In the small beds, with only room between them to weed and to gather the blooms, were all the different flowers she preferred, dwarf yellow pansies and periwinkles and many

Mother and child on Telegraph Hill after the earthquake, 1906. Photograph by J. B. Monaco.

kinds of sweet peas. I once said to her, You have such lovely watery periwinkle blue eyes. You mean, dearest, liquid eyes, she corrected. The flowers filled the house with their perfume and color.

One autumn we stayed at a hop ranch in the Snoqualmie Valley for several weeks. A young squaw came and asked us for a pair of shoes in which to bury her child who had always gone barefoot. A beautiful Southern girl who was staying at the ranch gave her a pair of very high-heeled white satin slippers.

My mother and little brother spent a few weeks every year with my grandfather in San Francisco. I followed during my vacation. When I was there one year I received a wire from my mother saying that the Misses Cochrane were giving up their school and I should see Miss Sarah Hamlin at once. She would coach me to pass the entrance examinations at the university. Sarah Hamlin had brought the Pundita Ramabei to the United States to lecture against the sacrifice of young Hindu widows on the funeral pyres of their husbands. Every morning at eight o'clock she put me through a course of algebra and trigonometry, sufficient for her to be able to recommend me to the University of Washington.

The winter at the university was a lively one. There were new friends, there were dances and parties on the lake when the weather permitted. It would have been a happy year if my mother's health had not worried us.

The next spring she had an unsuccessful operation. My father decided we should return to San Francisco, where surgeons could be consulted. The furniture was packed, my mother, my father and I and my little brother, my mother's trained nurse and my father's hunting dog took the train. We found a house, a simple home where we were comfortable.

Another operation advised by the best surgeons was not successful and my mother was never strong again. One of her uncles called for us frequently to drive us through Golden Gate Park to the Cliff House. This became too great an exertion for my mother, and the following spring she died. It was a terrible blow for us.

My grandfather persuaded us to move to his home where he lived with his brother Mark and where the house was frequently filled with the cousins from the San Joaquin Valley. The Spanish-American

War broke out soon after we moved. As the troops marched down Van Ness Avenue from the Presidio on their way to embark for the Philippines, I could hear their bugles. I would hurry up Van Ness Avenue to say good-bye to the soldiers of the Washington and California regiments. They were the boys with whom I had danced. They were very young and cheerful, very unlike the soldiers of the two World Wars. Those from the San Joaquin Valley would get leave to have a meal with us. The cook and I made great quantities of doughnuts for them to take back to distribute in camp.

My grandfather took me to Southern California to meet his friends of the pioneer days. We went by carriage, by buckboard, by horseback and by muleback. It was amusing but fatiguing. My grandfather, however, was never fatigued. Upon our return at Thanksgiving, we went to the San Joaquin Valley to look at his land.

I had received a parchment certifying me as a bachelor of music. Now I commenced to study piano with Otto Bendix, a pupil of Liszt, and harmony with Oscar Weil. A talented and lovely pupil of theirs, Elizabeth Hansen, became my friend.

Mrs. Moore and her children, who had gone to Europe, now returned. When Clare was preparing for college a tragedy occurred. Jeannie, the second daughter, was burned to death. Her lace dress caught fire in the candles on her dressing table and it was too late before help came. Jeannie had been beautiful, charming, fascinating. Mrs. Moore was prostrate, and Clare became the head of the family. Not long after this they went to Europe again.

I went on with my piano lessons with Otto Bendix. I went to Seattle where Elizabeth Hansen lived and where she and I gave a concert. It was a quite ambitious program of which I only remember that we played Schumann's variations for two pianos. Upon my return to San Francisco I played the Schubert *Wanderer* with orchestra. Soon after that, Otto Bendix died and my musical career came to an end.

My grandfather caught cold, which developed into influenza, and within a week he died. In his will he left a quarter of his estate to my aunt and a quarter to each of his three grandchildren. My father proposed that we should go south for a rest, and close up the big house and move to a smaller one upon our return. We found a pleasant house overlooking the Presidio.

It was an agreeable life. I saw a great deal of Clare's friend Eleanor Joseph. She had a caustic wit and had said of an old classmate, He said, 'Come into the garden, Maud,' and Maud went. I nicknamed her California Nell, and I called her Nellie.

Harriet Levy, who had lived next door to us on O'Farrell Street, returned from Europe where, in Florence, she had met Gertrude Stein and Gertrude's brother Leo. Both were interested in painting. Charles Loeser had introduced them to the pictures of Cézanne. Leo planned to go to Paris to paint, where Gertrude and he would begin to collect pictures. Gertrude Stein went often to the Pitti and Uffizi galleries, and in the heat of the summer would fall asleep stretched out on one of the benches. She said it was pleasant to wake up with the pictures about her.

In Egypt Harriet had met at a dinner party an Englishman who asked her, Tell me, how much do you pay now to kill a Chinaman in California? Harriet was aghast. I never heard of such a thing, she said. You pay ten dollars to shoot a Chinaman in San Jose, said the Englishman.

The Moores returned again from Europe. Paula, the oldest daughter, did not return with them. She had married a Dr. Wicksteed in London. When he and his brothers were still little boys someone drove up to them while they were walking in the garden and asked them, Does Mr. Wicksteed live here? They answered in chorus, We are the Mr. Wicksteeds.

To have a man at the head of the family, Clare had married William de Gruchy, a French-Canadian raised in Boston, who had settled in San Francisco.

Life went on calmly until one morning we and our home were violently shaken by an earthquake. Gas was escaping. I hurried to my father's bedroom, pulled up the shades, pulled back the curtains and opened the windows. My father was apparently asleep. Do get up, I said to him. The city is on fire. That, said he with his usual calm, will give us a black eye in the East.

Our servant was heating water in the kitchen on an alcohol stove to make coffee. The chimneys had fallen, the pipes were disrupted, there would be no baths. I walked up the hill to the entrance of the Presidio, where in the early morning light General Funston was marching his troops into the city where fires were commencing to burn.

My father, who had at last risen, walked down to the business quarter to see if the vaults of his bank were holding. Convinced that they were, he returned with four hundred cigarettes, all he could find. For Nellie, for Clare and for you, he explained.

I sent the servant to buy such provisions as she could find and I went to see how Nellie had fared. Her two Chinese servants were cooking on an improvised stove on the street. Nellie, with some novels, was distracting her mind as usual in her darkened library.

When I got home, Clare and Harriet were there. After a picnic lunch on the sidewalk, Clare left to join her mother and brother in Sausalito and Harriet went over to Oakland.

Paul Cowles of the Associated Press had met newspapermen at noon at the Fairmount Hotel on Nob Hill. They had asked him if they should meet there again tomorrow. To which Paul replied, If there is a tomorrow.

In the afternoon I packed the family silver in a Chinese chest and had my brother dig a deep hole in the garden into which we put it. The chest we covered with enough earth to protect the silver in case the fire spread. Working on the ground I felt slight tremors from time to time.

My father and brother arranged to spend the night in the nearby Presidio and I was to pass the night with some friends of a woman I knew, in Berkeley. There were no lights, and it was a long and difficult walk to the ferry.

The city was in darkness when we got to the ferry building. I asked if the trains were running on the other side of the bay. Sure, a voice answered from the darkness. People were herded onto the ferry, but there was no confusion. I fortunately was unable to look back upon burning San Francisco from the crowded boat.

At Berkeley there was still a long climb up the hill to the home of the Sidney Armers where they welcomed us, gave us a hot meal and comfortable beds. I slept fitfully and woke early. The Berkeley newspapers were alarming. There was no wire or telephone communication with San Francisco so I went back to San Francisco at once, leaving my friend to be cared for by the Armers.

The crossing, both by train and boat, was more normal than the night before. Passengers were not herded. The Portuguese musicians on the ferry were playing their usual diverting music. I met two of my former teachers from Miss Lake's School, hurrying back to see what remained of their little home.

The city was still burning. The water front and all the way to Van Ness Avenue was in ruins. People would advise one on where it was easiest and safest to walk, yet it took over an hour to get to the house.

My father and brother had not remained long in the Presidio. It seemed safer for one's possessions to remain with them, so they had returned home.

After a cold water sponge I went off again. Passing Annie Fabian's I stopped to ask how they had fared. She was a great carnation specialist and had created many new varieties. The heat of the flames was forcing her many thousands of plants into quicker blooming than a hothouse. Annie could not keep up with the necessary budding and told me I might gather as many as I could carry, which I did to take to Nellie.

Nellie, her sister, her two brothers, Clare, and Frank Jacot, whom Nellie was later to marry, were there. Nellie's oldest brother, who had managed their mother's estate, was depressed. Their income had disappeared in the fire. Nothing but their home remained. It was impossible for the four of them to live on its rent.

Over in Sausalito Clare had found a couple of packages of Venus de Milo cigarettes, which we naturally had never smoked. Then I produced several packages of my father's contribution, which we were pleased to have.

Nellie's Chinese cook prepared an excellent lunch for us. It was not until some weeks later that he told Nellie some thirty cousins of his had come up as refugees from their burning homes in Chinatown. He had gotten sacks of rice and dried Chinese food for them and had put them, the cousins and the food, into Nellie's basement where they lived so quietly for several weeks that no one in the house suspected their presence.

When I returned home my father told me that our landlord had made arrangements with working men to repair the chimneys within a few days, but it would be a while longer before the water mains would be repaired.

I got to work with the servant to clean the house. It was black with soot from the flames. In cleaning a drawer I found two tickets for the performance Sarah Bernhardt was to give of *Phèdre* at the Greek amphitheatre at the University of California. I had forgotten about that. I would go over to Oakland, have a bite and a bath at Harriet's sister's and take her niece with me for the performance. I could not decide whether the performance or the bath was the most alluring.

Bernhardt's voice was as exciting as I remembered it from my youth. On that day there was an especial example. Alone on the stage at the end of the first act. Phèdre gives an anguished cry as she disappears. Evidently Bernhardt had had no rehearsals, nor had she studied the large stage. Her arms outstretched, with her piercing cry she backed forever towards the curtained door. She prolonged the cry, the golden voice continued. The audience was breathless. Finally she reached the curtain and disappeared. I had seen her in many of her poignant roles but was never more moved than then.

After the performance, by great good luck we were near Bernhardt when she was getting into an open barouche in which she was to be driven away. The students from the university had unhitched the horses and were going to draw her. She fearlessly faced the California sun, her head thrown back with her famous radiant smile. I noticed, however, her visibly large teeth.

Life with chimneys and water mains finally repaired seemed normal, though of course it was far from being so. Nellie as usual sat a great part of the day in the darkened library. She was selecting the books she would sell.

Clare and her husband took a flat on Pacific Avenue beyond the fire area. We were all living in an extravagant and at the same time economical way. Later Frank Jacot called us The Necessary Luxury Company. We went to theatres, we went automobiling, we went to the Little Palace Café and Hotel which had become a fashionable shopping district where one could buy Paris clothes and perfume if one could afford it, and even if one could not.

The Michael Steins—Gertrude's elder brother and his wife—had hurried out to San Francisco from Paris to see what repairs would be necessary to their income-bearing flats. They had brought with them the "Portrait à la Raie Verte," of Madame Matisse with a green line down her face. It and the other paintings they brought were the first by Matisse to cross the Atlantic. The portrait impressed me immensely, as "La Femme au Chapeau" had impressed Gertrude Stein when she saw it at the vernissage of the Salon d'Automne of 1905 and bought it at once.

Mrs. Michael Stein followed Gertrude Stein's purchases but did not like the Picasso pictures. Neither did Matisse. Neither the subjects nor the paintings were to his taste. Mrs. Stein followed Matisse blindly. Mr. Stein believed in his wife and whatever she believed in.

Mr. Stein was a gentle creature. One day I was wearing a silver South Sea Island belt with a blue stone on its clasp. When Mike Stein's eye caught the blue stone, he brought from his pocket a small magnifying glass. Examining the stone he said, Ancient Asiatic glass.

My father met me walking with the Steins on Van Ness Avenue one afternoon. At home later he asked me, with all a Pole's prejudice, Who did you say was the German memorial monument you were with today?

Mrs. Stein wanted me to return to Paris with them when she heard from Harriet Levy that some day she and I should go together. I was cool about accepting this invitation, so they compromised with a more accommodating and charming young girl.

Harriet had often spoken of our going to Paris. It was time now to speak to my father about our plans. On the day I did, his first response was a noncommittal sigh. He would close the house and move to his club, he finally said. My brother could live in Berkeley for his two remaining years at the University of California.

We did not get off until September, 1907. It was hot crossing the continent, and while the porter was cleaning our compartment Harriet and I sat in a car where Harriet and the head of the Psychology Department at the University of Edinburgh got into conversation. Thereafter they had long conversations together.

In New York we stayed at an agreeable hotel where Lillian Russell was dining at a roof garden where we dined.

Nellie had by now married Frank Jacot and they were already in New York. Nellie took me the next afternoon to see Nazimova in *A Doll's House.* Her Slav temperament did not suit the role of Nora. It was the last performance of Ibsen I was ever to see.

The next day we drove down to the steamer past the enormous

excavations where myriads of men were working and which were to become Grand Central Terminal. It was quite biblical.

Nellie had sent flowers, books, magazines and fruit to the steamer for the voyage. I had Flaubert's letters, and Harriet had a copy of *Lord Jim* that she considered a tactless choice by the friend who had sent it.

On board was a distinguished oldish man, a commodore, who got into conversation with me when I was reading on the deck after lunch. We spent the greater part of the voyage together. Harriet did not speak to me of the episode but I could see that she considered that I lacked discretion. The commodore and I said a calm good-bye before we got on the launches that were taking us into the harbor of Cherbourg.

We were indeed in France. It was a fête day and there was dancing in the open air. We decided not to take the crowded boat train in the heat of the day but to stay the night in Cherbourg and take a morning train to Paris. Under the hotel window French voices were singing French songs in the mild French air.

1963

HUNTER S. THOMPSON

Generation of Swine

HOME MEDICINE is a big industry these days. A recent network survey by one of the major evangelical organizations indicates that one out of every three Americans will experiment this year with a variety of do-it-yourself home cures and quack remedies ranging from self-induced vomiting kits to alpha/beta brain wave scans and multihead, blood-magneto suction-drums to measure percentage of true body fat.

Others will test themselves daily, in towns and ghettos all over the republic, for potentially fatal levels of blood glucose, or use strange and expensive litmus tests to screen each other for leg cancer in the femurs and the ankles and knees.

We are all slaves to this syndrome, but in some ways it is a far, far better thing. . . . Last Saturday night I went out to the snack bar at the Geneva Drive-In near the Cow Palace and performed tests on a random selection of customers during the intermission period between "Rocky IV" and "Pale Rider."

The results were startling. . . .

Huge brains, small necks, weak muscles and fat wallets—these are the dominant physical characteristics of the '80s . . . The Generation of Swine.

"Rocky IV" runs about 91 minutes, but it seems more like 19 or 20. We had barely settled in—with a flagon of iced Near Beer and a full dinner of Spicy Hot nuggets from the Kentucky Fried Chicken people in lower Daly City—when a series of horrible beatings climaxed abruptly in a frenzy of teen-age political blather from Sylvester Stallone, and then the movie was over.

The only excitement came when Sly beat the huge Russky like a mule and the whole crowd of fog-windowed cars in the audience, as it were, came alive with a blast of honking horns and harsh screams.

I joined in, leaning heavily on the horn of my fully loaded Camaro, but when I tried to get out of the car and speak seriously with the other patrons I was menaced by a pack of wild dogs that had gathered around my car to gnaw on the fresh chicken bones.

I kicked one in the throat and seized another by the forelegs and bashed it against a nearby Datsun pickup with three women in the front seat. One of them rolled down the window and cursed me as the truck roared suddenly into action and screeched off in low gear, ripping the cheap metal speaker out by the roots. . . .

I moved the Camaro a few rows away and fled back through the darkness to the snack bar, where I found the heart-rate machine.

The directions were clear enough: "Deposit 25¢ and insert middle finger. As a rule, the lower your heart rate, the better your physical condition."

It had the look of state-of-the-art medical technology, a complex digital readout with ominous red numbers on a scale from 60 to 100. Anything under 60 was "athletic"; 60 to 70 was "well-conditioned"; 70 to 85 was "average"; and after that it got grim.

Between 85 and 100 was "below average," and over 100 said, "Inactive – consult your physician."

I tested Maria first, and she came in at 91, which shocked even casual onlookers. She wept openly, attracting the focus of a large crew-cut uniformed cop who said his name was Ray and asked me for some "personal or professional ID."

I had none. My attorney had run off, the night before, with all my credentials and press cards.

"Never mind that, Ray. Give me your hand," I said to him. "I need some human numbers for the baseline."

Meanwhile, I had laid my own middle finger into the slot and came up with a reading of 64, which visibly impressed the crowd. They moaned and jabbered distractedly as Ray moved into position, looking as spiffy and bristly and confident as a middle-aged fighting bull. I slapped another quarter into the slot and watched the test pattern seek out his number.

It was 105, and a hush fell over the crowd. Ray slumped in his uniform and muttered that he had to go out and check the lot for dope fiends and perverts and drunks.

"Don't worry," I called after him. "These numbers mean nothing. It could happen to anybody."

He eyed me sullenly and moved away, saying he would be back soon for another, more accurate reading. The crowd was thinning out; Maria had locked herself in the ladies' room and now I had nothing to work with except a few vagrant children.

I grabbed a small blond girl who said she was 10 years old and led her up to the machine. "I'm a doctor," I told her. "I need your help on this experiment."

She moved obediently into position and put her finger into the slot. The test pattern whirled and sputtered, then settled on 104. The child uttered a wavering cry and ran off before I could get her name. "Never mind this!" I shouted after her. "Children always run high on these things."

Her little sister spat at me as they backed away like animals.

I grabbed another one, a fat young lad named Joe, who turned out to be the son of Maggie, the night manager, who arrived just in time to keep Ray from calling in a SWAT team to have me locked up as a child molester.

Little Joe registered 126, a number so high that the machine offered no explanation for it. I gave him a quarter to go off and play the Donkey Kong machine on the other side of the aisle.

Ray was still hovering around with a worried look on his face. I was beginning to feel like the night stalker, a huge beast running loose in the neon swamp of the suburbs. Ray was still asking about my credentials, so I gave him one of my old business cards from the long-defunct National Observer.

"Not yet," I said. "I want to take another reading on myself." By that time I had loaded up on hot coffee and frozen my right index finger in a Styrofoam cup that Maggie had brought from the office.

Ray stood off, still confused by my relentless professional behavior, as I dropped my last quarter into the well-worn slot. The test pattern locked into a freeze pattern, unlike anything else we had seen to this point. The numbers rolled and skittered frenetically on the screen; people stood back and said nothing . . . and finally the test pattern settled on a number that nobody wanted to read.

It was double zero. I had no pulse. It was official — as final as some number carved in white granite on a tombstone on the outskirts of Buffalo.

The children stared blankly. I finished my hot dog and scurried off into the night . . . back to The City, back to the weird and sleazy streets where questions like these are not asked.

1985

When the Beatniks Were Social Lions

WHAT EVER happened to the Beat Generation? The question wouldn't mean much in Detroit or Salt Lake City, perhaps, but here it brings back a lot of memories. As recently as 1960, San Francisco was the capital of the Beat Generation, and the corner of Grant and Columbus in the section known as North Beach was the crossroads of the "beat" world.

It was a good time to be in San Francisco. Anybody with half a talent could wander around North Beach and pass himself off as a "comer" in the new era. I know, because I was doing it, and so was a fellow we'll have to call Willard, the hulking, bearded son of a New Jersey minister. It was a time for breaking loose from the old codes, for digging new sounds and new ideas, and for doing everything possible to unnerve the Establishment.

Since then, things have died down. The "beatnik" is no longer a social lion in San Francisco, but a social leper; as a matter of fact, it looked for a while as if they had all left. But the city was recently startled by a "rent strike" in North Beach and as it turned out, lo and behold, the strikers were "beatniks." The local papers, which once played Beat Generation stories as if the foundations of The System were crumbling before their very eyes, seized on the rent strike with strange affection—like a man encountering an old friend who owes him money, but whom he is glad to see anyway.

The rent strike lasted only about two days, but it got people talking again about the Beat Generation and its sudden demise from the

American scene – or at least from the San Francisco scene, because it is still very extant in New York. But in New York it goes by a different name, and all the humor has gone out of it.

One of the most surprising things about the rent strike was the fact that so few people in San Francisco had any idea what the Beat Generation was. An interviewer from a radio station went into the streets seeking controversy on "the return of the beatniks," but drew a blank. People remembered the term, and not much more.

But the Beat Generation was very real in its day, and it has a definite place in our history. There is a mountain of material explaining the sociological aspects of the thing, but most of it is dated and irrelevant. What remains are the people who were involved; most of them are still around, looking back with humor and affection on the uproar they caused, and drifting by a variety of routes toward debt, parenthood, and middle age.

My involvement was tangential at best. But Willard was in there at the axis of things, and in retrospect he stands out as one of the great "beatniks" of his time. Certainly San Francisco has good cause to remember him; his one and only encounter with the forces of law and order provided one of the wildest Beat Generation stories of the era.

Before San Francisco he had been in Germany, teaching English and cultivating an oriental-type beard. On his way out to the coast he stopped in New York and picked up a mistress with a new Ford. It was *de rigueur*, in those days, to avoid marriage at all costs. He came to me through the recommendation of a friend then working in Europe for a British newspaper. "Willard is a great man," said the letter. "He is an artist and a man of taste."

As it turned out, he also was a prodigious drinker in the tradition of Brendan Behan, who was said to have had "a thirst so great it would throw a shadow." I was making my own beer at the time and Willard put a great strain on the aging process; I had to lock the stuff up to keep him from getting at it before the appointed moment.

Sadly enough, my beer and Willard's impact on San Francisco were firmly linked. The story is a classic, and if you travel in the right circles out here you will still hear it told, although not always accurately. The truth, however, goes like this:

Willard arrived shortly before I packed up and left for the East; we had a convivial few weeks, and, as a parting gesture, I left him a five-gallon jug of beer that I did not feel qualified to transport across the nation. It still had a week or so to go in the jug, then another few weeks of aging in quart bottles, after which it would have had a flavor to rival the nectar of the gods. Willard's only task was to bottle it and leave it alone until it was ready to drink.

Unfortunately, his thirst threw a heavy shadow on the schedule. He was living on a hill overlooking the southern section of the city, and among his neighbors were several others of the breed, mad drinkers and men of strange arts. Shortly after my departure he entertained one of these gentlemen, who, like my man Willard, was long on art and energy, but very short of funds.

The question of drink arose, as it will in the world of art, but the presence of poverty cast a bleak light on the scene. There was, however, this five-gallon jug of raw, unaged home brew in the kitchen. Of course, it was a crude drink and might produce beastly and undesired effects, but . . . well. . . .

The rest is history. After drinking half the jug, the two artists laid hands on several gallons of blue paint and proceeded to refinish the front of the house Willard was living in. The landlord, who lived across the street, witnessed this horror and called the police. They arrived to find the front of the house looking like a Jackson Pollock canvas, and the sidewalk rapidly disappearing under a layer of sensual crimson. At this point, something of an argument ensued, but Willard is 6 feet 4, and 230 pounds, and he prevailed. For a while.

Some moments later the police came back with reinforcements, but by this time Willard and his helper had drunk off the rest of the jug and were eager for any kind of action, be it painting or friendly violence. The intrusion of the police had caused several mottos to be painted on the front of the house, and they were not without antisocial connotations. The landlord was weeping and gnashing his teeth, loud music emanated from the interior of the desecrated house, and the atmosphere in general was one of hypertension.

The scene that followed can only be likened to the rounding up of wild beasts escaped from a zoo. Willard says he attempted to flee, but floundered on a picket fence, which collapsed with his weight and that of a pursuing officer. His friend climbed to a roof and rained curses and shingles on the unfriendly world below. But the police worked methodically, and by the time the sun set over the Pacific the two artists were sealed in jail.

At this point the gentlemen of the press showed up for the usual photos. They tried to coax Willard up to the front of his cell to pose, but the other artist had undertaken to tip the toilet bowl out of the floor and smash it into small pieces. For the next hour, the press was held at bay with chunks of porcelain, hurled by the two men in the cell. "We used up the toilet," Willard recalls, "then we got the sink. I don't remember much of it, but I can't understand why the cops didn't shoot us. We were out of our heads."

The papers had a field day with the case. Nearly all the photos of the "animal men" were taken with what is known among press photographers as "the Frankenstein flash." This technique produces somewhat the same impression of the subject as a flashlight held under his chin, but instead of a flashlight, the photographer simply holds his flash unit low, so that sinister shadows appear on the face of a subject, and a huge shadow looms on the wall behind him. It is a technique that could make Caspar Milquetoast look like the Phantom of the Opera, but the effect, with Willard, was nothing short of devastating; he looked like King Kong.

Despite all the violence, the story has a happy ending. Willard and his friends were sentenced to six months in jail, but were quickly released for good behavior, and neither lost any time in fleeing to New York. Willard now lives in Brooklyn, where he moves from one apartment to another as walls fill up with paintings. His artistic method is to affix tin cans to a wall with tenpenny nails, then cover the wall with lumpy plaster and paint. Some say he has a great talent, but so far he goes unrecognized—except by the long-suffering San Francisco police, who were called upon to judge what was perhaps his most majestic effort.

Willard was as hard to define then as he is now; probably it is most accurate to say he had artistic inclinations and a superabundance of excess energy. At one point in his life he got the message that others of his type were gathering in San Francisco, and he came all the way from Germany to join the party.

Since then, things have never been the same. Life is more peaceful in San Francisco, but infinitely duller. That was pretty obvious when the rent strike cropped up; for a day or so it looked like the action was back in town, but it was no dice.

One of the "strikers," an unemployed cartoonist with a wife and a child and a rundown apartment for which he refuses to pay rent, summed up the situation. His landlady had declined to make repairs on the apartment, and instead got an eviction order. In the old days, the fellow would have stayed in the place and gotten tough. But the cartoonist is taking the path of least resistance. "It takes a long time to get people evicted," he says with a shrug, "and we're thinking of splitting to New York on a freight train anyway."

That's the way it is these days in the erstwhile capital of the Beat Generation. The action has gone East, and the only people who really seem to mourn it are the reporters, who never lacked a good story, and a small handful of those who lived with it and had a few good laughs for a while. If Willard returned to San Francisco today, he probably would have to settle for a job as a house painter.

1964

AMBROSE BIERCE

The Legatee

In fair San Francisco a good man did dwell,
And he wrote out a will, for he didn't feel well.
Said he: "It is proper, when making a gift,
To stimulate virtue by comforting thrift."

So he left all his property, legal and straight,
To "the cursedest rascal in all of the State."
But the name he refused to insert, for, said he:
"Let each man consider himself legatee."

In due course of time that philanthropist died,
And all San Francisco, and Oakland beside—
Save only the lawyers—came each with his claim,
The lawyers preferring to manage the same.

1882

The Van Nessiad

From end to end, thine avenue, Van Ness,
Rang with the cries of battle and distress!
Brave lungs were thundering with dreadful sound

The Palace of Fine Arts, Panama Pacific International Exposition, 1915.

And perspiration smoked along the ground!
Sing, heavenly muse, to ears of mortal clay,
The meaning, cause and finish of the fray.

Great Porter Ashe (invoking first the gods,
Who signed their favor with assenting nods
That snapped off half their heads—their necks grown dry
Since last the nectar cup went circling by)
Resolved to build a stable on his lot,
His neighbors fiercely swearing he should not.
Said he: "I build that stable!" "No you don't,"
Said they. "I can!" "You can't!" "I will!" "You won't!"
"By heaven!" he swore; "not only will I build,
But purchase donkeys till the place is filled!"
"Needless expense," they sneered in tones of ice—
"The owner's self, if lodged there, would suffice."
For three long months the awful war they waged:
With women, women, men with men, engaged,
While roaring babes and shrilling poodles raged!

Jove, from Olympus, where he still maintains
His ancient session (with rheumatic pains
Touched by his long exposure) marked the strife,
Interminable but by loss of life;
For malediction soon exhausts the breath—
If not, old age itself is certain death.
Lo! He holds high in heaven the fatal beam;
A golden pan depends from each extreme;
One feels of Porter's fate the downward stress,
One bears the destiny of all Van Ness.

Alas, the rusted scales, their life all gone,
Deliver judgment neither pro nor con:
The dooms hang level and the war goes on.
With a divine, contemptuous disesteem
Jove dropped the pans and kicked, himself, the beam:
Then, to decide the strife, with ready wit,
The nickel that he did not care for it
Twirled absently, remarking: "See it spin:
Head, Porter loses; tail, the others win."
The conscious nickel, charged with doom, spun round,
Portentously and made a ringing sound,
Then, staggering beneath its load of fate,
Sank rattling, died at last and lay in state.

Jove scanned the disk and then, as is his wont,
Raised his considering orbs, exclaiming: "Front!"
With leisurely alacrity approached
The herald god, to whom his mind he broached:
"In San Francisco two belligerent Powers,
Such as contended round great Ilion's towers,
Fight for a stable, though in either class
There's not a horse, and but a single ass.
Achilles Ashe, with formidable jaw
Assails a Trojan band with fierce hee-haw,
Firing the night with brilliant curses. They
With dark vituperation gloom the day.
Fate, against which nor gods nor men compete,
Decrees their victory and his defeat.
With haste, good Mercury, betake thee hence
And salivate him till he has no sense!"

§

Sheer downward shot the messenger afar,
Trailing a splendor like a falling star!
With dimming lustre through the air he burned,
Vanished, but with another sun returned.
The sovereign of the gods superior smiled,
Beaming benignant, fatherly and mild:
"Is Destiny's decree performed, my lad?—
And has he now no sense?" "Ah, sire, he never had."

1882

AMY TAN

Rules of the Game

I W A S six when my mother taught me the art of invisible strength. It was a strategy for winning arguments, respect from others, and eventually, though neither of us knew it at the time, chess games.

"Bite back your tongue," scolded my mother when I cried loudly, yanking her hand toward the store that sold bags of salted plums. At home, she said, "Wise guy, he not go against wind. In Chinese we say, Come from South, blow with wind–poom!–North will follow. Strongest wind cannot be seen."

The next week I bit back my tongue as we entered the store with the forbidden candies. When my mother finished her shopping, she quietly plucked a small bag of plums from the rack and put it on the counter with the rest of the items.

My mother imparted her daily truths so she could help my older brothers and me rise above our circumstances. We lived in San Francisco's Chinatown. Like most of the other Chinese children who played in the back alleys of restaurants and curio shops, I didn't think we were poor. My bowl was always full, three five-course meals every day, beginning with a soup full of mysterious things I didn't want to know the names of.

We lived on Waverly Place, in a warm, clean, two-bedroom flat that sat above a small Chinese bakery specializing in steamed pastries and dim sum. In the early morning, when the alley was still quiet, I could smell fragrant red beans as they were cooked down to a pasty sweetness. By daybreak, our flat was heavy with the odor of fried sesame balls and sweet curried chicken crescents. From my bed, I would listen as my father got ready for work, then locked the door behind him, one-two-three clicks.

At the end of our two-block alley was a small sandlot playground with swings and slides well-shined down the middle with use. The play area was bordered by wood-slat benches where old-country people sat cracking roasted watermelon seeds with their golden teeth and scattering the husks to an impatient gathering of gurgling pigeons. The best playground, however, was the dark alley itself. It was crammed with daily mysteries and adventures. My brothers and I would peer into the medicinal herb shop, watching old Li dole out onto a stiff sheet of white paper the right amount of insect shells, saffron-colored seeds, and pungent leaves for his ailing customers. It was said that he once cured a woman dying of an ancestral curse that had eluded the best of American doctors. Next to the pharmacy was a printer who specialized in gold-embossed wedding invitations and festive red banners.

Farther down the street was Ping Yuen Fish Market. The front window displayed a tank crowded with doomed fish and turtles struggling to gain footing on the slimy green-tiled sides. A hand-written sign informed tourists, "Within this store, is all for food, not for pet." Inside, the butchers with their blood-stained white smocks deftly gutted the fish while customers cried out their orders and shouted, "Give me your freshest," to which the butchers always protested, "All are freshest." On less crowded market days, we would inspect the crates of live frogs and crabs which we were warned not to poke, boxes of dried cuttlefish, and row upon row of iced prawns, squid, and slippery fish. The sanddabs made me shiver each time; their eyes lay on one flattened side and reminded me of my mother's story of a careless girl who ran into a crowded street and was crushed by a cab. "Was smash flat," reported my mother.

At the corner of the alley was Hong Sing's, a four-table café with a recessed stairwell in front that led to a door marked "Tradesmen." My brothers and I believed the bad people emerged from this door at night. Tourists never went to Hong Sing's, since the menu was printed only in Chinese. A Caucasian man with a big camera once posed me and my playmates in front of the restaurant. He had us move to the side of the picture window so the photo would capture the roasted duck with its head dangling from a juice-covered rope. After he took the picture, I told him he should go into Hong Sing's and eat dinner. When he smiled and asked me what they served, I shouted, "Guts and duck's feet and octopus gizzards!" Then I ran off with my friends, shrieking with laughter as we scampered across the alley and hid in the entryway grotto of the China Gem Company, my heart pounding with hope that he would chase us.

My mother named me after the street that we lived on: Waverly Place Jong, my official name for important American documents. But my family called me Meimei, "Little Sister." I was the youngest, the only daughter. Each morning before school, my mother would twist and yank on my thick black hair until she had formed two tightly wound pigtails. One day, as she struggled to weave a hard-toothed comb through my disobedient hair, I had a sly thought.

I asked her, "Ma, what is Chinese torture?" My mother shook her head. A bobby pin was wedged between her lips. She wetted her palm and smoothed the hair above my ear, then pushed the pin in so that it nicked sharply against my scalp.

"Who say this word?" she asked without a trace of knowing how wicked I was being. I shrugged my shoulders and said, "Some boy in my class said Chinese people do Chinese torture."

"Chinese people do many things," she said simply. "Chinese people do business, do medicine, do painting. Not lazy like American people. We do torture. Best torture."

My older brother Vincent was the one who actually got the chess set. We had gone to the annual Christmas party held at the First Chinese Baptist Church at the end of the alley. The missionary ladies had put together a Santa bag of gifts donated by members of another church. None of the gifts had names on them. There were separate sacks for boys and girls of different ages.

One of the Chinese parishioners had donned a Santa Claus costume and a stiff paper beard with cotton balls glued to it. I think the only children who thought he was the real thing were too young to know that Santa Claus was not Chinese. When my turn came up, the Santa man asked me how old I was. I thought it was a trick question; I was seven according to the American formula and eight by the Chinese calendar. I said I was born on March 17, 1951. That seemed to satisfy him. He then solemnly asked if I had been a very, very good girl this year and did I believe in Jesus Christ and obey my parents. I knew the only answer to that. I nodded back with equal solemnity.

Having watched the other children opening their gifts, I already knew that the big gifts were not necessarily the nicest ones. One girl my age got a large coloring book of biblical characters, while a less greedy girl who selected a smaller box received a glass vial of lavender toilet water. The sound of the box was also important. A ten-year-old boy had chosen a box that jangled when he shook it. It was a tin globe of the world with a slit for inserting money. He must have thought it was full of dimes and nickels, because when he saw that it had just ten pennies, his face fell with such undisguised disappointment that his mother slapped the side of his head and led him out of the church hall, apologizing to the crowd for her son who had such bad manners he couldn't appreciate such a fine gift.

As I peered into the sack, I quickly fingered the remaining presents, testing their weight, imagining what they contained. I chose a heavy, compact one that was wrapped in shiny silver foil and a red satin ribbon. It was a twelve-pack of Life Savers and I spent the rest of the party arranging and rearranging the candy tubes in the order of my favorites. My brother Winston chose wisely as well. His present turned out to be a box of intricate plastic parts; the instructions on the box proclaimed that when they were properly assembled he would have an authentic miniature replica of a World War II submarine.

Vincent got the chess set, which would have been a very decent present to get at a church Christmas party, except it was obviously used and, as we discovered later, it was missing a black pawn and a white knight. My mother graciously thanked the unknown benefactor, saying, "Too good. Cost too much." At which point, an old lady with fine white, wispy hair nodded toward our family and said with a whistling whisper, "Merry, merry Christmas."

When we got home, my mother told Vincent to throw the chess set away. "She not want it. We not want it," she said, tossing her head stiffly to the side with a tight, proud smile. My brothers had deaf ears. They were already lining up the chess pieces and reading from the dog-eared instruction book.

§

I watched Vincent and Winston play during Christmas week. The chessboard seemed to hold elaborate secrets waiting to be untangled. The chessmen were more powerful than Old Li's magic herbs that cured ancestral curses. And my brothers wore such serious faces that I was sure something was at stake that was greater than avoiding the tradesmen's door to Hong Sing's.

"Let me! Let me!" I begged between games when one brother or the other would sit back with a deep sigh of relief and victory, the other annoyed, unable to let go of the outcome. Vincent at first refused to let me play, but when I offered my Life Savers as replacements for the buttons that filled in for the missing pieces, he relented. He chose the flavors: wild cherry for the black pawn and peppermint for the white knight. Winner could eat both.

As our mother sprinkled flour and rolled out small doughy circles for the steamed dumplings that would be our dinner that night, Vincent explained the rules, pointing to each piece. "You have sixteen pieces and so do I. One king and queen, two bishops, two knights, two castles, and eight pawns. The pawns can only move forward one step, except on the first move. Then they can move two. But they can only take men by moving crossways like this, except in the beginning, when you can move ahead and take another pawn."

"Why?" I asked as I moved my pawn. "Why can't they move more steps?"

"Because they're pawns," he said.

"But why do they go crossways to take other men? Why aren't there any women and children?"

"Why is the sky blue? Why must you always ask stupid questions?" asked Vincent. "This is a game. These are the rules. I didn't make them up. See. Here. In the book." He jabbed a page with a pawn in his hand. "Pawn. P-A-W-N. Pawn. Read it yourself."

My mother patted the flour off her hands. "Let me see book," she said quietly. She scanned the pages quickly, not reading the foreign English symbols, seeming to search deliberately for nothing in particular.

"This American rules," she concluded at last. "Every time people come out from foreign country, must know rules. You not know, judge say, Too bad, go back. They not telling you why so you can use their way go forward. They say, Don't know why, you find out yourself. But they knowing all the time. Better you take it, find out why yourself." She tossed her head back with a satisfied smile.

I found out about all the whys later. I read the rules and looked up all the big words in a dictionary. I borrowed books from the Chinatown library. I studied each chess piece, trying to absorb the power each contained.

I learned about opening moves and why it's important to control the center early on; the shortest distance between two points is straight down the middle. I learned about the middle game and why tactics between two adversaries are like clashing ideas; the one who plays better has the clearest plans for both attacking and getting out of traps. I learned why it is essential in the endgame to have foresight, a mathematical understanding of all possible moves, and patience; all weaknesses and advantages become evident to a strong adversary and are obscured to a tiring opponent. I discovered that for the whole game one must gather invisible strengths and see the endgame before the game begins.

I also found out why I should never reveal "why" to others. A little knowledge withheld is a great advantage one should store for future use. That is the power of chess. It is a game of secrets in which one must show and never tell.

I loved the secrets I found within the sixty-four black and white squares. I carefully drew a handmade chessboard and pinned it to the wall next to my bed, where at night I would stare for hours at imaginary battles. Soon I no longer lost any games or Life Savers, but I lost my adversaries. Winston and Vincent decided they were more interested in roaming the streets after school in their Hopalong Cassidy cowboy hats.

On a cold spring afternoon, while walking home from school, I detoured through the playground at the end of our alley. I saw a group of old men, two seated across a folding table playing a game of chess, others smoking pipes, eating peanuts, and watching. I ran home and grabbed Vincent's chess set, which was bound in a cardboard box with rubber bands. I also carefully selected two prized rolls of Life Savers. I came back to the park and approached a man who was observing the game.

"Want to play?" I asked him. His face widened with surprise and he grinned as he looked at the box under my arm.

"Little sister, been a long time since I play with dolls," he said, smiling benevolently. I quickly put the box down next to him on the bench and displayed my retort.

Lau Po, as he allowed me to call him, turned out to be a much better player than my brothers. I lost many games and many Life Savers. But over the weeks, with each diminishing roll of candies, I added new secrets. Lau Po gave me the names. The Double Attack from the East and West Shores. Throwing Stones on the Drowning Man. The Sudden Meeting of the Clan. The Surprise from the Sleeping Guard. The Humble Servant Who Kills the King. Sand in the Eyes of Advancing Forces. A Double Killing Without Blood.

There were also the fine points of chess etiquette. Keep captured men in neat rows, as well-tended prisoners. Never announce "Check" with vanity, lest someone with an unseen sword slit your throat. Never hurl pieces into the sandbox after you have lost a game, because then you must find them again, by yourself, after apologizing to all around you. By the end of the summer, Lau Po had taught me all he knew, and I had become a better chess player.

A small weekend crowd of Chinese people and tourists would gather as I played and defeated my opponents one by one. My mother would join the crowds during these outdoor exhibition games. She sat proudly on the bench, telling my admirers with proper Chinese humility, "Is luck."

A man who watched me play in the park suggested that my mother allow me to play in local chess tournaments. My mother smiled graciously, an answer that meant nothing. I desperately wanted to go, but I bit back my tongue. I knew she would not let me play among strangers. So as we walked home I said in a small voice that I didn't want to play in the local tournament. They would have American rules. If I lost, I would bring shame on my family.

"Is shame you fall down nobody push you," said my mother.

During my first tournament, my mother sat with me in the front row as I waited for my turn. I frequently bounced my legs to unstick them from the cold metal seat of the folding chair. When my name was called, I leapt up. My mother unwrapped something in her lap. It was her *chang,* a small tablet of red jade which held the sun's fire. "Is luck," she whispered, and tucked it into my dress pocket. I turned to my opponent, a fifteen-year-old boy from Oakland. He looked at me, wrinkling his nose.

As I began to play, the boy disappeared, the color ran out of the room, and I saw only my white pieces and his black ones waiting on the other side. A light wind began blowing past my ears. It whispered secrets only I could hear.

"Blow from the South," it murmured. "The wind leaves no trail." I saw a clear path, the traps to avoid. The crowd rustled. "Shhh! Shhh!" said the corners of the room. The wind blew stronger. "Throw sand from the East to distract him." The knight came forward ready for the sacrifice. The wind hissed, louder and louder. "Blow, blow, blow. He cannot see. He is blind now. Make him lean away from the wind so he is easier to knock down."

"Check," I said, as the wind roared with laughter. The wind died down to little puffs, my own breath.

My mother placed my first trophy next to a new plastic chess set that the neighborhood Tao society had given to me. As she wiped each piece with a soft cloth, she said, "Next time win more, lose less."

"Ma, it's not how many pieces you lose," I said. "Sometimes you need to lose pieces to get ahead."

"Better to lose less, see if you really need."

At the next tournament, I won again, but it was my mother who wore the triumphant grin.

"Lost eight piece this time. Last time was eleven. What I tell you? Better off lose less!" I was annoyed, but I couldn't say anything.

I attended more tournaments, each one farther away from home. I won all games, in all divisions. The Chinese bakery downstairs from our flat displayed my growing collection of trophies in its window, amidst the dust-covered cakes that were never picked up. The day after I won an important regional tournament, the window encased a fresh sheet cake with whipped cream frosting and red script saying, "Congratulations, Waverly Jong, Chinatown Chess Champion." Soon after that, a flower shop, headstone engraver, and funeral parlor offered to sponsor me in national tournaments. That's when my mother decided I no longer had to do the dishes. Winston and Vincent had to do my chores.

"Why does she get to play and we do all the work?" complained Vincent.

"Is new American rules," said my mother. "Meimei play, squeeze all her brains out for win chess. You play, worth squeeze towel."

By my ninth birthday, I was a national chess champion. I was still some 429 points away from grand-master status, but I was touted as the Great American Hope, a child prodigy and a girl to boot. They ran a photo of me in *Life* magazine next to a quote in which Bobby Fischer said, "There will never be a woman grand master." "Your move, Bobby," said the caption.

The day they took the magazine picture I wore neatly plaited braids clipped with plastic barrettes trimmed with rhinestones. I was playing in a large high school auditorium that echoed with phlegmy coughs and the squeaky rubber knobs of chair legs sliding across freshly waxed wooden floors. Seated across from me was an American man, about the same age as Lau Po, maybe fifty. I remember that his sweaty brow seemed to weep at my every move. He wore a dark, malodorous suit. One of his pockets was stuffed with a great white kerchief on which he wiped his palm before sweeping his hand over the chosen chess piece with great flourish.

In my crisp pink-and-white dress with scratchy lace at the neck, one of two my mother had sewn for these special occasions, I would clasp my hands under my chin, the delicate points of my elbows poised lightly on the table in the manner my mother had shown me for posing for the press. I would swing my patent leather shoes back and forth like an impatient child riding on a school bus. Then I would pause, suck in my lips, twirl my chosen piece in midair as if undecided, and then firmly plant it in its new threatening place, with a triumphant smile thrown back at my opponent for good measure.

I no longer played in the alley of Waverly Place. I never visited the playground where the pigeons and old men gathered. I went to school, then directly home to learn new chess secrets, cleverly concealed advantages, more escape routes.

But I found it difficult to concentrate at home. My mother had

Shoppers in Chinatown, 1987. Photograph by Deanne Fitzmaurice.

a habit of standing over me while I plotted out my games. I think she thought of herself as my protective ally. He lips would be sealed tight, and after each move I made, a soft "Hmmmmph" would escape from her nose.

"Ma, I can't practice when you stand there like that," I said one day. She retreated to the kitchen and made loud noises with the pots and pans. When the crashing stopped, I could see out of the corner of my eye that she was standing in the doorway. "Hmmmph!" Only this one came out of her tight throat.

My parents made many concessions to allow me to practice. One time I complained that the bedroom I shared was so noisy that I couldn't think. Thereafter, my brothers slept in a bed in the living room facing the street. I said I couldn't finish my rice; my head didn't work right when my stomach was too full. I left the table with half-finished bowls and nobody complained. But there was one duty I couldn't avoid. I had to accompany my mother on Saturday market days when I had no tournament to play. My mother would proudly walk with me, visiting many shops, buying very little. "This my daughter Wave-ly Jong," she said to whoever looked her way.

One day, after we left a shop I said under my breath, "I wish you wouldn't do that, telling everybody I'm your daughter." My mother stopped walking. Crowds of people with heavy bags pushed past us on the sidewalk, bumping into first one shoulder, then another.

"Aiii-ya. So shame be with mother?" She grasped my hand even tighter as she glared at me.

I looked down. "It's not that, it's just so obvious. It's just so embarrassing."

"Embarrass you be my daughter?" Her voice was cracking with anger.

"That's not what I meant. That's not what I said."

"What you say?"

I knew it was a mistake to say anything more, but I heard my voice speaking. "Why do you have to use me to show off? If you want to show off, then why don't you learn to play chess?"

My mother's eyes turned into dangerous black slits. She had no words for me, just sharp silence.

I felt the wind rushing around my hot ears. I jerked my hand out of my mother's tight grasp and spun around, knocking into an old woman. Her bag of groceries spilled to the ground.

"Aii-ya! Stupid girl!" my mother and the woman cried. Oranges and tin cans careened down the sidewalk. As my mother stooped to help the old woman pick up the escaping food, I took off.

I raced down the street, dashing between people, not looking back as my mother screamed shrilly, "Meimei! Meimei!" I fled down an alley, past dark curtained shops and merchants washing the grime off their windows. I sped into the sunlight, into a large street crowded with tourists examining trinkets and souvenirs. I ducked into another dark alley, down another street, up another alley. I ran until it hurt and I realized I had nowhere to go, that I was not running from anything. The alleys contained no escape routes.

My breath came out like angry smoke. It was cold. I sat down on an upturned plastic pail next to a stack of empty boxes, cupping my chin with my hands, thinking hard. I imagined my mother, first walking briskly down one street or another looking for me, then giving up and returning home to await my arrival. After two hours, I stood up on creaking legs and slowly walked home.

The alley was quiet and I could see the yellow lights shining from our flat like two tiger's eyes in the night. I climbed the sixteen steps to the door, advancing quietly up each so as not to make any warning sounds. I turned the knob; the door was locked. I head a chair moving, quick steps, the locks turning – click! click! click! – and then the door opened.

"About time you got home," said Vincent. "Boy, are you in trouble."

He slid back to the dinner table. On a platter were the remains of a large fish, its fleshy head still connected to bones swimming upstream in vain escape. Standing there waiting for my punishment, I heard my mother speak in a dry voice.

"We not concerning this girl. This girl not have concerning for us."

Nobody looked at me. Bone chopsticks clinked against the insides of bowls being emptied into hungry mouths.

I walked into my room, closed the door, and lay down on my bed. The room was dark, the ceiling filled with shadows from the dinnertime lights of neighboring flats.

In my head, I saw a chessboard with sixty-four black and white squares. Opposite me was my opponent, two angry black slits. She wore a triumphant smile. "Strongest wind cannot be seen," she said.

Her black men advanced across the plane, slowly marching to each successive level as a single unit. My white pieces screamed as they scurried and fell off the board one by one. As her man drew closer to my edge, I felt myself growing light. I rose up into the air and flew out the window. Higher and higher, above the alley, over the tops of tiled roofs, where I was gathered up by the wind and pushed up toward the night sky until everything below me disappeared and I was alone.

I closed my eyes and pondered my next move.

1989

RUDYARD KIPLING

In San Francisco

He Arrives in the City

> "Serene, indifferent of fate,
> Thou sittest at the western gate,
> Thou seest the white seas fold their tents,
> Oh warder of two Continents.
> Thou drawest all thing small and great
> To thee beside the Western Gate."

THIS IS what Bret Harte has written of the great city of San Francisco, and for the past fortnight I have been wondering what made him do it. There is neither serenity nor indifference to be found in these parts; and evil would it be for the Continent whose wardship were intrusted to so reckless a guardian. Behold me pitched neck-and-crop from twenty days of the High Seas, into the whirl of California, deprived of any guidance, and left to draw my own conclusions. Protect me from the wrath of an outraged community if these letters be ever read by American eyes. San Francisco is a mad city–inhabited for the most part by perfectly insane people whose women are of a remarkable beauty. When the "City of Peking" steamed through the Golden Gate I saw with great joy that the block-house which guarded the mouth of the "finest harbour in the world, Sir" could be silenced by two gunboats from Hong Kong with safety, comfort and despatch.

Then a reporter leaped aboard, and ere I could gasp held me in his toils. He pumped me exhaustively while I was getting ashore, demanding, of all things in the world, news about Indian journalism. It is an awful thing to enter a new land with a new lie on your lips. I spoke the truth to the evil-minded Custom-house man who turned my most sacred raiment on a floor composed of stable-refuse and pine-splinters; but the reporter overwhelmed me not so much by his poignant audacity as his beautiful ignorance. I am sorry now that I did not tell him more lies as I passed into a city of three hundred thousand white men! Think of it! Three hundred thousand white men and women gathered in one spot, walking upon real pavements in front of real plate-glass windowed shops, and talking something that was not very different from English. It was only when I had tangled myself up in a hopeless maze of small wooden houses, dust, street-refuse, and children who play with empty kerosene tins, that I discovered the difference of speech.

"You want to go to the Palace Hotel?" said an affable youth on a dray. "What in hell are doing here, then? This is about the lowest place in the city. Go six blocks north to corner of Geary and Market; then walk around till you strike corner of Gutter and Sixteenth, and that brings you there."

I do not vouch for the literal accuracy of these directions, quoting but from a disordered memory.

"Amen," I said. "But who am I that I should strike the corners of such as you name? Peradventure they be gentlemen of repute, and might hit back. Bring it down to dots, my son."

I thought he would have smitten me, but he didn't. He explained that no one ever used the word "street," and that every one was supposed to know how the streets run; for sometimes the names were upon the lamps and sometimes they weren't. Fortified with these directions I proceeded till I found a mighty street full of sumptuous buildings four or five stories high, but paved with rude cobble stones in the fashion of the Year One. A cable-car without any visible means of support slid stealthily behind me and nearly struck me in the back. A hundred yards further there was a slight commotion in the street—a gathering together of three or four—and something that glittered as it moved very swiftly. A ponderous Irish gentleman with priest's cords in his hat and a small nickel-plated badge on his fat bosom emerged from the knot, supporting a Chinaman who had been stabbed in the eye and was bleeding like a pig. The bystanders went their ways, and the Chinaman, assisted by the policeman, his own. Of course this was none of my business, but I rather wanted to know what had happened to the gentleman who had dealt the stab. It said a great deal for the excellence of the municipal arrangements of the town that a surging crowd did not at once block the street to see what was going forward. I was the sixth man and the last who assisted at the performance, and my curiosity was six times the greatest. Indeed, I felt ashamed of showing it.

There were no more incidents till I reached the Palace Hotel, a seven-storied warren of humanity with a thousand rooms in it. All the travel-books will tell you about hotel arrangements in this country. They should be seen to be appreciated. Understand clearly—and this letter is written after a thousand miles of experiences—that money will not buy you service in the West.

When the hotel clerk—the man who awards your room to you and who is supposed to give you information—when that resplendent individual stoops to attend to your wants, he does so whistling or humming, or picking his teeth, or pauses to converse with someone he knows. These performances, I gather, are to impress upon you that he is a free man and your equal. From his general appearance and the size of his diamonds he ought to be your superior. There is no necessity for this swaggering, self-consciousness of freedom. Business is business, and the man who is paid to attend to a man might reasonably devote his whole attention to the job.

In a vast marble-paved hall under the glare of an electric light sat forty or fifty men; and for their use and amusement were provided spittoons of infinite capacity and generous gape. Most of the men wore frock-coats and top-hats,—the things that we in India put on at a wedding breakfast if we possessed them,—but they all spat. They spat on principle. The spittoons were on the staircases, in each bedroom—yea, and in chambers even more sacred than these. They chased one into retirement, but they blossomed in chiefest splendour round the Bar, and they were all used, every reeking one of 'em. Just before I began to feel deathly sick, another reporter grappled me. What he wanted to know was the precise area of India in square miles. I referred him to Whittaker. He had never heard of Whittaker. He wanted it from my own mouth, and I would not tell him. Then he swerved off, like the other man, to details of journalism in our own country. I ventured to suggest that the interior economy of a paper most concerned people who worked it. "That's the very thing that interests us," he said. "Have you got reporters anything like our reporters on Indian news papers?" "We have not," I said, and suppressed the "thank God" rising to my lips. "Why haven't you?" said he. "Because they would die," I said. It was exactly like talking to a child—a very rude little child. He would begin almost every sentence with: "Now tell me something about India," and would turn aimlessly from one question to another without the least continuity. I was not angry, but keenly interested. The man was a revelation to me. To his questions I returned answers mendacious and evasive. After all, it really did not matter what I said. He could not understand. I can only hope and pray that none of the readers of the "Pioneer" will ever see that portentous interview. The man made me out to be an idiot several sizes more drivelling than my destiny intended, and the rankness of his ignorance managed to distort the few poor facts with which I supplied him into large and elaborate lies. Then thought I: "The matter of American journalism shall be looked into later on. At present I will enjoy myself."

No man rose to tell me what were the lions of the place. No one volunteered any sort of conveyance. I was absolutely alone in this big city of white folks. By instinct I sought refreshment and came upon a bar-room, full of bad Salon pictures, in which men with hats on the backs of their heads were wolfing food from a counter. It was the institution of the "Free Lunch" that I had struck. You paid for a drink and got as much as you wanted to eat. For something less than a rupee a day a man could feed himself sumptuously in San Francisco, even though he be bankrupt. Remember this if ever you are stranded in these parts.

Later, I began a vast but unsystematic exploration of the streets. I asked for no names. It was enough that the pavements were full of white men and women, the streets clanging with traffic, and that the restful roar of a great city rang in my ears. The cable-cars glided to all points of the compass. I took them one by one till I could go no farther. San Francisco has been pitched down on the sand-bunkers of the Bikaneer desert. About one-fourth of it is ground reclaimed from the sea—any old-timer will tell you all about that. The remainder is ragged, unthrifty sand-hills, pegged down by houses.

From an English point of view there has not been the least attempt at grading those hills, and indeed you might as well try to grade the hillocks of Sind. The cable-cars have for all practical purposes made San Francisco a dead level. They take no count of rise or fall, but slide equably on their appointed courses from one end to the other of a six-mile street. They turn corners almost at right angles; cross other lines, and, for aught I know, may run up the sides of houses. There is no visible agency of their flight; but once in a while you shall pass a five-storied building, humming with machinery that winds up an everlasting wire-cable, and the initiated will tell you that here is the mechanism. I gave up asking questions. If it pleases Providence to make a car run up and down a slit in the ground for many miles, and if for two-pence-halfpenny I can ride in that car, why shall I seek the reasons of the miracle?

Rather let me look out of the windows till the shops give place to thousands and thousands of little houses made of wood – each house just big enough for a man and his family. Let me watch the people in the cars, and try to find out in what manner they differ from us, their ancestors. They delude themselves into the belief that they talk English, – "the" English, – and I have already been pitied for speaking with "an English accent." The man who pitied me spoke, so far as I was concerned, the language of thieves. And they all do. Where we put the accent forward, they throw it back, and vice versa; where we use the long "a," they use the short; and words so simple as to be past mistaking, they pronounce somewhere up in the dome of their heads. How do these things happen? Oliver Wendell Holmes says that Yankee schoolmarms, the cider, and the salt codfish of the Eastern States are responsible for what he calls a nasal accent. A Hindu is a Hindu and a brother to the man who knows his vernacular; and a Frenchman is French because he speaks his own language; but the American has no language. He is dialect, slang, provincialism, accent, and so forth. Now that I have heard their voices, all the beauty of Bret Harte is being ruined for me, because I find myself catching through the roll of his rhythmical prose the cadence of his peculiar fatherland. Get an American lady to read to you "How Santa Claus came to Simpson's Bar," and see how much is, under her tongue, left of the beauty of the original.

But I am sorry for Bret Harte. It happened this way. A reporter asked me what I thought of the city, and I made answer suavely that it was hallowed ground to me because of Bret Harte. That was true.

"Well," said the reporter, "Bret Harte claims California, but California don't claim Bret Harte. He's been so long in England that he's quite English. Have you seen our cracker-factories and the new offices of the Examiner?" He could not understand that to the outside world the city was worth a great deal less than the man.

He Meets a Bunco-Steerer

Night fell over the Pacific, and the white sea-fog whipped through the streets, dimming the splendours of the electric lights. It is the use of this city, her men and women, to parade between the hours of eight and ten a certain street, called Kearny Street, where the finest shops are situated. Here the click of heels on the pavement is loudest, here the lights are brightest, and here the thunder of the traffic is most overwhelming. I watched Young California and saw that it was at least expensively dressed, cheerful in manner, and self-asserting in conversation. Also the women are very fair. The maidens were of generous build, large, well-groomed, and attired in raiment that even to my inexperienced eyes must have cost much. Kearny Street, at nine o'clock, levels all distinctions of rank as impartially as the grave. Again and again I loitered at the heels of a couple of resplendent beings, only to overhear, when expected the level voice of culture, the staccato "Sez he, Sez I," that is the mark of the white servant-girl all the world over.

This was depressing because, in spite of all that goes to the contrary, fine feathers ought to make fine birds. There was wealth – unlimited wealth – in the streets, but not an accent that would not have been dear at fifty cents. Wherefore, revolving in my mind that these folk were barbarians, I was presently enlightened and made aware that they also were the heirs of all the ages, and civilized after all. There appeared before me an affable stranger of prepossessing appearance, with a blue and an innocent eye. Addressing me by name, he claimed to have met me in New York at the Windsor, and to this claim I gave a qualified assent. I did not remember the fact, but since he was so certain of it, why then – I waited developments. "And what did you think of Indiana when you came through?" was the next question. It revealed the mystery of previous acquaintance, and one or two other things. With reprehensible carelessness, my friend of the light-blue eye had looked up the name of his victim in the hotel register and read "India" for Indiana. He could not imagine an Englishman coming through the States from West to East instead of by the regularly ordained route. My fear was that in his delight at finding me so responsive he would make remarks about New York and the Windsor which I could not understand. And indeed, he adventured in this direction once or twice, asking me what I thought of such and such streets, which, from his tone, I gathered were anything but respectable. It is trying to talk unknown New York in almost unknown San Francisco. But my friend was merciful. He protested that I was one after his own heart, and pressed upon me rare and curious drinks at more than one bar. These drinks I accepted with gratitude, as also the cigars with which his pockets were stored. He would show me the Life of the City. Having no desire to watch a weary old play again, I evaded the offer, and received in lieu of the Devil's instruction much coarse flattery. Curiously constituted is the soul of man. Knowing how and where this man lied; waiting idly for the finale; I was distinctly conscious, as he bubbled compliments in my ear, of soft thrills of gratified pride. I was wise, quoth he, anybody could see that with half an eye; sagacious; versed in the affairs of the world; an acquaintance to be desired; one who had tasted the cup of Life with discretion. All this pleased me, and in a measure numbed the suspicion that was thoroughly aroused. Eventually the blue-eyed one discovered, nay insisted, that I had a taste for cards (this was clumsily worked in, but it was my fault, in that I met him half-way, and allowed him no chance of good acting). Hereupon, I laid my head to one side, and simulated unholy wisdom, quoting odds and ends of poker-talk, all ludicrously misapplied. My friend kept his countenance admirably; and well he might, for five minutes later we arrived, always by the purest of chances, at a place where we could play cards, and also frivol with Louisiana State Lottery tickets. Would I play? "Nay," said I, "for to me cards have neither meaning nor continuity; but let us assume that I am going to play. How would you and your friends get to work? Would you play a straight game, or make me drunk, or—well, the fact is I'm a newspaper man, and I'd be much obliged if you'd let me know something about bunco-steering." My blue-eyed friend cursed me by his gods,—the Right and the Left Bower; he even cursed the very good cigars he had given me. But, the storm over, he quieted down and explained. I apologised for causing him to waste an evening, and we spent a very pleasant time together. Inaccuracy, provincialism, and a too hasty rushing to conclusions were the rocks that he had split on; but he got his revenge when he said: "How would I play with you? From all the poppycock (Anglice: bosh), you talked about poker, I'd ha' played a straight game and skinned you. I wouldn't have taken the trouble to make you drunk. You never knew anything of the game; but the way I was mistaken in you makes me sick." He glared at me as though I had done him an injury. To-day I know how it is that, year after year, week after week, the bunco-steerer, who is the confidence-trick and card-sharper man of other climes, secures his prey. He slavers them over with flattery, as the snake slavers the rabbit. The incident depressed me because it showed I had left the innocent East far behind, and was come to a country where a man must look out for himself. The very hotel bristled with notices about keeping my door locked, and depositing my valuables in a safe. The white man in a lump is bad.

He Looks at Liquor and Politics

This brings me by natural sequence to the great drink question. As you know, of course, the American does not drink at meals as a sensible man should. Indeed, he has no meals. He stuffs for ten minutes thrice a day. Also he has no decent notions about the sun being over the yard-arm or below the horizon. He pours his vanity into himself at unholy hours, and indeed he can hardly help it. You have no notion of what "treating" means on the Western slope. It is more than an institution; it is a religion, though men tell me that it is nothing to what it was. Take a very common instance. At 10:30 a.m. a man is smitten with desire for stimulants. He is in the company of two friends. All three adjourn to the nearest bar,—seldom more than twenty yards away,—and takes three straight whiskies. They talk for two minutes. The second and third man then treat in order; thus each walks into the street, two of them the poorer by three goes of whiskey under their belt and one with two more liquors than he wanted. It is not etiquette yet to refuse a treat. The result is peculiar. I have never yet, I confess, seen a drunken man in the streets, but I have heard more about drunkenness among white men, and seen more decent men above or below themselves with drink, than I care to think about. And the vice runs up into all sorts of circles and societies. Never was I more astonished than at one pleasant dinner party to hear a pair of pretty lips say casually of a gentleman friend then under discussion, "He was drunk." The fact was merely stated without emotion. That was what startled me. But the climate of California deals kindly with excess, and treacherously covers up its traces. A man neither bloats nor shrivels in this dry air. He continues with the false bloom of health upon his cheeks, an equable eye, a firm mouth, and a steady hand till a day of reckoning arrives, and suddenly breaking up about the head, he dies, and his friends speak his epitaph accordingly. Why people who in most cases cannot hold their liquor should play with it so recklessly I leave others to decide. This unhappy state of affairs has, however, produced one good result which I will confide to you. In the heart of the business quarter, where banks and bankers are thickest, and telegraph wires most numerous, stands a semi-subterranean bar tended by a German with long blond locks and a crystalline eye. Go thither softly, treading on the tips of your toes, and ask him for a Button Punch. 'Twill take ten minutes to brew, but the result is the highest and noblest product of the age. No man but one knows what is in it. I have a theory it is compounded of the shavings of cherubs' wings, the glory of a tropical dawn, the red clouds of sunset, and fragments of lost epics by dead masters. But try you for yourselves, and pause a while to bless me, who am always mindful of the truest interests of my brethren.

But enough of the stale spilth of bar-rooms. Turn now to the august spectacle of a Government of the people, by the people, for the people, as it is understood in the city of San Francisco. Professor Bryce's book will tell you that every American citizen over twenty-one years of age possesses a vote. He may not know how to run his own business, control his wife, or instill reverence into his children, may be pauper, half-crazed with drink, bankrupt, dissolute, or merely a born fool; but he has a vote. If he likes, he can be voting most of his time—voting for his State Governor, his municipal officers, local option, sewage contracts, or anything else of which he has no special knowledge.

Once every four years he votes for a new President. In his spare moments he votes for his own judges–the men who shall give him justice. These are dependent on popular favor for re-election inasmuch as they are but chosen for a term of years–two or three, I believe. Such a position is manifestly best calculated to create an independent and unprejudiced administrator. Now this mass of persons who vote is divided into two parties–Republican and Democrat. They are both agreed in thinking that the other party is running creation (which is America) into red flame. Also the Democrat as a party drinks more than the Republican, and when drunk may be heard to talk about a thing called the Tariff, which he does not understand, but which he conceives to be the bulwark of the country or else the surest power for its destruction. Sometimes he says one thing and sometimes another, in order to contradict the Republican, who is always contradicting himself. And this is a true and lucid account of the forepart of American politics. The behind-part is otherwise.

Since every man has a vote and may vote on every conceivable thing, it follows that there exist certain wise men who understand the art of buying up votes retail, and vending them wholesale to whoever wants them most urgently. Now an American engaged in making a home for himself has not time to vote for turn-cocks and district attorneys and cattle of that kind, but the unemployed have much time because they are always on hand somewhere in the streets. They are called "the boys," and form a peculiar class. The boys are young men; inexpert in war, unskilled in labour; who have neither killed a man, lifted cattle, or dug a well. In plain English, they are just the men who can always be trusted to rally round any cause that has a glass of liquor for a visible heart. They wait–they are on hand–; and in being on hand lies the crown and the glory of American politics. The wise man is he who, keeping a liquor-saloon and judiciously dispensing drinks, knows how to retain within arm's reach a block of men who will vote for or against anything under the canopy of Heaven. Not every saloon-keeper can do this. It demands careful study of city politics, tact, the power of conciliation, and infinite resources of anecdote to amuse and keep the crowd together night after night, till the saloon becomes a salon. Above all, the liquor side of the scheme must not be worked for immediate profit. The boys who drink so freely will ultimately pay their host a thousand-fold. An Irishman, and an Irishman preeminently, knows how to work such a saloon parliament. Observe for a moment the plan of operations. The rank and file are treated to drink and a little money—and they vote. He who controls ten votes receives a proportionate reward; the dispenser of a thousand votes is worthy of reverence, and so the chain runs on till we reach the most successful worker of public saloons—the man most skillful in keeping his items together and using them when required. Such a man governs the city as absolutely as a king. And you would know where the gain comes in? The whole of the public offices of a city (with the exception of a very few where special technical skill is required) are short-term offices distributed according to "political" leanings. What would you have? A big city requires many officials. Each office carries a salary, and influence worth twice the pay. The offices are for the representatives of the men who keep together and are on hand to vote. The Commissioner of Sewage, let us say, is a gentleman who has been elected to his office by a Republican vote. He knows little and cares less about sewage, but he has sense enough to man the pumping-works and the street-sweeping-machines with the gentlemen who elected him. The Commissioner of Police has been helped to his post very largely by the influence of the boys at such and such a saloon. He may be the guardian of city morals, but he is not going to allow his subordinates to enforce early closing or abstention from gambling in that saloon. Most offices are limited to four years, consequently he is a fool who does not make his office pay him while he is in it.

The only people who suffer by this happy arrangement are, in fact, the people who devised the lovely system. And they suffer because they are Americans. Let us explain. As you know, every big city here holds at least one big foreign vote—generally Irish, frequently German. In San Francisco, the gathering place of the races, there is a distinct Italian vote to be considered, but the Irish vote is more important. For this reason the Irishman does not kill himself with overwork. He is made for the cheery dispensing of liquors, for everlasting blarney, and possesses a wonderfully keen appreciation of the weaknesses of lesser human nature. Also he has no sort of conscience, and only one strong conviction—that of deep-rooted hatred toward England. He keeps to the streets, he is on hand, he votes joyously, spending days lavishly,—and time is the American's dearest commodity. Behold the glorious result. To-day the city of San Francisco is governed by the Irish vote and the Irish influence, under the rule of a gentleman whose sight is impaired, and who requires a man to lead him about the streets. He is called officially "Boss Buckley," and unofficially the "Blind White Devil." I have before me now the record of his amiable career in black and white. It occupies four columns of small print, and perhaps you would think it disgraceful. Summarized, it is as follows: Boss Buckley, by tact and deep knowledge of the seamy side of the city, won himself a following of voters. He sought no office himself, or rarely: but as his following increased he sold their services to the highest bidder, himself taking toll of the revenues of every office. He controlled the Democratic party in the city of San Francisco. The people appoint their own judges. Boss Buckley's people appointed judges. These judges naturally were Boss Buckley's property. I have been to dinner parties and heard educated men, not concerned with politics, telling stories one to another of "justice," both civil and criminal, being bought with a price from the hands of these judges. Such tales they told without heat, as men recording facts. Contracts for road-mending, public buildings, and the like, are under the control of Boss Buckley, because the men whom Buckley's following sent to the City Council adjudicate on these contracts; and on each and every one of these contracts Boss Buckley levies his percentage for himself and his allies.

The Republican party in San Francisco also have their boss. He is not so great a genius as Boss Buckley, but I decline to believe that he is any whit more virtuous. He has a smaller number of votes at his command.

He Visits the Bohemian Club

There are no princes in America, at least with crowns on their heads; but a generous-minded member of some royal family received my letter of introduction. Ere the day closed I was a member of two clubs and booked for many engagements to dinner and party. Now this prince, upon whose financial operations be continual increase, had no reason, nor had the others, to put himself out for the sake of one Briton more or less; but he rested not till he had accomplished all in my behalf that a mother could think of for her debutante daughter. Do you know the Bohemian Club of San Francisco? They say its fame extends over the world. It was created somewhat on the line of the Savage by men who wrote or drew things, and it has blossomed into most unrepublican luxury. The ruler of the place is an owl—an owl standing upon a skull and cross-bones, showing forth grimly the wisdom of the man of letters and the end of his hopes for immortality. The owl stands on the staircase, a statue four feet high, is carved in the woodwork, flutters on the frescoed ceilings, is stamped on the note paper, and hangs on the walls. He is an Ancient and Honorable Bird. Under his wing 'twas my privilege to meet with white men whose lives were not chained down to routine of toil, who wrote magazine articles instead of reading them hurriedly in the pauses of office-work, who painted pictures instead of contenting themselves with cheap etchings picked up at another man's sale of effects. Mine were all the rights of social intercourse that India, stony-hearted step-mother of Collectors, has swindled us out of. Treading soft carpets and breathing the incense of superior cigars, I wandered from room to room studying the paintings in which the members of the club had caricatured themselves, their associates, and their aims. There was a slick French audacity about the workmanship of these men of toil unbending that went straight to the heart of the beholder. And yet it was not altogether French. A dry grimness of treatment, almost Dutch, marked the difference. The men painted as they spoke—with certainty. The club indulges in revelries which it calls "jinks," high and low, at intervals; and each of these gatherings is faithfully portrayed in oils by hands that know their business. In this club were no amateurs spoiling canvas because they fancied they could handle oils without knowledge of shadows or anatomy—no gentleman of leisure ruining the temper of publishers and an already ruined market with attempts to write "because everybody writes something these days." My hosts were working, or had worked, for their daily bread with pen or paint, and their talk for the most part was of the shop shoppy—that is to say, delightful. They extended a large hand of welcome and were as brethren, and I did homage to the Owl and listened to their talk. An Indian Club about Christmas-time will yield, if properly worked, an abundant harvest of queer tales; but at a gathering of Americans from the uttermost ends of their own continent the tales are larger, thicker, more spinous, and even more azure than any Indian variety. Tales of the War I heard told by an ex-officer of the South over his evening drink to a Colonel of the Northern army; my introducer, who had served as a trooper in the Northern Horse, throwing in emendations from time to time.

Other voices followed with equally wondrous tales of riata-throwing in Mexico or Arizona, of gambling at army posts in Texas, of newspaper wars waged in godless Chicago, of deaths sudden and violent in Montana and Dakota, of the loves of half-breed maidens in the South, and fantastic huntings for gold in mysterious Alaska. Above all, they told the story of the building of old San Francisco, when the "finest collection of humanity on God's earth, Sir, started this town, and the water come up to the foot of Montgomery Street." Very terrible were some of the tales, grimly humorous the others, and the men in broadcloth and fine linen who told them had played their parts in them.

"And now and again when things got too bad they would toll the city bell, and the Vigilance Committee turned out and hanged the suspicious characters. A man didn't begin to be suspected in those days till he'd committed at least one unprovoked murder," said a calm-eyed, portly old gentleman. I looked at the pictures around me, the noiseless, neat-uniformed waiter behind me, the oak-ribbed ceiling above, the velvety carpet beneath. It was hard to realize that even twenty years ago you could see a man hanged with great pomp.

They bore me to a banquet in honour of a brave Lieutenant, Carlin, of the "Vandalia," who stuck by his ship in the great cyclone at Apia and comported himself as an officer should. On that occasion I heard oratory with the roundest "o's"; and devoured a dinner the memory of which will descend with me into the hungry grave. There were about forty speeches delivered; and not one of them was average or ordinary. It was my first introduction to the American Eagle screaming for all it was worth. The Lieutenant's heroism served as a peg from which the silver-tongued ones turned themselves loose and kicked. They ransacked the clouds of sunset, the thunderbolts of Heaven, the deeps of Hell, and the splendours of the Resurrection, for tropes and metaphors, and hurled the result at the head of the guest of the evening. Never since the morning stars sang together for joy, I learned, had an amazed creation witnessed such superhuman bravery as that displayed by the American navy in the Samoa cyclone. Till earth rotted in the phosphorescent star-and-stripe slime of a decayed universe that God-like gallantry would not be forgotten. I grieve that I cannot give the exact words. My attempt at reproducing their spirit is pale and inadequate. I sat bewildered on a coruscating Niagara of—blatherumskite. It was magnificent—it was stupendous; and I was conscious of a wicked desire to hide my face in a napkin and grin. Then, according to the rule, they produced their dead, and across the snowy tablecloths dragged the corpse of every man slain in the Civil War, and hurled defiance at "our natural enemy" (England, so please you!) "with her chain of fortresses across the world." Thereafter they glorified their nation afresh, from the beginning, in case any detail should have been overlooked, and that made me uncomfortable for their sakes. How in the world can a white man, a Sahib of our blood, stand up and plaster praise on his own country? He can think as highly as he likes, but his open-mouthed vehemence of adoration struck me almost as indelicate. My hosts talked for rather more than three hours, and at the end seemed ready for three hours more. But when the Lieutenant—such a big, brave, gentle giant!—rose to his feet, he delivered what seemed to me as the speech of the evening. I remember nearly the whole of it, and it ran something in this way: "Gentlemen—it's very good of you to give me this dinner and to tell me all these pretty things, but what I want you to understand—the fact is—what we want and what we ought to get at once is a navy—more ships—lots of 'em—" Then we howled the top of the roof off, and I, for one, fell in love with Carlin on the spot. *Wallah!* He was a man.

The Prince among merchants bade me take no heed to the warlike sentiments of some of the old Generals. "The sky-rockets are thrown in for effect," quoth he, "and whenever we get on our hind legs we always express a desire to chaw up England. It's a sort of family affair."

And indeed, when you come to think of it, there is no other country for the American public speaker to trample upon.

France has Germany; we have Russia; for Italy, Austria is provided; and the humblest Pathan possesses an ancestral enemy. Only America stands out of the racket; and therefore, to be in fashion, makes a sandbag of the mother-country; and bangs her when occasion requires.

"The chain of fortresses" man, a fascinating talker, explained to me after the affair that he was compelled to blow off steam. Everybody expected it. When we had chanted "The Star Spangled Banner" not more than eight times, we adjourned. America is a very great country, but it is not yet Heaven with electric lights and plush fitting, as the speakers professed to believe. My listening mind went back to the politicians in the saloon who wasted no time in talking about freedom, but quietly made arrangements to impose their will on the citizens. "The Judge is a great man; but give thy presents to the Clerk," as the proverb saith.

He Meets the Ladies

I am hopelessly in love with about eight American maidens—all perfectly delightful till the next one comes into the room. O-Toyo was a darling, but she lacked several things; conversation, for one. You cannot live on giggles. She shall remain unmoved at Nagasaki while I roast a battered heart before the shrine of a big Kentucky blonde who had for a nurse, when she was little, a negro "mammy." By consequence she had welded on to Californian beauty, Paris dresses, Eastern culture, Europe trips, and wild Western originality, the queer dreamy superstitions of the negro quarters, and the result is soul-shattering. And she is but one of many stars. Item, a maiden who believes in education and possesses it, with a few hundred thousand dollars to boot, and a taste for slumming. Item, the leader of a sort of informal salon where girls congregate, read papers, and daringly discuss metaphysical problems and candy—a sloe-eyed, black-browed, imperious maiden. Item, a very small maiden, absolutely without reverence, who can in one swift sentence trample upon and leave gasping half a dozen young men. Item, a millionairess, burdened with her money, lonely, caustic, with a tongue keen as a sword, yearning for a sphere, but chained up to the rock of her vast possessions. Item, a typewriter-maiden earning her own bread in this big city, because she doesn't think a girl ought to be a burden on her parents. She quotes Theophile Gautier, and moves through the world manfully, much respected, for all her twenty inexperienced summers. Item, a woman from Cloudland who has no history in the past, but is discreetly of the present, and strives for the confidences of male humanity on the grounds of "sympathy." (This is not altogether a new type.) Item, a girl in a "dive" blessed with a Greek head and eyes that seem to speak all that is best and sweetest in the world. But woe is me!—she has no ideas in this world or the next, beyond the consumption of beer (a commission on each bottle), and protests that she sings the songs allotted to her nightly with no more than the vaguest notion of their meaning.

Sweet and comely are the maidens of Devonshire; delicate and of gracious seeming those who live in the pleasant places of London; fascinating for all their demureness the damsels of France clinging closely to their mothers, and with large eyes wondering at the wicked world; excellent in her own place and to those who understand her is the Anglo-Indian "spin" in her second season; but the girls of America are above and beyond them all. They are clever; they can talk. Yea, it is said that they think. Certainly they have an appearance of so doing. They are original, and look you between the brows as a sister might look at her brother. They are instructed in the folly and vanity of the male mind, for they have associated with "the boys" from baby-hood, and can discerningly minister to both vices, or pleasantly snub the possessor. They possess, moreover, a life among themselves, inde-pendent of masculine associations. They have societies and clubs and unlimited tea-fights where all the guests are girls. They are self-possessed without parting with any tenderness that is their sex-right; they understand; they can take care of themselves; they are superbly independent. When you ask them what makes them so charming, they say: "It is because we are better educated than your girls and we are more sensible in regard to men. We have good times all around, but we aren't taught to regard every man as a possible husband. Nor is he expected to marry the first girl he calls on regularly." Yes, they have good times, their freedom is large, and they do not abuse it. They can go driving with young men, and receive visits from young men to an extent that would make an English mother wink with horror; and neither driver nor drivee have a thought beyond the enjoyment of a good time. As certain also of their own poets have said:—

"Man is fire and woman is tow,
And the Devil he comes and begins to blow."

In America the tow is soaked in a solution that makes it fireproof, in absolute liberty and large knowledge; consequently accidents do not exceed the regular percentage arranged by the Devil for each class and climate under the skies. But the freedom of the young girl has its drawbacks. She is—I say it with all reluctance—irreverent, from her forty-dollar bonnet to the buckles in her eighteen-dollar shoes. She talks flippantly to her parents and men old enough to be her grandfather. She has a prescriptive right to the society of the Man who Arrives. The parents admit it. This is sometimes embarrassing, especially when you call on a man and his wife for the sake of information; the one being a merchant of varied knowledge, the other a woman of the world. In five minutes your host has vanished. In another five his wife has followed him, and you are left with a very charming maiden doubtless, but certainly not the person you came to see. She chatters and you grin; but you leave with a very strong impression of a wasted morning. This has been my experience once or twice. I have even said as pointedly as I dared to a man: "I came to see you." "You'd better see me in my office, then. The house belongs to my women-folk—to my daughter, that is to say." He spoke the truth. The American of wealth is owned by his family. They exploit him for bullion, and sometimes it seems to me that his lot is a lonely one. The woman get the ha'-pence; the kicks are all his own. Nothing is too good for an American's daughter (I speak here of the moneyed classes). The girls take every gift as a matter of course. Yet they develop greatly when a catastrophe arrives and the man of many millions goes up or down and his daughters take to stenography or type-writing. I have heard many tales of heroism from the lips of girls who counted the principals among their friends. The crash came; Mamie or Hattie or Sadie gave up their maid, their carriages and candy, and with a No. 2 Remington and a stout heart set about earning their daily bread.

"And did I drop her from the list of my friends? No, sir," said a scarlet-lipped vision in white lace. "That might happen to me any day."

It may be this sense of possible disaster in the air that makes San Franciscan society go with so captivating a rush and whirl. Recklessness is in the air. I can't explain where it comes from, but there it is. The roaring winds off the Pacific make you drunk to begin with. The aggressive luxury on all sides helps out the intoxication, and you spin for ever "down the ringing groves of change" (there is no small change, by the way, west of the Rockies) as long as money lasts. They make greatly and they spend lavishly; not only the rich but the artisans, who pay nearly five pounds for a suit of clothes and for other luxuries in proportion. The young men rejoice in the days of their youth. They gamble, yacht, race, enjoy prize-fights and cock-fights—the one openly, the other in secret—they establish luxurious clubs; they break themselves over horse-flesh and—other things; and they are instant in quarrel. At twenty they are experienced in business; and embark in vast enterprises, take partners as experienced as themselves, and go to pieces with as much splendour as their neighbours. Remember that the men who stocked California in the Fifties were physically, and as far as regards certain tough virtues, the pick of the earth. The inept and the weakly died en route or went under in the days of construction. To this nucleus were added all the races of the Continent— French, Italian, German, and of course, the Jew. The result you shall see in large-boned, deep-chested, delicate-handed women, and long, elastic, well-built boys. It needs no little golden badge swinging from his watch-chain to mark the Native Son of the Golden West—the country-bred of California. Him I love because he is devoid of fear, carries himself like a man, and has a heart as big as his boots. I fancy, too, he knows how to enjoy the blessings of life that his world so abundantly bestows upon him.

And what more remains to tell? I cannot write connectedly, because I am in love with all those girls aforesaid and some others who do not appear in the invoice. The type-writer girl is an institution of which the comic papers make much capital, but she is vastly convenient. She and a companion rent a room in a business quarter, and copy manuscript at the rate of six annas a page. Only a woman can manage a type-writing machine, because she has served apprenticeship to the sewing machine. She can earn as much as a hundred dollars a month, and professes to regard this form of bread-winning as her natural destiny. But oh how she hates it in her heart of hearts! When I had got over the surprise of doing business and trying to give orders to a young woman of coldly clerkly aspect, intrenched behind gold-rimmed spectacles, I made inquiries concerning the pleasures of this independence. They like it—indeed, they did. 'Twas the natural fate of almost all girls,—the recognised custom in America,—and I was a barbarian not to see it in that light.

"Well, and after?" said I. "What happens?"

"We work for our bread."

"And then what do you expect?"

"Then we shall work for our bread."

"Till you die?"

"Ye-es—unless—"

"Unless what? A man works till he dies."

"So shall we." This without enthusiasm—"I suppose."

Said the partner of the firm audaciously: "Sometimes we marry our employers—at least that's what the newspapers say."

The hand banged on half a dozen of the keys at once. "Yes, I don't care. I hate it—I hate it—I hate it, and you needn't look so!"

The senior partner was regarding the rebel with grave-eyed reproach.

"I thought you did," said I. "I don't suppose American girls are much different from English ones in instinct."

"Isn't it Theophile Gautier who says that the only differences between country and country lie in the slang and the uniform of the police?"

Now in the name of all the Gods at once, what is one to say to a young lady (who in England would be a Person) who earns her own bread, and very naturally hates the employ, and slings out-of-the-way quotations at your head? That one falls in love with her goes without saying; but that is not enough.

A mission should be established.

1889

JACK KEROUAC

October in the Railroad Earth

T H E R E   W A S   a little alley in San Francisco back of the Southern Pacific station at Third and Townsend in redbrick of drowsy lazy afternoons with everybody at work in offices in the air you feel the impending rush of their commuter frenzy as soon they'll be charging en masse from Market and Sansome buildings on foot and in buses and all well-dressed thru workingman Frisco of Walkup ?? truck drivers and even the poor grime-bemarked Third Street of lost bums even Negroes so hopeless and long left East and meanings of responsibility and *try* that now all they do is stand there spitting in the broken glass sometimes fifty in one afternoon against one wall at Third and Howard and here's all these Millbrae and San Carlos neat-necktied producers and commuters of America and Steel civilization rushing by with San Francisco *Chronicles* and green *Call-Bulletins* not even enough time to be disdainful, they've got to catch 130, 132, 134, 136 all the way up to 146 till the time of evening supper in homes of the railroad earth when high in the sky the magic stars ride above the following hotshot freight trains—it's all in California, it's all a sea, I swim out of it in afternoons of sun hot meditation in my jeans with head on handkerchief on brakeman's lantern or (if not working) on book, I look up at blue sky of perfect lostpurity and feel the warp of wood of old America beneath me and have insane conversations with Negroes in several-story windows above and everything is pouring in, the switching moves of boxcars in that little alley which is so much like the alleys of Lowell and I hear far off in the sense of coming night that engine calling our mountains.

But it was that beautiful cut of clouds I could always see above the little S.P. alley, puffs floating by from Oakland or the Gate of Marin to the north or San Jose south, the clarity of Cal to break your heart. It was the fantastic drowse and drum hum of lum mum afternoon nathin' to do, ole Frisco with end of land sadness – the people – the alley full of trucks and cars of businesses nearabouts and nobody knew or far from cared who I was all my life three thousand five hundred miles from birth-O opened up and at last belonged to me in Great America.

Now it's night in Third Street the keen little neons and also yellow bulblights of impossible-to-believe flops with dark ruined shadows moving back of torn yellow shades like a degenerate China with no money – the cats in Annie's Alley, the flop comes on, moans, rolls, the street is loaded with darkness. Blue sky above with stars hanging high over old hotel roofs and blowers of hotels moaning out dusts of interior, the grime inside the word in mouths falling out tooth by tooth, the reading rooms tick tock bigclock with creak chair and slantboards and old faces looking up over rimless spectacles bought in some West Virginia or Florida or Liverpool England pawnshop long before I was born and across rains they've come to the end of the land sadness end of the world gladness all you San Franciscos will have to fall eventually and burn again. But I'm walking and one night a bum fell into the hole of the construction job where they're tearing a sewer by day the husky Pacific & Electric youths in torn jeans who work there often I think of going up to some of 'em like say blond ones with wild hair and torn shirts and say "You oughta apply for the railroad it's much easier work you don't stand around the street all day and you get much more pay" but this bum fell in the hole you saw his foot stick out, a British MG also driven by some eccentric once backed into the hole and as I came home from a long Saturday afternoon local to Hollister out of San Jose miles away across verdurous fields of prune and juice joy here's this British MG backed and legs up wheels up into a pit and bums and cops standing around right outside the coffee shop – it was the way they fenced it but he never had the nerve to do it due to the fact that he had no money and nowhere to go and O his father was dead and O his mother was dead and O his sister was dead and O his whereabout was dead was dead – but and then at that time also I lay in my room on long Saturday afternoons listening to Jumpin' George with my fifth of tokay no tea and just under the sheets laughed to hear the crazy music "Mama, he treats your daughter mean," Mama, Papa, and don't you come in here I'll kill you etc. getting high by myself in room glooms and all wondrous knowing about the Negro the essential American out there always finding his solace his meaning in the fellaheen street and not in abstract morality and even when he has a church you see the pastor out front bowing to the ladies on the make you hear his great vibrant voice on the sunny Sunday afternoon sidewalk full of sexual vibratos saying "Why yes Mam but de gospel do say that man was born of woman's womb –" and no and so by that time I come crawling out of my warmsack and hit the street when I see the railroad ain't gonna call me till 5 a.m. Sunday morn probably for a local out of Bay Shore in fact always for a local out of Bay Shore and I go to the wailbar of all the wildbars in the world the one and only Third-and-Howard and there I go in and drink with the madmen and if I get drunk I git.

The whore who come up to me in there the night I was there with Al Buckle and said to me "You wanta play with me tonight Jim, and?" and I didn't think I had enough money and later told this to Charley Low and he laughed and said "How do you know she wanted money always take the chance that she might be out just for love or just out for love you know what I mean man don't be a sucker." She was a goodlooking doll and said "How would you like to oolyakoo with me mon?" and I stood there like a jerk and in fact bought drink got drink drunk that night and in the 299 Club I was hit by the proprietor the band breaking up the fight before I had a chance to decide to hit him back which I didn't do and out on the street I tried to rush back in but they had locked the door and were looking at me thru the forbidden glass in the door with faces like undersea – I should have played with her shurrouruuruuruuruuruuruurkdiei.

Despite the fact I was a brakeman making 600 a month I kept going to the Public restaurant on Howard Street which was three eggs for 26 cents 2 eggs for 21 this with toast (hardly no butter) coffee (hardly no coffee and sugar rationed) oatmeal with dash of milk and sugar the smell of soured old shirts lingering above the cookpot steams as if they were making skidrow lumberjack stews out of San Francisco ancient Chinese mildewed laundries with poker games in the back among the barrels and the rats of the earthquake days, but actually the food somewhat on the level of an old-time 1890 or 1910 section-gang cook of lumber camps far in the North with an oldtime pigtail Chinaman cooking it and cussing out those who didn't like it. The prices were incredible but one time I had the beefstew and it was absolutely the worst beefstew I ever et, it was incredible I tell you—and as they often did that to me it was with the most intensest regret that I tried to convey to the geek back of counter what I wanted but he was a tough sonofabitch, ech, ti-ti, I thought the counterman was kind of queer especially he handled gruffly the hopeless drooldrunks, "What now you doing you think you can come in here and cut like that for God's sake act like a man won't you and eat or get out-t-t-t-"—I always did wonder what a guy like that was doing working in a place like that because, but why some sympathy in his horny heart for the busted wrecks, all up and down the street were restaurants like the Public catering exclusively to bums of the block, winos with no money, who found 21 cents left over from wine panhandlings and so stumbled in for their third or fourth touch of food in a week, as sometimes they didn't eat at all and so you'd see them in the corner puking white liquid which was a couple quarts of rancid sauterne rotgut or sweet white sherry and they had nothing on their stomachs, most of them had one leg or were on crutches and had bandages around their feet, from nicotine and alcohol poisoning together, and one time finally on my way up Third near Market across the street from Breens, when in early 1952 I lived on Russian Hill and didn't quite dig the complete horror and humor of railroad's Third Street, a bum a thin sickly littlebum like Anton Abraham lay face down on the pavement with crutch aside and some old remnant newspaper sticking out and it seemed to me he was dead. I looked closely to see if he was breathing and he was not, another man with me was looking down and we agreed he was dead, and soon a cop came over and took and agreed and called the wagon, the little wretch weighed about 50 pounds in his bleeding count and was stone mackerel snotnose cold dead as a bleeding doornail—ah I tell you—and who could notice but other half dead deadbums bums bums bums dead dead times X times X times all dead bums forever dead with nothing and all finished and out—there—and this was the clientele in the Public Hair restaurant where I ate many's the morn a 3-egg breakfast with almost dry toast and oatmeal a little saucer of, and thin sickly dishwater coffee, all to save

14 cents so in my little book proudly I could make a notation and of the day and prove that I could live comfortably in America while working seven days a week and earning 600 a month I could live on less than 17 a week which with my rent of 4.20 was okay as I had also to spend money to eat and sleep sometimes on the other end of my Watsonville chaingang run but preferred most times to sleep free of charge and uncomfortable in cabooses of the crummy rack—my 26-cent breakfast, my pride—and that incredible semiqueer counter-man who dished out the food, threw it at you, slammed it, had a languid frank expression straight in your eyes like a 1930's lunchcart heroine in Steinbeck and at the steamtable itself labored coolly a junkey-looking Chinese with an actual stocking in his hair as if they'd just Shanghai'd him off the foot of Commercial Street before the Ferry Building was up but forgot it was 1952, dreamed it was 1860 goldrush Frisco—and on rainy days you felt they had ships in the back room.

I'd take walks up Harrison and the boomcrash of truck traffic towards the glorious girders of the Oakland Bay Bridge that you could see after climbing Harrison Hill a little like radar machine of eternity in the sky, huge, in the blue, by pure clouds crossed, gulls, idiot cars streak-ing to destinations on its undinal boom across shmoshwaters flocked up by winds and news of San Rafael storms and flash boats—there O I always came and walked and negotiated whole Friscos in one after-noon from the overlooking hills of the high Fillmore where Orient-bound vessels you can see on drowsy Sunday mornings of poolhall goof like after a whole night playing drums in a jam session and a morn in the hall of cuesticks I went by the rich homes of old ladies supported by daughters or female secretaries with immense ugly gar-goyle Frisco millions fronts of other days and way below is the blue passage of the Gate, the Alcatraz mad rock, the mouths of Tamalpais, San Pablo Bay, Sausalito sleepy hemming the rock and bush over yonder, and the sweet white ships cleanly cutting a path to Sasebo.—Over Harrison and down to the Embarcadero and around Telegraph Hill and up the back of Russian Hill and down to the play streets of Chinatown and down Kearny back across Market to Third and my wild-night neon twinkle fate there, ah, and then finally at dawn of a Sunday and they did call me, the immense girders of Oakland Bay still haunting me and all that eternity too much to swallow and not knowing who I am at all but like a big plump longhaired baby wor- walking up in the dark trying to wonder who I am the door knocks and it's the desk keeper of the flop hotel with silver rims and white hair and clean clothes and sickly potbelly said he was from Rocky Mount and looked like yes, he had been desk clerk of the Nash Buncome Association hotel down there in 50 successive heatwave summers without the sun and only palmos of the lobby with cigar crutches in the albums of the South and him with his dear mother waiting in a buried log cabin of graves with all that mashed past historied underground afoot with the stain of the bear the blood of the tree and cornfields long plowed under and Negroes whose voices long faded from the middle of the wood and the dog barked his last, this man had voyageured to the West Coast too like all the other loose American elements and was pale and sixty and complaining of sickness, might at one time been a handsome squire to women with money but now a forgotten clerk and maybe spent a little time in jail for a few forgeries or harmless cons and might also have been a railroad clerk and might have wept and might have never made it, and that day I'd say he saw the bridgegirders up over the hill of traffic of Harrison like me and woke up mornings with same lost, is now beckoning on my door and breaking in the world on me and he is standing on the frayed carpet of the hall all worn down by black steps of sunken old men for last 40 years since earthquake and the toilet stained, beyond the last toilet bowl and the last stink and stain I guess yes is the end of the world the bloody end of the world, so now knocks on my door and I wake up, saying "How what howp howelk howel of the knavery they've meaking, ek and won't let me slepit? Whey they drool? Whand out wisis thing that comes flarminging around my dooring in the mouth of the night and there everything knows that I have no mother, and no sister, and no father and no bot sosstle, but not crib" I get up and sit up and says "Howowow?" and he says "Telephone?" and I have to put on my jeans heavy with knife, wallet, I look closely at my railroad watch hanging on little door flicker of closet door face to me ticking silent the time, it says 4:30 a.m. of a Sunday morn, I go down the carpet of the skidrow hall in jeans and with no shirt and yes with shirt tails hanging gray workshirt and pick up phone and ticky sleepy night desk with cage and spittoons and keys hanging and old towels piled clean ones but frayed at edges and bearing names of every hotel of the moving prime, on the phone is the Crew Clerk, "Kerroway?" "Yeah." "Kerroway it's gonna be the Sherman Local at 7 a.m. this morning." "Sherman Local right." "Out of Bay Shore, you know the way?" "Yeah." "You had that same job last Sunday–Okay Kerroway-y-y-y-y." And we mutually hang up and I say to myself okay it's the Bay Shore bloody old dirty hagglous old coveted old madman Sherman who hates me so much especially when we were at Redwood Junction kicking boxcars and he always insists I work the rear end tho as one-year man it would be easier for me to follow pot but I work rear and he wants me to be right there with a block of wood when a car or cut of cars kicked stops, so they won't roll down that incline and start catastrophes, O well anyway I'll be learning eventually to like the railroad and Sherman will like me some day, and anyway another day another dollar.

And there's my room, small, gray in the Sunday morning, now all the franticness of the street and night before is done with, bums sleep, maybe one or two sprawled on sidewalk with empty poorboy on a sill–my mind whirls with life.

So there I am in dawn in my dim cell–2½ hours to go till the time I have to stick my railroad watch in my jean watchpocket and cut out allowing myself exactly 8 minutes to the station and the 7:15 train No. 112 I have to catch for the ride five miles to Bay Shore through four tunnels, emerging from the sad Rath scene of Frisco gloom gleak in the rainymouth fogmorning to a sudden valley with grim hills rising to the sea, bay on left, the fog rolling in like demented in the draws that have little white cottages disposed real-ecstatically for come-Christmas blue sad lights–my whole soul and concomitant eyes looking out on this reality of living and working in San Francisco with that pleased semi-loin-located shudder, energy for sex changing to pain at the portals of work and culture and natural foggy fear.–There I am in my little room wondering how I'll really manage to fool myself into feeling that these next 2½ hours will be well filled, fed, with work and pleasure thoughts.–It's so thrilling to feel the coldness of the morning wrap around my thickquilt blankets as I lay there, watch facing and ticking me, legs spread in comfy skidrow soft sheets with soft tears or sew lines in 'em, huddled in my own skin and rich and not spending a cent on—I look at my littlebook—and I stare at the words of the Bible.—On the floor I find last red afternoon Saturday's *Chronicle* sports page with news of football games in Great America the end of which I bleakly see in the gray light entering—the fact that Frisco is built of wood satisfies me in my peace, I know nobody'll disturb me for 2½ hours and all bums are asleep in their own bed of eternity awake or not, bottle or not—it's the joy I feel that counts for me.—On the floor's my shoes, big lumberboot flopjack workshoes to colomp over rockbed with and not turn the ankle—solidity shoes that when you put them on, yokewise, you know you're working now and so for same reason shoes not be worn for any reason like joys of restaurant and shows.—Night-before shoes are on the floor beside the Clunker-shoes a pair of blue canvas shoes à la 1952 style, in them I'd trod soft as ghost the indented hills sidewalks of Ah Me Frisco all in the glitter night, from the top of Russian Hill I'd looked down at one point on all roofs of North Beach and the Mexican nightclub neons, I'd descended to them on the old steps of Broadway under which they were newly laboring a mountain tunnel—shoes fit for watersides, embarcaderos, hill and plot lawns of park and tiptop vista.—Workshoes covered with dust and some oil of engines—the crumpled jeans nearby, belt, blue railroad hank, knife, comb, keys, switch keys and caboose coach key, the knees white from Pajaro Riverbottom finedusts, the ass black from slick sandboxes in yardgoat after yardgoat—the gray workshorts, the dirty undershirt, sad shorts, tortured socks of my life.—And the Bible on my desk next to the peanut butter, the lettuce, the raisin bread, the crack in the plaster, the stiff-with-old-dust lace drape now no longer laceable but hard as—after all those years of hard dust eternity in that Cameo skid inn with red eyes of rheumy oldmen dying there staring without hope out on the dead wall you can hardly see thru window-dusts and all you heard lately in the shaft of the rooftop middle way was the cries of a Chinese child whose father and mother were always telling him to shush and then screaming at him, he was a pest and his tears from China were most persistent and worldwide and repre-sented all our feelings in brokendown Cameo tho this was not admit-ted by bum one except for an occasional harsh clearing of throat in the halls or moan of nightmarer – by things like this and neglect of a hard-eyed alcoholic oldtime chorusgirl maid the curtains had now absorbed all the iron they could take and hung stiff and even the dust in them was iron, if you shook them they'd crack and fall in tatters to the floor and spatter like wings of iron on the bong and the dust would fly into your nose like filings of steel and choke you to death, so I never touched them. My little room at 6 in the comfy dawn (at 4:30) and before me all that time, that fresh-eyed time for a little coffee to boil water on my hot plate, throw some coffee in, stir it, French style, slowly carefully pour it in my white tin cup, throw sugar in (not California beet sugar like I should have been using but New Orleans cane sugar, because beet racks I carried from Oakland out to Watsonville many's the time, a 80-car freight train with nothing but gondolas loaded with sad beets looking like the heads of decapitated women) – ah me how but it was a hell and now I had the whole thing to myself, and make my raisin toast by sitting it on a little wire I'd especially bent to place over the hotplate, the toast crackled up, there, I spread the margarine on the still red hot toast and it too would crackle and sink in golden, among burnt raisins and this was my toast – then two eggs gently slowly fried in soft margarine in my little skidrow frying pan about half as thick as a dime in fact less a little piece of tiny tin you could bring on a camp trip – the eggs slowly fluffled in there and swelled from butter steams and I threw garlic salt on them, and when they were ready the yellow of them had been slightly filmed with a cooked white at the top from the tin cover I'd put over the frying pan, so now they were ready, and out they came, I spread them out on top of my already prepared potatoes which had been boiled in small pieces and then mixed with the bacon I'd already fried in small pieces, kind of raggely mashed bacon potatoes, with eggs on top steaming, and on the side lettuce, with peanut butter dab nearby on side. – I had heard that peanut butter and lettuce contained all the vitamins you should want, this after I had originally started to eat this combination because of the deliciousness and nostalgia of the taste – my breakfast ready at about 6:45 and as I eat already I'm dressing to go piece by piece and by the time the last dish is washed in the little sink at the boiling hotwater tap and I'm taking my lastquick slug of coffee and quickly rinsing the cup in the hot water spout and rushing to dry it and plop it in its place by the hot plate and the brown carton in which all the groceries sit tightly wrapped in brown paper, I'm already picking up my brakeman's lantern from where it's been hanging on the door handle and my tattered timetable's long been in my backpocket folded and ready to go, everything tight, keys, time-table, lantern, knife, handkerchief, wallet, comb, railroad keys, change and myself. I put the light out on the sad dab mad grub little diving room and hustle out into the fog of the flow, descending the creak hall steps where the old men are not yet sitting with Sunday morn papers because still asleep or some of them I can now as I leave hear beginning to disfawdle to wake in their rooms with their moans and yorks and scrapings and horror sounds, I'm going down the steps to work, glance to check time of watch with clerk cage clock – a hardy two or three oldtimers sitting already in the dark brown lobby under the tockboom clock, toothless, or grim, or elegantly mustached – what thought in the world swirling in them as they see the young eager brakeman bum hurrying to his thirty dollars of the Sunday – what memories of old homesteads, built without sympathy, horny-handed fate dealt them the loss of wives, childs, moons – libraries collapsed in their time – oldtimers of the telegraph wired wood Frisco in the fog gray top time sitting in their brown sunk sea and will be there when this afternoon my face flushed from the sun, which at eight'll flame out and make sunbaths for us at Redwood, they'll still be here the color of paste in the green underworld and still reading the same editorial over again and won't understand where I've been or what for or what – I have to get out of there or suffocate, out of Third Street or become a worm, it's alright to live and bed-wine in and play the radio and cook little breakfasts and rest in but O my I've got to tog now to work, I hurry down Third to Townsend for my 7:15 train – it's 3 minutes to go, I start in a panic to jog, goddam it I didn't give myself enough time this morning, I hurry down under the Harrison ramp to the Oakland-Bay Bridge, down past Schweibacker-Frey the great dim red neon printshop always spectrally my father the dead executive I see there, I run and hurry past the beat Negro grocery stores where I buy all my peanut butter and raisin bread, past the redbrick railroad alley now mist and wet, across Townsend, the train is leaving!

§

Fatuous railroad men, the conductor old John J. Coppertwang 35 years pure service on ye olde S.P. is there in the gray Sunday morning with his gold watch out peering at it, he's standing by the engine yelling up pleasantries at old hoghead Jones and young fireman Smith with the baseball cap is at the fireman's seat munching sandwich – "We'll how'd ye like old Johnny O yestiddy, I guess he didn't score so many touchdowns like we thought." "Smith bet six dollars on the pool down in Watsonville and said he's rakin' in thirty four." "I've been in that Watsonville pool –." They've been in the pool of life fleartiming with one another, all the long poker-playing nights in brownwood railroad places, you can smell the mashed cigar in the wood, the spittoon's been there for more than 750,099 yars and the dog's been in and out and these old boys by old shaded brown light have bent and muttered and young boys too with their new brakeman passenger uniform the tie undone the coat thrown back the flashing youth smile of happy fatuous well-fed goodjobbed careered futured pensioned hospitalized taken-care-of railroad men – 35, 40 years of it and then they get to be conductors and in the middle of the night they've been for years called by the Crew Clerk yelling "Cassady? It's the Maximush localized week do you for the right lead" but now as old men all they have is a regular job, a regular train, conductor of the 112 with goldwatch is helling up his pleasantries at all fire dog crazy Satan hoghead Willis why the wildest man this side of France and Frankincense, he was known once to take his engine up that steep grade – 7:15, time to pull, as I'm running thru the station hearing the bell jangling and the steam chuff they're pulling out, O I come flying out on the platform and forget momentarily or that is never did know what track it was and whirl in confusion a while wondering what track and can't see no train and this is the time I lose there, 5, 6, 7 seconds when the train tho underway is only slowly upchugging to go and a man a fat executive could easily run up and grab it but when I yell to Assistant Stationmaster "Where's 112?" and he tells me the last track which is the track I never dreamed I run to it fast as I can go and dodge people à la Columbia halfback and cut into track fast as off-tackle where you carry the ball with you to the left and feint with neck and head and push of ball as tho you're gonna throw yourself all out to fly around that left end and everybody psychologically chuffs with you that way and suddenly you contract and you like whiff of smoke are buried in the hole in tackle, cutback play, you're flying into the hole almost before you yourself know it, flying into the track I am and there's the train about 30 yards away even as I look picking up tremendously momentum the kind of momentum I would have been able to catch if I'd a looked a second earlier—but I run, I know I can catch it. Standing on the back platform are the rear brakeman and an old deadheading conductor ole Charley W. Jones, why he had seven wives and six kids and one time out at Lick no I guess it was Coyote he couldn't see on account of the steam and out he come and found his lantern in the igloo regular anglecock of my herald and they gave him fifteen benefits so now there he is in the Sunday har har owlala morning and he and young rear man watch incredulously this student brakeman running like a crazy trackman after their departing train. I feel like yelling "Make your airtest now make your airtest now!" knowing that when a passenger pulls out just about at the first crossing east of the station they pull the air a little bit to test the brakes, on signal from the engine, and this momentarily slows up the train and I could manage it, and could catch it, but they're not making no airtest the bastards, and I hek knowing I'm going to have to run like a sonofabitch. But suddenly I get embarrassed thinking what are all the people of the world gonna say to see a man running so devilishly fast with all his might sprinting thru life like Jesse Owens just to catch a goddam train and all of them with their hysteria wondering if I'll get killed when I catch the back platform and blam, I fall down and go boom and lay supine across the crossing, so the old flagman when the train has flowed by will see that everything lies on the earth in the same stew, all of us angels will die and we don't ever know how or our own diamond, O heaven will enlighten us and open your youeeeeeoueee—open our eyes, open our eyes—I know I won't get hurt, I trust my shoes, hand grip, feet, solidity of yipe and cripe of gripe and grip and strength and need no mystic strength to measure the musculature in my rib rack—but damn it all it's a social embarrassment to be caught sprinting like a maniac after a train especially with two men gaping at me from rear of train and shaking their heads and yelling I can't make it even as I halfheartedly sprint after them with open eyes trying to communicate that I can and not for them to get hysterical or laugh, but I realize it's all too much for me, not the run, not the speed of the train which anyway two seconds after I gave up the complicated chase did indeed slow down at the crossing in the airtest before chugging up again for good and Bay Shore. So I was late for work, and old Sherman hated me and was about to hate me more.

The ground I would have eaten in solitude, cronch—the railroad earth, the flat stretches of long Bay Shore that I have to negotiate to get to Sherman's bloody caboose on track 17 ready to go with pot pointed to Redwood and the morning's 3-hour work—I get off the bus at Bay Shore Highway and rush down the little street and turn in—boys riding the pot of a switcheroo in the yardgoat day come yelling by at me from the headboards and footboards "Come on down ride with us" otherwise I would have been about 3 minutes even later to my work but now I hop on the little engine that momentarily slows up to pick me up and it's alone not pulling anything but tender, the guys have been up to the other end of the yard to get back on some track of necessity—that boy will have to learn to flag himself without nobody helping him as many's the time I've seen some of these young goats think they have everything but the plan is late, the word will have to wait, the massive arboreal thief with the crime of the kind, and air and all kinds of ghouls—ZONKed! made tremendous by the flare of the whole prime and encrudalatures of all kinds—San Francisco and shroudband Bay Shores the last and the last furbelow of the eek plot pall prime tit top work oil twicks and wouldn't you?—the railroad earth I would have eaten alone, cronch, on foot head bent to get to Sherman who ticking watch observes with finicky eyes the time to go to give the hiball sign get on going it's Sunday no time to waste the only day of his long seven-day-a-week worklife he gets a chance to rest a little bit at home when "Eee Christ" when "Tell that sonofabitch student this is no party picnic damn this shit and throb tit you tell them something and how do you what the hell expect to underdries out tit all you bright tremendous trouble anyway, we's LATE" and this is the way I come rushing up late. Old Sherman is sitting in the crummy over his switch lists, when he sees me with cold blue eyes he says "You know you're supposed to be here 7:30 don't you so what the hell you doing gettin' in here at 7:50 you're twenty goddam minutes late, what the fuck you think this your birthday?" and he gets up and leans off the rear bleak platform and gives the high sign to the enginemen up front we have a cut of about 12 cars and they say it easy and off we go slowly at first, picking up momentum to the work, "Light that goddam fire" says Sherman he's wearing brand-new workshoes just about bought yestiddy and I notice his clean coveralls that his wife washed and set on his chair just that morning probably and I rush up and throw coal in the potbelly flop and take a fusee and two fusees and light them crack em Ah fourth of the July when the angels would smile on the horizon and all the racks where the mad are lost are returned to us forever from Lowell of my soul prime and single meditatee longsong hope to heaven of prayers and angels and of course the sleep and interested eye of images and but now we detect the missing buffoon there's the poor goodman rear man ain't even on the train yet and Sherman looks out sulkily the back door and sees his rear man waving from fifteen yards aways to stop and wait for him and being an old railroad man he certainly isn't going to run or even walk fast, it's well understood, conductor Sherman's got to get up off his switch-list desk chair and pull the air and stop the goddam train for rear man Arkansaw Charley, who sees this done and just come up lopin' in his flop overalls without no care, so he was late too, or at least had gone gossipping in the yard office while waiting for the stupid head brakeman, the tagman's up in front on the presumably pot. "First thing we do is pick up a car in front at Redwood so all's you do get off at the crossing and stand back to flag, not too far." "Don't I work the head end?" "You work the hind end we got not much to do and I wanta get it done fast," snarls the conductor. "Just take it easy and do what we say and watch and flag." So it's peaceful Sunday morning in California and off we go, tack-a-tick, lao-tichi-couch, out of the Bay Shore yards, pause momentarily at the main line for the green, ole 71 or ole whatever been by and now we get out and go swamming up the tree valleys and town vale hollows and main street crossing parking-lot last-night attendant plots and Stanford lots of the world—to our destination in the Poo which I can see, and, so to while the time I'm up in the cupolo and with my newspaper dig the latest news on the front page and also consider and make notations of the money I spent already for this day Sunday absolutely not jot spent a nothing—California rushes by and with sad eyes we watch it reel the whole bay and the discourse falling off to gradual gils that ease and graduate to Santa Clara Valley then and the fig and behind is the fog immemoriates while the mist closes and we come running out to the bright sun of the Sabbath Californiay—

At Redwood I get off and standing on sad oily ties of the brakie railroad earth with red flag and torpedoes attached and fusees in backpocket with timetable crushed against and I leave my hot jacket in crummy standing there then with sleeves rolled up and there's the porch of a Negro home, the brothers are sitting in shirtsleeves talking with cigarettes and laughing and little daughter standing amongst the weeds of the garden with her playpail and pigtails and we the railroad men with soft signs and no sound pick up our flower, according to same goodman train order that for the last entire lifetime of attentions ole conductor industrial worker harlotized Sherman has been reading carefully son so's not to make a mistake:

"Sunday morning October 15 pick up flower car
at Redwood, Dispatcher M.M.S."

1957

VIKRAM SETH

The Golden Gate

O n Sunday morning, groomed and waiting,
John sits in the Café Trieste.
A canny veteran of blind dating
(Twice bitten, once shy), it is best
To meet, he reckons, far from drama,
In daylight: less romantic, calmer,
And, if things should not turn out right,
Convenient for ready flight.
At noon, the meeting hour appointed,
A tall, fresh-faced blonde enters, sees
The suited John. "Excuse me, please . . .
(A little hesitant and disjointed)
. . . Would you be–John?" John smiles. "Correct.
And you're Elisabeth, I suspect."

"She's lovely," John thinks, almost staring.
They shake hands. John's heart gives a lurch.
"Handsome, all right, and what he's wearing
Suggests he's just returned from church. . . .
Sound, solid, practical, and active,"
Thinks Liz, "I find him quite attractive.
Perhaps. . . ." All this has been inferred
Before the first substantive word
Has passed between the two. John orders

A croissant and espresso; she
A sponge cake and a cup of tea.
They sit, but do not breach the borders
Of discourse till, at the same time,
They each break silence with, "Well, I'm—"

Both stop, confused. Both start together:
"I'm sorry—" Each again stops dead.
They laugh. "It hardly matters whether
You speak or I," says John: "I said,
Or meant to say—I'm glad we're meeting."
Liz quietly smiles, without completing
What she began. "Not fair," says John.
"Come clean. What was it now? Come on:
One confidence deserves another."
"No need," says Liz. "You've said what I
Would have admitted in reply."
They look, half smiling, at each other,
Half puzzled too, as if to say,
"I don't know why I feel this way."

Around them arias from Rossini
Resound from wall to wall. A bum
Unsoberly demands Puccini.
Cups clink. Aficionados hum
And sing along with Pavarotti,
Expatiate upon the knotty
Dilemmas of the world, peruse
The *Examiner* for sports or news
Or, best of all, the funny pages,

Golden Gate Bridge, 1987. Photograph by Deanne Fitzmaurice.

Where Garfield, the egregious cat,
Grows daily lazier and more fat,
And voluble polemic rages,
While praise by one and all's expressed
For the black brew of the Trieste.

The pair are now rapt in discussion.
Jan comes in, sees them, cannot hear
What they are saying—could be Russian
For all she knows; she does not steer
Too close, takes in the situation,
Sees John's face boyish with elation,
While Liz (Who's she?) with vibrant verve
In an exhilarating curve
Of explication or description
Looks radiant. Jan reflects, "Somehow
I feel . . . Oh Christ! . . . I feel, right now,
I don't want coffee. My Egyptian
Deities wait at home for food.
I'll come back when I'm in the mood."

Unnoticed, Janet leaves, abstracted
By her abortive coffee break.
Back in the café, Liz, attracted
By John's absorption, nibbles cake,
Sips tea, doffs her defensive armor
And, laughing, thinks, "This man's a charmer.
I like him, and he likes me, though
I can't imagine why it's so."
(O nightingales! O moon! O roses!)

In talk as heady as champagne
She mentions her cat, Charlemagne:
"A wondrous cat!" John laughs, proposes
A toast: "The King and Queen of France
And England. Far may they advance.

Well may they reign. Long may they flourish."
Happy (with just a dash of pain),
He drains his cup. "But now to nourish
My hopes of meeting you again—
What do you say—next Thursday—seven—
For dinner at the Tree of Heaven—
Say that you'll come—it's in the Haight—
A movie afterwards at eight?"
Liz thinks, "There's my gestalt group meeting.
I didn't go last week. I should
(The leader said) come if I could
This Thursday. . . ." But the thought is fleeting.
She says, "Thanks, John," and the pair parts
By shaking hands (with shaking hearts).

The days pass in a picosecond—
The days pass slowly, each a year—
Depending on how time is reckoned.
Liz, floating in the stratosphere
Of daydreams, sees the hours go flying.
For John they linger, amplifying
The interval until they meet.
The sun seems almost to retreat.
At last it's Thursday. John, ecstatic,

Arrives first, stares at the decor
(Arboreal), then at the door . . .
And Liz's entrance is dramatic:
A deep blue dress to emphasize
The sapphire spirit of her eyes.

Her gold hair's fashioned, not severely,
Into a bun. From a gold chain
A single pearl, suspended clearly,
Allures his eye. John, once again,
Can't speak for wonder and confusion:
A woman, or divine illusion?
He overcomes his vertigo
And stands. He mutters, "Liz, hello.
I hope . . . was it a hassle finding
This place?" His voice fails. He sits down.
Liz says, "You're nervous, Mr. Brown.
Don't worry; I too need reminding
That this is real." In an unplanned
Gesture of warmth, she takes his hand.

John looks downwards, as if admonished,
Then slowly lifts his head, and sighs.
Half fearfully and half astonished
They look into each other's eyes.
The waiter, bearded, burly, macho,
Says, "Madam, though it's cold, gazpacho
Is what I'd recommend. Noisettes
Of lamb, perhaps, or mignonettes
Of veal to follow. . . ." Unavailing

Are his suggestions. Nothing sinks
Into their ears. "Ah, well," he thinks,
"They're moonstruck. It'll be plain sailing.
Lovers, despite delays and slips
And rotten service, leave large tips."

Liz, floundering in a confusion
Of spirit, starts to speak: "Today
We fought a case about collusion. . . ."
John says, "I don't know what to say.
Liz, since we met, I think I'm losing
My mind—O God, it's so confusing—
I thought it was a joke, but when
We met, I realized—and then
Today, once more—it seems I'm flailing
Around for something—and I feel
An ache too desperate for repeal
Or cure—as if my heart were failing.
I was transported Sunday. Then
You left; the pain began again."

His voice is lowered, lost, appealing,
Rinsed of all wit, of all pretense.
Liz, helpless in a surge of feeling,
An undertow to common sense,
Finds that she has assumed the tender
Reincarnation of dream vendor.
Her eyes mist over with a glaze
Of sympathy. She gently says,
"Why do you find it so surprising

That you are happy? Are you sad
So often—tell me, John. I'm glad
That we've indulged in advertising,
But—having met you—it would seem
You feel all life's a shaky dream."

As in an airless room a curtain
Parts to admit the evening breeze,
So John's exhausted and uncertain
Tension admits a transient ease,
And Liz's lenient mediation
Smooths out his doubt and hesitation.
She looks at him: "Don't be afraid
I'll find what you say bland or staid."
Relieved of the unspoken duty
Of cleverness and coolness now
John brings himself to speak, somehow,
Of truth, ambition, status, beauty,
The hopes (or dupes) for which we strive,
The ghosts that keep the world alive.

But talk turns, as the meal progresses,
To (heart-unsettling) movie stars,
The chef's (mouth-watering) successes,
The ills (mind-boggling) of their cars,
To cats, to microchips, flotation
Of corporate bonds, sunsets, inflation,
Their childhoods . . . while, along the way,
A bountiful, rich cabernet
Bestows its warm, full-bodied flavor

On everything they touch upon,
But most of all on Liz and John
Who, fluent as the draught they savor,
In phrase both fulsome and condign
Sing praise of California wine.

Cut to dessert. An apt potation
Of amaretto. They forgo
The cinema for conversation,
And hand in hand they stroll below
The fog-transfigured Sutro Tower,
A masted galleon at this hour,
Adjourn for ice cream, rich and whole,
At Tivoli's, near Carl and Cole;
Next for a drive—refreshing drama
Of changing streets and changeless bay
And, where the fog has cleared away,
The exquisite bright panorama
Of streetlights, sea-lights, starlight spread
Above, below, and overhead.

The night is cold. It's late November.
They stand close, shivering side by side,
Chilled by the ice cream, yet an ember,
A flare, ignited by the ride,
This staring at the lights together,
Defends them from inclement weather.
They stand, half shivering, half still,
Below the tower on Telegraph Hill,
Not speaking, with a finger tracing

The unseen lines from star to star.
Liz turns. They kiss. They kiss, they are
Caught in a panic of embracing.
They cannot hold each other tight
Enough against the chill of night.

1986

H. L. MENCKEN

Romantic Intermezzo

TAKE WINE, women and song, add plenty of A-No. 1 victuals, the belch and bellow of oratory, a balmy but stimulating climate and a whiff of patriotism, and it must be obvious that you have a dose with a very powerful kick in it. This, precisely, was the dose that made the Democratic national convention of 1920, holden in San Francisco, the most charming in American annals. No one who was present at its sessions will ever forget it. It made history for its voluptuous loveliness, just as the Baltimore convention of 1912 made history for its infernal heat, and the New York convention of 1924 for its 103 ballots and its unparalleled din. Whenever I meet an old-timer who took part in it we fall into maudlin reminiscences of it, and tears drop off the ends of our noses. It came within an inch of being perfect. It was San Francisco's brave answer to the Nazi-inspired earthquake of April 18, 1906.

The whole population shared in the credit for it, and even the powers and principalities of the air had a hand, for they provided the magnificent weather, but chief praise went justly to the Hon. James Rolph, Jr., then and for eleven years afterward mayor of the town. In 1920, indeed, he had already been mayor for nine years, and in 1931, after five terms of four years each in that office, he was promoted to the dignity of Governor of California. He was a man of bold imagination and spacious ideas. More than anyone else he was responsible for the superb hall in which the convention was held, and more than any other he deserved thanks for the humane and enlightened entertainment of the delegates and alternates. The heart of that entertainment was a carload of Bourbon whiskey, old, mellow and full of pungent but delicate tangs – in brief, the best that money could buy.

The persons who go to Democratic national conventions seldom see such wet goods; in truth, they had never seen any before, and they have never seen any since. The general rule is to feed them the worst obtainable, and at the highest prices they can be cajoled and swindled into paying. Inasmuch as large numbers of them are Southerners, and most of the rest have Southern sympathies, it is assumed that they will drink anything, however revolting, provided only it have enough kick. In preparation for their quadrennial gathering to nominate a candidate for the Presidency the wholesale booze-sellers of the country ship in the dregs of their cellars—rye whiskey in which rats have drowned, Bourbon contaminated with arsenic and ptomaines, corn fresh from the still, gin that is three-fourths turpentine, and rum rejected as too corrosive by the West Indian embalmers. This stuff the Democrats put away with loud hosannas—but only for a few days. After that their livers give out, they lose their tempers, and the country is entertained with a rough-house in the grand manner. There has been such a rough-house at every Democratic national convention since Jackson's day, save only the Ja-convention at Chicago in 1940 and the incomparable gathering at San Francisco in 1920. The scene at the latter was one of universal peace and lovey-dovey, and every Democrat went home on his own legs, with his soul exultant and both his ears intact and functioning.

The beauty of this miracle was greatly enhanced by the fact that it was unexpected. Prohibition had gone into force only five months before the convention was scheduled to meet, and the Democrats arrived in San Francisco full of miserable forebodings. Judging by what they had already experienced at home, they assumed that the convention booze would be even worse than usual; indeed, most of them were so uneasy about it that they brought along supplies of their own. During the five months they had got used to hair oil, Jamaica ginger and sweet spirits of nitre, but they feared that the San Francisco booticians, abandoning all reason, would proceed to paint remover and sheep dip. What a surprise awaited them! What a deliverance was at hand! The moment they got to their hotels they were waited upon by small committees of refined and well-dressed ladies, and asked to state their desires. The majority, at the start, were so suspicious that they kicked the ladies out; they feared entrapment by what were then still called revenuers. But the bolder fellows took a chance—and a few hours later the glad word was everywhere. No matter what a delegate ordered he got Bourbon—but it was Bourbon of the very first chop, Bourbon aged in contented barrels of the finest white oak, Bourbon of really ultra and super quality. It came in quart bottles on the very heels of the committee of ladies—and there was no bill attached. It was offered to the visitors with the compliments of Mayor James Rolph, Jr.

The effects of that Bourbon were so wondrous that it is easy to exaggerate them in retrospect. There were, of course, other links in the chain of causation behind the phenomena I am about to describe. One, as I have hinted, was the weather—a series of days so sunshiny and caressing, so cool and exhilarating that living through them was like rolling on meads of asphodel. Another was the hall in which the convention was held—a new city auditorium so spacious, so clean, so luxurious in its comforts and so beautiful in its decorations that the assembled politicoes felt like sailors turned loose in the most gorgeous bordellos of Paris. I had just come from the Republican national convention in Chicago, and was thus keen to the contrast. The hall in Chicago was an old armory that had been used but lately for prize fights, dog shows and a third-rate circus, and it still smelled of pugs, kennels and elephants. Its walls and gallery railings were covered to the last inch with shabby flags and bunting that seemed to have come straight from a bankrupt street carnival. Down in the catacombs beneath it the victualling accommodations were of a grab-it-and-run, eat-it-if-you-can character, and the rooms marked "Gents" followed the primordial design of Sir John Harington as given in his "Metamorphosis of Ajax," published in 1596. To police this foul pen there was a mob of ward heelers from the Chicago slums, wearing huge badges, armed with clubs, and bent on packing both the gallery and the floor with their simian friends.

The contrast presented by the San Francisco hall was so vast as to be astounding. It was as clean as an operating room, or even a brewery, and its decorations were all of a chaste and restful character. The walls were hung, not with garish bunting, but with fabrics in low tones of gray and green, and in the whole place only one flag was visible. Downstairs, in the spacious basement, there were lunch-counters served by lovely young creatures in white uniforms, and offering the whole repertory of West Coast delicacies at cut-rate

Mayor James Rolph.

prices. The Johns were lined with mirrors, and each was staffed with shoe-shiners, suit-pressers and hat-cleaners, and outfitted with automatic weighing-machines, cigar-lighters, devices releasing a squirt of Jockey Club perfume for a cent, and recent files of all the principal newspapers of the United States. The police arrangements almost deserved the epithet of dainty. There were no ward heelers armed with clubs, and even the uniformed city police were confined to a few garrison posts, concealed behind marble pillars. All ordinary ushering and trouble-shooting was done by a force of cuties dressed like the waitresses in the basement, and each and every one of them was well worth a straining of the neck. They were armed with little white wands, and every wand was tied with a blue ribbon, signifying law and order. When one of these babies glided into a jam of delegates with her wand upraised they melted as if she had been a man-eating tiger, but with this difference: that instead of making off with screams of terror they yielded as if to soft music, their eyes rolling ecstatically and their hearts going pitter-pat.

But under it all, of course, lay the soothing pharmacological effect of Jim Rolph's incomparable Bourbon. Delegates who, at all previous Democratic conventions, had come down with stone in the liver on the second day were here in the full tide of health and optimism on the fifth. There was not a single case of mania à potu from end to end of the gathering, though the place swarmed with men who were subject to it. Not a delegate took home gastritis. The Bourbon was so pure that it not only did not etch and burn them out like the horrible hooches they were used to; it had a positively therapeutic effect, and cured them of whatever they were suffering from when they got to town. Day by day they swam in delight. The sessions of the convention, rid for once of the usual quarreling and caterwauling, went on like a conference of ambassadors, and in the evenings the delegates gave themselves over to amicable conversation and the orderly drinking of healths. The climax came on June 30, the day set apart for putting candidates for the Presidency in nomination. It was, in its way, the loveliest day of the whole fortnight, with a cloudless sky, the softest whisper of a breeze from the Pacific, and a sun that warmed without heating. As the delegates sat in their places listening to the speeches and the music they could look out of the open doors of the hall to the Golden Gate, and there see a fleet of warships that had been sent in by the Hon. Josephus Daniels, then Secretary of the Navy, to entertain them with salutes and manoeuvres.

There was an excellent band in the hall, and its leader had been instructed to dress in every speaker with appropriate music. If a gentleman from Kentucky arose, then the band played "My Old Kentucky Home"; if he was followed by one from Indiana, then it played "On the Banks of the Wabash." Only once during the memorable day did the leader make a slip, and that was when he greeted a Georgia delegate with "Marching Through Georgia," but even then he quickly recovered himself and slid into "At a Georgia Campmeeting." An entirely new problem confronted him as the morning wore on, for it was at San Francisco in 1920 that the first lady delegates appeared at a Democratic national convention. His test came when the earliest bird among these stateswomen got the chairman's eye. What she arose to say I do not recall, but I remember that she was a Mrs. FitzGerald of Massachusetts, a very handsome woman. As she appeared on the platform, the leader let go with "Oh, You Beautiful Doll!" The delegates and alternates, struck by the artful patness of the selection, leaped to their legs and cheered, and La FitzGerald's remarks, whatever they were, were received with almost delirious enthusiasm. The next female up was Mrs. Izetta Jewel Brown of West Virginia, a former actress who knew precisely how to walk across a stage and what clothes were for. When the delegates and alternates saw her they were stricken dumb with admiration, but when the band leader gave her "Oh, What a Pal Was Mary," they cut loose with yells that must have been heard half way to San José.

It was not these ladies, however, who made top score on that memorable day, but the Hon. Al Smith of New York. Al, in those days, was by no means the national celebrity that he was to become later. He had already, to be sure, served a year of his first term as Governor of New York, but not many people west of Erie, Pa., had ever heard of him, and to most of the delegates at San Francisco he was no more than a vague name. Thus there was little sign of interest when the Hon. W. Bourke Cockran arose to put him in nomination – the first of his three attempts upon the White House. Cockran made a good speech, but it fell flat, nor did the band leader help things when he played

"Tammany" at its close, for Tammany Hall suggested only Romish villainies to the delegates from the Bible country. But when, as if seeing his error, the leader quickly swung into "The Sidewalks of New York" a murmur of appreciation ran through the hall, and by the time the band got to the second stanza someone in a gallery began to sing. The effect of that singing, as the old-time reporters used to say, was electrical. In ten seconds a hundred other voices had joined in, and in a minute the whole audience was bellowing the familiar words. The band played six or eight stanzas, and then switched to "Little Annie Rooney," and then to "The Bowery," and then to "A Bicycle Built For Two," and then to "Maggie Murphy's Home," and so on down the long line of ancient waltz-songs. Here the leader showed brilliantly his subtle mastery of his art. Not once did he change to four-four time: it would have broken the spell. But three-four time, the sempiternal measure of amour, caught them all where they were tenderest, and for a solid hour the delegates and alternates sang and danced.

The scene was unprecedented in national conventions and has never been repeated since, though many another band leader has tried to put it on: what he lacked was always the aid of Jim Rolph's Bourbon. The first delegate who grabbed a lady politico and began to prance up the aisle was full of it, and so, for all I know, was the lady politico. They were joined quickly by others, and in ten minutes Al was forgotten, the convention was in recess, and a ball was in progress. Not many of the delegates, of course, were equal to actual waltzing, but in next to no time a ground rule was evolved which admitted any kind of cavorting that would fit into the music, so the shindig gradually gathered force and momentum, and by the end of the first half hour the only persons on the floor who were not dancing were a few antisocial Hardshell Baptists from Mississippi, and a one-legged war veteran from Ohio. For a while the chairman, old Joe Robinson, made formal attempts to restore order, but after that he let it run, and run it did until the last hoofer was exhausted. Then a young man named Franklin D. Roosevelt got up to second Al's nomination. He made a long and earnest speech on the heroic achievements of the Navy in the late war, and killed Al's boom then and there.

The great and singular day was a Wednesday, and the bosses of the convention made plans the next morning to bring its proceedings to a close on Saturday. But the delegates and alternates simply refused to agree. The romantic tunes of "East Side, West Side" and "A Bicycle Built For Two" were still sounding in their ears, and their veins still bulged and glowed with Jim Rolph's Bourbon. The supply of it seemed to be unlimited. Day by day, almost hour by hour, the ladies' committee produced more. Thus Thursday passed in happy abandon, and then Friday. On Saturday someone proposed boldly that the convention adjourn over the week-end, and the motion was carried by a vote of 998 to 26. That afternoon the delegates and alternates, each packing a liberal supply of the Bourbon, entered into taxicabs and set out to see what was over the horizon. San Francisco was perfect, but they sweated for new worlds, new marvels, new adventures. On the Monday following some of them were roped by the police in places more than a hundred miles away, and started back to their duties in charge of trained nurses. One taxicab actually reached Carson City, Nev., and another was reported, probably apocryphally, in San Diego. I myself, though I am an abstemious man, awoke on Sunday morning on the beach at Half Moon Bay, which is as far from San Francisco as Peekskill is from New York. But that was caused, not by Jim Rolph's Bourbon, but by George Sterling's grappo, a kind of brandy distilled from California grape skins, with the addition of strychnine.

After the delegates went home at last the Methodists of San Francisco got wind of the Bourbon and started a noisy public inquiry into its provenance. Jim Rolph, who was a very dignified man, let them roar on without deigning to notice them, even when they alleged that it had been charged to the town smallpox hospital, and offered to prove that there had not been a case of smallpox there since 1897. In due time he came up for reëlection, and they renewed their lying and unChristian attack. As a result he was reëlected almost unanimously, and remained in office, as I have noted, until 1931. In that year, as I have also noted, he was promoted by the appreciative people of all California to the highest place within their gift, and there he remained, to the satisfaction of the whole human race, until his lamented death in 1934.

1943

EDUARDO GALEANO

The Gold of California

FROM VALPARAÍSO, Chileans stream in. They bring a pair of boots and a knife, a lamp and a shovel.

The entry to San Francisco Bay is now known as "the golden gate." Until yesterday, San Francisco was the Mexican town of Yerbas Buenas. In these lands, usurped from Mexico in the war of conquest, there are three-kilo nuggets of pure gold.

The bay has no room for so many ships. An anchor touches bottom, and adventurers scatter across the mountains. No one wastes time on hellos. The cardsharp buries his patent leather boots in the mud:

"Long live my loaded dice! Long live my jack!"

Simply landing on this soil turns the bum into a king and the beauty who had scorned him dies of remorse. Vicente Pérez Rosales, newly arrived, listens to the thoughts of his compatriots: "Now I have talent! Because in Chile, who's an ass once he has cash?" *Here losing time is losing money.* Endless thunder of hammers, a world on the boil, birth-pang screams. Out of nothing rise the awnings under which are offered tools and liquor and dried meat in exchange for leather bags filled with gold dust. Crows and men squawk, flocks of men from all lands, and night and day eddies the whirlwind of frock coats and seamen's caps, Oregon furs and Maule bonnets, French daggers, Chinese hats, Russian boots, and shiny bullets at the waists of cowboys.

Under her lace sunshade, a good-looking Chilean woman smiles as best she can, squeezed by her corset and by the multitude that sweeps her over the sea of mud paved with broken bottles. In this port she is Rosarito Améstica. She was born Rosarito Izquierdo more years ago than she'll tell, became Rosarito Villaseca in Talcahuano, Rosarito Toro in Talca, and Rosarito Montalva in Valparaíso.

From the stern of a ship, the auctioneer offers ladies to the crowd. He exhibits them and sings their praises, one by one, *look gentlemen what a waist what youth what beauty what . . .*

"Who'll give more?" says the auctioneer. "Who'll give more for this incomparable flower?"

Levi's Pants

THE FLASHES of violence and miracles do not blind Levi Strauss, who arrives from far-off Bavaria and realizes at one blink that here the beggar becomes a millionaire and the millionaire a beggar or corpse in a click of cards or triggers. In another blink he discovers that pants become tatters in these mines of California, and decides to provide a better fate for the strong cloths he has brought along. He won't sell awnings or tents. He will sell pants, tough pants for tough men in the tough work of digging up rivers and mines. So the seams won't burst, he reinforces them with copper riveting. Behind, under the waist, Levi stamps his name on a leather label.

Soon the cowboys of the whole West will claim as their own these pants of blue Nîmes twill which neither sun nor years wear out.

The Road to Development

THE CHILEAN Pérez Rosales is looking for luck in the mines of California. Learning that, a few miles from San Francisco, fabulous prices are paid for anything edible, he gets a few sacks of worm-eaten jerky and some jars of jam and buys a launch. Hardly has he pushed off from the pier when a customs agent points a rifle at his head: *"Hold it there."*

This launch cannot move on any United States river *because it was built abroad and its keel is not made of North American wood.*

The United States had defended its national market since the times of its first president. It supplies cotton to England, but customs barriers block English cloth and any product that could injure its own industry. The planters of the southern states want English clothing, which is much better and cheaper, and complain that the northern textile mills impose on them their ugly and costly cloth from baby's diaper to corpse's shroud.

1984

KENNETH REXROTH

San Francisco Letter

T H E R E   H A S   been so much publicity recently about the San Francisco Renaissance and the New Generation of Revolt and Our Underground Literature and Cultural Disaffiliation that I for one am getting a little sick of writing about it, and the writers who are the objects of all the uproar run the serious danger of falling over, "dizzy with success," in the immortal words of Comrade Koba. Certainly there is nothing underground about it anymore. For ten years after the Second War there was a convergence of interest—the Business Community, military imperialism, political reaction, the hysterical, tear and mud drenched guilt of the ex-Stalinist, ex-Trotskyite American intellectuals, the highly organized academic and literary employment agency of the Neoantireconstructionists—what might be called the meliorists of the White Citizens' League, who were out to augment the notorious budgetary deficiency of the barbarously miseducated Southron male schoolmarm by opening up jobs "up N'oth." This ministry of all the talents formed a dense crust of custom over American cultural life—more of an ice pack. Ultimately the living water underneath just got so damn hot the ice pack has begun to melt, rot, break up and drift away into Arctic oblivion. This is all there is to it. For ten years or more, seen from above, all that could be discerned was a kind of scum. By very definition, scum, ice packs, crusts, are surface phenomena. It is what is underneath that counts. The living substance has always been there—it has just been hard to see—from above.

It is easy to understand why all this has centered in San Francisco. It is a long way from Astor Place or Kenyon College. It is one of the easiest cities in the world to live in. It is the easiest in America. Its culture is genuinely (not fake like New Orleans—white New Orleans, an ugly Southron city with a bit of the Latin past subsidized by the rubberneck buses) Mediterranean – *laissez faire* and *dolce far niente*. I for one can say flatly that if I couldn't live here I would leave the United States for someplace like Aix en Provence – so fast! I always feel like I ought to get a passport every time I cross the Bay to Oakland or Berkeley. I get nervous walking down the streets of Seattle with all those ghosts of dead Wobblies weeping in the shadows and all those awful squares peering down my neck. In New York, after one week of living on cocktails in taxicabs, I have to go to a doctor. The doctor always says – get out of New York before it kills you. Hence the Renaissance.

Most of the stuff written about San Francisco literary life has been pretty general, individuals have figured only as items in long and hasty lists. I want to talk at a little more length about a few specific writers and try to show how this disaffiliation applies to them, functions in their work.

In the first place. No literature of the past two hundred years is of the slightest importance unless it *is* "disaffiliated." Only our modern industrial and commercial civilization has produced an elite which has consistently rejected all the reigning values of the society. There were no Baudelaires in Babylon. It is not that we have lost sight of them in time. The nearest thing in Rome was Catullus, and it is apparent, reading him, that there stood behind him no anonymous and forgotten body of bohemians. He was a consort of the rich, of generals and senators, Caesar and Mamurra, and the girl he writes about as though she was, in our terms, an art-struck tart from the Black Cat, was, in fact, a notorious multimillionairess, "the most depraved daughter of the Clodian line." Tu Fu censured the Emperor, but he wanted to be recognized for it – he wanted to be a Censor. So the Taoism and Buddhism of Far Eastern culture function as a keel and ballast to the ship of state. The special ideology of the only artists and writers since the French Revolution who deserve to be taken seriously is a destructive, revolutionary force. They would blow up "their" ship of state – destroy it utterly. This has nothing to do with political revolutionarism, which in our era has been the mortal enemy of all art whatever. When the Bolsheviks, for a brief period, managed to persuade the culture bearers, demoralized by the world economic crisis and rising tide of political terrorism, that the political revolutionary and the artist, the poet, the moral *vates* were allies, Western European culture came within an ace of being destroyed altogether and finally. Capitalism cannot produce from within itself, from any of its "classes," bourgeois, petit-bourgeois, or proletariat, any system of values which is not in essence of itself. The converse is a Marxist delusion. This is why "Marxist aestheticians" have gone to such lengths to "prove" that the artist, the writer, the technical and professional intelligentsia, are *not* declassés in modern society, but members of the petit bourgeoisie, and must "come over," in the words of Engels' old chestnut, "to the proletariat," that is, become the prostitutes of their brand of State Capitalism. Nothing could be more false. Artist, poet, physicist, astronomer, dancer, musician, mathematician are captives stolen from an older time, a different kind of society, in which, ultimately, *they* were the creators of all primary values. They are exactly like the astronomers and philosophers the Mongols took off from Samarkand to Karakorum. They belong to the *ancien régime* – all *anciens régimes* as against the nineteenth and twentieth centuries. And so they could only vomit in the faces of the despots who offered them places in the ministries of all the talents, or at least they were nauseated in proportion to their integrity. The same principles apply today as did in the days of Lamartine. Caught in the gears of their own evil machinery, the bosses may scream for an Einstein, a Bohr, even an Oppenheimer; when Normalcy comes back, they kick them out and put tellers in their place. The more fools the Einsteins for having allowed themselves to be used – as they always discover, alas, too late.

You may not think all this has anything to do with the subject, but it is the whole point. Poets come to San Francisco for the same reason so many Hungarians have been going to Austria recently. They write the sort of thing they do for the same reason that Hölderlin or Blake or Baudelaire or Rimbaud or Mallarmé wrote it. The world of poet-professors, Southern Colonels and ex-Left Social Fascists from which they have escaped has no more to do with literature than do the leading authors of the court of Napoleon III whose names can be found in the endless pages of the *Causeries du lundi*. The *Vaticide Review* is simply the *Saturday Evening Post* of the excessively miseducated, and its kept poets are the Zane Greys, Clarence Budington Kellands and

J. P. Marquands of Brooks Brothers Boys who got an overdose of T. S. Eliot at some Ivy League fog factory. It is just that simple.

There are few organized systems of social attitudes and values which stand outside, really outside, the all corrupting influences of our predatory civilization. In America, at least, there is only one which functions on any large scale and with any effectiveness. This of course is Roman Catholicism. Not the stultifying monkey see monkey do Americanism of the slothful urban backwoods middle-class parish so beautifully satirized by the Catholic writer James Powers, but the Church of saints and philosophers – of the worker priest movement and the French Personalists. So it is only to be expected that, of those who reject the Social Lie, many today would turn towards Catholicism. If you have to "belong to something bigger than yourself" it is one of the few possibilities and, with a little mental gymnastics, can be made quite bearable. Even I sometimes feel that the only constant, consistent, and uncompromising critics of the secular world were the French Dominicans.

So, William Everson, who is probably the most profoundly moving and durable of the poets of the San Francisco Renaissance, is a Dominican Tertiary and oblate – which means a lay brother in a friary under renewable vows . . . he doesn't have to stay if he doesn't want to. It has been a long journey to this point. Prior to the Second War he was a farmer in the San Joaquin Valley. Here he wrote his first book of poems, *San Joaquin*. Like so many young poets he was naively accessible to influences his maturity would find dubious. In his case this was Jeffers, but he was, even then, able to transform Jeffers' noisy rhetoric into genuinely impassioned utterance, his absurd self-dramatization into real struggle in the depths of the self. Everson is still wrestling with his angel, still given to the long oratorical line with vague echoes of classical quantitative meters, but there is no apparent resemblance left to Jeffers. During the War he was in a Conscientious Objectors' camp in Oregon, where he was instrumental in setting up an off time Arts Program out of which have come many still active people, projects, and forces which help give San Francisco culture its intensely libertarian character. Here he printed several short books of verse, all later gathered in the New Directions volume, *The Residual Years*. Since then he has printed two books, *Triptych for the Living* and

A Privacy of Speech. In the tradition of Eric Gill and Victor Hammer, they are amongst the most beautiful printing I have ever seen. Since then – since entering the Order, he has published mostly in the *Catholic Worker.* In my opinion he has become the finest Catholic poet writing today, the best since R. E. F. Larsson. His work has a gnarled, even tortured, honesty, a rugged unliterary diction, a relentless probing and searching, which are not just engaging, but almost overwhelming. Partly of course this is due to the scarcity of these characteristics today, anything less like the verse of the fashionable quarterlies would be hard to imagine.

Philip Lamantia is generally considered by his colleagues in San Francisco to be another of the three or four leading poets of the community. He too is a Catholic. Unlike Everson, who is concerned primarily with the problems of moral responsibility, the World, the Flesh, and the Devil, Lamantia's poetry is illuminated, ecstatic, with the mystic's intense autonomy. Unfortunately, since his surrealist days, although he has written a great deal, he has published practically nothing. Poems he has read locally have been deeply moving, but each in turn he has put by and gone on, dissatisfied, to something else. As it is so often the case with the mystic temperament, art seems to have become a means rather than even a temporary end. I hope that soon he will find what he is seeking, at least in a measure, and then, of course, his previous work will fall into place and be seen as satisfactory enough to publish – I hope.

Of all the San Francisco group Robert Duncan is the most easily recognizable as a member of the international avant garde. Mallarmé or Gertrude Stein, Joyce or Reverdy, there is a certain underlying homogeneity of idiom, and this idiom is, by and large, Duncan's. But there is a difference, "modernist" verse tends to treat the work of art as purely self-sufficient, a construction rather than a communication. Duncan's poetry is about as personal as can be imagined. So it resembles the work of poets like David Gascoyne and Pierre Emmanuel, who, raised in the tradition, have seceded from it to begin the exploration of a new, dedicated personalism. What is the self? What is the other? These are the questions of those who have transcended "the existentialist dilemma" – Buber or Mounier. What is love? Who loves? Who is loved? Curiously, although Duncan is very far from being a Catholic, these are the leading problems of contemporary Catholic thought, as Gascoyne and Emmanuel are Catholics. Perhaps what this means is that, as I said at the beginning, the Church is one of the few places one can get away to and start asking meaningful questions. There is, however, no reason whatever why, if one is strong enough to stand alone, the same questions should not be asked independently. Duncan has written a large number of books; he started out very young (Gascoyne and Emmanuel were prodigies, too) as an editor of the *Experimental Review* with Sanders Russell, and later of *Phoenix* with the neo-Lawrentian Cooney. *Heavenly City, Earthly City; Fragments of a Disordered Devotion; Caesar's Gate; Medieval Scenes; Poems 1948–49* – the use of language may have changed and developed, but the theme is consistently the mind and body of love.

Allen Ginsberg's *Howl* is much more than the most sensational book of poetry of 1957. Nothing goes to show how square the squares are so much as the *favorable* reviews they've given it. "Sustained shrieks of frantic defiance," "single-minded frenzy of a raving madwoman," "paranoid memories," "childish obscenity"–they think it's all *so* negative. Also–which is much more important–they think there is something unusual about it. Listen you–do you *really* think your kids act like the bobby soxers in those wholesome Coca-Cola ads? Don't you know that across the table from you at dinner sits somebody who looks on you as an enemy who is planning to kill him in the immediate future in an extremely disagreeable way? Don't you know that if you were to say to your English class, "It is raining," they would take it for granted you were a liar? Don't you know that they never tell you nothing? That they can't? That faced with the system of values which coats you like the insulating rompers of an aircraft carrier's "hot papa"–they simply can't get through, can't, and won't even try any more to communicate? Don't you know this, really? If you don't, you're headed for a terrible awakening. *Howl* is the confession of faith of the generation that is going to be running the world in 1965 and 1975–if it's still there to run. "The Poetry of the New Violence"? It isn't at all violent. It is *your* violence it is talking about. It is Hollywood or the censors who are obscene. It is Dulles and Khrushchev who are childishly defiant. It is the "media" that talk with the single-minded frenzy of a raving madwoman. Once Allen is through telling you what you have done to him and his friends, he concerns himself with the unfulfilled promises of *Song of Myself* and *Huckleberry Finn,* and writes a *Sutra* about the sunflower that rises from the junk heap of civilization . . . your civilization. Negative? "We must love one another or die." It's the "message" of practically every utterance of importance since the Neolithic Revolution. What's so negative about it? The fact that we now live in the time when we must either mind it or take the final consequences? Curiously, the reviewers never noticed—all they saw was "total assault." All this aside, purely technically, Ginsberg is one of the most remarkable versifiers in America. He is almost alone in his generation in his ability to make powerful poetry of the inherent rhythms of our speech, to push forward the conquests of a few of the earliest poems of Sandburg and of William Carlos Williams. This is more skillful verse than all the cornbelt Donnes laid end to end. It is my modest prophecy, that, if he keeps going, Ginsberg will be the first genuinely popular, genuine poet in over a generation—and he is already considerably the superior of predecessors like Lindsay and Sandburg.

Lawrence Ferlinghetti runs the City Lights Pocket Bookshop, publishes the Pocket Poets Series, paints very well (a little like Redon), writes poetry (*Pictures of the Gone World*), and, with myself, has worked to bring about a marriage of poetry and jazz. He is a lazy-looking, good-natured man with the canny cocky eye of an old-time vaudeville tenor. Everybody thinks he's Irish. One of those Irish wops—like Catullus. He is actually French. I think he thinks he don't get enough done. Oh, yes, he teaches French, too. For several years after War Two he lived in Paris and his poetry, while quite, even very, American, is also quite French. He has translated most of the verse of Jacques Prévert and speaks of himself as influenced by him. Possibly, but I think he has moved up from his master into another qualitative realm altogether. Prévert is not, as some Americans seem to think, some sort of avant garde poet. He is their equivalent of our "*New Yorker* verse." This may be a sad comment on the comparative merits of two cultures, but this doesn't make Prévert any less journalistic—only a short distance above *Le Canard enchaîné* or Georges Fourrest. There is a lot more real bite to Ferlinghetti and a deeper humor. The French poet he resembles most is Queneau. It is possible to "disaffiliate," disengage oneself from the Social Lie and still be good tempered about it, and it is possible to bite the butt of the eternal Colonel Blimp with the quiet, penetrating tenacity of an unperturbed bull dog. This is Ferlinghetti's special talent and it is no mean one. e. e. cummings and James Laughlin have written this way, but few other Americans nowadays. His verse, so easy and relaxed, is constructed of most complex rhythms, all organized to produce just the right tone. Now tone is the hardest and last of the literary virtues to control and it requires assiduous and inconspicuous craftsmanship. Ferlinghetti is definitely a member of the San Francisco School—he says exactly what Everson, Duncan, Ginsberg say. I suppose, in a religious age, it would be called religious poetry, all of it. Today we have to call it anarchism. A fellow over in Africa calls it "reverence for life."

1957

LEWIS H. LAPHAM

Lost Horizon

FOR THE past six or seven weeks I have been answering angry questions about San Francisco. People who know that I was born in that city assume that I have access to confidential information, presumably at the highest levels of psychic consciousness. Their questions sound like accusations, as if they were demanding a statement about the poisoning of the reservoirs. Who were those people that the Reverend Jim Jones murdered in Guyana, and how did they get there? Why would anybody follow such a madman into the wilderness, and how did the Reverend Jones come by those letters from Vice-President Mondale and Mrs. Rosalynn Carter? Why did the fireman kill the mayor of San Francisco and the homosexual city official? What has gone wrong in California, and who brought evil into paradise? Fortunately I don't know the answers to these questions; if I knew them, I would be bound to proclaim myself a god and return to San Francisco in search of followers, a mandala, and a storefront shrine. Anybody who would understand the enigma of San Francisco must first know something about the dreaming narcissism of the city, and rather than try to explain this in so many words, I offer into evidence the story of my last assignment for the *San Francisco Examiner.*

I had been employed on the paper for two years when, on a Saturday morning in December of 1959, I reported for work to find the editors talking to one another in the hushed and self-important way that usually means that at least fifty people have been killed. I assumed that a ship had sunk or that a building had collapsed. The editors were not in the habit of taking me into their confidence, and I didn't expect to learn the terms of the calamity until I had a chance to read the AP wire. Much to my surprise, the city editor motioned impatiently in my direction, indicating that I should join the circle of people standing around his desk and turning slowing through the pages of the pictorial supplement that the paper was obliged to publish the next day. Aghast at what they saw, unable to stifle small cries of anguished disbelief, they were examining twelve pages of text and photographs arranged under the heading LOS ANGELES—THE ATHENS OF THE WEST. To readers unfamiliar with the ethos of San Francisco, I'm not sure that I can convey the full and terrible effect of this headline. Not only was it wrong, it was monstrous heresy. The residents of San Francisco dote on a romantic image of the city, and they imagine themselves living at a height of civilization accessible only to Erasmus or a nineteenth-century British peer. They flatter themselves on their sophistication, their exquisite sensibility, their devotion to the arts. Los Angeles represents the antithesis of these graces; it is the land of the Philistines, lying somewhere to the south in the midst of housing developments that stand as the embodiment of ugliness, vulgarity, and corruptions of the spirit.

Pity, then, the poor editors in San Francisco. In those days there was also a *Los Angeles Examiner,* and the same printing plant supplied supplements to both papers. The text and photographs intended for a Los Angeles audience had been printed in the Sunday pictorial bearing the imprimatur of the *San Francisco Examiner.* It was impossible to correct the mistake, and so the editors in San Francisco had no choice but to publish and give credence to despised anathema.

This so distressed them that they resolved to print a denial. The city editor, knowing that my grandfather had been mayor of San Francisco and that I had been raised in the city, assumed that he could count on my dedication to the parochial truth. He also knew that I had studied at Yale and Cambridge universities, and although on most days he made jokes about the future of a literary education, on this particular occasion he saw a use for it. What was the point of reading all those books if they didn't impart the skills of a sophist? He handed me the damnable pages and said that I had until five o'clock in the afternoon to refute them as false doctrine. The story was marked for page 1 and an eight-column headline. I was to spare no expense of adjectives.

The task was hopeless. Los Angeles at the time could claim the residence of Igor Stravinsky, Aldous Huxley, and Christopher Isherwood. Admittedly they had done their best work before coming west to ripen in the sun, but their names and photographs, together with those of a few well-known painters and a number of established authors temporarily engaged in the writing of screenplays, make for an impressive display in a newspaper. Even before I put through my first telephone call, to a poet in North Beach experimenting with random verse, I knew that cultural enterprise in San Francisco could not sustain the pretension of a comparison to New York or Chicago, much less to Periclean Athens.

Ernest Bloch had died, and Darius Milhaud taught at Mills College only during the odd years; Henry Miller lived 140 miles to the south at Big Sur, which placed him outside the city's penumbra of light. The Beat Generation had disbanded. Allen Ginsberg still could be seen brooding in the cellar of the City Lights Bookshop, but Kerouac had left town, and the tourists were occupying the best tables at Cassandra's, asking the waiters about psychedelic drugs and for connections to the Buddhist underground. Although I admired the work of Evan Connell and Lawrence Ferlinghetti, I doubted that they would say the kinds of things that the city editor wanted to hear. The San Francisco school of painting consisted of watercolor views of Sausalito and Fisherman's Wharf; there was no theater, and the opera was a means of setting wealth to music. The lack of art or energy in the city reflected the lassitude of a citizenry content to believe its own press notices. The circumference of the local interest extended no more than 150 miles in three directions – as far as Sonoma County and Bolinas in the north, to Woodside and Monterey in the south, and to Yosemite and Tahoe in the east. In a westerly direction the civic imagination didn't reach beyond the Golden Gate Bridge. Within this narrow arc the inhabitants of San Francisco entertained themselves with a passionate exchange of gossip.

At about three o'clock in the afternoon I gave up hope of writing a believable story. Queasy with embarrassment and apology, I informed the city editor that the thing couldn't be done, that if there was such a place as an Athens of the West – which was doubtful – then it probably was to be found on the back lot of a movie studio in Los Angeles. San Francisco might compare to a Greek colony on the coast of Asia Minor in the fourth century B.C., but that was the extent of it. The city editor heard me out, and then after an awful and incredulous silence, he rose from behind his desk and denounced me as a fool and an apostate. I had betrayed the city of my birth and the imperatives of the first edition. Never could I hope to succeed in the newspaper business. Perhaps I might find work in a drugstore chain, preferably somewhere east of St. Louis, but even then he would find himself hard-pressed to recommend me as anything but a liar and an assassin. He assigned the story to an older and wiser reporter, who relied on the local authorities (Herb Caen, Barnaby Conrad, the presidents of department stores, the director of the film festival), and who found it easy enough to persuade them to say that San Francisco should be more appropriately compared to Mount Olympus.

I left San Francisco within a matter of weeks, depressed by the dreamlike torpor of the city. Although in the past eighteen years I often have thought of the city with feelings of sadness, as if in mourning for the beauty of the hills and the clarity of the light in September when the wind blows from the north, I have no wish to return. The atmosphere of unreality seems to me more palpable and oppressive in San Francisco than it does in New York. Apparently this has always been so. Few of the writers associated with the city stayed longer than a few seasons. Twain broke camp and moved on; so did Bierce and Bret Harte. In his novel *The Octopus,* Frank Norris describes the way in which the Southern Pacific Railroad in the 1890s forced the farmers of the San Joaquin Valley to become its serfs. The protagonist of the novel, hoping to stir the farmers to revolt and to an idea of liberty, looks for political allies among the high-minded citizens of San Francisco. He might as well have been looking for the civic conscience in a bordello. A character modeled after Colis Huntington, the most epicurean of the local robber barons, explains to him that San Francisco cannot conceive of such a thing as social justice. The conversation takes place in the bar at the Bohemian Club, and the financier gently says to Norris's hero that "San Francisco is not a city . . . it is a midway plaisance."

The same thing can be said for San Francisco almost a hundred years later, except that in the modern idiom people talk about the city as "carnival." The somnambulism of the past has been joined with the androgynous frenzy of the present, and in the ensuing confusion who knows what's true and not true, or who's doing what to whom and for what reason? The wandering bedouin of the American desert traditionally migrate to California in hope of satisfying their hearts' desire under the palm tree of the national oasis. They seek to set themselves free, to rid themselves of all restraint, to find the Eden or the fountain of eternal youth withheld or concealed from them by the authorities (nurses, teachers, parents, caliphs) in the walled towns of the East. They desire simply to be, and they think of freedom as a banquet. Thus their unhappiness and despair when their journey proves to have been in vain. The miracle fails to take place, and things remain pretty much as they were in Buffalo or Indianapolis. Perhaps this explains the high rate of divorce, alcoholism, and suicide. The *San Francisco Examiner* kept a record of the people who jumped off the Golden Gate Bridge, and the headline always specified the number of the most recent victim, as if adding up the expense of the sacrifice to the stone-faced gods of happiness.

Given their suspicion of civilization, the wandering tribes have little patience with institutional or artistic forms, which they identify with conspiracy. Who dares to speak to them of rules, of discovering form and order in the chaos of feeling? Like the detectives in the stories by Dashiell Hammett and Raymond Chandler, the California protagonist belongs to no Establishment. He comes and goes as effortlessly as the wind, remarking on the sleaziness and impermanence of things, mocking the shabby masquerades (of governments and dictionaries) by which the prominent citizens in town cheat the innocent children of their primal inheritance. No matter how grandiose the facade, every door opens into an empty room. Without rules the bedouin's art and politics are as insubstantial as tissue paper or interior decoration, and in the extremities of their sorrow they have nothing to hold onto except the magical charms and amulets sold by mendicant prophets in the bazaars. Sometimes the prophets recommend extended vacations at transcendental dude ranches.

Maybe this is why the conversation in California is both so desperate and so timid. What passes for serious talk, at the Center for the Study of Democratic Institutions as well as in the cabanas around the pool at the Beverly Hills Hotel, has the earnest texture of undergraduate confession. Everybody is in the midst of discovering the obvious. Middle-aged producers, well known for their greed and cunning, breathlessly announce that politics is corrupt, that blacks don't much like whites, and that the wrong people get killed in the wrong wars. Women in sunglasses enter from stage left saying that they have just found out about Freud; somebody's literary agent astonishes the company with a brief summary of the French Revolution. Nobody wants to ask too many questions because usually it is preferable not to know the answers. More often than not the person to whom one happens to be speaking turns out to be playing a part in his own movie. Given the high levels of disappointment in California, people retire to the screening rooms of their private fantasy. The phantasmagoria that they project on the walls seldom bears much resemblance to what an uninitiated bystander might describe as reality. Thus, if a man says that he is a writer, it is possible that he writes notes to his dog, in green ink on a certain kind of yellow paper that he buys in Paris. If a woman says she's an actress, it is possible that she once stood next to Marlon Brando in an airport, and that he looked at her in such a way that she knew he thought she was under contract to Paramount. To ask such people many further questions, or to have the bad manners to remember what they were saying last week or last year, constitutes an act of social aggression.

California is like summer or the Christmas holidays. The unhappy children think that they are supposed to be having a good time, and they imagine that everybody else is having a better time. Thus the pervasive mood of envy and the feeling, common especially among celebrities, that somehow they have been excluded from something, that their names have been left off the guest list. In New York nobody wants to be David Rockefeller. They might want his money or his house in Maine, but they don't want to change places with the fellow, to actually wear his clothes and preside over the annual meeting of the Chase Manhattan Bank. But in California, people literally want to be Warren Beatty, or Teddy Kennedy, or Cher Bono. If only they could be Teddy or Warren or Cher, even for a few hours in a car traveling at high speed on Sunset Boulevard, then they would know true happiness and learn the secret of the universe.

In California so many people are newly arrived (in almost all declensions of that phrase) that their anxieties, like those of the parvenus in Molière's plays, provide employment for a legion of dancing masters (i.e., swamis, lawn specialists, hairdressers, spiritual therapists, swimming-pool consultants, gossip columnists, tennis professionals, et cetera, et cetera) who smile and bow and hold up gilded mirrors as false and flattering as the grandiose facades with which their patrons adorn the houses built to resemble a baroque chateau or a Spanish hacienda. The athletic coaches of the human-potential movements take the place of liveried servants in the employ of the minor nobility. Every season since the Gold Rush, California has blossomed with new money—first in gold, then in land, cattle, rail-roads, agriculture, film images, shipbuilding, aerospace, electronics, television, and commercial religions. The ease with which the happy few become suddenly rich lends credence to the belief in magical transformation. People tell each other fabulous tales of El Dorado. They talk about scrawny girls found in drugstores and changed over-night into princesses, about second-rate actors made into statesmen, about Howard Jarvis revealed as a savior of his people. Everybody is always in the process of becoming somebody else. If the transfor-mations can take place in the temporal spheres of influence, then why can't they also take place in the spiritual sectors?

Perhaps this is why California is so densely populated with converts of one kind of another. A young man sets out on the road to Ventura, but somewhere on the Los Angeles Freeway he has a vision. God speaks to him through the voice of a disc jockey broadcasting over Radio Free Orange County, and he understands that he has lived his life in vain. He throws away his credit cards and commits himself to Rolfing and salad. Thus, Jane Fonda discovers feminism and Tom Hayden declares his faith in "the system"; Eldridge Cleaver renounces the stony paths of radical politics and embraces the luxury of capitalism; Richard Nixon goes through as many conversions as he finds expedient; and Ronald Reagan begins as an ADA Democrat and ends as the conscience of the Republican rear guard. As with the prophets who gather the faithful in the compounds of pure truth, so the politicians conceive of politics not as a matter of practical compromise but as a dream of power and a fantasy of omnipotent wish.

Throughout the decade of the 1960s I kept reading in the newspapers about the revolutions coming out of California, about the free-speech movement at the University of California at Berkeley, about the so-called sexual revolution, about the counterculture and the "revolutionary life-styles" portrayed in the pages of *Vogue*. As recently as last year, people were talking about "the taxpayers' revolt," as if, once again, California were leading the nation forward into the future. Sometimes when reading these communiqués from the front I am reminded of Lenny Bruce and the bitter jokes with which he used to entertain the crowd at the hungry i in San Francisco. California sponsors no revolution and only one revolt. This is the revolt against time. In no matter what costumes the self-proclaimed revolutionaries dress themselves up, they shout the manifesto of Peter Pan. They demand that time be brought to a stop. They declare time to be circular, and they say that nothing ever changes in their perpetual summer, that they remain forever suspended in the enchantment of their innocent garden. History is a fairy tale, in which maybe they will consent to believe on the condition that the scripts have happy endings. The media advertise California as the image of the future, but to me the state is the mirror of the past—not the recent, historical past, but the ancient and primitive past of 90,000 years ago with the light of paleolithic fires flickering in the windows of the stores on Rodeo Drive.

Even the people who go to California to die hope to find a connection to another world. Maybe they will be initiated into the mysteries of reincarnation, or perhaps they will meet the pilot of a UFO. But most of the people who make the trek across the mountains expect that they will remain forever young. I remember once going to see Mae West in her shuttered house on the beach at Santa Monica. On a brilliantly blue afternoon the house was as dark as a nightclub. Miss West received me in a circle of candlelight and white satin, and although she was in her late seventies she affected the dress and mannerisms of a coquette. The effect was grotesque but only slightly more exaggerated than the disguises worn by people trying to look anywhere from ten to thirty years younger than their age. In California nobody is middle-aged. For as long as they can afford the cosmetics and the surgery, people pretend that they are still thirty-five; then one day all the systems fail and somebody else vanishes into the gulag of the anonymous old. I'm sure that the desire to obliterate time also has something to do with the weather. The absence of clearly defined seasons helps to sustain the illusion of the evangelical present. Perhaps this is also why people make such a solemn business of sport in California. Among people determined merely to be, and who therefore conceive of the world as a stadium, leisure acquires an importance equivalent to that of work. People get very serious about tennis because from the point of view of a child at play in the fields of the Lord, tennis is as serious as politics or blocks.

I left California because I didn't have the moral fortitude to contend with the polymorphousness of the place. It was too easy to lose myself behind a mask, and I had the feeling that I was wandering in a void, feeding on hallucinatory blooms of the lotus flower. The emptiness frightened me, and so did the absence of culture, of politics in the conventional sense, of art and conversation, of the social contrivances that make it possible to talk to other people about something else besides the degree of their God-consciousness, of all the makeshift laws and patched-together institutions with which men rescue themselves from their loneliness, their megalomania, and the seductions of self-annihilation. Had I been blessed with great genius, like Robinson Jeffers perched upon his rock in Carmel, I might have been able to make something out of nothing. But in San Francisco, as in Los Angeles, I woke up every morning thinking that I had to invent the wheel and discover the uses of fire. I needed the company of other men who had roused themselves from sleep and set forth on the adventure of civilization.

1979

Chinese family in Golden Gate Park, 1884. Photograph by A. J. Perkins.

FRANK CHIN

The Only Real Day

THE MEN played mah-jong or passed the waterpipe, their voices low under the sound of the fish pumps thudding into the room from the tropical fish store. Voices became louder over other voices in the thickening heat. Yuen was with his friends now, where he was always happy and loud every Tuesday night. All the faces shone of skin oily from the heat and laughter, the same as last week, the same men and room and waterpipe. Yuen knew them. Here it was comfortable after another week of that crippled would-be Hollywood Oriental-for-a-friend in Oakland. He hated the sight of cripples on his night and day off, and one had spoken to him as stepped off the A-train into the tinny breath of the Key System Bay Bridge Terminal. Off the train in San Francisco into the voice of a cripple. "Count your blessings!" The old white people left to die at the Eclipse Hotel, and the old waitresses who worked there often said "Count your blessings" over sneezes and little ouches and bad news. Christian resignation. Yuen was older than many of the white guests of the Eclipse. He washed dishes there without ever once counting his blessings.

"That's impossible," Huie said to Yuen.

Yuen grinned at his friend and said, "Whaddaya mean? It's true! You don't know because you were born here."

"Whaddaya mean 'born here'? Who was born here?"

"Every morning, I woke up with my father and my son, and we walked out of our house to the field, and stood in a circle around a young peach tree and lowered our trousers and pissed on the tree, made bubbles in the dirt, got the bark wet, splattered on the roots and watched our piss sink in. That's how we fertilized the big one the day I said I was going to Hong Kong tomorrow with my wife and son, and told them I was leaving my father and mother, and I did. I left. Then I left Hong Kong and left my family there, and came to America to make money," Yuen said. "Then after so much money, bring them over."

"Nobody gets over these days, so don't bang you head about not getting people over. What I want to know is did you make money?"

"Make money?"

"Yes, did you make money?"

"I'm still here, my wife is dead . . . but my son is still in Hong Kong, and I send him what I can."

"You're too good a father! He's a big boy now. Has to be a full-grown man. You don't want to spoil him."

Yuen looked up at the lightbulb and blinked. "It's good to get away from those *lo fan* women always around the restaurant. Waitresses, hotel guests crying for Rose. Ha ha." He didn't want to talk about his son or China. Talk of white women he'd seen changing in the corridor outside his room over the kitchen, and sex acts of the past, would cloud out what he didn't want to talk about. Already the men in the room full of fish tanks were speaking loudly, shouting when they laughed, throwing the sound of their voices loud against the spongy atmosphere of fish pumps and warm-water aquariums. Yuen enjoyed the room when it was loud and blunt. The fishtanks and gulping and chortling pumps sopped up the sound of the clickety clickety of the games and kept the voices, no matter how loud, inside. The louder the closer, thicker, fleshier, as the night wore on. This was the life after a week of privacy with the only real Chinese speaker being paralyzed speechless in a wheelchair. No wonder the boy doesn't speak Chinese, he thought, not making sense. The boy should come here sometime. He might like the fish.

"Perhaps you could," Huie said, laughing, "Perhaps you could make love to them, Ah-Yuen gaw." The men laughed, showing gold and aged yellow teeth. "Love!" Yuen snorted against the friendly laugh.

"That's what they call it if you do it for free," Huie said.

"Not me," Yuen said taking the bucket and water pipe from Huie. "Free or money. No love. No fuck. Not me." He lifted the punk from the tobacco, then shot off the ash with a blast of air into the pipe that sent a squirt of water up the stem. "I don't even like talking to them. Why should I speak their language? They don't think I'm anything anyway. They change their clothes and smoke in their slips right outside my door in the hallway, and don't care I live there. So what?" His head lifted to face his friends, and his nostrils opened, one larger than the other as he spoke faster. "And anyway, they don't care if I come out of my room and see them standing half-naked in the hall. They must know they're ugly. They all have wrinkles and you can see all the dirt on their skins and they shave their armpits badly, and their powder turns brown in the folds of their skin. They're not like Chinese women at all." Yuen made it a joke for his friends.

"I have always wanted to see a real naked American woman for free. There's something about not paying money to see what you see," Huie said. "Ahhh and what I want to see is bigger breasts. Do these free peeks have bigger breasts than Chinese women? Do they have nipples as pink as calendar girls' sweet suckies?" Huie grunted and put his hand inside his jacket and hefted invisible breasts, "Do they have . . . ?"

"I don't know. I don't look. All the ones at my place are old, and who wants to look inside the clothes of the old for their parts? And you can't tell about calendar pictures . . ." Yuen pulled at the deep smoke of the waterpipe. The water inside gurgled loudly, and singed tobacco ash jumped when Yuen blew back into the tube. He lifted his head and licked the edges of his teeth. He always licked the edges of his teeth before speaking. He did not think it a sign of old age. Before he broke the first word over his licked teeth, Huie raised his hand. "Jimmy Chan goes out with *lo fan* women . . . blonde ones with blue eyelids too. And he smokes cigars," Huie said.

"He smokes cigars. So what? What's that?"

"They light his cigars for him."

"That's because he has money. If Chinese have money here, everybody likes them," Yuen said. "Blue nipples, pink eyelids, everybody likes them."

"Not the Jews."

"Not the Jews." Yuen said. "I saw a cripple. Screamed 'Count your blessings!' Could have been a Jew, huh? I should have looked . . . Who cares? So what?"

"The Jews don't like anybody," Huie said. "They call us, you and me, the Tang people 'Jews of the Orient.' Ever hear that?"

"Because the Jews don't like anybody?"

"Because nobody likes the Jews!" Huie said. He pulled the tip of his nose down with his fingers. "Do I look like a Jew of the Orient, for fuckin out loud? What a life!" The men at the mah-jong table laughed and shook the table with the pounding of their hands. Over their laughter, Yuen spoke loudly, licking the edges of his teeth and smiling, "What do you want to be Jew for? You're Chinese! That's bad enough!" And the room full of close men was loud with the sound of tables slapped with night-pale hands and belly laughter shrinking into wheezes and silent empty mouths breathless and drooling. "We have a Jew at the Eclipse Hotel. They look white like the other *lo fan gwai* to me," Yuen said, and touched the glowing punk to the tobacco and inhaled through his mouth, gurgling the water. He let the smoke drop from his nostrils and laughed smoke out between his teeth, and leaned back into the small spaces of smoke between the men and enjoyed the whole room.

Yuen was a man of neat habits, but always seemed disheveled with his dry mouth, open with the lower lip shining, dry and dangling below yellow teeth. Even today, dressed in his day-off suit that he kept hung in his closet with butcher paper over it and a hat he kept in a box, he had seen people watching him and laughing behind their hands at his pulling at the shoulders of the jacket and lifting the brim of his hat from his eyes. He had gathered himself into his own arms and leaned back into his seat to think about the room in San Francisco; then he slept and was ignorant of the people, the conductor, and all the people he had seen before, watching him and snickering, and who might have been, he thought, jealous of him for being tall for a Chinese, or his long fingers, exactly what he did not know or worry about in his half-stupor between wakefulness and sleep with his body against the side of the train, the sounds of the steel wheels, and the train pitching side to side, all amazingly loud and echoing in his ears, through his body before sleep.

Tuesday evening Yuen took the A-train from Oakland to San Francisco. He walked to the train stop right after work at the restaurant and stood, always watching to the end of the street for the train's coming, dim out of the darkness from San Francisco. The train came, its cars swaying side to side and looked like a short snake with a lit stripe of lights squirming past him, or like the long dragon that stretched and jumped over the feet of the boys carrying it. He hated the dragon here, but saw it when it ran, for the boy's sake. The train looked like that, the glittering dragon that moved quickly like the sound of drum rolls and dangled its staring eyes out of its head with a flurry of beard; the screaming bird's voice of the train excited in him his idea of a child's impulse to run, to grab, to destroy.

Then he stood and listened to the sound of the train's steel wheels, the sound of an invisible cheering crowed being sucked after the lights of the train toward the end of the line, leaving the quiet street more quiet and Yuen almost superstitiously anxious. Almost. The distance from superstitious feeling could be a loss or an achievement, he wasn't sure.

He was always grateful for the Tuesdays Dirigible walked him to the train stop. They left early on these nights and walked past drugstores, bought comic books, looked into the windows of closed shops and dimly lit used bookstores, and looked at shoes or suits on dummies. "How much is that?" Yuen would ask.

"I don't know what you're talking," Dirigible, the boy of the unpronounceable name, would say. "I don't know what you're talking" seemed the only complete phrase he commanded in Cantonese.

"What a stupid boy you are; can't even talk Chinese," Yuen would say, and "Too moochie shi-yet," adding his only American phrase. "Come on, I have a train to catch." They would laugh at each other and walk slowly, the old man lifting his shoulders and leaning his head far back on his neck, walking straighter, when he remembered. The boy. "Fay Gay" in Cantonese, Flying Ship, made him remember.

A glance back to Dirigible as he boarded the train, a smile, a wave, the boy through the window a silent thing in the noise of the engines. Yuen would shrug and settle himself against the back, against the seat, and still watch Dirigible, who would be walking now, back toward the restaurant. Tonight he realized again how young the Flying Ship was to be walking home alone at night through the city back to the kitchen entrance of the hotel. He saw Dirigible not walking the usual way home, but running next to the moving train, then turning the corner to walk up a street with more lights and people. Yuen turned, thinking he might shout out the door for the boy to go home the way they had come, but the train was moving, the moment gone. Almost. Yuen had forgotten something. The train was moving. And he had no right. Dirigible had heard his mother say that Yuen had no right so many times that Dirigible was saying it too. In Chinese. Badly spoken and bungled, but Chinese. That he was not Yuen's son. That this was not China. Knowing the boy was allowed to say such things by his only speaking parent made Yuen's need to scold and shout more urgent, his silence in front of the spoiled punk more humiliating. Yuen was still and worked himself out of his confusion. The beginning of his day off was bad; nothing about it right or usual; all of it bad, no good, wrong. Yuen chewed it out of his mind until the memory was fond and funny, then relaxed.

"Jimmy Chan has a small Mexican dog too, that he keeps in his pocket," Huie said. "It's lined with rubber."

"The little dog?" Yuen asked. And the men laughed.

"The dog . . ." Huie said and chuckled out of his chinless face, "No, his pocket, so if the dog urinates . . ." He shrugged, "You know."

"Then how can he make love to his blonde *fangwai* woman with blue breasts if his pocket is full of dogpiss?"

"He takes off his coat!" The men laughed with their faces up into the falling smoke. The men seemed very close to Yuen, as if with the heat and smoke they swelled to crowding against the walls, and Yuen swelled and was hot with them, feeling tropically close and friendly, friendlier, until he was dizzy with friendship and forgot names. No, don't forget names. "A Chinese can do anything with *fan gwai* if he has money," Yuen said.

"Like too moochie shi-yet, he can," Huie shouted, almost falling off his seat. "He can't make himself white!" Huie jabbed his finger at Yuen and glared. The men at the table stopped. The noise of the mahjong and voices stopped to the sounds of rumps shifting over chairs and creaks of table legs. Heavy arms were leaned onto the tabletops. Yuen was not sure whether he was arguing with his friend or not. He did not want to argue on his day off, yet he was constrained to say something. He knew that whatever he said would sound more important than he meant it. He licked his teeth and said, "Who want to be white when they can have money?" He grinned. The man nodded and sat quiet a moment, listening to the sound of boys shouting at cars to come and park in their lots. "Older brother, you always know the right thing to say in a little pinch, don't you."

"You mother's twat! Play!" And the men laughed and in a burst of noise returned to their game.

The back room was separated from the tropical fish store by a long window shade drawn over the doorway. Calendars with pictures of Chinese women holding peaches the size of basketballs, calendars with pictures of nude white women with large breasts of all shapes, and a picture someone thought was funny, showing a man with the breasts of a woman, were tacked to the walls above the stacked glass tanks of warm-water fish. The men sat on boxes, in chairs, at counters with a wall of drawers full of stuff for tropical fish, and leaned inside the doorway and bits of wall not occupied by a gurgling tank of colorful little swimming things. They sat and passed the waterpipe and tea and played mah-jong or talked. Every night the waterpipe, the tea, the mah-jong, the talk.

"Wuhay! Hey, Yuen, older brother," a familiar nameless voice shouted through the smoke and thumping pumps. "Why're you so quiet tonight?"

"I thought I was being loud and obnoxious," Yuen said. "Perhaps it's my boss's son looking sick again."

"The boy?" Huie said.

Yuen stood and removed his jacket, brushed it and hung it on a nail. "He has this trouble with his stomach . . . makes him bend up and he cries and won't move. It comes and goes," Yuen said.

"Bring him over to me, and I'll give him some herbs, make him well in a hurry."

"His mother, my boss, is one of these new-fashioned people giving up the old ways. She speaks nothing but American if she can help it, and has *lo fan* women working for her at her restaurant. She laughs at me when I tell her about herbs making her son well, but she knows . . ."

"Herbs make me well when I'm sick."

"They can call you 'mass hysteria' crazy in the head. People like her mean well, but don't know what's real and what's phony."

"Herbs made my brother well, but he died anyway," Huie said. He took off his glasses and licked the lenses.

"Because he wanted to," Yuen said.

"He shot himself."

"Yes, I remember," Yuen said. He scratched his Adam's apple noisily a moment. "He used to come into the restaurant in the mornings. I'd fix him scrambled eggs. He always use to talk with bits of egg on his lips and shake his fork and tell me that I could learn English good enough to be cook at some good restaurant. I could too, but the cook where I wash dishes is Chinese already, and buys good meat, so I have a good life."

Huie sighed and said, "Good meat is important I suppose." Then put his mouth to the mouth of the waterpipe.

"What?" Yuen asked absently at Huie's sigh. He allowed his eyes to unfocus on the room now, tried to remember Huie's brother's face with bits of egg on the lips and was angry. Suddenly an angry old man wanting to be alone screamed. He wiped his own lips with his knuckles and looked back to Huie the herbalist. Yuen did not want to talk about Huie's brother. He wanted to listen to music, or jokes, or breaking bones, something happy or terrible.

"His fine American talk," Huie said. "He used to go to the Oakland High School at night to learn."

"My boss wants me to go there too," Yuen said. "You should only talk English if you have money to talk to them with . . . I mean, only fools talk buddy buddy with the *lo fan* when they don't have money. If you talk to them without money, all you'll hear is what they say behind your back, and you don't want to listen to that."

"I don't."

"No."

"He received a letter one day, did he tell you that? He got a letter from the American Immigration, and he took the letter to Jimmy Chan, who reads government stuff well . . . and Jimmy said that the Immigration wanted to know how he came into the country and wanted to know if he was sending money to Communists or not." Huie smiled wanly and stared between his legs. Yuen watched Huie sitting on the box; he had passed the pipe and now sat with his short legs spread slightly apart. He was down now, his eyes just visible to Yuen. Huie's slumped body looked relaxed, only the muscles of his hands and wrists were tight and working. To Yuen, Huie right now looked as calm as if he were sitting on a padded crapper. Yuen smiled and tried to save the pleasure of his day-off visit that was being lost in morbid talk. "Did he have his dog with him?" he asked.

"His dog? My brother never had a dog."

"I mean Jimmy Chan with his rubber pocket."

"How can you talk about Jimmy Chan's stupid dog when I'm talking about my brother's death?"

"Perhaps I'm worried about the boy," Yuen said. "I shouldn't have let him wait for the train tonight."

"Was he sick?"

"That too maybe. Who can tell?" Yuen said without a hint, not a word more of the cripple shouting "Count your blessings!" at the end of the A-train's line in Frisco. It wouldn't be funny, and Yuen wanted a laugh.

"Bring the boy to me next week, and I'll fix him up," Huie said quickly, and put on his glasses again. Yuen, out of his day-off, loud, cheerful mood, angry and ashamed of his anger, listened to Huie. "My brother was very old, you remember? He was here during the fire and earthquake, and he told this to Jimmy Chan." Huie stopped speaking and patted Yuen's knee. "Yes, he did have his little dog in his pocket . . ." The men looked across to each other, and Yuen nodded. They were friends, had always been friends. They were friends now. "And my brother told Jimmy that all his papers had been burned in the fire and told about how he came across the bay in a sailboat that was so full that his elbows, just over the side of the boat, were in the water, and about the women crying and then shouting, and that no one thought about papers, and some not even of their gold."

"Yes. I know."

"And Jimmy Chan laughed at my brother and told him that there was nothing he could do, and that my brother would have to wait and see if he would be sent back to China or not. So . . ." Huie put his hands on his knees and rocked himself forward, lifting and setting his thin rump onto the wooden box, sighed and swallowed, "my brother shot himself." Huie looked up to Yuen; they licked their lips at the same moment, watching each other's tongues. "He died very messy," Huie said, and Yuen heard it through again for his friend, as he had a hundred times before. But tonight it made him sick.

The talk about death and the insides of a head spread wet all over the floor, the head of someone he knew, the talk was not relaxing; it was incongruous to the room of undershirted men playing mah-jong and pai-gow. And the men, quieter since the shout, were out of place in their undershirts. Yuen wanted to relax, but everything was frantic that should not be; perhaps he was too sensitive, Yuen thought, and wanted to be numb. "You don't have to talk about it if it bothers," Yuen said.

"He looked messy, for me that was enough . . . and enough of Jimmy Chan for me too. He could've written and said my brother was a good citizen or something . . ." Huie stopped and flicked at his ear with his fingertips. "You don't want to talk anymore about it?"

"No," Yuen said.

"How did we come to talk about my brother's death anyhow?"

"Jimmy Chan and his Mexican dog."

"I don't want to talk about that anymore, either."

"How soon is Chinese New Year's?"

"I don't think I want to talk about anything anymore," Huie said, "New Year's is a long ways off. Next year."

"Yes, I know that."

"I don't want to talk about it," Huie said. Each man sat now, staring toward and past each other without moving their eyes, as if moving their eyes would break their friendship. He knew that whatever had happened had been his fault; perhaps tonight would have been more congenial if he had not taken Dirigible to the used bookstore where he found a pile of sunshine and nudist magazines, or if the cripple had fallen on his face, or not been there. Yuen could still feel the presence of the cripple, how he wanted still to push him over, crashing to the cement. The joy it would have given him was embarrassing, new, unaccountable, like being in love.

"Would you like a cigar, ah-dai low?" Huie asked, with a friendly Cantonese "Older Brother."

"No, I like the waterpipe." Yuen watched Huie spit the end of the cigar out onto the floor.

"You remind me of my brother, Yuen."

"How so?"

"Shaking your head, biting your lips, always shaking your

head . . . you do too much thinking about nothing. You have to shake the thinking out to stop, eh?"

"And I rattle my eyes, too." Yuen laughed, knowing he had no way with a joke, but the friendliness botched in expression was genuine, and winning. "So what can I do without getting arrested?"

"I don't know," Huie said and looked around, "Mah-jong?"

"No."

"Are you unhappy?"

"What kind of question is that? I have my friends, right? But sometimes I feel . . . Aww, everybody does . . ."

"Just like my brother . . . too much thinking, and thinking becomes worry. You should smoke cigars and get drunk and go help one of your *lo fan* waitresses shave her armpits properly and put your head inside and tickle her with your tongue until she's silly. I'd like to put my face into the armpit of some big *fangwai* American woman . . . with a big armpit!"

"But I'm not like your brother." Yuen said. "I don't shoot myself in the mouth and blow the back of my head out with a gun."

"You only have to try once."

Yuen waited a moment, then stood. "I should be leaving now," he said. Tonight had been very slow, but over quickly. He did not like being compared to an old man who had shot himself.

Huie stood and shook Yuen's hand, held Yuen's elbow and squeezed Yuen's hand hard. "I didn't mean to shout at you, dai low."

Yuen smiled his wet smile. Huie held onto Yuen's hand and stood as if he was about to sit again. He had an embarrassingly sad smile. Yuen did not mean to twist his friend's face into this muscular contortion; he had marred Huie's happy evening of gambling, hoarse laughter, and alcoholic wheezings. "I shouted too," Yuen said finally.

"You always know the right things to say, older brother." Huie squeezed Yuen's hand and said, "Goodnight dai low." And Yuen was walking, was out of the back room and into the tropical fish store. He opened the door to the alley and removed his glasses, blew on them in the sudden cold air to fog them, then wiped them clean.

For a long time he walked the always-damp alleys, between glittering streets of Chinatown. Women with black coats walked with young children. This Chinatown was taller than Oakland's, had more fire escapes and lights, more music coming from the street vents. He usually enjoyed walking at this hour every Wednesday of every week. But this was Tuesday evening, and already he had left his friends, yet it looked like Wednesday with the same paper vendors coming up the hills, carrying bundles of freshly printed Chinese papers. He walked down the hill to Portsmouth Square on Kearny Street to sit in the park and read the paper. He sat on a wooden bench and looked up the trunk of a palm tree, looking toward the sounds of pigeons. He could hear the fat birds cooing over the sound of the streets, and the grass snap when their droppings dropped fresh. Some splattered on the bronze plaque marking the location of the birth of the first white child in San Francisco, a few feet away. He looked up and down the park once, then moved to the other side of the tree out of the wind and sat to read the paper by the streetlight before walking. Tonight he was glad to be tired; to Yuen tiredness was the only explanation for his nervousness. Almost anger. Almost. He would go home early; there was nothing else to do here, and he would sleep through his day off, or at least, late into the morning.

1988

DORE ASHTON

An Eastern View of the San Francisco School

BOTH THE European and American art press, always avid for a controversy, have debated the existence of a San Francisco or Pacific Coast "school" of painting. Partisans of autonomy have claimed that San Francisco is entitled to a special section in the arena of contemporary American painting. Objectors insist that the San Francisco "school" is nothing other than a number of unrelated, talented individuals who happened to have worked in San Francisco during a special period roughly from 1945 to 1952.

In reality, there is no way to add up the idiosyncrasies which mark West Coast painting so that they constitute a genuine movement. Yet, San Francisco is separated from New York by a continent and from Europe by a sea. It is not so remarkable, then, that certain characteristics have become dominant enough in San Francisco painters to be considered the components of a "style." It is reasonable to acknowledge that from a general complex of new painting ideas which developed in the United States just after the war, San Francisco painters came to stress certain aspects while New York painters developed others. The psychological climate which nurtured San Francisco avant-garde artists was essentially the same as that in New York. It was a postwar climate of rebellion fed by the release of dammed up emotions and the inevitable hope for something fresh to come. Whatever the reasons, American painters, with mysterious solidarity, turned away from both their own tradition of realism and the European tradition of forty years standing of Cubism.

Between 1945 and 1950 there emerged three general tendencies which have remained salient in avant-garde painting throughout the United States. First, painters sought to revive the vigor of the oil medium, abandoning classical techniques. Variations ranged from the spontaneous application advocated by Hans Hofmann to the completely unorthodox "drip" technique of Jackson Pollock. As in contemporary poetry, where the act of making a poem interests the poet psychologically almost as much as the final product, so in painting the process became important. A new attitude to material added a dimension for the painter, which was to have direct bearing on his expression.

A second tendency was to break with conventional subject-matter. In New York as in San Francisco, painters moved as far from the subjects of the European painter as they could; they particularly avoided the subjects of the Cubists. The most congenial source for the American painter was a branch of Surrealism which advocated automatism. But for a time, it was in myth that the painters found escapes from conventional imagery. Painters like Rothko, Gottlieb, Still, and Pollock fell back on the unlimited possibilities of myth. And from the communal myth and the primordial associations artists sought to evoke, it was a short step, taken almost immediately, to the personal myth, the unabashedly subjective invention of content.

Finally, to accommodate the feelings released by the acceptance of subjective content, painters had to find a new formal approach. The logical, self-contained compositional devices of the Cubists hampered them. What was wanted was a totally new concept of space, one which gave the painter the possibility of expressing emotions unavailable to discursive reason.

It was this new attitude toward space which was developed with particular emphasis in San Francisco. Naturally, it simultaneously engaged the painters in New York. The treatment of the canvas as an extending plane surface rather than as a recession in the wall became marked around 1948. Critic Clement Greenberg was the first to note this in a provocative essay in *Partisan Review*, "The Crisis of the Easel Picture." He spoke mostly about Pollock, referring to "decentralized" and "polyphonic" composing. "The surface is knit together of a multiplicity of identical or similar elements; repeats itself without strong variations from one end of the canvas to the other and dispenses, apparently, with beginning, middle and ending."

Although Pollock's work was based on the arabesque which turned always on itself, the enormous scale of his canvases added a temporal factor related to the "open-form" concepts of the San Francisco painters. Possibly the Western space idea is closer to the

Oriental where there is a horizontal unfolding of space and little recession back from the picture plane. The time element, the rhythm of extension, plays a crucial part.

The San Francisco painter who made the most personal use of "unbound" space was Clyfford Still. It was Still, furthermore, who brought the ideas he had shared with New York painters to San Francisco in 1946. For a time he had worked along the same lines as the New York group showing in Peggy Guggenheim's Art of This Century Gallery. Among them, Still found affinity especially with Rothko, whom he later brought to the California School of Fine Arts as instructor. In 1946, Rothko wrote the foreword to Still's catalogue, pointing out that Still was among "the small band of Myth Makers who have emerged here during the war. . . . For me, Still's pictorial dramas are an extension of the Greek Persephone myth."

Both Still and Rothko were involved with memory and ancestral phantoms at the time, though interpretable literary reference grew fainter and fainter between 1945 and 1948. In 1945, for example, Still painted "The Specter and the Perroquet" in which a phallic vertical form was opposed to a haloed figure vaguely suggesting a bird. About a year later, the same picture appeared transformed into what became the autographic Still image: the specter became the vertical break-through in atmosphere, the shaft of light which pierces the top of the canvas; and the parrot became a flameline, a rent in the surface rather than a positive form.

Since then, Still has continued to dehydrate space, keeping his huge canvases nearly in a single plane. His great asphalt black works are densely worked with the knife, spreading in terrifyingly vast plains until the finger-like breakthroughs of form give the eye a momentary shock of space memory. Like atomic radiation, these paintings absorb the breathing atmosphere, sucking the spectator into a darkness and light nightmare replete with perilous chasms and flashes of hell-fire light. They engage the eye in a journey which cannot be avoided, and in the time the eye must wander in the shuddering plain, an emotion akin to anxiety and primordial fear is evinced. Space and time are ineffably linked in Still's work, as they are in the work of Mark Rothko.

The parallelism of the two painters appears even in their writings—the reluctant and defiant writings of men who insist that only their work must speak. In 1952, both Still and Rothko (as well as Pollock) were in the "Fifteen Americans" exhibition at the Museum of Modern Art. Their fiercely romantic philosophical stances were illustrated in their statements:

Rothko: "The progression of a painter's work, as it travels in time from point to point, will be toward clarity: toward the elimination of all obstacles between the painter and the idea, and between the idea and the observer. As examples of such obstacles, I give (among others) memory, history or geometry, which are swamps of generalization from which one might pull out parodies of ideas (which are ghosts) but never an idea in itself. . . .

"A picture lives by companionship, expanding and quickening in the eyes of the sensitive observer. It dies by the same token. It is therefore a risky act to send it out into the world. . . ."

(Note that Rothko considers his former preoccupation with memory an obstacle. Also, that the attitude of the painter as a "solitary," a man whose projections are unfairly exposed to a hostile world but whose protection is supreme integrity, is pronounced. It is an attitude widely held among San-Francisco-trained painters.)

Still: "That pigment on canvas has a way of initiating conventional reactions for most people needs no reminder. Behind these reactions is a body of history matured in dogma, authority, tradition. The totalitarian hegemony of this tradition I despise, its presumptions I reject. Its security is an illusion, banal and without courage. . . .

"We are now committed to an unqualified act, not illustrating outworn myths or contemporary alibis. One must accept total responsibility for what he executes. And the measure of his greatness will be in the depth of his insight and his courage in realizing his own vision. Demands for communication are both presumptuous and irrelevant. . . ."

In terms of the influence of his own style, Still was immensely important to younger painters, but it was probably in terms of his point of view that he made the most profound impression on his students. Still is a legitimate heir to the romantic tradition stemming from the French nineteenth-century poets. As an avant-gardist, or romantic, he drives on to the boundaries of the known, not afraid to take the crucial risk of passing beyond. Jacques Maritain has pointed out that the biggest development in poetry, as in the visual arts, was the growth of the awareness of self instigated by the nineteenth-century Romantics. The idea of the artist becoming a hero in his work and being sacrificed perhaps to the future is very active today among painters, though not exactly in the febrile way angelism occurs among poets. With Still, it is a necessary premise. Still's statement given above is not very different in tone from Rimbaud's *Lettre du Voyant* and from some of Baudelaire's pronouncements.

What Still and a few other avant-garde painters conveyed to younger artists was the importance of having courage and of exalting personal integrity. "One must accept total responsibility for what he executes." In some cases, student imitators made a parody of Still's stance. Unable to withdraw completely, these younger men were ambivalent in their pose as solitaries, keeping one eye cocked on the world. Of course, Still was not alone in having his tenets distorted. Hans Hofmann, whose influence has been sustained in San Francisco for many years, left behind a number of young painters who interpreted his dynamic philosophy in terms of unlimited license, and his vitality as the by-product of unreflected action.

Since I was never a resident of San Francisco, I hesitate to assess the role of other painters such as Hassel Smith, Elmer Bischoff, and younger men like Walter Kuhlman and Frank Lobdell, in advancing San Francisco painting. But it is safe to say the major figure in San Francisco was Clyfford Still.

Probably the impetus of the painting revolution there would not have been so great had there not been corresponding theoreticians energetically keeping up with the artists. The liveliest place in San Francisco between 1946 and 1952 was the California School of Fine Arts. Director Douglas McAgy, an articulate and ambitious intellectual, set a smart pace for art schools all over the country, engaging the best painters available as teachers and keeping the curriculum amazingly flexible. In complete sympathy with the painters, McAgy attempted to make students aware of the underlying philosophy of the avant-garde. In 1948, he wrote: "Artists, in coping with assumptions by which we live through the dimensional idiom space-time, are attacking another level." In the school, there were elaborate diagrams and constructions illustrating the space-time continuum to reveal to students "the new measure of life, as opposed to the Renaissance." Emphasis was placed on "non-rational truths" and students were encouraged to develop freely within a poetic realm. (Since 1954, the California School of Fine Arts has apparently reverted to the orthodox tradition and now plies its students with supplementary English, history, philosophy, and "design" courses.)

Everything in the good days was geared to the most intensely imaginative developments. Jean Varda, an eloquent, quick-witted cosmopolitan whose conversations are as famous in New York, London, and Paris as they are in San Francisco, exhorted his students to believe in painting as a self-sufficient way of life rather than as a tool. Varda would say, "Painting is a philosophical instrument of life . . . a painting has a cosmic reason for being; its creation is the result of the ecstatic moment at the peak of clarity of vision." Varda's well-developed philosophy, and the philosophies of Still and a few other older painters, conditioned the students at the California School of Fine Arts. Through their contacts with mature painters, they acquired a pride and boldness that enabled them later to move out on their own into unexplored areas.

A number of students and young instructors at the California School of Fine Arts eventually left San Francisco for Paris and New York where they exhibited their work. It is on the basis of these exhibitions that Europe and New York began to speak of the "San Francisco school." Although exhibitions of work by Sam Francis and Lawrence Calcagno in Paris, and Ed Corbett, Edward Dugmore, Richard Diebenkorn, Ernest Briggs, and a few others in New York, do not provide a basis of judgment of San Francisco painting, they do offer a basis for comparison between so-called "New York school" and San Francisco painting. And through comparison, it is possible to see characteristics which the San Francisco painters share. I am not suggesting that these painters have similar temperaments and sensibilities, but rather, that each has expanded some tenet discovered during the apprentice years in San Francisco. The painters I mention in the following paragraphs have established reputations recently, and in my opinion, they reflect their San Francisco background.

Ernest Briggs, who was a student of Still at the California School of Fine Arts where he studied from 1947 to 1951, shows a marked predilection for large scale and for the extension of laterally determined space. Briggs has absorbed Still's premises without being imitative. (Except perhaps in his statements. In the introduction to the "Twelve Americans" catalogue in 1956, he paraphrased Still: "For me the challenge of painting lies implicitly within the act—to penetrate inherited conceptual deposits and attempt the possible impingement of spirit, the personal image, remains the enduring command of conscience.")

Briggs regards the canvas as a vast plain on which to trace an emotional experience which, for want of a better term, might be called "flux." He tries to create continuous rhythms that seem to suggest rushing water by plaiting his color in sinuous ribbons. These rushes of color, perversely, flow upward in many of his recent canvases, creating a provoking derangement for the eye. His use of a diamond or spade-shaped stroke with a banked diagonal bias increases the rush of movement in much the same way as small elements served the Futurists. At his best, Briggs creates power with the veins of glistening reds, yellows, slate blues, and warm cedars, underswept with carbon blacks and overflecked with beads of light. And he sustains the movement of his forms on the large scale well. But there is an understandable repetition in his projections of movements in space (he is comparatively young as a painter), and he has not yet found a means of integrating figure with ground, or of suggesting profound space without using perspective to do so.

Sam Francis, who like Briggs was born in California in 1923 and was active in San Francisco from 1947 to 1950, established his reputation in France where his giant canvases were first remarked more for their novelty than for their esthetic value. Francis, perhaps even more than the others, has avoided any reference to natural phenomena, choosing a limited group of forms to express his moods. His canvases are scored with myriad small elements, roughly kidney shaped, which generally drift either to an evanescent horizon or to open areas at the side of the canvas. Francis' small elements which slide over thinly washed backgrounds are curiously related to the atomist's philosophy expounded by Mark Tobey. But in Francis' giant versions, the additive quality somehow loses its intensity. Without climax and lacking an underlying mystery, the monotonous surface patterning in Francis' work exhausts the eye long before the rest of the senses have a chance to be engaged.

Until very recently, Richard Diebenkorn's motif had always been landscape–landscape interpreted through a lusty sensibility stimulated during his period at the California School of Fine Arts, first as a student and then as a teacher. Diebenkorn, together with John Hultberg and Frank Lobdell, was an active *agent-provocateur* for the San Francisco brand of abstract expressionism; they were already established as promising younger painters by 1950. I first saw Diebenkorn's paintings, together with those of Ed Corbett, also an instructor at the California School of Fine Arts, in New Mexico in 1951. Although their techniques differed, both young painters had acquired a landscape concept which probably would never have materialized had they not been exposed both to the Southwestern scale and the teachings of Still. Corbett painted flat, shadowy landscapes seen as if from above, with atmospheric touches of light and a distinct reference to the expansive desert, infusing his canvases with a softened light and a deliberately stressed extension. Diebenkorn's were vaporous, suggestive compositions in the sandy, sunbleached colors of the desert.

In his first exhibition in New York last year, Diebenkorn showed paintings executed in a more fluent daring style, introducing dissonant color and accidental effects. The paintings presented a single landscape under various conditions. Some were obvious references to Pacific vistas in which an excited image was complete with explosively colorful sky (lusty pinks, orange yellows); a blue line symbolized horizon and grass-green shapes at the bottom underlined the landscape theme. Although he involved suggestive imagery, Diebenkorn nevertheless used a space related to that of other San Francisco painters, for all of his forms were kept in horizontal bands which could have been extended into infinity. Depth was indicated by tilting trapezoidal forms, but never very deeply. Like Corbett's paintings, Diebenkorn's give the impression of being seen from above, and are occultly balanced.

Diebenkorn's vitality was evident in his free stroking, his fearless color juxtapositions, and his generous disposition of space. His faults lay in indecision–a willingness to leave unresolved problems apparent on his canvases. Recently, Diebenkorn has rather abruptly turned away from abstraction. I have seen only one of his figurative paintings: a characterization of a man at table. Here, Diebenkorn's desire to portray inhibited his hand and definitely cramped his imagination.

Edward Dugmore is another painter who profited from contact with Clyfford Still during a crucial period in his painting life. Dugmore was in San Francisco from 1948 to 1950, long enough to free him from the restrictions of his classical training and to enable him to develop a powerful subjective style. At first, he explored the space possibilities opened in the work of Still and Rothko, seeking by means of large static, void areas to create the psychological illusion of unbounded space. Later, still using the lateral plane, Dugmore began to activate his canvases with textures, colors, and more defined forms. His canvases in his last exhibition at the Stable Gallery were sinewy compositions of drifts of vertical strokes. Dugmore's paintings are more closely composed than Brigg's and tend to be equilibrated by careful use of horizontal elements. Although Dugmore is not interested in "real" space, most of his works carry the sense of the baseboard, the horizontal place on which the spectator stands.

A deft painter, Dugmore has amplified his palette considerably in recent months, introducing many shades of soft gray, blue, cloudy white, and vermilion. His apprenticeship in San Francisco taught him the value of muscular, expansive painting. Now, he is elaborating, refining, calling in expanded associational references. He is a painter still deeply concerned with nature, but with the underlying structures and rhythms of nature felt out first in imaginative drawings, without ratiocination, then translated into a "mood" in his paintings.

Lately, I have seen a few other examples of work by San Francisco painters but none which equaled the work of the painters just discussed. Judging from paintings which slip into New York now and then, expressionist "action painting" is on the rise in San Francisco, while it is subsiding in New York. Students seem to have taken a fancy to the uninhibited gesture, the wildly seized moment— possibly a misinterpretation of the teachings of Hofmann.

With the absence of Still, who now works in strict seclusion in New York, and the return, four years ago, to figurative painting by David Park, Elmer Bischoff, and several others, activity in San Francisco appears to be less inspired, less significant. Nevertheless, it is still, after New York, the major source of avant-garde painting of quality. There are still many exceptional exhibitions, excited arguments, and strong stands taken by artists. In a letter written in February, 1957, Hubert Crehan, former editor of *Art Digest* and a painter in the Still tradition, commented on the current situation. I quote most of the letter, for Crehan has lived on and off in San Francisco for years, was a close friend of Dugmore and Briggs, and is the author of a much-discussed essay in *Art News* debating the existence of the San Francisco school. His letter is somewhat partisan, influenced no doubt by his own commitment as a painter, but I think offers a lively impression of San Francisco today:

> Things have changed in San Francisco within the past five to eight years. The center of creative work has shifted from the California School of Fine Arts to the University of California. This is probably symptomatic of a lot of things which I've not gone into too deeply. . . . More or less they are in competition though I don't believe that the CSFA will ever put Cal. U. out of business. At Cal, where the department is headed by Erle Loran, a scholar and a gentleman, the aura of influence remains—as it has been for almost twenty years—Hofmannesque with variations. . . .
>
> There has been in San Francisco, as in New York, a movement among some painters who once played with "free forms" back to figurative representation. Led by David Park, the ideological leader of this local movement, it superficially appears to have won the day, but that's only because people are inclined to accept the honors handed out by juries without really looking at the work or inquiring into the motives of jurors. Elmer Bischoff is a cohort of Park: they have recently taken Richard Diebenkorn into camp as well as Paul Wonner and several others. These older painters are all teachers and wield influence at the grass roots as well as through their tactics of awarding each other top prizes as they take turns on juries. . . .
>
> There've been several one-man shows which reveal the basic ground swell of abstract expressionism in these parts, shows presented both at the CSFA and the DeYoung Museum. . . . Earlier this year Sonia Getchoff showed a selection of her aggressively large canvases. . . . Her husband, James Kelley, showed earlier too at the CSFA. They both paint free forms, although despite acknowledging their force and

potential, their paintings are not wholly realized. Their shows, like most of the paintings, did not hang together for want of unity of style and clarity of vision. . . . While there is not very much direct Oriental influence here, contrary to what one might expect, there are two young Japanese women, Emika Nakano and Nora Yamamoto, who exhibit interesting paintings.

There's a group of underground painters and sculptors who don't play the museum and gallery game, and presumably, they might be the most exciting of the artists. Frank Lobdell did show a selection of figurative works (at the Triangle Gallery) that was a surprise. . . . In group shows I've seen single paintings of Byron McClintock, John Saccaro, Julius Wasserstein, David Kasmore, Felex Ruvolo, and Hassel Smith that I appreciated.

I should mention that the second generation, so to speak, of the original San Francisco nonobjective movement, people like Ernest Briggs and Edward Dugmore, has exerted an influence that is plainly visible in the work of younger artists. This I believe is all to the good. It counteracts the Park ideology and carries on the spirit of Clyfford Still.

1957

Fireboats in front of the Bay Bridge, 1986. Photograph by Steve Ringman.

CZESLAW MILOSZ

Where I Am

*It has been said that the problems that face California today, America must
meet tomorrow. The waves of the future break first on the rocky California
coast, change comes most rapidly. There is truth in this. It misses the point
a little, because no place is like any other place, and California is in many
ways unique. Yet no one can afford to be unaware of the changes and
difficulties that confront California. They are too likely to be the problems of
all the civilized world.*

Raymond F. Dassmann
The Destruction of California

W A L K I N G   A L O N G   the street, I raise my eyes and
see the nuclear laboratories glowing among the eucalyptus trees in
the folds of a hill. I turn, and there is San Francisco Bay, metallic and
darkening now, taking only some of the sky's green, yellow, and
carmine. Berkeley clings to hills which face west, toward the Pacific,
and its best hours–afternoon, dusk, the famous sunsets, evening–are
unspoiled by sea fog. There are many cities and countries in my mind,
but they all stand in relation to the one which surrounds me every day.
The human imagination is spatial and it is constantly constructing an
architectonic whole from landscapes remembered or imagined; it
progresses from what is closest to what is farther away, winding layers
or strands around the single axis, which begins where the feet touch
the ground. Many consequences flow from the spatial nature of the
imagination, and I will return to them frequently. Now I will limit
myself to saying that for me, awake or dreaming, the four corners of
the world begin with the forms almost within reach of my hand. To
the west, the islands and promontories of the bay, the bridges–two
dinosaurs–San Francisco's clustered skyscrapers, the Golden Gate
flaring and fading in the regular intervals of light on steel threads too

fine to be seen, and, beyond the bridge, the open sea. To the east, roads that follow the cliffs, the eucalyptus trees on the slopes, scree the color of a rattlesnake, a tunnel, and empty hills banked up to the horizon – pale green hills tending to rose and violet for a few months a year, then flaxen under the brilliant blue sky, rarely reached by the fog from the sea. To the south, a flat sterile plane inhabited by a million people, the city of Oakland, and above it, the elliptical concrete bands which lead southward to San Jose and Los Angeles. The north, too, is marked by bands bearing three lanes of traffic toward the wine country around Napa and Santa Rosa, and then come the coniferous forests of northern California, where eagles circle above chasms of mist.

My imagination does not venture very far west, where there is nothing but thousands of miles of ocean forever the same; nor does it roam farther east than the Sacramento Valley and its pass in the Sierra Nevadas. Past the Sierra Nevadas it encounters a zero – the empty, wrinkled surface of the planet crossed by jets in a matter of hours. On the other hand, my imagination likes to play with images – it constantly shifts the great deserts of southern California and Arizona, rearranges the rocks (cathedrals? petrified, primeval lizards?) jutting out from the water by the wild Oregon coast, and toys with the orchards in Washington near the Mt. Rainier glacier.

No, picture postcards in prose are not my specialty. But still I find something oppressive in the virginity of this country, virgin in the sense that it seems to be waiting for its names. America was not slowly and gradually put into words over the centuries; and if somebody tried to render it in words, the changes were so great, twenty years much the equal of two hundred elsewhere, that the slate was always being wiped clean. Both here, on the West Coast, and everywhere in America, one is faced with something that is impossible to define by allusions to the "humanistically formed imagination" – something incomprehensible in regard both to the forms taken in by the eye and to the attempt to connect those forms to the lives of human beings. Our species is now on a mad adventure. We are flung into a world which appears to be a nothing, or, at best, a chaos of disjointed masses we must arrange in some order, in some relation to one another – this to the right of that, that to the left of this – using a map's abstract planes.

The disturbing freedom of encountering a plateau, river canyon, or crater where nobody has been before or has at least left no discernible traces . . . which demands an arbitrary choice, not subject to any verification.

1975

RANDY SHILTS

No Cross, No Crown

T H E G L I M M E R of dawn was obscured by a dark curtain of clouds hanging over San Francisco.

Dan White had stayed up all night, eating cupcakes, drinking Cokes, and finally watching the sun work its way over the horizon. White was still moping around the house when Mary Ann woke to go to work at the fried potato stand. She dressed the baby and left for the babysitter's at 7:30 a.m.

White's aid, Denise Apcar, called at 9 a.m. to tell Dan that a group of his supporters planned to present Mayor Moscone with petitions and letters of support from District 8 voters. Since Mary Ann had the car, Dan asked if Denise would come and take him to City Hall. White hung up the phone, showered, shaved, and slipped into his natty three-piece tan suit. He walked downstairs to his basement den and picked up his .38 Smith & Wesson, the Chief's Special model so favored by police officers. He checked the chamber; it was loaded. Stepping into a small closet off the den, he reached to the top shelf and pulled down a box of Remington hollow-headed bullets. He methodically pulled each bullet from the Styrofoam case where they were individually packed. He counted out ten, two chambers' full, slipped the gun into his well-worn holster, snapped the holster to his belt, and then carefully tucked the gun under his vest.

Cyr Copertini, George Moscone's appointments secretary, was surprised to see the mayor's black Lincoln limousine parked by the Polk Street entrance of City Hall when she arrived to work at 8:40 a.m. The mayor rarely arrived before her, but then she remembered today was to be a special day at City Hall. Cyr found her boss ebuliant that morning. He'd gotten a good response to his private soundings about appointing a liberal neighborhood activist to Dan White's supervisorial seat. He'd finally have his working majority on the board. Moscone had originally planned a 10 a.m. press conference to announce the appointment, but he asked Cyr to delay the gathering until 11:30. George decided to take care of some phone work before then.

A cadre of Dan White's supporters were waiting in the mayor's office when Cyr arrived. They wanted to present a stack of petitions to the mayor. Cyr offered to take the papers to him. No, they insisted, they wanted to see Moscone. Copertini returned to her office. George told her he did not want to see the delegation. Copertini was not surprised. Moscone was by nature a jovial man who avoided potentially nasty confrontations at all costs. He still had not told Dan White that he would not be reappointed. Copertini went back to White's supporters, told them the mayor was busy, and promised to give them a receipt swearing that Moscone would have the petitions on his desk within minutes of when they handed them over to her. They relented and gave Cyr the petitions, shortly after 9 a.m.

At about the same time, George Moscone dialed Dianne Feinstein's Pacific Heights home. No, he was not going to reappoint White, he explained, even though the former supervisor insisted he would physically take his seat at that day's board meetings, whether he got it back or not. George returned to writing out by hand his comments for the press conference. Later that morning, his close ally, Assemblyman Willie Brown, dropped in briefly and the two made arrangements to do some Christmas shopping that weekend.

A worried Dianne Feinstein was sitting in her small City Hall office a half hour after talking to Moscone. As president of the board, the decorum-minded Feinstein felt it was her responsibility to prevent the kind of donnybrook that might arise when two men, both claiming to be supervisor from District 8, tried to get in the same chair at that afternoon's board meeting. She called a hurried meeting with a deputy city attorney and the board clerk to see if there were any legal tactics that could circumvent the problem. Finally, she decided she would try to dissuade White from forcing his way into the chambers. She told her aides to try to find White, and tell him she'd like to have a chat before the meeting.

§

Dick Pabich and Jim Rivaldo had rarely seen Harvey in as good a mood as when he bounded into the office at 9 a.m. He was always bouncy on Monday mornings, since each board meeting gave him the chance to put on another show, but that morning, Harvey seemed particularly cheerful. Funding for a gay community center would be voted on that day, and Harvey figured he finally had his sixth vote. He chatted briefly with Jim and Dick, then strolled over to the mayor's office where Moscone told him the news he wanted to hear–Dan White would not get his seat back. Buoyant, Harvey walked down the grand marble staircase and started to make his way toward a cafeteria where he could have his morning roll.

Doug Franks had been thinking about Harvey all morning. Just couldn't get him off his mind, even as he left the senior citizens center where he worked and headed for the library. He was surprised when he ran into Harvey striding down the street.

"I've never seen you so radiant," Doug told him.

"I am," Harvey said. "I'm happy. I just came from George's office. He's not going to reappoint Dan White."

Milk wasn't sure whom the mayor would appoint, but he knew he had the gay center vote and he was confident he had a sixth vote for many other decisions to come. The couple walked together to the cafeteria for breakfast. Harvey spent most of the next fifteen minutes talking excitedly about the march on Washington. No senators or congressmen could speak, he decided, unless they came out. They walked back to Civic Center, where Doug turned to go to the library and Harvey to City Hall. They agreed to get together that night for dinner after the board meeting.

Denise Apcar told Dan White she had seen Harvey leave the mayor's office when she picked White up, about 10:15. Dan told her he wanted to see both George and Harvey once he got to City Hall. Denise noted he was rubbing his hands together and blowing on his fingertips as he talked. "I'm a man. I can take it," he told her. "I just want to talk with them, have them tell me to my face why they won't reappoint me."

Denise dropped White off at City Hall and left to gas up her car. William Melia, a city engineer with a lab overlooking the supervisors' parking lot, first noticed a nervous young man pacing by his window at about 10:25. The man walked back and forth, anxiously glancing into the window where Melia was working. The phone rang and Melia stepped briefly into another room to take the call. As soon as he left the room, he heard the lab window open and the sound of someone jumping to the floor and running out of the lab and into the hall.

"Hey, wait a second," Melia shouted. He knew such an entrance was a sure way to avoid passing through the metal detectors at the public entrances of City Hall.

"I had to get in," White explained. "My aide was supposed to come down and let me in the side door, but she never showed up."

"And you are –"

"– I'm Dan White, the city supervisor. Say, I've got to go." With that, White spun on his heel and left the office.

Mildred Tango, a clerk-typist in the mayor's office, saw White hesitating near the main door of the mayor's office as if he didn't want to use that entrance. Inside sat the mayor's police bodyguard; White knew that, since he had once worked the relief shift as the mayor's police bodyguard during the Alioto administration. White saw Tango unlocking a side door to the mayor's office on her rounds to collect the morning mail. She recognized White and let him follow her into the hallway that led to the mayor's suite. White presented himself at Cyr Copertini's desk at about 10:30 a.m.

"Hello, Cyr. May I see the mayor?"

"He has someone with him, but let me go check."

Moscone grimaced at the news. He was clearly uncomfortable with the idea of a confrontation on what promised to be such a splendid morning.

"Give me a minute to think," the mayor said. "Oh, all right. Tell him I'll see him, but he'll have to wait a minute."

Cyr asked if George wanted someone to sit in on the meeting. Press secretary Mel Wax often served such duty to make sure disgruntled politicos did not later lay claim to specious mayoral promises.

"No. No," George said, "I'll see him alone."

"Why don't you let me bring Mel in?" Copertini persisted.

"No, no. I will see him alone."

Copertini told White the mayor would be a few minutes. Dan seemed nervous.

"Would you like to see a newspaper while you're waiting?" Copertini asked.

He didn't.

"That's all right. There's nothing in it anyway, unless you want to read about Caroline Kennedy having turned twenty-one."

"Twenty-one? Is that right?" White shook his head. "Yeah. That's all so long ago. It's even more amazing when you think that John-John is now eighteen."

Moscone buzzed for White.

"Good girl, Cyr," Dan White said.

An aide told Dianne Feinstein that he had just seen Dan go into the mayor's office. She sent her administrative assistant, Peter Nardoza, to find White. As an extra precaution, Feinstein opened her office door so she could see him if he slipped into the long hallway on which the supervisors' offices were clustered.

Around the same time Dan White walked into George Moscone's office, Harvey Milk was stepping up the marble staircase to his aides' offices. Dick Pabich was working on correspondence. Jim Rivaldo was talking to a gay lawyer, who, Harvey knew, had a fondness for leather during his late-night carousing.

"Well, where are your leathers?" Milk asked.

"Don't worry," Jim joked. "He's got leather underwear on."

Milk excused himself to go to the bank. He was expecting Carl Carlson with the cashier's check. Jim and Harvey agreed to get together again at 11:30 so they could go to the swearing-in of the new supervisor.

Harvey walked to his office, but Carlson hadn't arrived yet. Harvey was on the phone when he came in, about 10:50; Carl sat down to do some typing until Harvey was finished.

Dan White and Moscone hadn't been in the mayor's large ceremonial office more than five minutes before Cyr heard White's voice raised, shouting at Moscone. George hated scenes and decided to try to mollify the former supervisor by inviting him to a small den off his office where he kept a wet bar. He lit a cigarette, poured two drinks, and turned to see White brandishing a revolver. White pulled the trigger and fired a bullet into Moscone's arm, near the shoulder, and immediately shot a second slug into the mayor's right pectoral. Moscone sank to the floor as the second bullet tore into his lung. Dan White knelt next to the prostrate body, poised the gun six inches from the right side of Moscone's head, and fired a bullet that ripped through Moscone's earlobe and into his brain. He pulled the trigger again and another bullet sped from the revolver, through Moscone's ear canal and into the brain.

White methodically emptied the four spent cartridges and the one live bullet from his Smith & Wesson and crammed them into the right pocket of his tan blazer. He had special bullets for his next task; the hollow-headed dum-dum bullets that explode on impact, ripping a hole into the victim two to three times the size of the slug itself. White slipped the five bullets into the revolver's chamber, stepped out a side door, and dashed toward the other side of City Hall where the supervisors' offices were.

The four dull thuds sounded like a car backfiring, Cyr thought, so she looked out her office window, but saw nothing. Rudy Nothenberg, Moscone's top deputy, had an 11 a.m. appointment with the mayor. He was ready to cancel it when he noted that George's meeting with White was taking longer than expected. He was relieved when he saw White hurriedly leave the office; he'd get his chance to talk to the mayor after all.

Dick Pabich saw White dashing toward the supervisorial offices. What a jerk, Pabich thought, running around here like he's still somebody important.

Peter Nardoza saw him rushing into the hallway outside Dianne Feinstein's office.

"Dianne would like to talk to you," Nardoza said.

"Well, that will have to wait a couple of moments," White answered sharply.

Feinstein heard the exchange, then saw White flash by her office door.

"Dan," she called.

"I have something to do first," White said.

Harvey and Carl were getting ready to go to the bank when White stuck his head into Milk's office.

"Say, Harv, can I see you?"

"Sure."

White took Harvey to his old office across the hall. He noticed that his name plate had already been removed from the door. Once Milk stepped inside, White planted himself between him and door. He drew his revolver and fired. A sharp streak of pain sped through Harvey.

"Oh no," Milk shouted. "N–" He reflexively raised his hand to try to protect himself.

White knew that bullets went through arms, and he fired again, cutting short Harvey's cry. The slug tore into Harvey's right wrist, ripped into his chest and out again, finally lodging near his left elbow. Another dum-dum bullet pounded Milk in the chest. He was falling now, toward the window. As he crumpled to his knees, Dan White took careful aim from across the office. The first three bullets alone would not have killed Harvey. White took careful aim at the staggering figure and fired a fourth bullet which sliced into the back of his head and out the other side, spraying blood against the wall. The shots sounded so loud they startled White; louder than the shots in Moscone's office. Harvey had fallen to the floor. White gripped the revolver's handle and pulled the trigger once more. The bullet left only a dime-sized wound on the outside of Harvey's skull, but shards from its hollow tip exploded when they struck Harvey's skull, tearing and ripping into his brain. Harvey Milk died at approximately 10:55 a.m. on the dark gray morning of November 27, 1978, a year and half short of his fiftieth birthday.

Dianne Feinstein had heard the first shot and known exactly what it was–Dan White had committed suicide. Then she heard more shots and felt an unspeakable horror. She had to get up from her desk. She had to force her brain and body to function together, to move her out of her chair, out of her office. But she felt she was going too slow, too slow, she had to go faster. She saw White walk by her door. She couldn't move fast enough as she smelled the odor of gunpowder that wafted down the hall.

Carl Carlson thought at first maybe the sounds were firecrackers, but he had heard Harvey shout and knew it was not firecrackers. Carlson stepped out of Harvey's office in time to see White walk out of his office, pull the door shut behind him, glance coldly at Carlson, then walk calmly down the hall. Feinstein joined Carl at the door to White's office.

Feinstein shoved the door open and saw Harvey's body sprawled out, his face toward the window, lying in a spreading pool of blood. Feinstein's mind shifted into automatic. All her emergency medical training told her to take the injured man's pulse. She knelt to take Harvey's arm; she put her finger to Harvey's wrist and it quickly oozed into the wound left by the second bullet. Blood and tissue engulfed her finger.

White ran into Denise Apcar's office. "Give me the keys," he shouted to her. "Give me the keys."

Apcar nervously handed White her car keys and he dashed out the door.

Only two or three minutes had passed since Dan White had left the mayor's office. Rudy Nothenberg was waiting for George to buzz him for their 11 a.m. appointment. It didn't make sense – Rudy had seen Dan White leave. What was taking George so long? Tentatively he stuck his head in Moscone's main office, then walked into the adjoining den and saw George's feet. He figured Moscone had fainted until he got closer and saw the blood flowing from his head onto the carpet. Moscone still held a lit cigarette in his right hand; it was burning a hole into the back of his tie.

"Get in here," he shouted to Cyr. "Call an ambulance. Get the police."

Dianne Feinstein bounded into Harvey's office with Carl. She grabbed a phone, frantically called the police chief. The chief's lines, however, were all busy with calls from the mayor's office, but Feinstein didn't know that and kept dialing desperately. What's the matter she thought. Why can't I get through?

A few blocks away, Dan White was at a fast-food joint calling Mary Ann. Something happened, he said. He needed to meet her right away at St. Mary's Cathedral.

§

Carl Carlson was on Harvey's other phone, buzzing Dick Pabich. Dick had just come into his office telling Jim Rivaldo how weird White had looked. He answered Carl's call.

"Harvey's been shot. Call an ambulance."

"Oh, sure," Pabich answered sarcastically.

"No time for messing around. I'm serious."

"What?"

Pabich jumped from his desk and raced toward Harvey's office. Rivaldo followed him into the corridor and saw a cadre of armed police racing toward the mayor's office. He followed them, thinking that was the best way to find the source of the ruckus, when Pabich ran back and shouted at the officers, "No, no. It's not the mayor's office. It's down here." Several officers split off and followed Pabich to the supervisors' offices. Chief Gain arrived shortly after and sought out Feinstein, telling her the mayor had been killed too.

"Oh, no," Feinstein gasped.

Aides now circled Dan White's office door. Dick Pabich remembered seeing White rush by and arrived at the obvious conclusion. "Dan White did it," he said. A conservative board clerk who had never had much use for either Milk or his gay entourage scolded Dick: "How can you say such a thing?"

Mary Ann White left the cab and hurried across the wide brick terrazo that stretches in front of the modernistic St. Mary's Cathedral. She quickly spotted her husband in the chapel.

"I shot the mayor and Harvey," he told her.

They talked for a few minutes. Mary Ann said she'd stand by him through any ordeal. They started walking the few blocks to Northern Station, the police station where White had once worked as a member of the San Francisco Police Department. As they walked, Mary Ann kept her hand around Dan White's waist, holding firmly onto the revolver in the belt holster, fearing he might suddenly grab the gun and shoot himself.

Hundreds of reporters were rushing to City Hall. Stories were muddled. Was the mayor shot? Was he dead? No, it was Harvey Milk. Milk and one of his aides? Were they dead? And, of course, the question that immediately came to all the reporters' minds: Were the shootings the work of a Peoples Temple hit squad? Jim Jones's code word for the suicide rituals–"white night"–was also supposed to trigger cadres of Peoples Temple assassins, according to reports from Jonestown. Had they started doing their bloody work?

At 11:20 a.m., a shaken Dianne Feinstein stepped from the supervisors' offices to make the announcement. Her face looked haggard; Police Chief Gain had to support her as she spoke.

"As president of the board of supervisors, it my duty to inform you that both Mayor Moscone and Supervisor Harvey Milk have been shot and killed."

The reporters recoiled with a collective gasp that nearly drowned out Feinstein's next words.

"Supervisor Dan White is the suspect."

Across City Hall, outside the mayor's office, press secretary Mel Wax made the same announcement to another knot of reporters. Wax added that under the provisions of the city charter, Board of Supervisors President Feinstein was now acting mayor.

Doug Franks easily found the book he sought in the library, checked it out, and walked the five blocks back to the senior center where he worked. When he arrived, he saw that somebody had taken a portable television to the living room where the seniors now huddled, murmuring in shock. He heard the announcer's raspy voice: "Again, Supervisor Milk and Mayor Moscone have been killed."

Doug stumbled; he felt he was going to faint; he had just hugged Harvey, checked out a book, walked five blocks and now Harvey was dead. That's all the time it took–and someone you love is dead.

At 11:25 a.m., Dan and Mary Ann White arrived at Northern Station.

"It's there," White said, pointing to his right hip.

The officer took the revolver from White's belt and the four spent .38 special casings and one bullet from his blazer pocket. White wanted to turn himself in at Northern Station because his friend, Paul Chignell, the vice-president of the Police Officers' Association, worked there. White asked Chignell to make sure the press stayed away from his wife.

White seemed calm and detached, not particularly distraught, Chignell noted. White asked, "Is he dead, Paul?"

Police and officials from the coroner's office busily snapped pictures of the two undisturbed bodies for nearly an hour. Cleve Jones and Scott Smith arrived at City Hall shortly after the shootings. At first, wary supervisors' aides would not admit Smith to Harvey's office; nobody recognized him. Jones finally pulled Scott into the secured area, where grim-faced police mixed with sobbing board clerks and the small group of Harvey's stunned aides.

"It's over. We've lost it," Jim Rivaldo kept muttering to no one in particular. He felt drawn to the door of Dan White's office where Harvey still lay. The police officer at the door warned him away from the grisly sight, but Rivaldo felt he needed to connect with the physical reality of Harvey's death. He stood outside the door as policemen were turning the corpse over to put it in the black rubber body bag. Jones stepped up and peered over Rivaldo's shoulder as the officers struggled with Milk's lanky frame. Harvey was blue now, his discolored head rolling limply, his suit and thick dark hair stained with clots of blood. Jim stared at the bloodstained wall and tried to retrace the path of Harvey's stumble to calculate what Milk had seen last. Harvey had fallen facing the window, so that before Dan White had pumped the last bullets into his staggering victim, Harvey could have looked out the window and seen the grand facade of the San Francisco War Memorial Opera House across the street.

The police finally succeeded in getting Harvey's body into the bag, which was then put on a gurney, covered with a crisp, creased hospital sheet and pushed down the hallway past his old office. At noon, the doors of the supervisors' offices opened and police wheeled the gurney into a nearby elevator—the elevator Harvey had always forsaken in favor of the grand staircase—then out a side entrance of City Hall into a waiting coroner's ambulance.

At about the same time Milk's body was being slipped on a rack beneath the stretcher bearing George Moscone, Dan White was sitting down with homicide inspectors Ed Erdelatz and Frank Falzon. Falzon had attended St. Elizabeth's Grammar School with White and later coached him on the police softball team; Dan had been his star player. Falzon read White his Miranda rights and then taped his twenty-four-minute confession. The interrogation of White – or, some said, the lack of it – would later prove to be one of the most controversial aspects of the murder case.

By noon, a small silent crowd was gathering outside City Hall, standing below the dome, staring dumbly at the police, reporters, and city officials who scurried up the wide stairs. The golden-bordered city flag above the portico was pulled to half-mast as the crowd grew. Some dropped flowers on the steps. Before long, a mound grew and an angry young man put a hand-lettered sign amid the blossoms: "Happy, Anita?"

The EXTRA editions were hitting the newstands on Castro Street with their bold headlines: "Mayor, Milk Slain; Dan White Seized." Knots of Castro residents clustered on the corners, reading the newspapers in disbelief. Many of the bars and businesses quickly closed their doors and hung black bunting at their entrances. Black-bordered pictures of Harvey appeared in shop windows, store clerks slipped on black armbands. People started coming to Castro Street, to gather where they had so many times before in past crises.

Frank Robinson had spent the morning working on his new submarine disaster novel when he took his afternoon break and heard the news from a restaurant waitress. He went home, tuned into a news radio station, and started taking the dozens of calls from Harvey's other friends. He remembered the early days he and Harvey had spent bullshitting about politics on the old maroon couch in the funky Victorian storefront on Castro Street. A sense of isolation gripped Robinson as he realized this all was over now. He had no anger or hatred for Dan White. For Frank, White did not even exist as a person; White was just a tool, he thought. It was the whole society that hated gays; the game had always been stacked. You could be the best man in the world, he thought, and still the society would crucify you.

A few blocks away, Harvey's political friends from the San Francisco Gay Democratic Club were conferring at Harry Britt's house. They decided to respond to the assassinations just as they had responded to the crises of past years – a march from Castro Street to City Hall. The permits, details, and announcements fell into place as the afternoon wore on. They asked mourners to bring candles.

President Carter's statement that afternoon expressed "a sense of outrage and sadness at the senseless killing" of the two men. He praised Supervisor Milk as a "hard-working and dedicated supervisor, a leader of San Francisco's gay community, who kept his promise to represent all constituents."

The board met briefly for its regularly scheduled Monday meeting at 2 p.m. "This is an unparalleled time for San Francisco, and we need to keep together," said Acting Mayor Feinstein. "I think we all have to share the same sense of outrage, the same sense of shame, the same sense of sorrow and the same sense of anger." Feinstein urged the public to "go into a state of very deep and meaningful mourning and to express its sorrow with a dignity and an inner examination. . . ."

Medora Payne was on her lunch break at Lowell High School when a friend told her that Harvey and the mayor had been killed by Dan White. She had to be kidding, Medora thought, but her chemistry teacher confirmed the news. Medora could tell by the look in her teacher's eyes that it was true. She broke into tears, apologized to her friend for not believing her, and asked if she would stay with her while she wept for the funny man she had met so many years before when she took her parents' film to get developed at Castro Camera. She spent the next few hours walking around the high school's cinder track, crying and remembering the nights she had spent licking envelopes and handing out brochures for Harvey Milk.

Tom O'Horgan heard the news in New York City only hours before he went to the mailbox to find the letter Harvey had posted after he went to the opera, the letter ending with the exclamation – "Life is worth living." A few hours later, Jack McKinley, hysterical from grief, joined him. O'Horgan loaned him the money to make the trip to San Francisco.

Mrs. Gina Moscone and the mayor's mother were attending a cousin's funeral seventy miles north of San Francisco when the assassinations occurred. The mayor's four children had converged on their home from their various schools by 1 p.m., when they finally arrived home. Gina took a few steps from her car and collapsed into a friend's arms. She had heard of the news of her husband's killing on the car radio.

"This is Harvey Milk, speaking on Friday, November 18, 1977. This is to be played only in the event of my death by assassination. I've given considerable thought to this, not just since the election. I've been thinking about this for some time prior to the election and certainly over the years. I fully realize that a person who stands for what I stand for, an activist, a gay activist, becomes the target or potential target for a person who is insecure, terrified, afraid, or very disturbed with themselves. Knowing that I could be assassinated at any moment or any time, I feel it's important that some people should understand my thoughts, so the following are my thoughts, my wishes, my desires, whatever, and I'd like to pass them on and played for the appropriate people."

Most of the people in the room had known Harvey had made this tape. Now, only three hours after the shootings, they were following Harvey's wish that it be played. Harvey knew enough about the machinations of City Hall politics to understand that the outer trappings of sorrow would not keep politicos from immediately maneuvering to grab his seat. He had made the tape to ensure that his post would not fall into the hands of the gay moderates, whom he had so long opposed. Pabich, Rivaldo, Jones, Carlson, and Scott Smith, along with a handful of others, had originally walked into Harvey's office to play the tape, but Scott had seen Harvey's honorary clown certificate and the memorabilia cluttering Harvey's walls and could not bear to stay in the room, so they now huddled in Supervisor Carol Ruth Silver's cubicle, listening to Harvey's political will.

"I stood for more than just a candidate. I think there was a strong differential between somebody like Rick Stokes and myself. I have never considered myself a candidate. I have always considered myself part of a movement, part of a candidacy. I've considered the movement the candidate. I think there's a distinction between those who use the movement and those who are part of the movement. I think I was always part of the movement. I wish that I had time to explain everything I did. Almost everything was done with an eye on the gay movement."

Harvey launched into vociferous attacks on the four people who he said should not succeed him: Jim Foster, Rick Stokes, Jo Daly, and Frank Fitch, all past presidents of the Alice Toklas Democratic Club Harvey had battled so long. He then listed the four people who he said should be considered as replacements, strongly praising Frank Robinson and Bob Ross, his first choices, suggesting Harry Britt as a third choice, and offhandedly mentioning Anne Kronenberg as well. Scott sat through the tapes silently, still numbed by the killing. Cleve broke into sobs as Harvey's voice talked on. Jim Rivaldo, meanwhile, began to marvel at the perfection of the destiny Harvey had created for himself. There Harvey was, carefully instructing his friends on what to do next, weighing the political situation and prodding his allies to keep up the fight. Rivaldo felt torn between the tragedy of the day and this sense of marvel that Harvey was living out an extraordinary final act. He had known that his death would be another step in a historical process, and was even now counseling his associates in how to use it. Rivaldo began to think less of Harvey, a man who had been killed, than Harvey the actor, still performing exquisite political theater.

Even as they listened to the tape, reporters were clamoring for a statement from Harvey's friends. In the next paragraphs, they found it.

"The other aspect of the tapes is the business of what would happened should there be an assassination. I cannot prevent some people from feeling angry and frustrated and mad, but I hope they will take that frustration and that madness and instead of demonstrating or anything of that type, I would hope they would take the power and I would hope that five, ten, one hundred, a thousand would rise. I would like to see every gay doctor come out, every gay lawyer, every gay architect come out, stand up and let that world know. That would do more to end prejudice overnight than anybody would imagine. I urge them to do that, urge them to come out. Only that way will we start to achieve our rights."

Harvey closed his tape with the lecture most in the room had heard many times before; maybe that's why it wasn't included in the press release that Harvey's lawyer, John Wahl, read to reporters soon afterward. The last words that most of them would ever hear Harvey Milk speak concerned the one commodity he believed he had brought to gays— hope: "I ask for the movement to continue, for the movement to grow because last week I got the phone call from Altoona, Pennsylvania, and my election gave somebody else, one more person, hope. And after all, that's what this is all about. It's not about personal gain, not about ego, not about power—it's about giving those young people out there in the Altoona, Pennsylvanias hope. You gotta give them hope."

At Harry Britt's house, the leaders of the San Francisco Gay Democratic Club were beginning to arrive at the same consensus developing in Harvey's office about who should follow Milk as supervisor. Frank Robinson, Harvey's first choice, had neither the experience nor the desire to be a supervisor. The second choice, Bob Ross, had never been close to Harvey's younger political coterie. They worried his instincts were more conservative than their own liberalism, so they decided to try to engineer the selection away from him. Few of Harvey's intimates took Harry Britt seriously as a potential successor. His political experience was largely limited to Milk's campaigns and their own fledging Democratic club. His long sideburns and west Texas drawl convinced most that he was an unrefined yahoo, ill-suited for the role as the city's chief gay spokesperson. That left Anne Kronenberg. As Harvey's aide and former campaign manager, Anne knew many of the political connections who would be necessary to persuade the next mayor. Though the group making the decision was almost exclusively male, most liked the idea of advancing a lesbian for the job, since lesbian-feminists frequently carped that the gay movement seemed dominated by men. Slowly, with many phone calls between Britt's house and City Hall, the consensus began to build for Kronenberg who was then on a plane, flying home from a visit with her parents.

Joe Campbell saw a bold headline mentioning something about a mayor, but since stories about mayors usually meant talk about politics, Joe didn't bother to give the paper an extra glance. He wasn't interested in politics. Later that same Monday afternoon, he was driving toward his isolated Marin County home when he picked up a hunky young hitchhiker.

"Too bad about the mayor and that other guy," the rider casually said.

"What about?"

"You haven't heard? They got shot. The mayor and some other guy. He was a supervisor."

"Milk?"

"Yeah, that's it. Harvey Milk."

"Are you sure he's dead?"

"Yeah. Shot in the head."

Campbell careened his station wagon to the shoulder of the gravel road and collapsed into tears.

"That's my lover," he sobbed.

The hitchhiker held Campbell for five minutes as Joe wept for the man he had lived with for six years in what seemed like another lifetime. As the late afternoon sun began to set over the Pacific, Campbell began his frantic drive into San Francisco.

Though most of his friends at City Hall spent much of the day saying how shocked they were that Dan White would kill the mayor and supervisor, Undersheriff Jim Denman had no trouble believing that Dan White was capable of the crime. Denman had spent years working with the police subculture and his brief meetings with Dan White had indicated the former supervisor fit the police mold well – rigid, conservative, and anti-gay. But White was also a prisoner who needed protection. With the image of Jack Ruby shooting Lee Harvey Oswald haunting him, Denman personally supervised Dan White's first day in jail. Denman was not particularly surprised that police treated White with deference, though he was taken aback when one policeman gave White a pat on the behind, as if the killer had just scored the winning touchdown for the high school football team. What did amaze Denman was the cool calm with which White handled himself. He was controlled, businesslike, and exceedingly polite. If he was in shock, Denman thought, it was at best a very mild shock. The only time White showed any sign of emotion was when he called his mother. "Hi, mom, how you doing?" he said. "I guess you heard." A few minutes into the conversation, White's voice turned soft and caring, like it might crack – and then White caught himself and his voice turned hard again.

When the cell door slammed behind him, White betrayed no hint of emotion. He simply laid back on his cot, folded his arms behind his

The funeral of Mayor George Moscone and Supervisor Harvey Milk at the City Hall Rotunda, 1978. Photograph by Arthur Frisch.

head and stared at the ceiling. For three days Denman watched White for any sign that he understood what he had done. Never did a tear, a questioning glance, or any sign of remorse cross the former policeman's face.

From radio reports, Joe Campbell learned of a memorial service for Harvey at a makeshift gay community center near City Hall. He sat near the back of the hall, still in shock, and overheard someone whisper that Harvey's lover was in the front row. Campbell glanced to Doug Franks but couldn't think of anything to say. As the service began, Campbell realized that the speakers were talking about a man he didn't know, certainly not about the Harvey Milk he had met at Riis Park Beach in 1956. Joe never understood what Harvey meant with all his politics business, but he had no doubt that it wasn't anything worth getting shot about. He was still dazed when he left the service. Since Joe knew little of Castro Street or the marches, he didn't know that as he left the memorial service, thousands were converging on Castro Street. Instead, Joe drifted to a friend's apartment, where he spent the night.

The crowd started gathering at 7:30 p.m. on the corner of Castro and Market Streets, the place that would one day be called Harvey Milk Plaza. Hundreds, then 5000 and soon 10,000 came with their candles. From a nearby balcony came the mournful wail of a conch shell as the crowd silently grew. The businesses had all closed now, their commercial displays replaced with tributes to Harvey Milk and George Moscone. Cleve Jones and his street radical friends had been training monitors all afternoon at Jones's apartment a block up Castro. The police were worried about violence, but the throng, which had been so rambunctious during protests over gay rights referenda, needed little quelling as it stood dumbly, waiting for direction. A bank of television lights flicked on across Market Street and the crowd started moving toward it. The monitors, however, were not yet in place. As titular leader of street marches, Jones scrambled to a promontory where he could soothe the crowd. From a bullhorn, he shouted words from a folk song by lesbian singer Meg Christian:

Can we be like drops of water
Falling on the stone
Splashing, breaking, dispersing in air
Weaker than the stone by far
But be aware that as time goes by
The rock will wear away.

The crowd stopped and stared mutely at Jones while the monitors raced into position.

Three men, carrying the American, California, and San Francisco flags, took their places at the beginning of the procession, flanked by a lone drummer, slowly thrumping a muffled beat while in the night, the sound of a distant trumpet murmured the old Bob Dylan song "Blowin' in the Wind." Slowly, the march pushed down the boulevard, stretching for five and then ten blocks while thousands more were still arriving on Castro Street. Then tens of thousands of candles glimmered in the night, their flickers merging with the lights on the hills around Castro Street so that from a distance it appeared that a thousand stars had fallen onto the avenue and were moving slowly toward City Hall, flowing from the hills of San Francisco and the dark night above.

1982

North Beach burning after the earthquake, 1906. Photograph by J. B. Monaco.

JACK LONDON

The Fire

THE EARTHQUAKE shook down in San Francisco hundreds of thousands of dollars' worth of walls and chimneys. But the conflagration that followed burned up hundreds of millions of dollars' worth of property. There is no estimating within hundreds of millions the actual danger wrought. Not in history has a modern imperial city been so completely destroyed. San Francisco is gone. Nothing remains of it but memories and a fringe of dwelling-houses on its outskirts. Its industrial section is wiped out. Its business section is wiped out. Its social and residential section is wiped out. The factories and warehouses, the great stores and newspaper buildings, the hotels and the palaces of the nabobs, are all gone. Remains only the fringe of dwelling houses on the outskirts of what was once San Francisco.

Within an hour after the earthquake shock the smoke of San Francisco's burning was a lurid tower visible a hundred miles away. And for three days and nights this lurid tower swayed in the sky, reddening the sun, darkening the day, and filling the land with smoke.

On Wednesday morning at a quarter past five came the earthquake. A minute later the flames were leaping upward. In a dozen different quarters, south of Market Street, in the working-class ghetto, and in the factories, fires started. There was no opposing the flames. There was no organization, no communication. All the cunning adjustments of a twentieth century city had been smashed by the earthquake. The streets were humped into ridges and depressions, and piled with the debris of fallen walls. The steel rails were twisted into perpendicular and horizontal angles. The telephone and telegraph systems were disrupted. And the great water-mains had burst. All the shrewd contrivances and safeguards of man had been thrown out of gear by thirty seconds' twitching of the earth-crust.

The Fire Made Its Own Draft.

By Wednesday afternoon, inside of twelve hours, half the heart of the city was gone. At that time I watched the vast conflagration from out on the bay. It was dead calm. Not a flicker of wind stirred. Yet from every side wind was pouring in upon the city. East, west, north and south, strong winds were blowing upon the doomed city. The heated air rising made an enormous suck. Thus did the fire itself build its own colossal chimney through the atmosphere. Day and night this dead calm continued, and yet, near to the flames, the wind was often half a gale, so mighty was the suck.

Wednesday night saw the destruction of the very heart of the city. Dynamite was lavishly used, and many of San Francisco's proudest structures were crumbled by man himself into ruins, but there was no withstanding the onrush of the flames. Time and again successful stands were made by the fire-fighters, but every time the flames flanked around on either side, or came up from the rear, and turned to defeat the hard-won victory.

An enumeration of the buildings destroyed would be a directory of San Francisco. An enumeration of the buildings undestroyed would be a line and several addresses. An enumeration of the deeds of heroism would stock a library and bankrupt the Carnegie medal fund. An enumeration of the dead—will never be made. All vestiges of them were destroyed by the flames. The number of the victims of the earthquake will never be known. South of Market Street, where the loss of life was particularly heavy, was the first to catch fire.

Remarkable as it may seem, Wednesday night, while the whole city crashed and roared into ruin, was a quiet night. There were no crowds. There was no shouting and yelling. There was no hysteria, no disorder. I passed Wednesday night in the path of the advancing flames, and in all those terrible hours I saw not one woman who wept, not one man who was excited, not one person who was in the slightest degree panic-stricken.

Before the flames, throughout the night, fled tens of thousands of homeless ones. Some were wrapped in blankets. Others carried bundles of bedding and dear household treasures. Sometimes a whole family was harnessed to a carriage or delivery wagon that was weighted down with their possessions. Baby buggies, toy wagons, and go-carts were used as trucks, while every other person was dragging a trunk. Yet everybody was gracious. The most perfect courtesy obtained. Never, in all San Francisco's history, were her people so kind and courteous as on this night of terror.

A Caravan of Trunks.

All night these tens of thousands fled before the flames. Many of them, the poor people from the labor ghetto, had fled all day as well. They had left their homes burdened with possessions. Now and again they lightened up, flinging out upon the street clothing and treasures they had dragged for miles.

They held on longest to their trunks, and over these trunks many a strong man broke his heart that night. The hills of San Francisco are steep, and up these hills, mile after mile, were the trunks dragged. Everywhere were trunks, with across them lying their exhausted owners, men and women. Before the march of the flames were flung picket lines of soldiers. And a block at a time, as the flames advanced, these pickets retreated. One of their tasks was to keep the trunk-pullers moving. The exhausted creatures, stirred on by the menace of bayonets, would arise and struggle up the steep pavements, pausing from weakness every five or ten feet.

Often, after surmounting a heart-breaking hill, they would find another wall of flame advancing upon them at right angles and be compelled to change anew the line of their retreat. In the end, completely played out, after toiling for a dozen hours like giants, thousands of them were compelled to abandon their trunks. Here the shopkeepers and soft members of the middle class were at a disadvantage. But the workingmen dug holes in vacant lots and backyards and buried their trunks.

The Doomed City.

At nine o'clock Wednesday evening I walked down through the very heart of the city. I walked through miles and miles of magnificent buildings and towering skyscrapers. Here was no fire. All was in perfect order. The police patrolled the streets. Every building had its watchman at the door. And yet it was doomed, all of it. There was no water. The dynamite was giving out. And at right angles two different conflagrations were sweeping down upon it.

At one o'clock in the morning I walked down through the same section. Everything still stood intact. There was no fire. And yet there was a change. A rain of ashes was falling. The watchmen at the doors were gone. The police had been withdrawn. There were no firemen, no fire-engines, no men fighting with dynamite. The district had been absolutely abandoned. I stood at the corner of Kearny and Market, in the very innermost heart of San Francisco. Kearny Street was deserted. Half a dozen blocks away it was burning on both sides. The street was a wall of flame. And against this wall of flame, silhouetted sharply, were two United States cavalrymen, sitting their horses, calmly watching. That was all. Not another person was in sight. In the intact heart of the city two troopers sat their horses and watched.

Surrender was complete. There was no water. The sewers had long since been pumped dry. There was no dynamite. Another fire had broken out further uptown, and now from three sides conflagrations were sweeping down. The fourth side had been burned earlier in the day. In that direction stood the tottering walls of the Examiner building, the burned-out Call building, the smoldering ruins of the Grand Hotel, and the gutted, devastated, dynamited Palace Hotel.

The following will illustrate the sweep of the flames and the inability of men to calculate their spread. At eight o'clock Wednesday evening I passed through Union Square. It was packed with refugees. Thousands of them had gone to bed on the grass. Government tents had been set up, supper was being cooked, and the refugees were lining up for free meals.

At half-past one in the morning three sides of Union Square were in flames. The fourth side, where stood the great St. Francis Hotel, was still holding out. An hour later, ignited from top and sides, the St. Francis was flaming heavenward. Union Square, heaped high with mountains of trunks, was deserted. Troops, refugees, and all had retreated.

A Fortune for a Horse.

It was at Union Square that I saw a man offering a thousand dollars for a team of horses. He was in charge of a truck piled high with trunks from some hotel. It had been hauled here into what was considered safety, and the horses had been taken out. The flames were on three sides of the Square, and there were no horses.

Also, at this time, standing beside the truck, I urged a man to seek safety in flight. He was all but hemmed in by several conflagrations. He was an old man and he was on crutches. Said he: "Today is my birthday. Last night I was worth thirty thousand dollars. I bought five bottles of wine, some delicate fish, and other things for my birthday dinner. I have had no dinner, and all I own are these crutches."

I convinced him of his danger and started him limping on his way. An hour later, from a distance, I saw the truck-load of trunks burning merrily in the middle of the street.

On Thursday morning, at a quarter past five, just twenty-four hours after the earthquake, I sat on the steps of a small residence on Nob Hill. With me sat Japanese, Italians, Chinese, and negroes—a bit of the cosmopolitan flotsam of the wreck of the city. All about were the palaces of the nabob pioneers of Forty-nine. To the east and south, at right angles, were advancing two mighty walls of flame.

I went inside with the owner of the house on the steps of which I sat. He was cool and cheerful and hospitable. "Yesterday morning," he said, "I was worth six hundred thousand dollars. This morning this house is all I have left. It will go in fifteen minutes." He pointed to a large cabinet. "That is my wife's collection of china. This rug upon which we stand is a present. It cost fifteen hundred dollars. Try that piano. Listen to its tone. There are few like it. There are no horses. The flames will be here in fifteen minutes."

Outside, the old Mark Hopkins residence, a palace, was just catching fire. The troops were falling back and driving the refugees before them. From every side came the roaring flames, the crashing walls, and the detonations of dynamite.

The Dawn of the Second Day.

I passed out of the house. Day was trying to dawn through the smoke-pall. A sickly light was creeping over the face of things. Once only the sun broke through the smoke-pall, blood-red, and showing a quarter of its usual size. The smoke-pall itself, viewed from beneath, was a rose color that pulsed and fluttered with lavender shades. Then it turned to mauve and yellow and dun. There was no sun. And so dawned the second day on stricken San Francisco.

An hour later I was creeping past the shattered dome of the City Hall. Than it there was no better exhibit of the destructive force of the earthquake. Most of the stone had been shaken from the great dome, leaving standing the naked framework of steel. Market Street was piled high with the wreckage, and across the wreckage lay the overthrown pillars of the City Hall, shattered into crosswise sections.

This section of the city, with the exception of the Mint and the Postoffice, was already a waste of smoking ruins. Here and there through the smoke, creeping warily under the shadows of tottering walls, emerged occasional men and women. It was like the meeting of the handful of survivors after the day of the end of the world.

On Mission Street lay a dozen steers, in a neat row stretching across the street, just as they had been struck down by the flying ruins of the earthquake. The fire had passed through afterward and roasted them. The human dead had been carried away before the fire came. At another place on Mission Street I saw a milk-wagon. A steel telegraph pole had smashed down sheer through the driver's seat and crushed the front wheels. The milk cans lay scattered around.

All day Thursday, and all Thursday night, all day Friday and Friday night, the flames still raged.

Friday night saw the flames finally conquered, though not until Russian Hill and Telegraph Hill had been swept and three-quarters of a mile of wharves and docks had been licked up.

The Last Stand.

The great stand of the fire-fighters was made Thursday night on Van Ness avenue. Had they failed here, the comparatively few remaining houses of the city would have been swept. Here were the magnificent residences of the second generation of San Francisco nabobs, and these, in a solid zone, were dynamited down across the path of the fire.

1906

KAY BOYLE

Seeing the Sights in San Francisco

THERE ARE any number of unique spots of interest in this vicinity that are, unfortunately, not known to the majority of tourists who flock throughout the year to our beautiful and festive city. I have jotted down a few notes about two or three of these off-the-beaten-track places which vacationers should not fail to see.

Last year I frequently suggested to sojourners in these parts that Sunday was the best day of the week to make a tour of the fabulous Golden Gate Cemetery which lies in all its verdant beauty in the rolling countryside just beyond South San Francisco. On Sunday, one did not at that time run the weekday risk of being delayed an hour or more at the gates by half a dozen or so hearses bearing flag-draped coffins, and by the unavoidable accompanying press of the cars of families and friends.

Happily, this year the same problem does not exist on any day of the week, for practically every well-tended inch of that vast, flowering expanse is now symmetrically covered with gleaming white headstones. As of late June, only the dependents of servicemen already resting there are being accepted, and this makes for a far more leisurely atmosphere. Thus a visit may be planned for any day that suits the sightseer's schedule. On one side, under the bluest of California skies, he will see the sparkling waters of the Pacific, and on the other, beyond the flowering area, he will see, rising in dramatic contrast, the wild, barren hills that the government hopes soon to be able to procure for further cultivation.

On arrival at this scenic wonderland, it will be well worth your while to leave your car or bus and stroll down the spacious, well-kept avenues that wind around and almost seem to embrace the grassy slopes. Thanks to the noted clemency of our winters, an endless profusion of gladioli, irises, roses in a variety of colors, and gold and white chrysanthemums presents a year-round breathtaking horticultural display.

Indeed, the abundance of flowers often makes it difficult to find the temporary markers which supply the names of those who lie under these freshly spread coverlets. But if you take a moment to kneel down and push aside some of the floral offerings you may read on neatly typed cards framed in metal and covered with sturdy transparent plastic, that Pfc. Stuart Hawkins, for instance, of the U.S. Infantry died on May 20, 1967, and was laid to rest here on May 26, 1967; or that Lt. David O'Hara of the U.S. Marines died on June 18, 1967, and was interred in this beautiful spot on June 23. It may cross your mind before you get up from your knees that just six weeks or so ago Pfc. Hawkins and Lt. O'Hara were walking around the streets of Saigon or Danang or somewhere like that, and this is quite an arresting thought. Indeed, after visiting this and other out-of-the-way sites, you will have an endless stream of unusual memories to take home with you.

Background to this particular offbeat outing is readily available to tourists who can spare the time for a brief visit to the mortuary home on Valencia, situated in the famous Mission District of the city. One of the interesting sights there is the arrival of Navy trucks from Travis Air Force Base several times a day. Each truck is equipped with tiers of shelves, or berths resembling those of a sleeping car, on which have been placed long aluminum containers, conveniently numbered and tagged. On each container, stenciled in black, are the words, DO NOT TIP. This is because the contents have been packed in ice at the Tan Son Nhut Air Base in Saigon, and, despite the high degree of refrigeration, there may be some loose water in the container by the time it reaches its destination. The Travis Mortuary Affairs office, however, is justifiably proud of the fact that never during the course of any previous war have erstwhile combatants been transported with such a short lapse of time from the battlefield to the embalmer's table. It is not at all unusual for the remains of returning servicemen to reach the base three or four days after demise in Vietnam.

Travis Air Force Base itself should not be overlooked as a site of truly exceptional interest. It has the distinction of being the one base to receive *all* the containers flown in from Southeast Asia. They travel on C-141-A jets, poetically known as Starlifters, and these giant military birds, carrying a mixed cargo, touch down on the runway at the rate of thirty or forty every twenty-four hours. The containers, speedily emptied of their contents at the Valencia funeral parlor, are then returned by truck to Travis, loaded on to Starlifters, and rushed back to Tan Son Nhut Air Base to serve again. Some of them—and this is reassuring confirmation of the rigid economy practiced by our military—have been in use since the Korean War.

Another example of the forethought with which this operation is handled may be noted in the fact that, the embalming completed, a one-man military escort accompanies each individual flag-draped coffin to its home destination. That destination may be as far from San Francisco as New Jersey or Rhode Island, or as close as Nevada or Washington State, but there is no doubt in the minds of the military authorities, or in that of the director of the funeral home, that wherever the young man's family may reside, this official gesture is highly valued. The military escort usually spends the night in the former serviceman's home, and it is customary for a brief notice to this effect to appear in the social column of the local paper. "It's a kind of status thing, and the family appreciates it very much," the director of the Valencia funeral parlor told me.

It is also fascinating to watch the sleek Navy limousines making their daily deliveries to this efficiently run funeral home. Each limousine, fitted with clothes-racks, brings as many as twelve or fifteen fine new uniforms to the mortuary. Dark blue and trimmed in scarlet and gold, they are carried with scrupulous care into the tastefully decorated interior of the funeral parlor. On one of my visits there, I learned that there is frequently not enough left of the young serviceman himself to fit into the uniform the army provides. The director, a personable young man with three young children and an attractive wife who live in the funeral home with him, was kind enough to invite me in to view some of the remains so that I might understand the problems with which he is faced. "It is far from being an enjoyable business," he confided.

If the interested visitor wishes to explore even further behind the scenes, he will learn that competitive bidding in the San Francisco funeral-services world has been brisk. But the director of the

Hippies waiting in line for a Rolling Stones concert, 1972. Photograph by Dave Randolph.

particular home on Valencia, who got the government contract in 1966, maintains that it is not as profitable a deal as the number of bodies processed every week might lead one to believe. "By the time they are ready to go home, they all look just as lifelike as the art we practice can make them," one of the embalming assistants told me. "We give the same care and attention to the preparation of servicemen as we would if they were on a retail basis. We feel we owe it to the boy's family that he goes home looking just as good as he did when he went away—and sometimes even better."

For a complete change of scene, I would suggest a day at Port Chicago on the other side of the bay. This sleepy little town is a pleasant hour-and-a-half drive from downtown San Francisco, and natives claim that it enjoys the best climate in the whole of Northern California. So as to take advantage of every moment of sunlit air and lively sea breezes, it is recommended that you take a box lunch with you. The seasoned traveler will not feel self-conscious about eating it quite openly, even though a number of hardy visitors who stand before the Naval Weapons Station may be observing a twenty-four-hour fast. Few signs are displayed by this handful of young people, and their presence can be easily overlooked. If questioned, they will be glad to tell you that nine percent of all the explosives sent to Vietnam, including napalm bombs, leave from this busy port.

The Naval Station is a leisurely ten-minute walk from the town of Port Chicago, and you will not, of course, be permitted to enter the confines of the station, which is designated as government property, but the distant masts and rigging of the docked munition ships silhouetted against the clear blue sky is the most picturesque of sights.

If taking your lunch with you presents a problem, a simple regional meal may be procured at modest cost in the little restaurant in the heart of town. Lunching there also offers the attraction of firsthand contact and conversation not only with longtime residents of Port Chicago, but also with merchant seamen off cargo ships that have just returned from Vietnam. Enter into the free and easy atmosphere that prevails, and you will come away with a wealth of interesting information. For instance, the property owners of the town are wholly absorbed in a united effort to frustrate the navy's plans to buy out the town so as to take over the entire area for increased shipping facilities. As one store owner put it to me, "I don't care what happens in Vietnam, but I'm not going to sell my four lots to the navy for $700 each when each one of them is worth $1,200." Another resident said he had no intention of selling his $30,000 home for $11,000, which is what the navy is offering.

The seamen, speaking in their quaint dialects (many come from the Deep South), will tell you of the difficulties that are encountered in getting crews together. Despite the high pay and the generous bonuses, it is not an easy matter to man the munition freighters. But now and then a note of true jubilation is sounded by those seamen who have amassed small fortunes in war-zone pay. They will now be able to purchase homes for their families, and even finance a son's or daughter's college education. For untrained, unskilled men, such rewards were merely pipe dreams before. So even war has its unexpected compensations. On one occasion a totally illiterate seaman regaled me with a hilarious story of his attempts, on the trip he had just returned from, to get transportation from Saigon to Danang, through enemy lines, to see his GI son who was in an army hospital there.

Among the many unusual visitors you will see standing before the gates of the Naval Weapons Station, the most impressive is a blond young man of proud and distinctive bearing who is known to one and all as "Larry." Because he has been seen standing there for over a year now, Larry Cooper has become a familiar landmark. The town sheriff, quite a personable young man himself, will stop his official car beside Larry and smile as he greets him, and Larry will lean in through the car window and have a pleasant five-minute chat with this officer of the law. Although Larry's hair is longish, it is neatly trimmed, and although he does have a bright blond Van Dyke beard, he is in no sense a hippie. Indeed, his dignified figure suggests that of an old-time, frontier preacher who has strayed for a moment from the Hollywood set where a Western is being filmed.

Larry describes himself as "a non-Christian minister of truth," and he says that his hope is to be "a point of light and truth for others to see the dignity of Man." It would be easy to picture him in his dark suit and white shirt, a soft-brimmed hat on his blond head, stepping out of an ambushed stagecoach in the wild and woolly days of the old West and persuading the shamefaced stickup men to lower their guns and let the stage continue on its way.

Other young people standing there before the gates, through which passes a constant stream of armored trucks marked EXPLOSIVES, will tell you Larry is a graduate of a California ministerial school, and indeed there is a suggestion of benediction in the friendly hand he raises in greeting to all who pass. Larry will tell you that it was a merchant seaman he ran into in San Francisco in the spring of 1966 who told him about the shipments from Port Chicago. (The man had made two or three trips to Vietnam and his conscience was beginning to bother him.) And everyone, including the sheriff, knows that Larry stopped a running napalm truck last summer by standing before it, and that he still has a weekend or two to serve in jail to complete his fifteen-day sentence.

Everyone also knows that Larry has to come out from San Francisco by bus now, as in August of this year the two cars he used to bring visitors over for a day's outing were, one after another, destroyed by fire. The names of the young men from Port Chicago who destroyed the cars are known to Larry, and he raises his hand in greeting to them as well when they roar past in their jalopies, their spit often striking his face or the faces of other visitors standing before this vast expanse of government property.

Before setting out at the end of the day on the beautiful return drive to San Francisco, take a moment or two to pick up a memento from the debris of bright, discarded cans, flowering cactus, and broken bottles tossed by passing motorists. You will find bits and pieces of the shattered frames of what were placards in their time, charred syllables of words which once spelled "women" or "children" or "Vietnam." On my first visit to Port Chicago I had the good luck to find five words intact on a cardboard placard otherwise nearly destroyed by fire. They said, MEN ARE NOT OUR ENEMIES. . . . The partially burned and scattered lexicon you can salvage there will always make a fascinating conversation piece and may even prove one day a unique supplementary document to our current history.

If you feel so disposed before you go, do help Larry pick up the

Pepsi-Cola and lemon-pop bottles that didn't break when they were thrown. He turns them in at the Port Chicago grocery store, and the refunded deposit money goes toward paying his bus fare back to town. "For the most part everyone's been very helpful," he will tell you. "Marines as well as the workers who load the ships came out and expressed their sympathy about the destruction of the cars. The men working here and the navy personnel know we aren't going to be frightened off, and they respect that. They know now that whatever happens, we're here to stay."

1967

LAWRENCE FERLINGHETTI

In Golden Gate Park That Day...

I n Golden Gate Park that day
>   a man and his wife were coming along
> thru the enormous meadow
>   which was the meadow of the world
He was wearing green suspenders
>   and carrying an old beat-up flute
>   in one hand
> while his wife had a bunch of grapes
>   which she kept handing out
>   individually
>   to various squirrels
>   as if each
>   were a little joke

And then the two of them came on
>   thru the enormous meadow
which was the meadow of the world
>   and then
>   at a very still spot where the trees dreamed
>   and seemed to have been waiting thru all time
>   for them
>   they sat down together on the grass
>   without looking at each other

and ate oranges

without looking at each other

and put the peels

in a basket which they seemed

to have brought for that purpose

without looking at each other

And then

he took his shirt and undershirt off

but kept his hat on

sideways

and without saying anything

fell asleep under it

And his wife just sat there looking

at the birds which flew about

calling to each other

in the stilly air

as if they were questioning existence

or trying to recall something forgotten

But then finally

she too lay down flat

and just lay there looking up

at nothing

yet fingering the old flute

which nobody played

and finally looking over

at him

without any particular expression

except a certain awful look

of terrible depression

1957

ANNE LAMOTT

Almost 86*'ed*

Love is not kind or honest and does not contribute to happiness in any reliable way.

Alice Munro

A N D   S O   we all know, neither does wealth or fame, neither does being an artist. Show me a group of at least reasonably successful writers, actors, filmmakers, fine artists, and dancers, and I'll show you a litter of weird, tortured puppies.

For one thing, they have to spend a lot of time alone. Some say Too Much Time–thinking, shaping, creating, creatively destroying, reshaping, alone except for the tools of their trades, and other inanimate objects, and various leering specters. None of these are on the side of the artist. Take the walls of one's work space, for instance. After Too Much Time alone, hour after hour, day after day, the walls warp, pulse contract, taunt, in cahoots with the ghost of Edgar Allan Poe. And critics perch on the artist's shoulders, like the angel and the devil of conscience in cartoons. Somebody once said, "A critic is someone who comes onto the battlefield after the battle is over and shoots the wounded." So the artist cries out, The *hell* with the critics, and the critics smile.

Just get the work done, we cry to ourselves and each other. Keep the faith! Trust in GM and take short views! Onward! And one has to pretend that it doesn't matter what happens when the final project comes out of the chute–whether in the public eye one emerges sovereign or goat. No, this doesn't matter; what matters is the process, the artistic growth, the integrity, the vision. Work is the gimbal of the artist's life–Matisse, when asked if he believed in God, replied, "Yes, when I work."

Even if one receives praise and attention, the artist may end up feeling like the squat and pompous Renaissance king in the old *New Yorker* cartoon, who is studying a just-completed royal portrait of himself in which he is depicted in all his squat pomposity, with angels soaring down to greet him, singing hallelujahs. "More angels!" he cries to the painter, who stands beside him at the easel. "And make them happier to see me!"

So when the work is done for the day and the project is still spinning around the artist's medicine-ball head—spinning like a Tibetan prayer wheel, to the exclusion of being able to care much about anything else—the artist heads for the places where his or her cronies hang out, fellow artistic sociopaths and sympathizers. Who listen, commiserate, gossip, exhort, share the excitement or despair.

North Beach San Francisco's Tosca Cafe has always been one of the prime places where artists of one persuasion or another met in the evenings, from the Beats in the fifties to the local movie luminaries in the eighties. It has also always been a place for hip San Franciscans, for North Beach regulars, and socialites, upwardly mobile aging youth, business gentility, local politicians, and illustrious visitors. Mailer used to drop by in the sixties, Louis Malle was there the other day. People all over the world know about it and come by for a drink when in town. It is a grand old place, beautifully lit, with opera on the jukebox and a long, fine bar with ancient towering espresso machines at either end. Behind the bar are fresh flowers, and Mario, arguably the world's most perfect bartender, who has been here since 1946.

Jeannette Etheredge has been the owner since 1980. Her mother, Armen Bali, the legendary benefactor of the great Russian ballet stars, brings them by when they are in town, and Francis Coppola, whose Zoetrope Studio is in the Sentinel Building one block away, brings his people by. In 1982, when production of *The Right Stuff* began in San Francisco, director Phil Kaufman and his actors—Sam Shepard, Ed Harris, Fred Ward—began hanging out there nightly. Hunter Thompson, Robin Williams, Harry Dean Stanton . . . Tosca is a confluence of artistic greats—actors, directors, dancers, writers—and sophisticated San Franciscans. People feel special there. They belong.

What a lovely hat belonging is! You walk into the right room, and you pick up this hat and put it on, this hat of belonging, and you wonder, What was all that fuss about? The anguish, the loneliness, the lack of connectedness.

It is an exciting and secure feeling to belong at Tosca.

I used to, pretty much, more or less. Until February 5.

Jeannette is a powerful, attractive woman in her forties, a rabid fan of movies and ballet. She has an exemplary relationship with her employees, and entertains her friends, famous or not, with concern and generosity, six nights a week (Tosca is closed on Mondays). It is rare that a customer acts up: on those rare occasions, Jeannette can deliver a look of pure, withering, horrified disdain. She is like the woman in the P.G. Wodehouse story, "known in native bearer and half-caste trader circles as 'Mgobo-'Mgumbi, which may be loosely translated as She On Whom It Is Unsafe To Try Any Oompus-Boompus."

She does not like drunks, or drunk people. We have discussed this on a number of occasions (previous to the incident on February 5, an event to which I shall return). Granted, there probably aren't a lot of bar owners who rejoice when a group of loud, mindless drunks arrive at their bars, but Jeannette *really* doesn't like drunks. As much as anything (she has told me), she can't stand to see what they do to themselves. She has created an atmosphere where civilized people can drink in a grand old bar with an illustrious history, where they can safely assume that the other customers will not start acting up. (On occasions when customers at the bar started becoming obnoxious, Mario has been known to sidle over and casually mention his large son, a large son to whom Mario must still show a thing or two.)

So you go in to talk to Mario and Jeannette and your cronies, and maybe you go in because there are apt to be some celebrities there, and you go in to have a drink, or two. Tosca is, after all, a bar, and bars are about alcohol.

Alcohol is a drug dealing with one's sense of personal power. It seems to me that two kinds of people drink a lot: those who feel powerless, and those granted an irrational amount of power. For the former, alcohol diminishes the feeling of powerlessness; it makes you feel more capable, while, ironically, it is making you less so. It gives you the feeling that you can do it, which is what power is all about. And for the latter, those with an irrational amount of power—doctors, lawyers, the rich and/or famous – it takes away the guilt, the internal squirminess. It makes you feel a benevolent amusement about your power. It makes you feel that it is okay.

In this scheme of things, it is still a great advantage to be a male.

I have been at any number of parties and bars, full of erudite and successful people, where popular, powerful men arrived, or ended up, drunk – I mean, really drunk, three sheets to the wind drunk – and proceeded to tear up the pea patch. I have repeatedly heard them spout words so crude, rude and socially unacceptable that they made what I said to Jeannette on February 5 sound like something by Kahlil Gibran. These men ruin evenings, and they keep getting invited back. They are men, breadwinners, they are just blowing off steam. They can also let themselves go, can bloat, sag, wrinkle, gray, whatever, and still be thought attractive, more powerful with every passing year. But woman with however much power and fame damn well better stay attractive – so what kind of real power is this? As Roy Blount Jr. wrote, "Power that worries about whether its hiney is beautiful is not power."

(And furthermore: have you ever noticed that if you're a man with badly pockmarked skin, you can still be an actor – whom women will desire? Bill Murray and the head of the vice squad on "Miami Vice" come to mind. Can you think of any pockmarked actresses? I rest my case.)

Jeannette and Tosca offer you shelter from the storm: Reagan will almost surely send us to war in Nicaragua, and your shy neighbor may be constructing a huge sex box, and if he doesn't kill you, your cheese might, and the book and movie industries are, for the most part, run by men with the vision and honor of cattle ticks, and too many people out there are hungry and homeless and decompensating. Outside all hell seems to be breaking loose, so what are you going to do?

Go inside.

The lighting in Tosca is golden, elegant, and there are, as always, fresh flowers behind the bar, and Mario is zizzing up one of Tosca's famous brandy-laced cappuccinos, and there is Francisco gentility in the clothes and carriage of the people who sit at the bar or at the red Formica tables and Naugahyde booths in the big room, talking. There is opera on the jukebox, and Caruso does not yet have to compete with the blaring disco which will start up downstairs when the Palladium nightclub opens. (When it does, its beat will have a congealing effect on the opera in here, not unlike the liturgical sound track in movies like *The Omen* or *Damien: Omen Two* when the adorable young anti-Christ begins to act up.) But for now, the opera adds to the atmosphere of animated civility.

My cronies are here, the people I "run into" rather than "have to dinner." Tony Dingman tells me about the movie his boss Coppola is making; Sara Strom—Francis's secretary—and I discuss a wonderful slutty nail polish I have discovered; Al Wiggins discusses Stanley Cavell for a while and then tells me that people who come to Tosca before 8:30 are like the people in Elmore Leonard who get to airports an hour or more before departure time, they are People who do not have enough to do. I greet Jeannette, who is at her stool by the espresso maker at the far end of the bar. She asks me about my work. I tell her, and ask if I can cash a check. Yes, of course, she says. I talk to Curt Gentry about J. Edgar Hoover, wonderful squalid stuff, and then to Peggy Knickerbocker about a mutual friend of ours, and about meat loaf. I ask Jeannette if I can practice pool by myself in the back. She says, Yes, of course.

I belong, pretty much, more or less.

I play pool by myself for a while, and then, lonely, go back to the bar. Everyone in the place is talking or listening, or, as Fran Lebowitz suggests, talking and waiting.

Half of the people who are listening (or waiting) appear to be meeting the eyes of whoever is talking to them, but they are wearing psychic bifocal contact lenses: they can look into their friend's eyes while at the same time peer through the bottom part of the contacts to check out their friend's teeth, or neckline, or lack of it thereof. Then they can look through the top part of the contacts to see if there is someone more interesting around, or if anyone famous has arrived.

I am aware of what they are up to because I am doing the same thing.

I can't help it. It is an automatic response. I do not like to admit this, but I am, in a figurative sense, a star-shtupper. Many of us here tonight are. It is another major reason we hang out at Tosca. Maybe coming in here caters to everything cheap in us—the desire to see celebrities, the desire to be seen as a local celebrity. Maybe if you are mentally sound – if you have a reasonably healthy balance of confidence and humility, you do not have these needs. I have a friend who knows one of you. But most of the people I know are driven by a blend of arrogance and secret, crippling self-doubt, and many of the people I know are star-shtuppers. I'm not sure that this is a bad thing – I mean, it's not as bad as putting people into huge sex boxes, and it's not even as bad as going to the movies wearing digital watches that go off every half hour. It's just sort of silly or sort of sad or something. (One of my best friends – a brilliant and discerning man in his late forties, a man who has read *Ulysses* half a dozen times – recently covered a day's shooting of "Dynasty," and wrote in a letter to me, "Linda Evans wasn't there, drat, because I was sure she would fall in love with me; poor Mickey.")

Watching for stars at Tosca is like watching for whales from the Point Reyes lighthouse: it is a splendid place to be even when you don't see any spouts or tails, but when you do, when all of a sudden *fush!*, you see the geyser of a whale, it makes the world bigger for a moment. Or when all of a sudden Sam Shepard comes in, and you've been in awe of his pure, beautiful writing, and his charisma as an actor, and he's standing a few feet away, talking to Jeannette: it rolfs the Sam Shepard file in your head, and all those memories of awe and admiration rush out like bubbles.

Memories of the great good people who happen to be famous are like Fabergé eggs: in Marin this spring. Huey Lewis draping the gold medal around the neck of a retarded ten-year-old sprinter at the Special Olympics – "Chariots of Fire" blasting from speakers behind them, ecstasy on the girl's face when he kisses her cheek. Ecstasy on my face at ten years old, when Vivian Vance dropped by for a visit. (She was married to John Dodds, who was my father's editor at the time, and she was dressed to the nines and wearing this marvelous fandango eye makeup. Ethel Mertz! The three little Lamotties, raised to be Politeness Children, greeted them ladies first, of course – I had been trained to curtsy, and the Politeness Boys to bow at the waist. And then when we turned to greet Mr. Dodds, Vivian waved away the very *idea*, as if it were smoke, and, with her head held high, announced, "Oh, but you don't even have to bother with him: *I'm* the famous one.")

I cannot remember to whom I lent my only suitcase three months ago, but I can perfectly remember the exact shade of Vivian's eye shadow.

Tosca is a place where San Franciscans can feel special, aristocratic in an egalitarian kind of way, and it is a place where celebrities can go and for the most part avoid being pestered by star-shtupping people like me. Jeannette protects her friends, both by offering them sanctuary in the private room in the back where the pool table is, and by making it quite clear that they are not to be bothered when they are hanging out at the bar or in a booth. They are here, but not really approachable.

I, on the other hand, being a medium-small fish, am approachable by people who recognize me from dust-jacket photos. All right, maybe it doesn't happen all that often, but they do come up from time to time at Tosca, and they say nice things about my books, and I hang my head and shuffle, and then begin bowing and scraping with embarrassed pleasure. I think I must look like a trained horse answering the question, How much is three plus three? (But then there was the time a rich and slightly scary-looking woman came up and asked, "Are you Anne Lamott?" and I nodded, and she said, "You wrote *Rosie*," and I nodded and blushed and began the bowing and scraping. "God," she said. "I just *hated* it.")

But if you're famous, Jeannette can and will protect you. During the Democratic National Convention, any number of stars hung out, either with her at the far end of the bar, or in the poolroom. The place was packed. Hunter Thompson was there, Robin Williams was there, and Ronald Reagan Jr. was there. I watched him mingle nicely with Jeannette and the other stars, and it was perfectly clear that I must not approach him. Must keep my distance. ("Hey! You're Ron Reagan, right? God, I just *hate* your father.")

Tosca can be a magical and relaxed place, whether or not any stars come in. The only thing you have to do to be a part of this exclusive club is to not act up. That is the only rule, and I broke it.

Imagine if you will a meter such as the one on the old "Queen for a Day" show that registered the misery applause, only in this case it will measure Human Excellence. If the needle moves all the way to the right, you've got a person whose life personifies grace and excellence: David Niven, say, or Chris Evert, or Yehudi Menuhin, or E.B. White. If the needle moves all the way to the left, you've got Muamar al-Qaddafi, or people who blow up cats.

My performance at Tosca on the evening of February 5 sent the needle racing over to the left: it stopped in the area occupied by the scores of Martha in *Who's Afraid of Virginia Woolf?* and Linda Blair toward the end of *The Exorcist,* and Frances Farmer out on the town a few years before the lobotomy.

I went to Tosca that night with my friend Curt Gentry, with whom I had had several drinks at Gino and Carlo. It was a quiet night. Jeannette was playing dominoes with an elegant male friend. We said hello, and she invited us to a party the following night, a party at Tosca to welcome Tony Dingman home from Rio. Some of our cronies were there. We mingled nicely. Then Curt left, and another friend arrived, and I had a couple more with him, and regaled him with stories of the twenty-two-hour Greyhound bus trip I had taken from Seattle the day before. I had begun to crack in Portland; Portland is only an hour away from Seattle. He bought me another drink, and left for the bathroom, at which point I took the opportunity to traipse over to Jeannette, and—under the illusion that I was continuing to mingle nicely—began making jocular comments.

For some reason it seemed amusing to call Jeannette unprintable names, in front of her friend. The terms of endearment my best friends use with me, along the lines of "you ignorant slut" and "you incurable troglodyte" and "you godforsaken moron" and worse. I was gregariously insensitive to the fact that Jeannette was having to sit there being verbally attacked by a loud, mindless drunk, in front of a friend.

Then I dusted off my hands and left for home.

The next morning I did not remember those last fifteen minutes at Tosca.

I was looking forward to the party for Tony all day.

When I walked into Tosca that night, around seven, Jeannette was sitting with Curt Gentry and Peggy Knickerbocker at the far end of the bar. I said hello to each of them in turn. Peggy and Curt said hello back. "Aren't you going to say hello?" I asked Jeannette, only somewhat nervous. "No," she said.

Curt and Peggy, stiffly, anxiously, turned to each other and began discussing the weather.

"Well, why not?" I asked.

And she began to tell me just how profoundly uncute and unfunny I had been the night before, and how I had humiliated her in front of her friend, and just what a general ass I had made of myself, and then she nailed me on two or three of my gravest personality defects. It was almost uncanny.

I stood listening, in a rapt, wired state of Cobra Hypnosis.

Then I apologized six ways from Sunday; I was nauseated with remorse. I bowed and scraped, and sort of begged for forgiveness. Jeannette cleared her throat, and said, "Well," and then Tony and some more of our cronies arrived.

We all hugged him and said welcome back. I began to cry. Curt got out his handkerchief and mopped me up. I made small jokes and told Tony about my twenty-two-hour Greyhound bus ride, and tears kept pouring down my face, and Curt kept mopping me up, and I kept making little jokes and really mingling rather nicely, under the circumstances. And then I thought, well maybe I'll go home now and have a nice glass of Drano.

I went up to Jeannette, apologized some more, and said I could not remember feeling so ashamed, and she ended up accepting my apology: she was really pretty nice about the whole thing.

But things just haven't been the same between us since.

I've gone in about once a month since then, and I sit miserably behind the espresso machine at Mario's end of the bar, and I talk to him or to Tony Dingman or to Curt or whomever, and it is clear that Jeannette does not want anything to do with me. I have not yet been eighty-sixed, but I am on the bad persons list, and I worry every time that Mario will come over to tell me about his big son.

1985

HERB CAEN

That Was San Francisco

EVEN VETERAN world travelers, well-seasoned in their salt-and-pepper tweeds, seem to agree that it was quite a town in the olden, golden days. "The greatest city I ever visited," one global gadabout once told me, "was San Francisco–a city that died in 1906."

That, of course, is the rather annoying attitude of the super-sentimentalist, who looks at yesterday with longing and at today with disdain. For "old" San Francisco still lives, in out-of-the-way corners, in endless conversations among today's graybeards, in the musty attics of many a memory. Today, it is a city that continues to grow–chained always to the past–a past that is ever present.

Old San Francisco. "The city that was never a small town" definitely had something, and whatever it was, they still talk about it. Not in the manner of the historians, with meaningless dates and esoteric anecdotes, but in an endless mumble-jumble of names and places and happenings that still seem tinged with a special kind of brightness.

"Do you remember?" the old-timer always demands. Yes, remember:

When a jockey named "Snapper" Garrison rode the great horse Boundless to an amazing victory in the Ninety-three Fair–giving birth to the term "Garrison finish." When a gang of pioneer ruffians used to shout "huddle 'em, huddle 'em!" as they crowded around their victims–thus coining the word "hoodlum." When a gambler who hung around the Cliff House used to challenge his fellow bettors in a loud phrase that he invented to live forever: "All right, put up or shut up!"

Remember the old Orpheum on O'Farrell Street? Its regular customers held their regular seats for the gala Sunday-night performances year after year–and the great ambition of every prominent San Franciscan was to get a permanent pass to the theater. So one day Charles

Enrico Caruso as Don Jose in *Carmen,* his last performance in San Francisco on the eve of the 1906 earthquake.

L. Ackerman, president of the Orpheum, bestowed this most princely of favors upon Horace Platt, president of the now also defunct Geary Street Railway. Platt was overjoyed until he noticed, in small letters at the bottom of the pass, the following legend: "Not good on Saturdays, Sundays, or holidays."

So he had a special Geary Street Railway pass made for Ackerman. On the bottom of the card was printed, in equally small letters: "Not good going east or west" – the only directions traveled by his company.

The old Orpheum. A lot of tears have been shed over it. When he appeared for the last time on its stage, Ted Lewis had to pull his old silk hat down over his eyes – to hide his grief. Today, there is nothing to mark its site. Where a generation of San Franciscans enjoyed the greatest performers of the age only a parking lot stands, or sits. Perhaps the last San Franciscan to "enjoy" the Orpheum was a real estate operator named Maurice Moskovitz. Just before the wreckers went to work, he sneaked inside, found his old "permanent" chair, and sat there alone for a few minutes. Yes. He cried too.

The City That Was. Remember when all the horsecars were converted to cables – sometime in the Nineties, wasn't it? – and hundreds of homeless families flocked to buy the suddenly outmoded conveyances? These they hauled out to the sand dunes near Ocean Beach to convert into homes, and overnight the "city" of Carville was born.

For years the horsecarmmunity flourished. Potted geraniums flowered in the streetcar windows, and the wealthier squatters blossomed out with lace curtains. Where the well-to-do of today sport two automobiles, the aristocrats of Carville owned two horsecars, tacked together to form a single dwelling.

But Carville was doomed around 1910, when the city decided to grade the Great Highway that runs grandly along the ocean front. The horsecar forerunner of the Sunset District was condemned, and the squatters sadly gathered their pitiful baggage and trooped desolately across the sands in a new pilgrimage to poverty.

But San Francisco had an especially gala Fourth-of-July celebration that year. As massed thousands watched from the surrounding dunes, the Fire Department destroyed Carville in a blaze that still burns in the memories of oldsters. Trumpeted the mayor as the embers glowed to death: "May San Franciscans never again be reduced to living under such miserable conditions."

(Brave words those. But today many a San Franciscan, living in an unlighted basement, would welcome a horsecar to call home . . .)

The old days. Once you start dreaming, the recollections come flittering back in clusters.

Those Sunday mornings in the Ferryboat Era, when you met your friends under the Ferry Building's clock, and flipped coins to decide which ride to take. If you felt like a long trip, there were the *Gold* and the *Petaluma,* which made the thirty-eight-mile run to Petaluma in six or eight hours, depending on how long you had to wait for the Black Point Bridge to open. Or you had your choice of the Monticello Steamship Company's *Ashbury Park* and *General Frisbee,* waiting to take you in elegant style to Vallejo.

At Pier 3 you might pause for a look at the *J. D. Peters* and the *Port of Stockton,* or nearby the *Delta King* or *Delta Queen,* on the memorable Sacramento River run. (Ah, those moonlit prohibition nights along the Sacramento, with one of the big *Deltas* majestically rounding a bend, her white wake dotted with empty bottles bobbing up and down in an endless string!)

But usually, after you counted your small change, you compromised on the best nickel ride in the world — on the Creek Route's *Encinal* or *Thorofare,* fifty minutes from the south end of the Ferry Building to First and Broadway in Oakland, with good meals and plenty of time to eat them.

The vanished ferryboats. For long, slow-moving decades they seemed rooted permanently to the Bay, the mobile counterparts of Goat Island and Angel Island and Alcatraz. There was much talk of bridges, but such miracles seemed centuries away. Surely there would always be the ferries, the white ones and the orange ones, hauling sleepy-eyed commuters in the morning and tired-eyed commuters in the evening, bleating around in the fog at half-speed and only occasionally nudging into the steel wall of a tanker, lugging knicker-clad hikers to Marin County every Sunday for a hike up Tamalpais, lazing around on moonlit nights in the blessed pre-jukebox days as a three-piece orchestra played dreamy Viennese waltzes and young couples sat staring into space on the deck with their fingers tightly interlocked.

Old San Francisco. So much to remember.

Jack Johnson, the great fighter, training at the Beach, and the mobs that gathered, at fifty cents a head, to watch him work out on a punching bag. At the end of the session he'd unlease his mighty muscles and knock the bag off its moorings and into the crowd— finders keepers.

Rosetta Duncan, later to become famous playing "Topsy" to her sister Vivian's "Eva," doing a little Dutch-boy act at John Tait's O'Farrell Street café—and quitting when he refused a five-dollar-a-week raise. The late great movie comedian, "Fatty" Arbuckle, showing that he had a heart somewhere in his heft by buying new mattresses for every prisoner in the county jail. Jack Warner, now one of Hollywood's powerful Warner Brothers, running a tiny theater on Fillmore Street near Sutter—and having the nightly receipts changed into nickels so he could count them out with his now-forgotten partner ("one for you, one for me"). The pretty little usherette at the Castro Theater, whose name meant nothing then; a few years later every movie-goer was talking about Janet Gaynor.

The memorable night when Tessie Wall, the madame, shot her estranged husband, Frankie Daroux, in Anna Lane—then calmly awaited arrest and later offered to save his life by donating her blood. The great fighter, Stanley Ketchel, showing up at Shreve's swank jewelry store on the morning after a successful fight, wearing a dressing gown and escorting a beautiful woman for whom he'd casually select expensive trinkets. "Dasher Jack" Cannon, the Beau Brummell of the Police Department, who always carried an ultra-thin, silver-plated gun, a gift from a visiting celebrity named Rudolf Valentino, who was impressed with the officer's impeccable clothes and insisted that the ordinary service revolver caused an unsightly bulge.

The names, the faces, the places that stick in your mind! Charlie Chaplin, Gentleman Jim Corbett, and the Great Fitzsimmons, giving free shows every Sunday at the Chutes on Haight Street. The block bounded by Powell, Ellis, Mason, and Eddy, containing more nationally known cafés than any other block in the country—the Louvre with its imported beers, the Oriental, Teddy Lundstet's, Shiff & Dow's, the Langam, Pratt & Tierney's, Spider Kelly's, Jack Morgan's, the Inverness, Haymarket, and the original Techau Tavern. Louis Coutard, the chef at the old Poodle Dog, proudly concocting the delicacy that still bears his name—Crab Louis.

The celebrated sea lion, Ben Butler, that used to sit in front of the Cliff House and patiently shake flippers with thousands of local yokels each Sunday. And the two trained canaries that were the cutest sight to see at Sutro Baths (one of the birds would pull the lanyard of a tiny cannon, whereupon the other one would fall "dead" into a miniature coffin). The great sensation of 1910: Jim Woods, manager of Hotel St. Francis, making the public pronouncement that henceforth women would be allowed to smoke in the lobby and hallways. And creating no sensation at the 1915 Fair—a young, curly-haired man playing the piano in front of Sid Grauman's Chinese concession; today you know him as Harry Richman.

Colorful characters, colorful customs, colorful costumes.

That favorite South o'Market celebrity, "Uncle Sam," the candy man, dressed to the hilt in top hat, starred coat, and striped pants; in one hand he carried a bunch of toy balloons that "cried" as the air slowly escaped from them, and in the other he clutched an ugly blacksnake whip to use on the hoodlums who heckled him.

The second largest gambling casino in the world—the Café Royal, in the basement of what is now the Pacific Building at Fourth and Market; only the casino at Monte Carlo was bigger. Its bouncer was the handsome Paddy Ryan, whom John L. Sullivan defeated for the championship in 1882, and who wore, while on bouncing duty, a silk hat, cutaway coat, flowered vest, and striped pants. But fancy clothes were the rule. Remember when John L. and Jim Corbett fought a four-round exhibition at the Grand Opera House—in swallowtail coats?

And the old Palace Hotel, for decades the most elegant hostelry west of Chicago, full of history and historic incidents. Like the time President Ulysses S. Grant, on his first visit to San Francisco, received such a mighty acclaim as he drove into the rotunda that a Chinese waiter on an upper balcony leaned over to see what all the shouting was about. Only one thing was wrong with this understandable gesture: the waiter forgot he had a tray full of dishes on top of his head. They landed squarely in the President's lap.

And around the Palace they still talk about the day a white man and his Indian wife arrived from Alaska, where he had just dug up a fortune in gold. He wanted nothing but the best, or better, so the manager installed the couple in an elegant suite on the top floor. But lo, the poor Indian wife of the rich miner was so unnerved by the elevator ride that when dinner time came she told her husband to go ahead. She preferred to walk down to the dining room.

A few minutes later she joined her husband at his table, holding a large hunting knife in her hand. Her explanation was simple: "I blaze trail down to dining room so could find way back after dinner." For six floors she had hacked chunks out of the expensive woodwork and banisters!

Yes, characters, always characters. The tough old-time cops who used to discourage known pickpockets by breaking their hands with one blow from their billies. The Superior Court judges who were known as "Crying Eddie" Shortall (he whined slightly while dressing down attorneys); "Ethical Edgar" Zook (the loophole boys had a tough time with him); and "Rain-in-the-Face" Treadwell, who was part Indian, wore a high collar and shoestring tie, and chewed a mighty wad of tobacco (a man of deadly aim). Scholer Bangs, most renowned of the old lamplighters, who used to fire up the street lamps along Webster Street between California and Sutter, followed by hordes of kimono-clad Japanese kiddies, all chanting: "Limpy, limpy lamplighter, California fleabiter, when the lamps begin to light, then the fleas begin to bite!"

Even at the tender age of six a San Franciscan might well be a character. About to make his first appearance with Alfred Hertz and the San Francisco Symphony, Violinist Yehudi Menuhin decided it was too warm under the spotlights on the Civic Auditorium stage—and made everybody wait while he calmly put down his bow and fiddle, peeled off his white sweater, handed it across the footlights to his father, and then nodded that he was ready to launch his professional career.

§

Memories of April 18, 1906, too, the day of the earthquakes and fires and the death of an era. They still talk about John Tait running out of his Powell Street apartment seconds before the building collapsed and dashing like a crazy man to his great café. He stood outside a few seconds and cried with relief because it was still standing. Then he unlocked the front door and walked in – to find that everything but the front wall had been demolished.

They still talk, after all these years, of Tenor Enrico Caruso picking himself up from the floor after the first shock had thrown him out of bed and vowing in a loud and frightened voice: "I will never set foot in San Francisco again!"(Although, obviously, a foot was not what he was setting on San Francisco at the moment.) The little-known sequel to this gaudy fable being that he was all set for a triumphal "homecoming" concert in San Francisco some fifteen years later – only to die an untimely death in Italy.

They like to tell the story of John Barrymore, still clad in white tie and tails, wandering about the shattered city on the morning of April 18 and talking a newspaperman into sending an emergency wire for him to his uncle, John Drew, and his sister, Ethel, in New York. In the telegram John fabricated a doleful tale of jolted out of bed, wandering around the city in a daze, and being forced by a brutal soldier to grab a shovel and work for twelve solid hours. In New York, Ethel read the wire, turned to Uncle John, and smiled: "Do you believe it?" Answered Drew firmly: "Every word. It took an act of God to get him out of bed and the United States Army to put him to work!"

And, if their memories are especially good, they might smile about the opening, just after the fire, of a makeshift opera season at the Chutes Theater at Fulton and Tenth Avenue. It was *Lohengrin,* starring the ultra-buxom Mme. Lucille Nordica. During the performance she fell down a flight of stairs, shaking the stage so palpably that the whole audience rushed frantically into the street, thinking it was another earthquake.

But always, when they talk about the events of April 18, they talk about the courage of the survivors. Few tributes were more to the point than that of Major General A. W. Greeley, the martial law administrator, who wrote: "It is safe to say that 200,000 people were brought to a state of complete destitution. Yet I never saw a woman in tears, nor heard a man whine over his losses."

But it remained for a young man named Larry Harris to capture best the proud, cocky spirit of San Francisco in 1906. He did it with a poem called "The Damndest Finest Ruins," which, I'm sorry to say, few of the city's present generation seem to have heard of. It goes like this:

The Damndest Finest Ruins

Put me somewhere west of East Street where there's nothin' left but
    dust,
Where the lads are all a bustlin' and where everything's gone bust,
Where the buildin's that are standin' sort of blink and blindly stare
At the damndest finest ruins ever gazed on anywhere.

Bully ruins–bricks and wall–through the night I've heard you call
Sort of sorry for each other cause you had to burn and fall,
From the ferries to Van Ness you're a God-forsaken mess,
But the damndest finest ruins–nothin' more or nothin' less.

The strangers who come rubberin' and a huntin' souvenirs,
The fools they try to tell us it will take a million years
Before we can get started, so why don't we come live
And build our homes and factories upon land they've got to give.

"Got to give!" why, on my soul, I would rather bore a hole
And live right in the ashes than even move to Oakland's mole,
If they'd all give me my pick of their buildin's proud and slick
In the damndest finest ruins still I'd rather be a brick!

1949

WILLIAM SAROYAN

Blood of the Lamb Gospel Church, Turk Street off Fillmore, San Francisco, 1929

I N 1 9 2 9 , after my return from failure in New York, I used to seek free diversion wherever I might be able to find it, for the simple reason that I did not have the price of any other kind, and so I learned to find restoration of the soul in walking, looking at people and houses and animals and trees, or in visiting the places to which admission was both free and eagerly sought: the Public Library, the museums, the art galleries, the department stores, and the churches.

The Blood of the Lamb Gospel Church was actually an empty store on Turk Street. The plate-glass windows were whitened with Bon Ami, so that the services might be conducted in private. From the third-floor flat at 2378 Sutter Street the little store-church was a leisurely evening's walk of under fifteen minutes. After supper I frequently set out for a walk of restoration, thought, and peace, having in mind that I might just go into the little church and take a chair in the last row, and look and listen for a while. It was a church founded by several black people, and one frequently heard grateful references to Brother Hutchins, Elder Montgomery, Gospel Singer Sister Ellison, and Sexton Graves. There was no preacher, as such, or rather there was no official or ordained minister. But everybody seemed to be equal to giving either a testimonial about his life and transformation, a reading with asides from the Good Book, a loud prayer, a very lively dance, or a recitation in Tongues.

It was this last, which I heard and witnessed by good luck on my very first visit in January of 1929, that sent me back, in the hope that I might see and hear another version of it. The man who had been Talking in Tongues before my arrival was standing, his fists clenched, his eyes shut, sweat rolling down his tan face. It took me two or three minutes to understand that he was not preaching, not praying, and not testifying – and furthermore that he was not speaking English, Spanish (which I imagined he *was* speaking, from the sound and rhythm and usage of the words), French, Italian, German, or any other language spoken by mortals. He was speaking in the language of the angels. He was possessed. I found that I did not consider that he was sick or mad. On the contrary, although he looked pretty wrought up, I felt that he was a kind of genius, a little freakish but no less authentic on that account. He talked and the congregation listened and cried "Yes," "Hallelujah," "Glory," "That's right," and other expressions of appreciation, as if they understood perfectly what he was saying.

I can't pretend that I didn't understand, for it seemed to me that he was simply demonstrating a little more of the mystery of the human being and the human soul. I studied his language, the rhythm and the words, hoping to type them out and to see if I could track them down. They seemed to be rooted in very real languages. From memory I will put down something like what he said: Esposa conta falla almahada opalappa dablu. Said of course with expression, emphasis, and all of the vocal shadings by which spoken words in a sentence take on form. And his own emotional involvement in what he was saying or thinking or communicating rose and fell, so that he was frequently highly excited, that is even more than he was at the outset, even more than anybody in a trance is, and then subsided to more controlled, unemotional, rather intelligent gibberish.

Best of all, though, I went to this church to hear the songs, and to join in the singing: "There is power in the power house." I loved this song because of its proud and loud happiness. And of course there were several songs about being washed in the blood of the lamb.

1929

MARK TWAIN

Early Rising as Regards Excursions to the Cliff House

> Early to bed, and early to rise,
> Makes a man healthy, wealthy and wise.
> > Benjamin Franklin.

> I don't see it.
> > George Washington.

N O W   B O T H   of these are high authorities—very high and respectable authorities—but I am with General Washington first, last, and all the time on this proposition.

Because I don't see it, either.

I have tried getting up early, and I have tried getting up late—and the latter agrees with me best. As for a man's growing any wiser, or any richer, or any healthier, by getting up early, I know it is not so; because I have got up early in the station-house many and many a time, and got poorer and poorer for the next half a day, in consequence, instead of richer and richer. And sometimes, on the same terms, I have seen the sun rise four times a week up there at Virginia, and so far from my growing healthier on account of it, I got to looking blue, and pulpy and swelled, like a drowned man, and my relations grew alarmed and thought they were going to lose me. They entirely despaired of my recovery, at one time, and began to grieve for me as one whose days were numbered—whose fate was sealed—who was soon to pass away from them forever, and from the glad sunshine, and the birds, and the odorous flowers, and murmuring brooks, and whispering winds, and all the cheerful scenes of life, and go down into the dark and silent tomb—and they went forth sorrowing, and jumped a lot in the graveyard, and made up their minds to grin and bear it with that fortitude which is the true Christian's brightest ornament.

You observe that I have put a stronger test on the matter than even Benjamin Franklin contemplated, and yet it would not work. Therefore, how is a man to grow healthier, and wealthier, and wiser by going to bed early and getting up early, when he fails to accomplish these things even when he does not go to bed at all? And as far as becoming wiser is concerned, you might put all the wisdom I acquired in these experiments in your eye, without obstructing your vision any to speak of.

As I said before, my voice is with George Washington's on this question.

Another philosopher encourages the world to get up at sunrise because "it is the early bird that catches the worm."

It is a seductive proposition, and well calculated to trap the unsuspecting. But its attractions are all wasted on me, because I have no use for the worm. If I had, I would adopt the Unreliable's plan. He was much interested in this quaint proverb, and directed the powers of his great mind to its consideration for three or four consecutive hours. He was supposing a case. He was supposing, for instance, that he really wanted the worm—that the possession of the worm was actually necessary to his happiness—that he yearned for it and hankered after it, therefore, as much as a man *could* yearn for and hanker after a worm under such circumstances—and he was supposing, further that he was opposed to getting up early in order to catch it (which was much the more plausible of the two suppositions). Well, at the end of three or four hours' profound meditation upon the subject, the Unreliable rose up and said: "If he were so anxious about the worm, and he couldn't get along without him, and he didn't want to get up early in the morning to catch him—why then, by George, he would just lay for him the night before." I never would have thought of that. I looked at the youth, and said to myself, he is malicious, and dishonest, and unhandsome, and does not smell good—yet how quickly do these trivial demerits disappear in the shadow, when the glare from this great intellect shines out above them!

I have always heard that the only time in the day that a trip to the Cliff House could be thoroughly enjoyed was early in the morning (and I suppose it might be as well to withhold an adverse impression while the flow-tide of public opinion continues to set in that direction).

I tried it the other morning with Harry, the stock-broker, rising at 4 a.m., to delight in the following described things, to wit:

A road unencumbered by carriages, and free from wind and dust; a bracing atmosphere; the gorgeous spectacle of the sun in the dawn of his glory; the fresh perfume of flowers still damp with dew; a solitary drive on the beach while its smoothness was yet unmarred by wheel or hoof, and a vision of white sails glinting in the morning light far out at sea.

These were the considerations, and they seemed worthy a sacrifice of seven or eight hours' sleep.

We sat in the stable, and yawned, and gaped, and stretched, until the horse was hitched up, and then drove out into the bracing atmosphere. (When another early voyage is proposed to me, I want it understood that there is to be no bracing atmosphere in the pro-gramme. I can worry along without it.) In half an hour we were so thoroughly braced up with it that it was just a scratch that we were not frozen to death. Then the harness came unshipped, or got broken, or something, and I waxed colder and drowsier while Harry fixed it. I am not fastidious about clothes, but I am not used to wearing fragrant, sweaty horse-blankets, and not partial to them, either; I am not proud, though, when I am freezing, and I added the horse-blanket to my overcoats, and tried to wake up and feel warm and cheerful. It was useless, however—all my senses slumbered and continued to slumber, save the sense of smell.

When my friend drove past suburban gardens and said the flowers never exhaled so sweet an odor before, in his experience, I dreamily but honestly endeavored to think so too, but in my secret soul I was conscious that they only smelled like horse-blankets. (When another early voyage is proposed to me, I want it understood that there is to be no "fresh perfume of flowers" in the programme, either. I do not enjoy it. My senses are not attuned to the flavor—there is too much horse about it and not enough eau de cologne.)

The wind was cold and benumbing, and blew with such force that we could hardly make headway against it. It came straight from the ocean, and I think there are icebergs out there somewhere. True, there was not much dust, because the gale blew it all to Oregon in two minutes; and by good fortune, it blew no gravel-stones, to speak of—

only one of any consequence, I believe—a three-cornered one—it struck me in the eye. I have it there yet. However, it does not matter—for the future I suppose I can manage to see tolerably well out of the other. (Still, when another early voyage is proposed to me, I want it understood that the dust is to be put in, and the gravel left out of the programme. I might want my other eye if I continue to hang on until my time comes; and besides, I shall not mind the dust much hereafter, because I have only got to shut one eye, now, when it is around.)

No, the road was not encumbered by carriages—we had it all to ourselves. I suppose the reason was, that most people do not like to enjoy themselves too much, and therefore they do not go out to the Cliff House in the cold and the fog, and the dread silence and solitude of four o'clock in the morning. They are right. The impressive solemnity of such a pleasure trip is only equalled by an excursion to Lone Mountain in a hearse. Whatever of advantage there may be in having that Cliff House road all to yourself we had—but to my mind a greater advantage would be in dividing it up in small sections among the entire community; because, in consequence of the repairs in progress on it just now, it's as rough as a corduroy bridge—(in a good many places) and consequently the less you have of it, the happier you are likely to be and the less shaken up and disarranged on the inside. (Wherefore, when another early voyage is proposed to me, I want it understood that the road is not to be unencumbered with carriages, but just the reverse—so that the balance of the people shall be made to stand their share of the jolting and the desperate lonesomeness of the thing.)

From the moment we left the stable, almost, the fog was so thick that we could scarcely see fifty yards behind or before, or overhead; and for a while, as we approached the Cliff House, we could not see the horse at all, and were obliged to steer by his ears, which stood up dimly out of the dense white mist that enveloped him. But for those friendly beacons, we must have been cast away and lost.

I have no opinion of a six-mile ride in the clouds; but if I ever have to take another, I want to leave the horse in the stable and go in a balloon. I shall prefer to go in the afternoon, also, when it is warm, so that I may gape, and yawn, and stretch, if I am drowsy, without disarranging my horse-blanket and letting in a blast of cold wind.

Cliff House, 1896.

We could scarcely see the sportive seals out on the rocks, writhing and squirming like exaggerated maggots, and there was nothing soothing in their discordant barking, to a spirit so depressed as mine was.

Harry took a cocktail at the Cliff House, but I scorned such ineffectual stimulus; I yearned for fire, and there was none there; they were about to make one, but the bar-keeper looked altogether too cheerful for me—I could not bear his unnatural happiness in the midst of such a ghastly picture of fog, and damp, and frosty surf, and dreary solitude. I could not bear the sacrilegious presence of a pleasant face at such a time; it was too much like sprightliness at a funeral, and we fled from it down the smooth and vacant beach.

We had that all to ourselves, too, like the road—and I want it divided up, also, hereafter. We could not drive in the roaring surf and seem to float abroad on the foamy sea, as one is wont to do in the sunny afternoon, because the very thought of any of that icy-looking water splashing on you was enough to congeal your blood, almost. We saw no white-winged ships sailing away on the billowy ocean, with the pearly light of morning descending upon them like a benediction— "because the fog had the bulge on the pearly light," as the Unreliable observed when I mentioned it to him afterwards; and we saw not the sun in the dawn in his glory, for the same reason. Hill and beach, and sea and sun were all wrapped in a ghostly mantle of mist, and hidden from our mortal vision. (When another early voyage is proposed to me, I want it understood that the sun in his glory, and the morning light, and the ships at sea, and all that sort of thing are to be left out of the programme, so that when we fail to see them, we shall not be so infernally disappointed.)

We were human icicles when we got to the Ocean House, and there was no fire there, either. I banished all hope, then, and succumbed to despair; I went back on my religion, and sought surcease of sorrow in soothing blasphemy. I am sorry I did it, now, but it was a great comfort to me, then. We could have had breakfast at the Ocean House, but we did not want it; can statues of ice feel hunger? But we adjourned to a private room and ordered red-hot coffee, and it was a sort of balm to my troubled mind to observe that the man who brought it was as cold, and as silent, and as solemn as the grave itself.

His gravity was so impressive, and so appropriate and becoming to the melancholy surroundings, that it won upon me and thawed out some of the better instincts of my nature, and I told him he might ask a blessing if he thought it would lighten him up any—because he looked as if he wanted to, very bad—but he only shook his head resignedly and sighed.

That coffee did the business for us. It was made by a master artist, and it had not a fault; and the cream that came with it was so rich and thick that you could hardly have strained it through a wire fence. As the generous beverage flowed down our frigid throats, our blood grew warm again, our muscles relaxed, our torpid bodies awoke to life and feeling, anger and uncharitableness departed from us and we were cheerful once more. We got good cigars, also, at the Ocean House, and drove into town over a smooth road, lighted by the sun and unclouded by fog.

Near the Jewish cemeteries we turned a corner too suddenly, and got upset, but sustained no damage, although the horse did what he honestly could to kick the buggy out of the State while we were grovelling in the sand. We went on down to the steamer, and while we were on board, the buggy was upset again by some outlaw, and an axle broken.

However, these little accidents, and all the deviltry and misfortune that preceded them, were only just and natural consequences of the absurd experiment of getting up at an hour in the morning when all God-fearing Christians ought to be in bed. I consider that the man who leaves his pillow, deliberately, at sun-rise, is taking his life in his own hands, and he ought to feel proud if he don't have to put it down again at the coroner's office before dark.

Now, for that early trip, I am not any healthier or any wealthier than I was before, and only wiser in that I know a good deal better than to go and do it again. And as for all those notable advantages, such as the sun in the dawn of his glory, and the ships, and the perfume of the flowers, etc., etc., etc., I don't see them, any more than myself and Washington see the soundness of Benjamin Franklin's attractive little poem.

If you go to the Cliff House at any time after seven in the morning, you cannot fail to enjoy it—but never start out there before daylight, under the impression that you are going to have a pleasant time and come back insufferably healthier and wealthier and wiser than your betters on account of it. Because if you do you will miss your calculation, and it will keep you swearing about it right straight along for a week to get even again.

Put no trust in the benefits to accrue from early rising, as set forth by the infatuated Franklin—but stake the last cent of your substance on the judgment of old George Washington, the Father of his Country, who said "he couldn't see it."

And you hear me endorsing that sentiment.

1864

The Fashions

I ONCE made up my mind to keep the ladies of the State of Nevada posted upon the fashions, but I found it hard to do. The fashions got so shaky that it was hard to tell what was good orthodox fashion, and what heretical and vulgar. This shakiness still obtains in everything pertaining to a lady's dress except her bonnet and her shoes. Some wear waterfalls, some wear nets, some wear cataracts of curls, and a few go bald, among the old maids; so no man can swear to any particular "fashion" in the matter of hair.

The same uncertainty seems to prevail regarding hoops. Little "highflyer" schoolgirls of bad associations, and a good many women of full growth, wear no hoops at all. And we suspect these, as quickly and as naturally as we suspect a woman who keeps a poodle. Some who I know to be ladies, wear the ordinary moderate-sized hoops, and some who I also know to be ladies, wear the new hoop of the "spread-eagle" pattern—and some wear the latter who are not elegant and virtuous ladies—but that is a thing that may be said of any fashion whatever, of course. The new hoops with a spreading base look only tolerably well. They are not bell-shaped—the "spread" is much more abrupt than that. It is tent-shaped; I do not mean an army tent, but a circus tent—which comes down steep and small half way and then shoots suddenly out horizontally and spreads abroad. To critically examine these hoops—to get the best effect—one should stand on the corner of Montgomery and look up a steep street like Clay or Washington. As the ladies loop their dresses up till they lie in folds and festoons on the spreading hoop, the effect presented by a furtive glance up a steep street is very charming. It reminds me of how I used to peep under circus tents when I was a boy and see a lot of mysterious legs tripping about with no visible bodies attached to them. And what handsome vari-colored, gold-clasped garters they wear now-a-days! But for the new spreading hoops, I might have gone on thinking ladies still tied up their stockings with common strings and ribbons as they used to do when I was a boy and they presumed upon my youth to indulge in little freedoms in the way of arranging their apparel which they do not dare to venture upon in my presence now.

But as I intimated before, one new fashion seems to be marked and universally accepted. It is in the matter of shoes. The ladies all wear thick-soled shoes which lace up in front and reach half way to the knees. The shoe itself is very neat and handsome up to the top of the instep—but I bear a bitter animosity to all the surplus leather between that point and the calf of the leg. The tight lacing of this legging above the ankle-bone draws the leather close to the ankle and gives the heel an undue prominence or projection—makes it stick out behind and assume the shape called the "jay-bird heel" pattern. It does not look well. Then imagine this tall shoe on a woman with a large, round, fat foot, and a huge, stuffy, swollen-looking ankle. She looks like she had on an elbow of stovepipe. Any foot and ankle that are not the perfection of proportion and graceful contour look surpassingly ugly in these high-water shoes. The pretty and sensible fashion of looping up the dress gives one ample opportunity to critically examine and curse an ugly foot. I wish they would cut down these shoes a little in the matter of leggings.

1866

Farewell

*M*Y FRIENDS *and Fellow-Citizens:* I have been treated with extreme kindness and cordiality by San Francisco, and I wish to return my sincerest thanks and acknowledgments. I have also been treated with marked and unusual generosity, forbearance and good-fellowship, by my ancient comrades, my brethren of the Press—a thing which has peculiarly touched me, because long experience in the service has taught me that we of the Press are slow to praise but quick to censure each other, as a general thing—wherefore, in thanking them I am anxious to convince them, at the same time, that they have not lavished their kind offices upon one who cannot appreciate or is insensible to them.

"I am now about to bid farewell to San Francisco for a season, and to go back to that common home we all tenderly remember in our waking hours and fondly revisit in dreams of the night—a home which is familiar to my recollection, but will be an unknown land to my unaccustomed eyes. I shall share the fate of many another longing exile who wanders back to his early home to find gray hairs where he expected youth, graves where he looked for firesides, grief where he had pictured joy—everywhere change! remorseless change where he had heedlessly dreamed that desolating Time had stood still!—to find his cherished anticipations a mockery, and to drink the lees of disappointment instead of the beaded wine of a hope that is crowned with its fruition!

"And while I linger here upon the threshold of this, my new home, to say to you, my kindest and my truest friends, a warm good-bye and an honest peace and prosperity attend you, I accept the warning that mighty changes will have come over this home also when my returning feet shall walk these streets again.

"I read the signs of the times, and I, that am no prophet, behold the things that are in store for you. Over slumbering California is stealing the dawn of a radiant future! The great China Mail Line is established, the Pacific Railroad is creeping across the continent, the commerce of the world is about to be revolutionized. California is Crown Princess of the new dispensation! She stands in the centre of the grand highway of the nations: she stands midway between the Old World and the New, and both shall pay her tribute. From the far East and from Europe, multitudes of stout hearts and willing hands are preparing to flock hither; to throng her hamlets and villages; to till her fruitful soil; to unveil the riches of her countless mines; to build up an empire on these distant shores that shall shame the bravest dreams of her visionaries. From the opulent lands of the Orient, from India, from China, Japan, the Amoor; from tributary regions that stretch from the Arctic circle to the equator, is about to pour in upon her the princely commerce of a teeming population of four hundred and fifty million souls. Half the world stands ready to lay its contributions at her feet! Has any other State so brilliant a future? Has any other city a future like San Francisco?

"This straggling town shall be a vast metropolis: this sparsely populated land shall become a crowded hive of busy men: your waste places shall blossom like the rose and your deserted hills and valleys shall yield bread and wine for unnumbered thousands: railroads shall be spread hither and thither and carry the invigorating blood of commerce to regions that are languishing now: mills and workshops, yea, and *factories* shall spring up everywhere, the mines that have neither name nor place to-day shall dazzle the world with their affluence. The time is drawing on apace when the clouds shall pass away from your firmament, and a splendid prosperity shall descend like a glory upon the whole land!

"I am bidding the old city and my old friends a kind, but not a sad farewell, for I know that when I see this home again, the changes that will have been wrought upon it will suggest no sentiment of sadness; its estate will be brighter, happier and prouder a hundred fold than it is this day. This is its destiny, and in all sincerity I can say, So mote it be!"

1866

Author Biographies

Art critic DORE ASHTON briefly visited San Francisco in 1957. She was on assignment for the *Evergreen Review*, charged with evaluating the city's art scene; "An Eastern View of the San Francisco School" is her report.

Muckraking journalist AMBROSE BIERCE was a regular columnist for the *San Francisco Examiner* and the *Wasp* from the Civil War to World War I. When he wasn't digging scandal out of the crevices of City Hall, he wrote now-obscure poems—the two included haven't been published since 1911.

Novelist and essayist KAY BOYLE lived as an expatriate in Paris for several years and now lives in San Francisco. Her essays for the *New Yorker* and the *Nation* on postwar Europe, McCarthyism, and Civil Rights have gained her wide acclaim. "Seeing the Sights in San Francisco" is excerpted from *Words That Must Somehow Be Said*, a collection of her essays from the past fifty years.

HERB CAEN is a San Francisco fixture who, for the past fifty years, has churned out a daily three-dot column for the *San Francisco Chronicle*. "That Was San Francisco" is from his 1949 collection of columns, *Baghdad-by-the-Bay*.

FRANK CHIN is normally a playwright. The release of his first collection of short stories, *The Chinaman Pacific & Frisco R.R. Co.* earned him an American Book Award. He currently lives on I-5 between Los Angeles and Seattle.

Poet LAWRENCE FERLINGHETTI contributed significantly to San Francisco's Beat spirit when he opened City Lights Pocket Book Shop in the '50s, soon the hangout for all the Beats. Ferlinghetti can still be found there, usually arguing about Central America.

FRANCES FITZGERALD is a Pulitzer-Prize–winning essayist and a regular contributor to the *New Yorker*. "The Castro" first appeared in the *New Yorker* and is collected in her book of essays, *Cities on a Hill*.

Uruguayan novelist EDUARDO GALEANO's trilogy, *Memory of Fire*, chronicles, in brief vignettes, the entire history of the Americas. The San Francisco selections are from the second volume, *Faces and Masks*, covering 1701 to 1900.

JACK KEROUAC, along with Neal Cassady, constituted the heart of the Beat generation. His novels *On the Road, The Dharma Bums,* and *The Subterraneans* were largely set in San Francisco and described his and fast-talking Cassady's exploits. Kerouac was working in China Basin for Southern Pacific Railroad when he wrote "October in the Railroad Earth."

British novelist and storyteller RUDYARD KIPLING visited San Francisco in the 1880s to pitch a manuscript, "Light That Failed," to *The San Francisco Chronicle*. It was rejected.

ANNE LAMOTT is a Marin County writer whose novels include *Hard Laughter, Rosie*, and, most recently, *All New People*. "Almost 86'ed" first appeared in *California* magazine.

LEWIS LAPHAM's grandfather was mayor of San Francisco. Despite being from an old local family, Lapham swore off the city and headed east, eventually to edit *Harper's* magazine, where he is today. "Lost Horizons" tells why.

JACK LONDON was a native San Franciscan known for his riveting adventure novels *The Call of the Wild, John Barleycorn*, and *The Sea Wolf*. When the 1906 earthquake struck, he was working as a reporter for the local *Argonaut* and filed this story on the fire.

H. L. MENCKEN was a journalist, critic, and editor of the *Smart Set* and the *American Mercury* magazines. He first visited San Francisco in 1920, to cover the Democratic National Convention. He had a good time.

Polish Nobel Prize winner CZESLAW MILOSZ has lived in California since 1960. He teaches at University of California, Berkeley. "Where I Am" is from *Visions from San Francisco Bay,* a collection of his essays.

ISHMAEL REED is an Oakland-based novelist, poet, and essayist. For the past twenty years he divided his time between lecturing at UC Berkeley and chronicling black life in the Bay Area and the south. "The Moochers Have a Crisis" is from his 1974 novel *The Last Days of Louisiana Red.*

KENNETH REXROTH was a poet, essayist, critic, translator, and unwilling father to the Beats. His clear, hip poems and essays like "San Francisco Letter" (from a 1957 *Evergreen Review*) inspired a whole generation of Beat writers.

WILLIAM SAROYAN's short stories, such as "The Daring Young Man on the Flying Trapeze," and plays, such as *The Time of Your Life,* brought him a Pulitzer Prize, which he refused. Living in the Sunset district, Saroyan chronicled the colorful side of the city, from dark taverns to wild church meetings.

Poet VIKRAM SETH was born in Calcutta in 1952 and now lives in San Francisco. His widely acclaimed *The Golden Gate* is a lengthy narrative poem, set in his adopted home.

RANDY SHILTS is a journalist for the *San Francisco Chronicle* and author of *And the Band Played On.* His groundbreaking reporting on the AIDS crisis has made him a respected spokesman on gay issues. "No Cross, No Crown" is from his book on Harvey Milk, *The Mayor of Castro Street.*

ROBERT LOUIS STEVENSON arrived broke in San Francisco in 1879. He rented a room on Bush Street and set to writing—mostly from a bench in Portsmouth Square. "Arriving in San Francisco" chronicles his first glimpse of the Bay Area.

AMY TAN's first novel, *The Joy Luck Club,* was last year nominated for the National Book Award. "Rules of the Game" is an excerpt about growing up in shadowy 1950s Chinatown.

The legendary Welsh poet DYLAN THOMAS was mesmerized by San Francisco while interviewing for a guest lecturer post at the Berkeley English Department.

Muckraking journalist HUNTER S. THOMPSON established "Gonzo Journalism" when he reported on the death of the Beats for the *Nation* in 1964. After years of Fear and Loathing with the Hell's Angels, Dallas Cowboys, and Richard Nixon, he resurfaced as a columnist for the *San Francisco Examiner*, this time covering San Francisco in the 1980s, or as he dubs it, The Generation of Swine.

ALICE B. TOKLAS was born in San Francisco; she was living with her father on California Street when the 1906 earthquake hit. She fled to Europe the next year, then returned with Gertrude Stein in the mid-1930s. The included earthquake account is from her 1963 autobiography, *What Is Remembered*.

Novelist ANTHONY TROLLOPE regularly toured the world, intricately detailing his voyages. In 1875, returning from the Sandwich Islands and apparently in a bad mood, he released the included dispatch on San Francisco. It was first published by Colt Press, a small press in San Francisco, in 1946.

MARK TWAIN, aka Samuel Clemens, came to San Francisco to escape the Civil War. Arriving in the city, he likened it to home ("it's like being on Main Street in Hannibal and meeting old familiar faces"). Soon he was reporting on political corruption, fashion, and fog for the *San Francisco Chronicle,* the *Call*, and the *Golden Era* newspapers. In the Montgomery Street Turkish Baths, he played penny ante with a man named Tom Sawyer.

TOM WOLFE came to San Francisco in 1967 as a reporter for *New York* magazine. His dispatches of the happenings aboard Ken Kesey's magic bus eventually became *The Electric Kool-Aid Acid Test,* a hallmark book of New Journalism.

Credits

"Black Shiny FBI Shoes" from *The Electric Kool-Aid Acid Test* by Tom Wolfe. Copyright © 1968 by Tom Wolfe. Reprinted by permission of Farrar, Straus and Giroux, Inc.

Dylan Thomas letters reprinted with permission of Macmillan Publishing Company from *The Collected Letters of Dylan Thomas*, Paul Ferris, Editor. Copyright © 1985 by The Trustees for the Copyrights of Dylan Thomas.

"The Moochers Have a Crisis" reprinted with permission of Atheneum Publishers, an imprint of Macmillan Publishing Company from *The Last Days of Louisiana Red* by Ishmael Reed. Copyright © 1989 by Ishmael Reed.

"The Castro" is reprinted with permission of Simon & Schuster, Inc., from *Cities on a Hill*, copyright © 1987 by Frances Fitzgerald.

"What Is Remembered" is excerpted from *What Is Remembered*, copyright © 1963, 1985 by Alice B. Toklas. Published by North Point Press and reprinted by permission.

"A Generation of Swine" is reprinted with permission of Summit Books, a division of Simon & Schuster, from *A Generation of Swine*, copyright © 1988 by Hunter S. Thompson.

"When Beatniks Were Social Lions" is reprinted with permission of Summit Books, a division of Simon & Schuster, from *The Great Shark Hunt*, copyright © 1979 by Hunter S. Thompson.

"Rules of the Game" is reprinted by permission of the Putnam Publishing Group from *The Joy Luck Club* by Amy Tan, copyright © 1989 by Amy Tan.

"October in the Railroad Earth" is reprinted by permission of Grove Press, a division of Wheatland Corporation. Copyright © 1957 by Jack Kerouac.

San Francisco Stories was designed by Herman + Company, San Francisco, California. Cover design by Karen Pike. Cover photograph, *Seal Rocks*, by Laura Volkerding. Set in Perpetua by TBH/Typecast Inc., Cotati, California.